AMONG
THE
BURNING

A SKYGLASS NOVEL

First published by Kindle Direct Publishing 2024.

First Edition
ISBN paperback: 979-8-9877402-6-2
ISBN ebook: 979-8-9877402-7-9

Visit Caytlyn Brooke's website:
http://caytlynbrooke.wixsite.com/booksbycaytlyn

Editor: Chelsea Cambeis
Proofreader: Samantha Moran
Cover Designer: Neil J Hart

OTHER WORKS

Dark Flowers

Wired

Among the Hunted

The Baker's Wife

Crimson Crisp

Hush Little Baby

*For everyone who chose the bear, because
we know that real monsters smile.*

CONTENT WARNING

Among the Burning is a sequel in the Skyglass Series and continues to be an anthem for survivors of sexual assault. Sexual assault, violence, animal deaths, death, attempted rape, mentions of incest, verbal assault, and flashbacks to previous assaults are included in this novel to bring awareness to survivors' experiences, as well as to start the conversation of how damaging assault is, both physically and mentally for the victims. None of the aforementioned are graphic; however, the character's experiences are expressed on the page and may be triggering for some readers. This book is intended to strengthen survivors' voices and allow everyone a safe space to feel rage, shame, guilt, confusion, forgiveness, and anything else they may be struggling with on their own personal healing journey after assault.

RAINN National Sexual Assault Hotline
1-800-656-4673
Or chat online at: online.rainn.org

National Sexual Violence Resource Center
resources@nsvrc-respecttogether.org
877-739-3895

CHAPTER 1

Rough fingers encircled Kait's throat, squeezing until black stars stole her vision. She pushed off the wall, but her tormentor was ready. His other hand gripped her hips and wrenched her body against his.

"You wanted a monster. Here I am."

Kait's eyes drank in darkness. Gone was the cave, the threat, but her fear remained and curled around her heart like barbed wire.

"He's dead. Zeus is dead," Kait whispered and placed her hands on her sweating temples.

It had been three months since she'd helped rid the realms of the dangerous immortal, but the dread of his inevitable return seeped into her subconscious and painted poisonous strokes across her dreams.

Kait exhaled a steadying breath and settled back against the soft moss of her pillow. Silver moonlight kissed her face as the wind ushered the clouds away, bleaching her dark bed stark white. She turned away and buried her face in the crook of her elbow, but light continued to bathe the insides of her eyelids. She clenched her eyes tighter.

"Just an hour of sleep. That's all I want," Kait moaned as she imagined the hectic day awaiting her.

In response, the moonlight blinked as a shadow danced across and doused the earth in darkness. A delighted chuckle wormed into Kait's ear and echoed dangerously. The fine hairs coating her arms prickled as the feeling of being watched transformed her cozy hammock into a claustrophobic net of tangled silk. She kicked the smothering blanket off her legs and melted into the wind. The breeze cradled her and circled the suspended branches of the wide tree she and several other aurais slept in.

The other wind nymphs dozed peacefully as Kait alighted from the air, her bare feet depressing frost-coated blades of grass, to search for anything amiss in the clear night. "You're being paranoid. There's no one here." She scanned the tree line once more, then pivoted on her heels. Just beyond the towering cypress trees of the north wood, a twig snapped, disturbing the quiet. Kait held her breath as the residual fear from her dream spiked.

"Hello?"

The same ghostly laughter from before echoed across the small meadow. Kait glanced at the moon. It was nearly full, the beautiful white light surrounding it almost a perfect match to the soft glow that radiated from her own flesh—her halo, the physical embodiment of a nymph's connection to her elemental magic and the ethereal realm. "This is Olean, your home. Immortals cannot enter. There is nothing to be afraid of," she chided herself.

Kait bit the inside of her cheek and wandered toward the sound, eager to quiet her doubts for good. It was probably a hungry deer scouring the pine needles, but sleep would continue to evade her if she didn't make sure.

Wet grass licked the soles of her feet and clung to her bare skin. Kait reached the edge of the small forest and peered inside, but the thick foliage was too dense for the moon to illuminate. Blackness stretched, morphing innocent tree limbs and transforming brush into sinister figures. She swallowed uneasily and took a step back.

A flurry of feathers brushed her cheek and drew a startled cry from her lips. A gray-and-white speckled hawk scolded her from above, its beady eyes narrowed and accusatory—as if *she* had startled *it*. Kait placed a hand over her racing heart and gulped in the early morning air.

A bird. Just a bird. She sighed.

The hawk clicked its sharp beak and chortled for attention. Kait looked again, but this time, the bird appeared smug, its gaze brimming with excitement. She wrinkled her brow. Another twig cracked, followed by the thud of deliberate footsteps. She peered into the shadows once more, hoping to identify the early riser.

Drag, stomp. Drag, stomp. Drag, moan, stomp.

Kait couldn't understand the pattern. She watched the hawk out of the corner of her eye. From its agitated movements, she knew whatever it was drew closer. In response to her climbing anxiety, the wind kicked up loose dirt and twigs to create an eddy of debris. The air tasted wrong, like rotting leaves. Her fingers twisted in an intricate dance, and she vanished. Her elemental form would be far more defensive against whatever stalked her.

Drag, moan, stomp. Drag, moan, stomp.

Kait ascended, dressed in the comfort of the night sky, and wove through the naked fingers of the tree branches. With renewed confidence, she flew farther into the woods. Several yards off, she caught sight of a dark figure shuffling along the ground but couldn't make out the nymph's face. The only feature visible was glossy black hair that hung to the middle of her back. The nymph ambled along, seemingly lost and directionless as she moaned in pain. Without pause, Kait left the air and alighted onto a pile of dead foliage. A loud crunch announced her presence, but she was no longer concerned with remaining hidden.

"Excuse me?" Kait called as she closed the short distance between them until a decaying log blocked her path. "Do you need help?"

The nymph stopped her slow progression at the sound of Kait's voice. Her shoulders flinched, and her neck snapped to the right. Kait hesitated, sniffed the air again, and frowned. The nymph was the source of the strange odor. "Did you hurt your leg?" she asked, wondering if the wound may be infected.

The nymph moaned in reply as a snarl built behind her teeth. Kait could only see a sliver of her face as stringy hair draped across her cheek. Her eye gleamed wetly in the darkness.

Kait shivered, and her confidence shrank, no longer seeing a sickly creature, but a potential violent predator. "Are you all right?"

The nymph didn't answer, but the hawk shrieked from its perch. Kait leapt back at the unexpected cry. Her foot slipped on slick moss, and she collapsed to the forest floor.

The nymph hissed and lurched forward, hands curling like eager talons. Dragging her injured leg behind her, the nymph clambered over the thick log between them. Kait stared, too shocked by the nymph's erratic behavior to think straight. She grimaced as the nymph's bones cracked and popped, jutting out at odd angles as she clawed her way over the decayed bark. Disturbing mewls emanated from her throat, spilling over diseased gums and a slack jaw. What few teeth the nymph retained were yellowed and broken, surrounded by gaping black holes where the others used to sit.

Kait scuttled backward a few inches, transfixed. Before, she'd thought the nymph had been moaning in pain, but as she watched her tear feverishly at the obstacle between them, she realized the nymph was suffering from a different affliction: hunger.

Kait's terrified scream pierced the night as the nymph's broken fingers fumbled for her ankles. Kait pulled her legs up and dug her knees into the wet earth as she crawled out of her attacker's grasp. The nymph roared and lunged again, and her dirt-encrusted nails carved angry red lines into Kait's flesh.

With a jerk, Kait slammed her foot into the nymph's jaw and bucked her backward with enough force to sever her grip. For a moment, the endless moans emanating from the nymph's mouth ceased—only to increase tenfold. With renewed vigor, the nymph wrenched her twisted body off the ground and charged. Kait's eyes bulged at the nymph's speed and intensity. She leapt to her feet and entwined her fingers to cast, intending to disappear into the wind, but the nymph was faster.

She slammed into Kait with surprising force, and the pair crashed to the ground. Skeletal limbs and gnarled fingers tried to latch on while the nymph's gnashing teeth created an eerie melody for the chaotic scene. Kait wrapped her hands around the nymph's throat to hold her off, but she fought back like a rabid dog, arching her back and thrashing her head from side to side. She smelled horrendous, and up close, Kait realized why.

The nymph's flesh was in a state of interrupted decomposition and infested with wriggling maggots. Their milky bodies fell onto Kait's chest like fat raindrops.

Plop, plop, plop.

Kait clenched her jaw to keep from gagging and squeezed the nymph's throat tighter. If she could cut off her air supply long enough, she might slip into unconsciousness. She clawed the nymph's rotting skin until she felt her spine beneath her fingertips, but still the nymph fought, unaffected. Her flesh flaked off in large patches as jellylike blood pooled to the surface.

"Help! Someone, help me!" Kait's grip loosened as the squishy blood slipped underneath her fingertips. "Help!"

Unable to hold on any longer, Kait released her and rolled to the right. The nymph fell to the ground and unleashed a guttural scream. In a blink, she scrambled back up and onto Kait's chest, then pinned her down with her knees.

Help will never come for you, a voice said. *This is the future. This is your future. I'm afraid it's very bleak.*

Kait tried to pull herself free, but the nymph was too heavy. She twisted her neck, searching for the speaker, but nothing but shrinking shadows greeted her as dawn approached. Warm pink color crested over the hills, spilling light into the woods like an overturned bucket of paint. Coral rays illuminated the nymph and allowed Kait to view her features for the first time.

Scraggly brown hair framed her face in thin greasy stands, and her scalp sported multiple bald patches from the hair either having been torn free or fallen out. Most of her bottom lip was missing, and the flayed skin around it scabbed and oozed a green pus. The skin on her face was rotten, and her cheekbones were visible through the thin flesh.

Kait wiggled her fingers where they were pinned against her hips. She had to get in the air. The nymph hissed and dug her knees harder into Kait's side to prevent escape.

"Please. Don't do this." Kait recalled the words spoken inside her mind moments ago.

This is your future.

A sickening dread clenched her stomach as the nymph's ravenous smile was highlighted by the first rays of sunlight. Kait stopped struggling, looked in her eyes, and glimpsed the same violet color reflected in her mirror every morning.

"Oh, goddess."

The nymph's grin stretched, her jaw clicking as it fought to remain attached at the joint. With a moan that resembled laughter, the nymph doubled over and buried her teeth in the base of Kait's throat.

Help will never come for you.

CHAPTER 2

A hard slap jolted Kait away from the gnashing teeth and crunch of bone.

"Open your eyes," a husky voice commanded.

Kait obeyed and braced herself for the horrific sight of her rotting visage. Instead, Anamalla, a strong aurai leader, stood over her, her dark satin skin a welcome sight.

"What's going on? What happened?" Kait asked as she pushed herself onto her elbows. Several aurais hovered around her hammock, staring at her with a mixture of concern and bewilderment.

"I think we should be asking you that question," Anamalla stated. "You were screaming like Hades was burning you alive. I wouldn't be surprised if you woke the queen herself."

"Screaming? I was screaming?" Kait's fingers danced over the silk threads of the hammock that cradled her. She was suspended beneath the sparse leaves of a large maple tree in the same bunk she'd fallen asleep in last night. "I'm not in the infirmary?"

Anamalla crossed her arms. "Why would you be?"

"I was attacked last night. I heard someone wandering around the woods." Kait pointed ahead. "I thought she needed help, but when I called to her, she charged and bit me."

"Who was it?" Gleena asked, wrinkling her thin eyebrows.

Kait paused. "Uh, I think it was supposed to be me, but . . . she was more like a walking corpse."

Anamalla dropped her arms and rolled her eyes. "As fascinating as that sounds, I don't have time to listen to bad dreams. Come on, ladies. It's time to get to work. Report to me for your assignments." The graceful aurai spun away from Kait, dismissing her fears as easily as an annoying fly.

"A dream? It wasn't a dream," Kait argued as the rest of the nymphs descended to the ground. "It was too real." She raised her hands and scrutinized the smooth flesh. Moments ago, they had been covered in blood, and a diseased nymph had been about to devour her . . . but she wasn't lying on the forest floor in an eviscerated pile. Never had she experienced such a powerful dream. It didn't make sense. If she did wander into a nightmare, it usually centered on Zeus, not flesh-eating monsters.

Kait shook her head while dread wormed its way into her heart. She slid out of bed into the crisp morning air and let her body fall. For a minute, she was free, untethered by worry or fear before the ground rose to catch her. Her bare feet easily rode the cool current and she filed in at the back of the line.

A mourning dove cooed, long and sorrowful. Kait scanned the tall pines that surrounded the valley as the nymphs shuffled forward. Vaguely, she heard Anamalla's orders for those in front of her, but she didn't pay attention, too focused on finding the bird amongst the dark green limbs. The memory of the eerie hawk from her dream swirled in her mind, and she was plagued with unease that she was missing something important.

"Kaitaini."

Anamalla's crisp tone shattered Kait's wonderings. Her head snapped to the front, and her brows arched. Only she and Anamalla remained. She brushed her dark brown curls behind her ears and stepped before the waiting aurai.

"Sorry," Kait said.

Anamalla's lips pursed and she consulted her notes. "You'll be in Equine today with Dion and her team. A geyser erupted last night." She cast a doubtful look in Kait's direction. "It's a very physical assignment. Will you be able to handle that?" The judgment in her voice was clear.

Kait straightened as a spark of ire flickered in her gut. "Absolutely. I'll dress and report immediately."

"All right," Anamalla said with a curt nod.

Kait started walking across the meadow, but her gaze flickered back to the trees.

It was a dream. Forget it.

She pushed doubt to the corners of her mind, and followed the rest of the aurais to the hot pools, trying to take her own advice.

"Contain it! Contain it!"

Water lashed out violently and pushed the naiads back. The small group of water nymphs dug their heels into the slick mud, grunting as the spray peppered their faces. "Kait, what are you waiting for?" Dion cried.

Kait hovered above the wild geyser, her arms spread wide as she commanded the wind. Her hands swirled, funneling the current into a powerful tornado. If she could contain the gushing water in an impenetrable bubble, the naiads could tame the source below. The small team had been battling the powerful force for an hour now, trying to prevent a catastrophic flood.

Expanding her fingers so wide they hurt, Kait surrounded the thirty-foot spout and fit the air as close as possible to the endless droplets. Cinching her fingers into a closed fist, she suffocated the water, inch by inch, until it coalesced into a writhing sphere.

"Perfect!" Dion shouted. "Hold it! Keep it steady while we seal the interior breach!"

A naiad with a black braid melded with the pooling water at their feet and slid into the long crack on top of the plateau. Kait had no idea how she planned to fix the leak, but she knew how devastating failure would be. Already, the fields were saturated, causing irreparable damage to the crops the creatures depended on.

Kait's hands shook as the water bucked against its invisible prison. She squeezed her fists tighter, and her nails dug into her palms. She couldn't let go, especially not with a naiad submerged below the surface. The water kicked again and wrenched her off-balance. She narrowed her gaze and rolled her arms one over the other in rapid succession. Mirroring her actions, the violent sphere started to rotate, spinning ferociously. Within seconds, the writhing current within calmed, no longer able to exert force on its prison bars.

A satisfied smile danced on Kait's lips. They were going to succeed, and the good creatures of Equine could replant and salvage something for their harvest. For the first time that morning, hope surged within her chest.

A gray flash drew Kait's attention away from the water to the other side of the plateau where the naiads waited. At first, she assumed it was another nymph coming to help, but her movements were too disjointed. Blond hair was plastered to her neck and clung to her bare shoulders like seaweed. Kait frowned as the new arrival advanced on Dion, whose focus was on her soldier below. The nymph opened her mouth. Her jaw clicked as a chilling moan danced on the wind, flavoring the air with the unmistakable scent of death. Too late, Kait understood. Hunger twisted the nymph's features as she bared her teeth and threw her arms around Dion's neck.

"No!" Kait abandoned her task and transformed into the wind. A cannonball of water swallowed her as the giant sphere dropped out of the sky. She tried to break free, but the liquid held her captive and plummeted to the earth like a missile.

"Look out!" the naiads screamed. Some rolled out of the water's direct path, while a few vanished, transforming into the same element that threatened to impale them.

Red rocks loomed close and unforgiving. Kait forced herself to relax and floated to the surface with the rest of the air bubbles. As if aware of her intent to flee, the sphere dove faster and exploded on the flat plateau with enough force to shake the mountainside the nymphs clung to. Kait emerged within seconds of impact and shifted from her elemental form to her physical shape once again. Water ricocheted off the rocks, soaking her jumpsuit.

Swiping droplets out of her eyes, Kait ran and slipped on the mud-covered stones. Fresh cuts stung the flesh on her legs, but she ignored the pain.

Where's Dion? Where did that thing go? Thoughts tore through her mind like lightning bolts as she searched in the chaos she had created. Naiads struggled to their feet, their hair coiled about their bodies like serpents as they nursed dislocated shoulders and sprained wrists. Wails of pain haunted the scene. At last, her gaze found Dion lying face down in a scarlet puddle.

"Please, no." Kait sprinted to the naiad's side. "Dion! Dion, can you hear me?" Gingerly, she slid her hands beneath the nymph's shoulders and flipped her onto her back. A deep gash cut across her forehead, and blood trickled over her eyelids. Kait studied the wound. It didn't look like a bite. "Dion. Dion?"

The naiad's eyes fluttered open and blinked against the blood. "Ow, what happened? Why did you do that?"

"Where did she go?" Kait's eyes roamed the rest of Dion's body for a bite. "The nymph who attacked you, did you see where she went?"

Dion pressed her hand to her head and winced as her fingers skimmed a tender spot. "What are you talking about? No one attacked me. Where's Nina?

Did she get out? Has anyone seen her?"

"I'm here," a freckled nymph called from a few yards away. "I found a pocket in time, but I couldn't complete the seal. I have to go back in."

All three nymphs turned toward the fissure where water had resumed spewing in a vast geyser that nearly blocked out the sun.

Dion sighed, her frustration palpable. She climbed to her feet. "What happened, Kait? Why did you stop holding the water? Do you realize what you've done? You could have gotten someone killed."

Kait stood as well and scanned the hobbling nymphs for the infected one with blond hair. "I'm so sorry, Dion. I wasn't thinking about the water. I saw the nymph bite you and had to help."

Dion scoffed in disgust. "Been indulging in some nectar this morning, aurai? No one bit me. I wasn't attacked. What is wrong with you? You not only put our lives in danger but the lives of these citizens, as well. If we don't fix this, they starve. Don't you get it?" Her voice was ice, hard and crisp.

"But I saw her come from behind that rock and pull you down. Why would I make that up?"

"I don't know, but until you're checked out, you're off my team. Report to Tahlia and have her send another aurai in your stead. One that's sane." Dion spat at her feet.

"But . . . I saw her. Please, something isn't right."

Dion held up a silencing hand. "Get back to Olean and talk to a healer about your hallucinations. I need to make sure my team is safe." She turned her back on Kait and hurried to a naiad holding her bleeding leg.

Kait bit her lip. She was tempted to argue further, but the finality in Dion's eyes was clear. Shame burned her cheeks as she lifted into the air, grateful she could disappear. Maybe it *had* been a hallucination, but why would her subconscious conjure something so terrifying? She drifted toward the portal. First Anamalla and now Dion. If she wasn't careful, by nightfall, all of Olean would think she had gone mad.

CHAPTER 3

Kait stepped through the shimmering portal onto the platform in the town square. The sun shone brightly, reflecting off small mounds of snow that lingered from the last storm. She crossed to the railing, eager to feel the rays on her skin, but the moment she stepped into the light, thick clouds formed and left her in shadow. Her heart fell. She had disappointed everyone, and now even the sun refused to grant her its grace.

Kait's teeth worried at her bottom lip as she left the platform, anxious to escape the bustling square and retreat to solitude where she would only have to face the judgment of her own reflection. Dion's order rang in her head as she hurried toward the ancient oak tree that housed Tahlia's rooms. Her pace slowed as she wove beneath the trellis. The winding vines that usually tickled her cheek were long shriveled, lying dead and forgotten atop the wooden beams. Kait yearned for spring when the harsh warden of winter relaxed its hostile hold over the world. An image of her elder's stern countenance dominated her thoughts. Her news would no doubt etch an even deeper frown across Tahlia's lips, but Kait was nearly two hundred years old; her wounded pride was the least of her worries.

Kait knocked. A minute passed, and silence was her only hostess. "Perhaps she's with the queen." Kait tamed her imagination before it could dredge up another mirage. There was no reason to suspect foul play; it was simply poor timing.

Pivoting on the smooth stone threshold, Kait retreated down the path and veered left. Since intelligence and compassion were traits of anthousais, healing and knowledge of the body came naturally to them, whereas the other clans had to work much harder to achieve similar results. Most of the apothecaries and healing centers were in Olean's western quadrant where the majority of earth nymphs resided, but another trauma center had been recently added just half a mile from the main square, close to the Hall of Portals. If a nymph was injured in another realm, the proximity to a healer often meant life or death.

Kait walked the short distance and reached the healer's hut a few minutes later. She breezed through the dark green door and peered inside the warm front room. It was empty. "Hello? Healer, are you available?" Another tepid silence greeted her.

Help will never come for you.

The memory of those hushed words chilled Kait, and the wind surged, reading her anxiety. "They're busy. That's all. Don't let it get in your head."

Kait abandoned the second dwelling and stepped back into winter's cold embrace. She tried to recall where Anamalla was stationed today, but the fierce nymph hadn't shared that information with her. With few options, she resumed her walk. Goddess willing, she'd cross paths with one of the nymphs she sought, but in the meantime, she could use the break to figure out why she seemed to be losing her mind.

Keeping her eyes trained on the muddy trails ahead, Kait left the square and its chattering occupants behind. She considered transitioning to the air, but it felt good to move. Not allowing thoughts to form, she pushed her legs until her muscles burned and focused on her breathing. In the back of her mind, her exhalation grew louder and resembled a steady raspy moan.

Kait shifted to a sprint and ran as fast as her legs could carry her, as though she could outrun the sound and her frightening dream. When she left the square, she'd had a destination in mind, but now, it felt wrong to stop. Nowhere in her beloved Olean was safe. Maybe if she kept going, her dark thoughts would be unable to keep up with her velocity.

But nymphs were not blessed with boundless energy, and soon Kait's body grew weak from the intense exertion. She collapsed at the edge of a small frozen pool and rolled onto her back. She closed her eyes as her chest heaved and her heart thumped wildly. After a few minutes, the ice crystals beneath her melted and absorbed into her dress like a sponge. Kait didn't notice the cold—temperature didn't affect a nymph's system like it did a human's—but the clinging feeling of the damp fabric was distracting. With a sigh, she sat up and rubbed her eyes with her palms.

"Kaitaini?" someone called behind her.

Kait caught sight of her elder's olive-green robes over her shoulder. "Oh,

Tahlia. You scared me."

Tahlia paused a few feet away and cocked her head. "I was on my way back from a meeting with the elders and saw you sitting here. What's going on? I assigned you to Dion's team today. Did you already seal the geyser?" The elder aurai fixed Kait with a pointed expression. Her eyes didn't stray to the beauty of the frozen pool. Instead, they remained on her, heavy with concern.

A long white cloud of vapor escaped from between Kait's lips as she wrapped her arms around her body, unsure where to begin. "I was in Equine, but something strange happened to me last night. I saw a nymph stumbling around. When I tried to help, she attacked me. When I got close enough to see her face, I realized . . . It was me."

Tahlia absorbed the words. "That's an intense dream."

"No, I was awake. I remember the pain as she sank her teeth into me. Her putrid smell . . . It wasn't a dream. It was too real."

"I don't see a bite on you now," Tahlia countered.

"I awoke in my hammock, but I swear it happened."

"I don't understand. How do you know it wasn't a bad dream?"

"I saw the creature again, not even an hour ago. Another wild nymph rushed down the mountain and attacked Dion, but when I arrived at her side, the nymph was gone."

"What did Dion say?"

Color flooded Kait's cheeks. "She didn't see anyone. Nothing attacked her. She was angry because I dropped the water I was responsible for and injured several naiads. I tried to find you at home to send a replacement in my stead, but you were out."

"Injured? Kait, this is serious. How long have they been waiting? Why didn't you assign another aurai yourself? You're more than capable."

"I'm sorry. I wasn't thinking clearly. Everyone says I'm hallucinating, but I swear the deranged nymphs were as real as you and me. Please, Tahlia, you have to believe me."

Tahlia sighed and turned away from Kait's pleading gaze. "I don't know what to say. Frankly, I'm shocked by your behavior. You know better than to abandon your team. You should have tried harder to locate me."

"I know, and I apologize. But Tahlia, this dream—"

"Sounds highly improbable, Kait. When was the last time you took a break? Ever since you returned from the human realm, you've hardly slept. Working yourself to the bone won't dull the memories. Exhaustion only gives them the strength to haunt you at night. You should talk to someone and eliminate the burden. *Forgive* yourself. You went through an incredible ordeal. It's okay to admit you need time to heal."

"I stopped by a healer today before I came here, but she wasn't in either." Kait's violet eyes focused on a pair of cardinals swooping in dizzying patterns over the still pool.

Tahlia touched her shoulder, and her tone softened. "That's good. Try again and make an appointment. I think your mind and body are telling you to slow down. What do your sisters think about these . . . visions?"

"I haven't seen them. Bia is involved in the realm of Madik's development. Ever since we defeated Zeus, I can hardly keep her in Olean for a few hours."

"She likes her freedom," Tahlia said with a smile. "And Jezlem? I know she's adjusting to life as a mortal after the loss of her halo, but I'm sure she'd still be interested."

"Maybe." Kait cleared her throat and stood. "I'll recruit another aurai to send in my place. Dion is still waiting."

"I'll take care of that. I want you to relax, take a break. Leave Olean and deal with whatever stressors are causing these violent apparitions. Once you've established harmony within yourself, come to me. If you pass my evaluation, then you can return to assignments, but until then, my dear, your behavior is too unpredictable. Do you understand?"

Kait gaped, dumbstruck. No one, not even Tahlia, believed her.

No help will ever come for you.

The words wove through her mind like a poisonous fog, already proving true.

"I understand," Kait said, her voice barely audible.

Tahlia nodded, then leapt into the air and disappeared on the wind like a fading ghost, leaving Kait alone with only her thoughts to keep her company, and as the elder had suggested, that was a very dangerous place indeed.

A frigid wind greeted Kait as she stepped onto the muddy shore of the mortal world. The landscape had changed drastically since fall and appeared even more barren than Olean. Rather than the beautiful colors of rust and sunshine that had previously adorned them, the trees were stripped bare, without even the sparkle of frost painting the cracked bark. She shivered and took another step. It felt as if hundreds of eyes were trained on her. Passing beneath the skeletal trees, she pulled her arms tight to her sides to avoid their gnarled fingers and pointed thorns.

Although the landscape was bleak, Kait recognized the lake where she first met Blake—the mortal who had helped rescue her from Zeus three months ago. He'd thought her dead when he first saw her. Truthfully, it would have been easier for him if she had been. Instead of a quick phone call to the police and a story to tell his friends, Blake and his best friend Joel had been coerced into a deadly game with the gods.

Kait didn't find out until they had returned to Olean how close to death all of them had come after Zeus captured her and held her imprisoned in the mountains. The small rescue party had battled through a blizzard, defeated the god's vicious spiked tiger-like creature called a piriol, and somehow managed to cut down the titan Atlas with help from Layla, a rare shifter nymph who had brewed the boys a regenerative draught to equal the playing field.

Kait recalled the moment she saw Blake in Atlas's cavern amidst the carnage. It seemed as if the sweet mortal she'd met just a week prior had aged fifty years. She could hardly recognize him under the layers of blood, sweat, and grime as he clutched his sword and charged Zeus. Even as his deep gashes wept, Blake fought, her shield until his heart struggled to beat and his soul slipped from his lips.

Guilt twisted Kait's stomach as she pictured his face and remembered the sound of his last breath. Bia had miraculously healed him, but not once since they'd parted had Kait tried to contact him, let alone visit. Did he hate her? Think her cruel or ungrateful that he had risked his life for her—died to prevent Zeus from taking her body and reducing her to a mortal, as he did to Jezlem?

Kait forced her wandering thoughts to evaporate the moment they settled on anything of substance. It was easier to remain aloof, detached. Blake didn't belong in her world, and she had no idea how to exist in his. Dancing in a crowded club with strangers was one thing, but slowing down and forming a relationship with a mortal was totally different. They were from opposite worlds. Shared trauma wasn't exactly a solid foundation for a budding romance.

Kait shook her head and exhaled, trying to rid her chest of the tightness that clenched it whenever she thought of Blake. Memories of his closed eyes assailed her, the bloody gashes that scarred his hands, and the feeling of his cool skin as his soul slipped away. He'd sacrificed everything to help, and ironically, it was this level of commitment that scared her.

Blake hadn't hesitated to jump into an unimaginable world of fantasy when he'd learned of her fate. So why couldn't Kait bring herself to leap as well? The image of her and Blake sitting on the edge of his bed caused her nerves to flutter. Before Zeus pulled them into his dark game, she had allowed herself to let go. In his warm cluttered room, she wasn't a nymph and Blake wasn't mortal. It hadn't mattered that they were different. For just a moment, she was able to breathe and confide in someone without fear of judgment. Blake had listened and even revealed a sliver of his own demons.

Images of bloody scars across Blake's body shrank back, replaced by the few innocent freckles that sprinkled his wrist. Kait recalled the feeling of his thigh pressed against hers and flushed at the heat the simple touch had wrought. For a century, she'd closed herself off to love and intimacy, terrified of the horrors hidden within false promises. Yet when she looked into Blake's eyes, heard his story, the frozen wall she'd thrust her heart behind after Hermes started to thaw.

It had been a century since that terrible night at the speakeasy. After weeks of sneaking into the mortal club with her friend Willow and dancing with the charming god, Kait had foolishly believed Hermes when he whispered he loved her. Willow had tried to keep her from going back, from believing the immortal's silver tongue. Gods only cared about the hunt, about attaining euphoria—the glorious high when they coupled with a nymph and absorbed her connection to the ethereal realm, her halo. But Kait hadn't listened. The next thing she knew, Hermes had her pinned against a wall while Apollo ravaged her best friend.

Tears welled in Kait's eyes and her chest constricted with rage every time she recalled the feeling of her friend's ragged screams as she fought to break free from Apollo's silencing magic. The image of Willow fighting beneath the god as he forced himself on her was forever branded in her memory. His assault left her body broken beyond a healer's repair. He killed her. Kait vowed from that moment on to never trust a man with her heart, or anything else for that matter.

No, Kait wasn't in love with Blake. But his sacrifice and courage introduced her to the idea that good men could exist and opened her to the chance that maybe she wouldn't have to be alone for the rest of her life. The only problem now was convincing her mind to give her heart a little freedom, but that was easier said than done.

"Of course, Jez lives here. Of all the places in the mortal world, she chose to build her life two blocks away from Blake." Kait groaned and hiked up the hill toward the small Vermont town. "Maybe Ionna's sensors were mistaken, and she traced a different mortal here."

Kait knew her musings were in vain. She'd seen the way her sister had looked at Blake's friend Joel. She'd only been around the pair for a few hours, but their attraction was tangible. Begrudgingly, she followed the anthousai's directions and emerged from the woods. Bennington was quaint, hosting less than ten thousand people.

A few hundred feet away, motorists went about their day. Thick coats, wool hats, and knitted scarves were securely wrapped around each pedestrian to protect against winter's touch. Kait glanced down at her own attire. Shimmering golden fabric hung from her neck and ended just above her knees. Her chocolate hair billowed over her back, and her feet were bare atop the snow.

"Great," Kait muttered, following the path. Her feet crunched over the frozen white landscape. The last time she'd traversed the forest road, it was well-trodden by those seeking the wood's serenity. Today, however, it lay before her pure and untouched. Kait frowned. The same uneasy feeling that had assailed her during her dream licked her exposed skin, searching for a weakness to exploit. She shivered and picked up the pace.

CHAPTER 4

A copper bell clanged overhead as Kait entered the little store. The scent of smoky pine permeated the warm space as candles competed for dominance with the aroma of the pizza parlor next door. Brushing errant snowflakes off her hair, she meandered through the eclectic rows. Flashlights stood beside a waffle iron, and fishing poles and scarves hung suspended from the water-stained ceiling, while a rack of winter coats was crammed between a collection of bicycles on the left and a small rack of children's books on the right.

"Afternoon."

Kait spun around to find an elderly man with a faded baseball cap and bright blue eyes surrounded by deep wrinkles stocking Beanie Babies in a pile next to cereal boxes. "Oh, uh, hi there."

"I'd ask if I could help you find anything, but I'm betting you're in the market for a good coat."

Kait glanced down at her thin romper. "Ah, yes. I was at a party and misplaced mine."

The man arranged a stuffed cow atop a flamingo and waved her forward. "A party, huh? Fancy. Come on back. The coats are over here." He shuffled along the linoleum while his liver- spotted hands slightly shook.

Kait crossed her arms over her chest and feigned a shiver. "It was a birthday thing," she explained, though the clerk didn't seem to care that she was dressed like an imbecile.

He paused in front of the bookshelf and ran a hand over the few coats. They swayed gently on their hangers. "I don't have much left. I've been meaning to box these up and ship 'em back. Most folks already got their winter gear this time of the year, see?"

Kait nodded. She rifled through the slim selection until her fingers hovered over a dark turquoise parka with black faux fur. It was the only one without a T after the size. "I'll take this one."

"Good choice." The clerk nodded and fixed his cap. Raising two fingers, he waved her onward again and headed toward the back wall. Kait followed and tucked the parka under her arm. "I've got one or two pairs of boots, too. They're men's, but I figure it beats your toes falling off."

Kait curled her bare toes atop the linoleum. "Oh, yeah. You're probably right."

"You forget your shoes at this party, too?"

Kait grimaced. Because nymphs transitioned to their elements so often, the less clothing they donned, the smoother the metamorphosis. In Olean, hardly anyone wore shoes—a practice that clearly made her stand out here. "There was a lot going on."

The clerk grunted low in his throat and tossed her a fleece-lined pair with navy blue rubber soles. "Take these. They'll be big on you, but they're better than what you got."

"Thank you," Kait said, withdrawing the boots from the box.

"Is there anything else you were needing today? Anyone I can call for you?" His eyes lingered on the four scars that knotted the skin on her neck.

Kait paused with the left boot in her hand. She knew he was asking a different question, but she couldn't exactly explain the scars were from a piriol's teeth, a forever reminder that she wasn't strong enough to prevent Zeus from assaulting Jezlem. Instead, she pasted a bright smile on her face and tucked her chin, hoping to erase the man's concerns. "Thank you, but I'm fine. I'm heading over to the little pub down the road to meet up with my sister."

The man grunted once more before giving a definitive nod. "All right. Let's get you on your way, then." He slid behind the register and began to type numbers into a machine.

Kait's stomach dropped.

"I'm so sorry. I—I can't pay for these. I don't have any money." Kait placed the box on the counter and draped the coat on top. "Sorry for wasting your time." Heat blossomed on her cheeks at her stupidity. The armories spread throughout Olean offered any article of clothing one could wish for—gowns, leather, even jeans—all at no cost. She had been so distracted by her conversation with Tahlia that she hadn't thought to stop and dress appropriately for the mortal realm. She only intended to visit with Jez for a few minutes, but the trip was turning into a nightmare. She hunched her shoulders to hide behind her curls. Her hand grazed the metal handle when the clerk called out.

"Wait, darling. I can't let you go outside dressed like that."

Kait paused and looked at him over her shoulder. What was she supposed to do? "Um, I can see if my sister has some money?"

The clerk shook his head. "Nah, nah. Come on back here."

Kait's fingertips slipped off the handle, and she clasped her hands together in front of her as she made her way back to the register. Brushing hair out of her face, she fixed the clerk with a quizzical stare.

"Put these on," the clerk instructed.

"But I don't—"

"I know, but my wife would divorce me if she learned I let you go out there like that over a few bucks."

"Thank you, but I can't accept them."

"Sure you can, and you will. I told you earlier—I was about to ship them back to the warehouse. You're doing me a favor." His skin crinkled as he gave her a warm smile.

Kait smiled in return, touched by his generosity. She reached for the coat and burrowed into the soft fluff surrounding the hood. Next, she took out the boots, surprised at how sturdy yet comfortable they were. Pink color returned to her cheeks. The items weren't cheap.

The clerk gave a genuine chuckle. "There now. That's better. I can sleep easy tonight."

"Thank you so much. I appreciate your kindness."

The clerk waved his hand in front of his face. "No worries. Like I said, you're doing me a favor. You go have fun with your sister now and maybe keep your wits about you at the next party." He raised his eyebrows as he gave her a wide smile.

"Yes, sir. Thank you. Bye."

"Nice meeting you, darling."

The brass bell dinged as she pulled the door open to exit. Kait didn't feel the cold, and although the wind enveloped her rather than bit into her like the mortals complained, she couldn't disagree that the parka and boots were a welcome addition to her thin wardrobe as the down-filled sleeves hugged her frame. The image of Blake sitting beside her sparked again. What would it feel like to be held by him?

With a deep exhale, Kait continued down the sidewalk toward the pub where Jezlem worked. The sunset cast the snow-covered hills in a rosy glow as the rays flickered like a dying fire.

A sturdy brick building awaited her on the other side of the street. Through the large front window, she could see the small restaurant was packed with hungry diners eager to escape the cold. Kait lifted her boot but hesitated as fear wormed its way into her heart. It was too alive inside, too loud. How was she going to find Jez? Then, a mess of blond hair bounced into view as her sister passed the window, one hand balancing a large serving tray loaded down with glasses, the other perched on her hip. Jezlem laughed, her eyes bright with joy at something a customer said. She looked happy. Kait crossed the street.

Guilt clenched her stomach again. What was she doing there? Jez was mortal. She didn't need to be drawn back into an ethereal nightmare. Kait sighed, and her breath spidered across the glass in a hazy fog.

At least say hello. You came all this way.

Kait swallowed her trepidation and left her worries clinging to the windowsill, edging her way past a group of people smoking outside the doorway. The pleasant aroma of baking bread and a symphony of spices collided with the bitter scent of nicotine.

"How many in your party?" a young girl asked from behind a wooden podium.

"Ah, just me."

"Is a seat at the bar okay?" the hostess asked, bending down to grab a laminated menu.

"A bar? Um, I was hoping to sit where I could talk to Jezlem," Kait said, unsure if her sister was even using her real name in the human realm.

The hostess glanced at a sheet marked with numerous Xs. "Of course. Everyone always wants Jez. Her tables are full, but since it's just you, I can probably put you on the outskirts of her section. Okay?"

Kait's head spun as she tried to understand the girl's jargon. She nodded and followed, caught off guard by her sister's nickname coming from a human's lips. She shed her hood and squeezed through the dozens of bodies lingering around a broad horseshoe-shaped table. Two men tossed bottles into the air, barely catching them before they spiraled back up.

"Jared and Danny. They took the World Bartender Championship last year. Here's your table. I'll let Jez know you're over here, and she'll be with you in a few minutes," the girl said sweetly and handed her a stiff menu.

"Thanks."

Kait shrugged out of her new coat and slid onto the wooden seat. She stared at the words on the menu and images of greasy hunks of crumbled pink meat. Her stomach knotted. Apart from the fish naiads supplied for the realm, nymphs didn't eat meat.

"Evening! Welcome to Philly's. My name is Jez, and I'll be your server. Can I get you started with a margarita or glass of wi—" Jez stopped. "Kait? What are you doing here?"

Kait lowered the menu and smiled. "I was in the area and thought I'd say hi."

Jezlem was silent for a moment while she studied Kait's face. "In the area? Why were—you know what? It doesn't matter. I can't believe you're here. Give me a hug."

Kait stood and wrapped her arms around her sister, burrowing her face in her bushy ponytail. "It's so good to see you," she whispered, fighting back tears.

Jezlem pulled away, and her red lips frowned. "What happened? What's wrong?"

Kait glanced around at the rambunctious restaurant. Standing there, it was hard to believe the ethereal world existed or that darkness followed her. She opened her mouth to reply when another server whizzed by, supporting an impossible number of plates.

"Jez, table seven is looking for you, and your cheese fries are dying in the window," the girl called.

Jezlem glanced toward the kitchen. "Don't leave, please. Let me finish this rush, and then we'll talk, okay?" Kait nodded as Jezlem broke their embrace. "Eat something. Have a drink."

Kait gestured to the vast menu. "What should I get?"

"Don't worry. I'll bring you something good," Jezlem said with a grin, though her eyes were tight with worry. "Sit tight. I'll be back soon."

"Okay."

Kait resumed her seat and wrapped her arms around herself, watching Jezlem melt into the crowd. True to her word, she returned a short while later with a glass filled with pale yellow liquid, a basket of fried sticks, and a black bundle shoved under her arm.

"Lemonade," Jezlem said, setting down the glass. "Think of it like juju berries with more sugar, and these are steak fries. Dip them in this." She dragged a red bottle from the far side of the table. "They're amazing."

"Thanks," Kait said. "What's that?"

Jezlem glanced at the object under her arm. "Oh, this is for you. Drape it around your shoulders." She leaned forward and placed the soft fabric around Kait's neck.

"Why? I'm not cold." Kait touched the scarf.

Jezlem's eyes flickered back and forth as she bent over the table. "Your halo is attracting some stares."

Kait's cheeks burned. In her haste to see Jezlem, she had forgotten about the golden aura that radiated from her skin. Glancing around the room, she quickly saw what Jez meant. Several guys at the bar were looking in her direction.

"Is it bad?" Kait asked as she spread the scarf as wide as possible.

"Not really. I suspect they're just working up the nerve to come say hi, but when the lights dim, people will notice for sure. This way, you'll be prepared." Jezlem patted her shoulder.

"They won't come over here, will they?"

"Don't worry. If one of them works up the courage, which I doubt, just pretend you don't speak English," Jezlem answered. "I've got to help run some platters. If you need anything, wave me down."

Kait gave her an uneasy smile and held up her lemonade. "I will, and thanks for this."

"No problem. I'll bring you something heavier a little later," Jezlem called over her shoulder.

Kait sighed, her anxiety slowly easing as she took a sip of the exotic drink. The sides of her tongue tingled when the alien flavor rushed down her throat. "Whoa." She laughed and set it back down on the wooden tabletop in exchange for one of the crispy fries. She brought it to her lips and nibbled the edge, tasting butter and garlic. It was delicious. She consumed the whole basket, and only when she reached the bottom of the grease-stained paper did she realize she'd forgotten to try them with the red sauce.

"Here's a fresh batch for you," an attractive server with glasses said. Grabbing the empty basket, he placed another full one before her. "Jez said you'd like them." He winked and spun around, gone before she could open her mouth.

"Thank you!" she called, though the upbeat jazz music overhead drowned her out.

Kait picked up another fry and took a bite. He was handsome, with a nice jawline. Her stomach tightened uncomfortably as she thought of Blake. What if he were there, watching her from another table? Would he recognize her? Talk to her? Her nerves prickled, and she shivered. "Don't think about him. Don't think," she admonished and placed another fry between her teeth. She forced her mind to go blank and focused on watching the humans corralled beside her—anything to keep from looking back at herself.

CHAPTER 5

It was a little after ten when Jezlem collapsed into the seat beside Kait two hours later. Her upper body flopped across the tabletop as she cradled her chin in her hand and unleashed her pent-up curls from the elastic band.

"Goddess, that feels better," Jezlem ran her fingers through the creases. "What a night. I'm sorry it took me so long. Another server called off, so I got stuck covering her section. Did you like the chicken?"

"Yeah, it was different but tasty."

"Tell me about it. I refused at first, but Joel eventually convinced me."

"How's that going? How's all of it going? You seem happy, in your element again."

Jezlem's shoulders shook with a light snort. "Sure, rather than controlling rivers, I now wield platters of chicken alfredo like a beast."

Kait's voice softened. "You know what I mean. You may not have your connection to the water like before, but you've always been a natural leader. You seem so comfortable around the mortals, too."

Jezlem untied her stained apron and set it in a heap in front of her. "I wasn't at first. I couldn't keep the orders straight and dumped soup all over a woman's lap. It helped that I'd waited tables back down in Florida after everything with Zeus, but it was still a huge adjustment. Especially leaving the beach. When I moved up here, it felt like losing my connection all over again, but Joel helped a lot. I would have been lost without him."

Kait swallowed a growing lump in her throat and shifted in her seat. "That's wonderful. I'm glad you're doing so well."

"Joel even talked me into applying to a few colleges. I got my first acceptance letter last week." Her cheeks turned a soft pink.

"College? What's that?"

"School. They're all over the country. Students can learn about anything. Once they've gained enough knowledge on a particular subject, they graduate and get a job. I think I want to be a history teacher or work in a museum."

"History? Whose history?"

"Ours. Well, sort of," Jezlem explained with a laugh. "Apparently, Greek mythology is a thing amongst the mortals. Who better to talk about the gods than me?"

Kait's eyebrows shot up at the irony. Jezlem's students would certainly get a unique perspective on the myths. "That sounds amazing. Which one are you going to attend?"

Jezlem shrugged. "I'm not sure yet. I got into Syracuse, but Joel said it's in New York. I'd rather be somewhere warm and close to the beach. We sent a few applications to schools down south, too, so we'll see."

"We?" Kait posed, already knowing the answer.

"Joel and I applied to all the same schools. We . . . Well, we want to stay together." Jezlem blushed.

"Wow, you guys are getting more serious than I thought." Kait tried to keep her tone neutral, but even she could hear the judgment. She'd only met Joel the one time before he and Blake returned to the human realm, but battling sadistic gods hadn't left a lot of opportunity to get to know him.

"What do you mean?"

"Nothing. It's just . . . You've only been together three months. I'm worried about what will happen if it doesn't work out. You shouldn't tether yourself."

Jezlem narrowed her eyes. "You think he's going to leave me? Use me like Zeus and desert me when he finds someone better?"

The cozy atmosphere plunged. Kait had forgotten her sister's quick temper. "No, I didn't mean that. I'm sure Joel is great. I just don't want him to hurt you."

Jezlem leaned away from the table and fixed Kait with a pointed stare. "When was the last time you saw Blake? In the mountains after he died rescuing you? Talk about getting hurt."

"I'm sorry." Kait's neck flushed a deep pink.

Jezlem grumbled under her breath and pushed back her chair. "Come on. They're getting ready to close. We should go."

Kait followed soundlessly after they slipped into their coats and left the warm pub. The starry night welcomed them with an icy bite. Jezlem shivered beside her as they walked past darkened businesses, but Kait barely registered the chilling winds. She thought back to the kind store clerk and zipped the coat higher.

They walked in silence until the end of the block as Jezlem led the way. "So, why haven't you talked to him?" she asked.

Snow crunched under their boots. "I don't know," Kait mumbled. "I've thought about it, but when I imagine seeing him again, I back out. What can I say? What would we do? I don't want to start hanging out with him and give him the wrong idea. We're too different. I don't belong in his world."

"And yet, here you are, traversing the mortal world as easily as me."

"Yeah, well, my being here has nothing to do with him this time."

Jezlem paused and placed her hand on Kait's arm. "Earlier, when I first saw you, something was wrong."

Kait bit the inside of her cheek. She wanted to confess everything, but after their tense moment in the restaurant, it no longer felt like the right time. Their relationship had been strained for as long as she could remember. Since they were young, Jez had adopted the role of maternal protector out of the three sisters. Gentle Bia hadn't seemed to mind Jez's domineering guidance as they learned pankration fighting techniques, sparred with their elements, and studied the last sister trio that comprised the Triad and their fulfillment of the prophecy with the victory of the Titan War.

From the moment of their rare creation when three sisters had manifested instead of one from a drop of the mother goddess Gaia's blood, they'd been told they were destined to bring about another powerful change to the ethereal realms. But Kait had rebelled against the prophecy's destined demands of greatness from her until Willow's death, as well as Jezlem's strict expectations for how a nymph of the Triad should behave. Kait recalled dozens of times their elders had to step in and break up an altercation between the two of them.

"Oh, no. Everything is fine. I was just . . . overwhelmed seeing you. I'm sorry I didn't visit sooner."

Jezlem stared. "You know, you've always been a terrible liar. I can see it now. Something has you spooked."

Kait laughed nervously, trying to brush off Jezlem's concern. "It's nothing, just—" She hesitated, searching for an adequate excuse. "I keep thinking about Zeus. I want the memories to go away."

Her sister's face softened, and her suspicion vanished. "I'm sorry, Kait. I wish there were something I could do to help."

"Thanks." Over Jezlem's shoulder, shadows shifted as a figure snuck through the lightly falling snow. Kait swept her arms out and herded Jezlem behind her.

"What are you doing?" Jezlem asked as she tripped up the curb.

"Quiet. Something is following us."

"Where?"

Kait didn't answer. Her eyes focused on the pockets of darkness that hugged the nearby buildings and parked cars while her ears strained for the dreaded moans or stunted limp that accompanied the diseased nymphs. Holding her breath, she waited, her fingers eager to cast.

The sound of thudding footsteps, along with ragged breathing, caused Kait's heart rate to jump. She spun around, but all she could see were snowflakes as they fell and obscured her sight lines.

"Kait, what's going on?"

A shadow flickered across the back window of a silver Jeep to their left, followed by a raspy gurgle. Kait didn't hesitate. She touched the tips of her fingers together in rapid succession and forced her palms open to unleash an explosion of energy. The wind shot forward and pummeled the creature just as the top of its head slunk into view. Twirling her hands, she wrenched it off its feet to hang suspended in the air.

"Kait! Are you crazy? You can't cast in the mortal realm! What if someone sees?" Jezlem cried, glancing down the empty street. "The Immortal Council will—"

"Self-defense, Jez."

"Against what?"

"Help! Get me down!" the creature yelled as a black brick rained from its upturned pocket.

"Joel?" Jezlem called. "Kait, put him down!"

Kait's racing pulse calmed and she lowered her hands. Joel's soles grazed the sidewalk a moment later. "Oops, sorry. Hey, Joel."

"Ah, no worries. Nothing's broken. Wait . . . Kait? Wow, hey. It's been a while." Joel moved forward as if to give her a hug but hesitated, no doubt frightened she might throw him into the air again.

"Yeah, sorry. I came to say hi to Jez, and I thought you were something . . . else."

"I get it. Now I know to never sneak up on a nymph." He bent down, scooping his fallen phone out of the snow.

Jezlem slipped her hands into his and stepped close, like one magnet seeking out another. "What are you doing here, goofball?"

"I came from Philly's. I wanted to walk you home, but Ray said I just missed you." Joel kissed the tip of her nose.

"Aren't you sweet?" Jezlem sighed, kissing him back.

Joel tucked Jezlem's arm in his. "Geez, it's cold out here. Let's get you guys back to your place before we get frostbite."

"Good idea." Kait stepped aside to allow the couple to lead the way. She kept her eyes downcast on the accumulating snow, but she could feel Jezlem's stare. Her reaction had been way over the top. Had she even heard the moans? The raspy breaths? Or was it another hallucination? Falling into step behind them, she vaguely listened to Joel's chattering as her eyes flickered back and forth, examining each shadow and crevice they passed. She took a deep breath; she was being irrational. The gods would never allow those creatures into the human realm. Maybe it *was* all in her head.

"How long are you staying?" Joel asked before he raised a cup of hot chocolate to his lips.

"Just a few hours, I think." Kait wrapped her hands around her own mug.

A look of disappointment crossed Joel's face. "Really? That's too bad. I know Blake would love to see you."

Kait tilted her head and took a sip, shrugging to acknowledge the poor timing.

Jezlem ambled into the small living room and sat down next to Joel, then draped her legs over his. "You should stay. At least for the night. They're forecasting the snow will turn to ice soon."

Kait rolled her eyes. "When has that ever stopped me?"

Jezlem sighed and fluffed her voluminous hair over her shoulder. "Come on. Even as the wind, getting hit in the face with ice isn't pleasant. Plus, you'll barely be able to find the portal in this mess. It's settled. You're sleeping over."

"Fine," Kait relented as she sank deeper into the narrow armchair. Then, she steered the conversation away from herself. "This is a cute place."

"Thanks." Jezlem beamed with pride. "Joel helped me find it. The lady who lives downstairs is older. Her son lived up here for a bit, but then he got a job and moved out. The rent is cheap, and it's warm, so I'm happy. Plus, I had the best time finding all the furniture."

Joel groaned. "Yeah, if you like trekking in and out of Goodwill and the Salvation Army for an entire weekend."

Jezlem elbowed him and pursed her lips. "You had fun."

Joel snorted. "Sure. Mainly, I was trying to keep you from buying everything. You're only going to be here for a few months."

"That doesn't matter. I want it to feel like home."

"What do you mean?" Kait asked, having trouble following.

"I move out of here at the beginning of August. Well, once we pick a school."

"Yup," Joel said. "Then, it's just you and me." Jezlem nuzzled into Joel's embrace as he wrapped his arms more tightly around her.

Kait hid behind her mug as she swallowed the tiny grains of chocolate that clung to the bottom. The desire to leave was stifling. Sitting across from the happy couple made her feel as if she were intruding on their private world. She stared at her sister. Although she had been reduced to a mortal, she hadn't given up. She wasn't wandering the human world, lost and confused. She had goals, a purpose, and hope.

What do I have? Ghoulish dreams and an empty sky.

"So, what do you think, Kait? If the town is snowed in tomorrow, you want to go?" Jezlem's cheery voice roused Kait from her thoughts.

"Yeah, that sounds fine," Kait answered, even though she hadn't heard what plans they were discussing.

"Awesome. I can't wait to see the look on his face," Joel said as he rose to his feet. "Well, it's closing in on midnight. I better head home."

Jezlem pulled him around to face her. "Will you be okay walking back? Want me to come?"

"I'll be fine. It's just a couple blocks. Stay here where it's warm." Joel leaned down and kissed Jezlem on the lips, lingering an extra second. "I love you." With a final peck, he slipped away from the couch and shrugged into his coat and hat.

"I love you, too," Jezlem called, and a radiant smile danced on her lips.

"Love you more. Good to see you, Kait. I'll meet you guys tomorrow.

Night!" Joel waved and disappeared out the door, closing it tight behind him.

Jezlem stared at the now empty entryway while happiness and concern warred in her eyes.

Kait set her cup down. "Are you all right?"

Jezlem snapped her gaze back to her. "Yeah. I get nervous when he walks home this late. He lives less than a mile away, but you never know how long it might take in this weather."

"I'm sure he'll be okay," Kait replied, unable to keep the annoyance out of her tone. She had never seen her sister like this. Jezlem was strong and independent. It was strange to see her in the new role of sappy-eyed lover. "What's happening tomorrow?"

A devilish grin leapt onto Jezlem's face. "I knew you weren't paying attention. Now, you'll have to wait and see."

Kait groaned. "Just tell me."

"Fine. If classes are canceled because of the storm, you, me, Joel, and Blake are going to hang out."

Kait's heart leapt at the betrayal. "Wait, what? Blake? Why would you do that? You know I'm not comfortable seeing him."

Jezlem shrugged. "You were going to talk to him sooner or later, so I made the decision for you."

"Great, while you and Joel drool over one another, Blake and I will be stuck making small talk about the weather."

"It doesn't have to be like that. Blake is nice. Stop thinking about how different you two are and focus on getting to know him. Now, what's really going on with you?"

Kait wrinkled her nose. "I told you. I don't know what to say to him."

Jezlem waved her hand. "No, not that. I saw the way you acted outside before Joel showed up. You were ready to attack him. Who did you think was coming?"

Kait frowned. She had been so eager to discuss the strange happenings with Jez when she first arrived, but now, her throat grew dry. Everyone else had dismissed her claims; part of her was scared her sister would do the same. "No one. He caught me off guard is all."

Jezlem shook her head. "No, it's more than that. Just like there's more behind the reason you came here. I know you, Kait. You've never been . . . sentimental. You didn't come because you missed me. What happened?"

Kait wrung her hands, half-tempted to fade into the air to escape the conversation. But Jezlem was right. Maybe she *would* believe her. "Okay," she started tentatively. "Last night, I saw something. A nymph walking in the woods. Her gait made me think she needed help, but when I got closer, she attacked me. When I saw her face . . . It was me. A rotten version of me. Then, I saw another one later that day. It attacked Dion at the falls in Equine. I don't know what they are, but they're following me. No one believes me. They all say it's stress after what happened with Zeus, but this is different. This is scary. It feels like an—"

"An omen," Jezlem finished, her eyes wide. "That's why you thought something was following us before."

"Yeah." Kait exhaled, relieved. "Have you ever heard of this?"

Jezlem pulled her legs off the floor and tucked them underneath her as if the frightening creatures lurked beneath the worn couch. She leaned toward Kait, her voice a whisper. "Omens are a very powerful form of premonition, usually sent to lower beings from an immortal. When a patron is favored, omens relay good fortune coming their way."

"And if the patron has offended the god?"

"A dark omen is sent, typically to tell of an impending threat. Someone is messing with your head. Forcing visions upon you to drive you mad and seclude you from others."

"Who would do that? This doesn't feel like Zeus."

"No, you're right. It's not his style. But there are other gods who could easily infiltrate your mind and play with your fears."

"They wouldn't send them into the human realm, would they?"

Jezlem bit her lip. "If these creatures are solid projections from *your* mind, then yes. They can terrorize you anywhere you are. Right now, they're only real to you. We need to pray whoever is behind this keeps it that way."

"You're saying this could manifest into something tangible?" Kait shook her head. "What does that mean?"

Jezlem swallowed, and her once serene features clouded with despair. "That everyone we love is in danger."

CHAPTER 6

This is such a bad idea. Why are you doing this?

Kait surged through the swirling wind. Jezlem's prediction had come true. The little Vermont town was covered under a thick blanket of snow. Most of its residents continued to doze, surrounded by sweet dreams of a possible lazy day in the middle of the week.

Kait wasn't sure of the time. The slate-gray sky softened as she materialized atop the fluffy snow. Hopefully, Blake would be awake. If not, she prayed he'd think of her appearance as more of a dream than a nightmare. She danced lightly across the powder to press the palm of her hand against the wooden door of the yellow house and closed her eyes, letting the wind be her ears. Within, she identified two sets of even breathing. She took a step back and contemplated returning to Jezlem's apartment. Maybe leaving this early wasn't such a good idea. If Jez woke to find her gone, especially after Kait had revealed the omens last night, she might freak out.

"Just leave," Kait whispered. "He doesn't have to know you were here."

The idea was tempting, but Jezlem was right. Blake had journeyed halfway across the world to save her. At the very least, she owed him an explanation, and the idea of doing it in front of an audience made it even worse. No, she wasn't running again.

Kait fanned her fingers in a swift pattern. Her skin vaporized into the cold air and funneled up to the roof. With ease, she directed the current into the chimney and a moment later stood in the small living room. She surveyed the space, remembering the way the throw pillow had felt beneath her cheek before she'd bolted. It felt like a lifetime ago.

Zeus is gone, his soul suspended in limbo until Hades releases it. He's not here.

Kait stepped out of the wind's hold and moved silently through the sleeping house. With a gentle wave of her hands, she rose into the air and ascended the stairs, not willing to risk a squeaky step giving away her presence until she hovered outside Blake's door. It was slightly ajar. From her angle, she could make out his sleeping form draped across the mattress.

Just do it. Get it over with.

She stepped inside and smirked at the unruly chaos. Careful to avoid a half-eaten sandwich and stale potato chips, Kait slunk toward the bed and perched on the edge. Her weight eased onto the mattress and her back pressed against one of Blake's legs. He didn't move. In the dim light, she studied his face and compared it to the image stored in her memory.

His black hair was longer and now grazed the middle of his forehead. Several zits dotted his jaw, and he sported a greenish bruise on his left cheekbone, but he still took her breath away as she recalled the way he had faced the most powerful god in the heavens. He never quit, never backed down. She ran her fingertips along the top of the comforter above his stomach. Had his wounds healed or did his interaction with the ethereal realm leave deep scars? Part of her was tempted to look, but the idea of Blake catching her peeking at his bare flesh smothered any interest.

Kait withdrew her hand and pressed the heels of her palms into her eyes, trying to rub away her conflicting emotions. She hated to admit cowardice, but how could she wake him? He was doing fine without her. Her gaze slid to the window and the awaiting woods beyond.

I'll just talk to him later with Jez and Joel.

Rising from the bed, she refused to acknowledge the lie. The moment she left, she wouldn't return. Kait took a step toward the window, but soft fingers clasped her narrow wrist.

"Please stay," Blake whispered, peering at her drowsily.

"I thought you . . . I was . . . I have to get . . ." Kait tried to form an excuse, but she was too surprised to think straight. "Okay."

Blake pulled her back to the bed and shifted over toward the wall. Kait allowed him to guide her onto the mattress, where she laid her head beside his on the pillow.

What are you doing? Get out of here!

Kait closed her eyes, trying to shut off her thoughts, her conscience. What was she doing? How did this make things less complicated? Blake mumbled while his arms wrapped around her. His embrace wasn't hostile, but protective, a shield against probing nightmares. She ignored the reality of how awkward the late morning would be, settled deeper into Blake's arms, and for the first time in weeks, drifted away into a peaceful sleep.

A restful groan, along with shifting limbs, roused Kait an hour later. She shook the clinging webs of sleep from her fuzzy brain and rolled over, confused as to why her hammock felt so sturdy. Bright light fought to slip under her lashes, pulling her closer to the surface of consciousness. She sighed in defeat, and her eyes fluttered open. She squinted toward the sun streaming through the window.

"I thought I was dreaming," a deep voice whispered beside her.

Kait rolled toward the speaker. Memories of the early morning slithered back. "Blake."

He stared, green eyes drowsy with sleep, as if he wasn't entirely convinced she was real.

"I, uh, came to talk to you. To apologize for not . . . Well, for doing nothing these past few months. For abandoning you." Her words rushed out before she could think of a more eloquent way to explain.

"You came to apologize? To me?" Blake cocked his visible eyebrow.

Kait cleared her throat, suddenly too warm and too close to Blake in his narrow bed. What had she been thinking? "Yes. I meant to visit sooner, but . . . things got in the way."

Blake frowned and moved his arm from beneath her head to prop up his own. "I get it. I never thought I'd see you again."

"Why?"

Blake shrugged and withdrew his other arm off Kait's waist. She watched pink color warm his cheeks as he realized with startling clarity that she really was lying beside him. "I guess because I don't really know you. Why would you come back? Zeus is gone. I assumed you'd return to whatever it was you were doing before him."

"I tried. I tried harder than you can imagine to settle back into the same routine, but it felt wrong. I felt empty. It wasn't enough anymore."

"Well, I don't think getting captured by another crazy god is a good remedy for that."

Kait scoffed and pushed his shoulder. "Yeah, because that's where I was headed."

Blake's lips cracked into a crooked grin, and her breathing stuttered.

What are you doing? Why are you flirting?

Biting the inside of her cheek, Kait slipped out from beneath the tangled covers and stood on the carpeted floor to distance herself as far from Blake as the disheveled room allowed. She didn't want to laugh with him. Didn't want to lead him on. She was a nymph of the ethereal realm, and he was human. He was right. They didn't know much about one another, and it had to stay that way.

But would it be so bad?

Before her thoughts could grow dangerous, Kait ran a hand through her tousled hair and fixed her eyes on a pile of crumpled shirts at her feet. "Sorry about all that. Again, I just wanted to apologize. I should go." She took a step toward the door but then remembered his mother. She shifted her weight toward the window instead. "I'll go this way."

"Do you want to take a walk?" Blake pushed himself into a seated position and stared at her with easy confidence.

"A walk? I don't know. There's a lot of snow out there."

Blake smirked. "That's what boots are for. If you don't want to, don't worry about it. You just seemed like you had more you wanted to talk about."

"I did? What I mean—"

"Relax, Kait. If you'd rather not go, it's no big deal." He leaned his head against the wall, and the comforter fell forward and exposed his bare chest.

Kait smiled and averted her gaze to the floorboards. "A walk sounds nice."

"Great," Blake said and then scooted off the bed. Kait took a step back to allow him more room, but his long stride still put him only inches away from her. "Can you go out the window and knock on the front door in five minutes? I'd rather not explain this to my mom."

Kait nodded. "Uh, yeah, sure. I mean, of course."

"Okay, see ya," Blake said with another crooked smile. He padded away and disappeared out the door.

Kait exhaled and crossed to the window, opening it only a sliver to avoid welcoming the frigid breeze inside. "What are you doing?" she asked herself. "He's mortal. It will never work. Make sure he understands that and get back to

Olean." She evaporated into the air and slipped through the mesh grates of the screen into the overcast sky, leaving behind thoughts of a possible tomorrow with Blake on the warm sheets.

CHAPTER 7

Kait's knuckles rapped on the plum door as more snow began to fall. The tidy little porch she huddled on did little to keep the elements away. She swatted clinging flakes off her eyelashes as the door swung open.

An older woman with light brown hair streaked with white answered the door. "May I help you?" The resemblance to Blake was uncanny. The woman shared the same slender nose and high cheekbones. Sophisticated wrinkles ringed her green eyes, resulting in an air of wisdom. Kait's heart broke. She recognized the pain in her tight smile, for the same wariness plagued her.

"Morning. Is Blake in?" Kait asked as she pulled her coat collar tighter around her.

Blake's mother looked Kait up and down, surprise evident in her eyes. "I think he's getting out of the shower. Hang on. Blake!" she cried over her shoulder.

The living room was visible behind her. A side table lamp cast the small space in a cozy glow. It evoked a feeling of warmth and love, but the memory Blake had shared with her of his abusive father darkened the scene. She was glad the woman before her had found a way out from under him.

Blake's muted reply floated down the stairs. "What?"

"You've got a visitor!" His mother turned back to face Kait with a curious smile on her face. "What's your name, dear? Are you a senior with Blake?" She crossed her arms and scanned the snowy road, presumably for Kait's car.

"Yeah. My name is Kait."

"Did you just move here?"

"A couple weeks ago."

"Oh, really? From where?" The sound of hurried footsteps stomping down the stairs saved Kait from having to answer. "Slow down. How many times have I told you not to run in the house?"

Blake's head popped into view as he covered it with a red knit cap. "Sorry, Mom. We're going for a walk. Be back later."

"All right, but don't stay out too long. The weather said we're supposed to get another four inches before lunch. And keep that hat on. You'll get pneumonia with your hair soaking wet like that," his mother warned as he snuck past her.

"Sure, Mom. See ya." He waved.

"Have fun." Her lips twitched with amusement as she followed their retreat from the porch.

"Sorry about that."

"It's okay. Your mom is nice," Kait said, plunging her hands into her pockets as she and Blake fell into step. "Why was she smiling like that?"

Blake snorted. "She's wondering what a beautiful girl is doing knocking on my door during a snowstorm. She's been trying to convince me to go out with someone ever since my girlfriend and I split two years ago. I think she's a little excited."

"She thinks I'm your girlfriend?"

"Nah, don't worry about her. That's how moms are. I'll reassure her you're just a friend." Blake led them down a quiet road.

Just a friend. The comment stung more than it should. *What else would he think? He hasn't seen you in months. You're barely an acquaintance.*

Kait licked a few snowflakes off her lips as she pictured Blake with a cute bubbly girl from his school. The image made her stomach hurt.

"So, where are we going?" Kait asked, shaking the thoughts away.

"Nowhere. It just feels good to walk, especially in all this snow. It's like we're the only two people here."

Kait looked into the swirling sky and blinked as chunky flakes kissed her face. "Like a winter wonderland."

"Exactly." Blake pointed his feet to the side of the road, where slender brown trees cloaked in white waited for them to pass beneath their leaning trunks. "What have you been up to? Besides being plagued with guilt?" he teased.

"What? That's not it," Kait said. "I'm just . . . glad you're happy. I didn't want you to be—"

"Missing you?" Blake turned to face her. The movement carried him so close that the cold vapor from their breaths mingled in a plume of white smoke. He shook his head and leaned away. "As cool as it was battling gods, I was more than happy to return to my boring life."

"Oh, good."

Blake resumed his pace, and his boots crunched through a thin layer of ice atop the snow. Kait didn't know what to think, what to feel. This boy had risked everything and traveled thousands of miles to rescue her; yet, he treated her indifferently, like an older sister who had finally come home to visit.

"This is embarrassing," Blake said, stopping suddenly in his tracks, "but do you mind waiting here for a second?"

Kait wrinkled her brow, caught off guard by his strange outburst. "Why?"

"I need to . . . do something quick. Sorry, something just came over me." His face had turned a brilliant shade of red.

"Sure, I can wait here," Kait said, averting her gaze from his flaming cheeks.

"Thanks. I'll be right back." Blake raced off into the trees as fast as the thick snow would allow.

Kait bit her lip to keep from laughing. Blake's humiliation was almost tangible. To pass the time while he tended to his bodily needs, she angled her head and squinted up into the delicate flakes. A blanket of peace settled atop her shoulders. It felt as if the rest of the world had paused and this beautiful moment was solely for her—a tiny sliver of hope amidst the tumultuous visions and accusations.

"Sorry!" Blake yelled, shattering the peaceful reverie a minute later. He jogged back along the path he'd carved and buried his hands in his pockets, clearly trying to appear as nonchalant as possible. At least his cheeks had cooled. "So, what have you been up to?"

"Not much. I've bounced around to different realms to help repair issues that have come up, like taming geysers, altering cold air currents, stuff like that."

"Yeah, sounds like normal everyday tasks." Blake laughed and crouched down, brushing the accumulated snow off a covered log with his glove. "Let's sit. It's hard to talk to you when I'm focused on not falling into some creature's hidden den."

Kait took the cleared spot and stretched her legs in front of her, then glanced at Blake out of the corner of her eye. "Thanks. This is nice."

Blake bit his lip. "Back in my room, you said you felt empty. What did you mean?"

She traced her palm over the snow-covered wood. "It's hard to explain."

"Take your time. I don't need to be anywhere."

Kait inhaled and narrowed her gaze. "After everything calmed down, I realized how alone I was. Before, I was always looking after Bia or working with Jez and basically trying to prove to everyone what a strong soldier I could be. Now my sisters are gone, off on new and exciting adventures, while I'm stuck at home twiddling my thumbs."

"Why don't you leave, too? Why didn't you go with Bia?"

Kait opened her mouth to respond, then closed it, at a loss for what to say. "I have no idea. That never occurred to me. Bia was so determined and anxious to leave Olean. She didn't have any fear. It's different for me. Everywhere I go, I feel as if I'm being watched, like someone is bidding their time to strike. Being somewhere new and unfamiliar only makes me feel more vulnerable."

"Then, why come here? Aren't you vulnerable in my world?" Blake asked.

"Yeah, but so are the gods. There are rules for Earth. Their magic is just as limited as mine here. Your world is a kind of neutral zone. Unless we're in danger, nymphs aren't allowed to use magic, especially in front of humans. Our world can't be exposed."

"But that didn't stop Hera from attacking us before."

"What?" Unease prickled the back of her neck. Bia had never mentioned that Hera had physically crossed into the mortal realm to assault them, but Blake wouldn't make that up. There were rules—hard limits governed by the Immortal Council—that held all ethereal creatures accountable. Exposure of their world was forbidden, as was harming a mortal. Had Hera been able to use her clout and bribe the other ancients to turn a blind eye? Kait's head spun.

"Sorry, I didn't mean to scare you. I just meant that you can't shut everyone out. You can't stop living because of something that *might* happen. Both joy and terror exist everywhere."

A loud flutter of wings clapped, and Kait snapped her head to the right. A mass of birds lifted into the white sky, their wings pumping hard as if to escape an unknown threat. The same hideous chuckle from her dream drifted through the trees. Acting on instinct, Kait jumped to her feet.

"What?"

"There is another reason I came here. Quick, get up."

Blake complied, searching the still trees for an unknown catalyst. "What's going on?"

"Someone is wielding dark magic to target me and send horrible visions. So far, they've manifested in diseased nymphs, hell-bent on devouring flesh. Jez is right. You both are. I think whoever is behind them is waiting until I'm most vulnerable." Her eyes widened with a sick revelation. "It's a trap." Kait pulled her hands out of her pockets as fear spiked like an icicle through her heart.

This can't be happening. This can't be real.

Snapping twigs exploded in her ears as a pale silhouette rushed through the trees with savage speed. Kait threw out her arm to shield Blake as an infected nymph charged from out of nowhere, sprinting atop the snow. She was a good twenty yards away, but there was no mistaking her identity. Red hair streamed behind the nymph like a dancing flame as she leapt over buried logs, her amber eyes diluted by hunger. Her once scarlet dress was now ragged and torn, filthy and soiled with blood and dirt.

"Is that—"

"Bia." Kait's voice broke as her sister belched an inhuman snarl. "Run!"

Kait grabbed Blake's hand, yanking him after her. The once quiet wood now rang with shrill gasps and ragged breaths as Kait pushed her legs harder, but the heavy snowdrifts pulled her down faster than quicksand. "Hurry!" She squeezed Blake's hand tighter as he collapsed to his knees.

"It's no use." Blake struggled to stand as his hands punched through the unstable floor.

"No, we can outrun her. Come on! Get back on your feet!"

"But I don't want to." Blake dug his nails into Kait's flesh, then laughed loudly when she cried out.

"Blake! What are you doing? We have to get out of here." Kait eyed Bia's fast-approaching form over his shoulder.

"You're not going anywhere," Blake hissed. With surprising strength, Blake wrenched her arm forward and threw her back.

Kait sailed through the air, blinded by the falling snow until her head collided with a nearby tree trunk. The impact stole her breath, and her vision blurred. What was happening? Kait reached up to cradle a tender spot on the back of her scalp. Warm liquid soaked her hair as heat spread over her palm and blood stained the white powder beneath her.

Blake snickered. "You're even weaker than I thought."

Kait winced and glanced up. Bia stood beside Blake, licking her lips as her broken fingers twitched at her sides. "What's going on?"

"Did you really think you could escape my nightmares in the mortal world?" Blake spat. "The gods' powers are limited, are they? Well, what do you make of this?" He gestured to the decayed nymph at his side, his eyes hard chips. "Would you like to feel her teeth? Or do you still think it's all in your head?"

"Who are you?"

"That's right. We've never been properly introduced. But I do believe you know my husband." Blake's features flickered like a hologram experiencing a momentary surge. When they settled again, his green eyes were gone, replaced by cool gray irises dappled with silver bursts. His jawline softened and his high cheekbones curved gracefully beneath flawless skin. His hair lengthened under the knit cap and transformed into lush golden curls. "Well, you *knew* my husband. I believe you helped slay him."

"Hera?" Kait asked incredulously as she surveyed the quiet woods. "What did you do to Blake?"

"Relax, nymph. Your precious mortal no longer interests me. When he left you to relieve himself after my magic targeted his bladder, he suffered a minor head wound. I imagine he'll come to after we've concluded our business . . . unless the snow buries him first." A devilish grin pulled at the corner of her mouth. "Adopting his visage was nothing more than a simple parlor trick. I found your reunion this morning quite touching, but I must admit, I was surprised you stuck around. You strike me as the flighty type."

Kait ground her teeth and readied her palms. "Why? Because I had to keep evading your husband's disgusting advances? Return to Olympus. You can't be here. You can't use magic. The Council forbade—"

"Oh, but I can. The Council doesn't have the power to watch all of Earth at once. If I keep my power low, they'll never know," Hera purred, ignoring Kait's jab with a soft flutter of her lashes.

Kait recalled dappled feathers and a hawk's piercing cry from her nightmare. "The bird. That was you. All along, it was you."

"Correct," Hera cooed. "All immortals have an animal familiar, but rarely do they indulge. I've found the form allows me to travel anywhere I desire."

Kait's eyes flickered to the infected nymph, who shifted her weight back and forth as if desperate to resume the hunt. "You sent the visions."

"Wow. Did you piece that together all by yourself?" Hera scoffed. "Indeed. I wanted you to be the first to witness what the new nymph race will look like. An improvement, don't you agree?"

Kait swallowed. "What do you mean?"

"Once my virus is released, there isn't a nymph alive who will be safe." Hera smiled, circling like a predator. "Soon, your entire race will be reduced to drooling groaning corpses until the infection runs its course. Then, the ethereal realm will be cleansed, reserved only for the immortals who are worthy of its beauty and riches. No more filthy whores to pollute my perfect world."

"Whores? Do you realize it's your husbands, sons, and brothers who are to blame? For centuries, we have begged to be left alone! The Council created Olean as a sanctuary away from your kind, but still the gods stalk us into mutual realms while we facilitate nature's growth to take our halos and indulge in euphoria by force. Yet there you stand, blaming us for the men you've raised like wild dogs, letting them mount whatever moves as long as they come whimpering back to you."

Hera leapt forward and flashed her teeth as her elegant silver dress billowed atop the snow. "You speak loudly for one so young. Seems you think yourself free of blame. Just a poor victim. Yet, look at what you're wearing beneath that coat. Fabric so sheer you leave nothing to the imagination and the cut so low your breasts are practically falling out. What do you expect?" She reared back as if Kait carried a disease she might catch. "The Council was foolish for gifting you Olean. Having sanctuary allowed Gaia to create an endless horde of you. You're nothing but an imitation. A beautiful flawless version of immortals with the added enticement of being forbidden to touch. The treaty between us is pointless—a line of red tape to duck beneath."

Kait steeled herself as her hands shook with anger. "My attire doesn't impact anyone but me. I wear this because it's easier to shift from my element and because I enjoy it, not because I'm asking to be assaulted. Do you hear yourself? You're delusional, especially if you think you're going to succeed in this wretched endeavor."

Hera spat, the volatile stream just missing Kait's boots. "Oh, I'm not worried. I've made arrangements that will ensure no one interferes with my plans."

Kait hissed. "Have you?"

Hera chuckled, and it was a beautiful whimsical sound. "You've got fire. I see why my Zeus was drawn to you. Pity his lust guided him rather than his mind. A mind is a glorious asset, especially when you learn to manipulate those you want to *hurt.*"

Hera completed her circle as she came to a stop behind the grotesque figure of Bia. Gently, she placed her hand on Bia's shoulder and stroked her greasy hair.

"The nymphs you saw were a projection. Nightmares with legs. They can't cause true harm, but the fear they evoke is hard to forget, isn't it? I created them to test their effectiveness, and you were a most willing subject. You taught me what worked and what needed to be improved. Increased speed, more teeth, things like that. Now that my nightmares have been perfected, the real threat will soon be ready." Hera smiled, her eyes flickering like a snake's. "Guess who I've chosen as the first victim to fall?"

Kait's lips parted as she pictured herself stumbling around, lost and broken, fueled only by the savage need to eat. Her gaze wandered back to Hera, and the goddess stared back innocently. The tips of her fingers traced the dead nymph's jaw and brushed her lips. The truth dawned on Kait and stole her breath.

"No, please. Leave her alone," Kait begged, hardly able to form the words.

Hera threw back her shining hair as a high-pitched laugh emitted from her throat. "Finally. Didn't I tell you? The power to manipulate is wonderous. Do you know where your sister is? From our conversation back there, it doesn't seem so." Hera leaned forward and ran her mouth along Bia's bruised neck like a lover. "I'd take a good look at this one if I were you. At least she's breathing. Bye now."

With one last wicked grin, Hera spun on her heels and vanished into the folds of her skirts. The crisp pleats transformed into sleek feathers, and with a cry that echoed like laughter, the goddess shot into the air. In seconds, the hawk's compact body blended into the falling snow.

Kait tore her eyes away from the bright flakes and stumbled back as the infected nymph remained planted before her, grinning like a dog let off its leash. The nymph didn't hesitate.

Launching forward, she sliced at the air with decayed fingers, shiny white bone visible beneath the gray flesh. Kait was ready. With a swift spin, she evaporated as the wind enveloped her and carried her high into the skeletal treetops.

Below, the enraged nymph moaned, stumbling around like a rat trapped in a maze. Kait's heart hammered at her narrow escape. The breeze gathered, ready to usher her away, but what of the nymph? She couldn't leave her to wander into town.

It's not real. There's no danger.

Even though the nymph didn't exist outside her own mind, Kait's senses betrayed her. She was convinced her ragged breaths and putrid scent were those of a concrete being. If someone were attacked, she would be wholly responsible. Maybe that's exactly what Hera desired.

I have to kill her.

Kait glanced around at the barren woods. There wasn't much to use for a weapon. Summoning the power of the wind, she flexed her fingers over and over, gathering strength. She could feel the magic pulse between her palms. On the ground, the nymph craned her neck. She threw her body against the tree and dug her exposed bones into the smooth bark while she searched the skies blindly for prey. Frustrated moans poured from her throat as her teeth gnashed what remained of her lower lip.

The ground trembled, and Kait raised her hands, tugging anything that wasn't rooted to the earth into the air. Dozens of rocks, big and small, along with tree limbs, hovered in the white sky, waiting for the command to strike. She looked down and wrinkled her nose in disgust as black blood trailed down the nymph's chin from her self-inflicted injuries. She clearly didn't feel pain, didn't feel remorse. She only knew hunger and the one source that would satisfy it.

Barely able to control her magic, Kait lifted her gaze to the nymph's eyes. They were cloudy with death, but the soft amber color made her catch her breath. She had Bia's eyes.

It's not Bia. Hera said so. Kill it and be done. Kill it so you can save her.

Kait slammed her hands together and shut her eyes as the powerful blast of magic exploded and ricocheted. The air roared, filling her ears with its strength as it heaved the objects forward, their target oblivious to the impending danger. Numerous thuds echoed before silencing the nymph's cries. Kait grimaced. She felt every hit, every vibration as the rocks collided, and the sharp limbs penetrated and cut. She opened her eyes and shivered at the slaughter.

The nymph lay in a crumpled heap. Her septic blood pooled beneath her body, melting the snow into a gray puddle to match her flesh. Nature's weapons littered the ground around her, but Kait spied the murder weapon amongst them. A large jagged rock the size of her fist rolled a few feet away from the deceased nymph. Its fatal edge pointed to the sky, the bulbous protrusion a perfect match to the nymph's concave skull.

Kait funneled downward and stepped onto the blood-splattered snow, heaving with relief and disgust. She'd done it. She'd killed one of Hera's horrible creatures. She averted her gaze from the nymph's vacant stare. Snowflakes danced on her eyes as if trying to remedy the horrific scene by burying it with beauty. Kait wished to rest now, to run back to Blake and bury her head beneath his warm covers again.

Hera won't delay. You need to find Bia and warn the others.

Forcing her legs away from the spreading blood, Kait pushed her hands and cupped the air. In response, a large drift of snow rose and crested like a giant wave before it slammed down atop the nymph's still form.

"Be at peace," Kait whispered. Guilt tugged at her heart. She should have buried the nymph properly, but the ground was frozen, and outside of her mind, none of it existed anyway. Blake was safe. Jez was safe. But only if Kait stayed far away from them.

Kait narrowed her gaze at the wind-blown tundra, searching for any sign of Blake. "Blake! Blake, can you hear me?" Her heart raced. To kill an innocent was inexcusable, punishable by an eternity in Tartarus, yet that threat hadn't made Hera hesitate when she'd targeted Blake and his friend a few months ago.

Kait scanned the snowy woods again. She had no idea where Blake was. Hera had mentioned knocking him out. Was he still unconscious? She took a few steps through the thick snow, but panic tugged her in the opposite direction, back toward the portal home. Olean needed her. The nymphs needed to know the horrors that were coming.

A faint cry reached her, and a spot of red appeared one hundred yards away. Relief flooded Kait's chest as Blake walked parallel to her location, no doubt trying to find her. But he was alive. The magnetic pull of the portal rippled through her frame. She promised herself she'd return and explain everything to Blake, but without a concrete timeline of Hera's judgment day, the threat to her realm was too close and immediate to delay.

"I'm coming, Bia."

Kait vanished into the air and directed the wind upward. She soared above the trees, anxious to reach the portal, but even as she ascended, her heart yearned to stay and sit with Blake just a little while longer.

Before Hera's impersonation, she'd barely said a dozen words to him, but the memory of his warm arms encasing her in his bed caused her to stutter in her escape. It would be so easy to linger, enjoy an uncomplicated afternoon, and pretend everything was okay. Unfortunately, her world—and the current threat against it—was anything but uncomplicated, and if she didn't prepare Olean, Jezlem's musing would come true. Everyone she loved would die.

CHAPTER 8

"Hmm, seems our little nymph has more fight in her than I anticipated," Hera said as she slid off the marble column that encircled her Skyglass. She shook her arms. The last few remaining feathers transitioned back to flesh as the winter woods blurred behind her. Lazy clouds replaced the barren scenery as the Skyglass portal emitted the goddess back to her private sanctuary on Olympus. "Not to worry, Ze-Ze." Hera ran her palm down the coiled body of her pet python, who waited on the floor far removed from the unforgiving drop. She'd never been keen on the reptiles, until she sent two to kill Zeus's bastard child, Hercules. The snakes had failed to destroy the child, but the serpents' cunning and ferocity were intriguing, and she adopted one of her own. "Let her scramble to protect her sister. All her effort will be for naught once my toxin is released. Come, we must speak with Ares."

Hera slipped both hands beneath the serpent's scales and heaved her bulk onto her shoulders. The great silver-and-black snake hissed sweetly, stretching along her mistress's skin like a glamorous necklace. Once Ze-Ze was settled, Hera pulled her golden tresses back and piled them atop her head in a messy crown. Several ringlets escaped the diamond band she secured it with and softened her face, hiding the dark intentions that lurked beneath her beauty.

Silver sandals peeked out beneath her floor-length dress as she ambled across the terrace at the edge of her gardens. Hera's quarters were coveted by other immortals for their seclusion and luxury, and she prided herself on her beautiful home. Many assumed after her marriage to Zeus that her gardens had been gifted to her. No one knew the sacrifices she had made, the amount of blood she'd spilled to be worthy of owning the lush plot.

She followed the marble steps down until they transitioned to soft grass that adorned the heart of the garden. Elaborate trellises curved with the land, each adorned with thick vines and exotic blooms. Hera passed beneath each one, stepping in and out of the brilliant sunlight. The rays chased her as her long skirts bent the stalks and created a gentle cadence as she sauntered toward the front exit.

Hera pulled the pearl gate aside and slipped onto the quiet street. Far removed from the main hub of Mount Olympus, she rarely ran into other immortals. She fought to keep her gaze focused on the alabaster shells that made up the road, but the pull was too great, and her eyes disobeyed and wandered right, toward her only neighbor.

Ornate golden posts punctured the clear sky and stood guard on either side of elegant double doors. Hera's breath caught as her lips trembled. The once meticulous entrance had receded into chaos. Aggressive weeds poured through tiny cracks in the crumbling granite, and the golden gates no longer shone under the rust and decay. It had been three months since Zeus's death, and the landscape had attacked with a vengeance. Wiping away a solitary tear, Hera tore her gaze away and hurried down the lane. She refused to let the memory of her husband's smile or his warm voice form. It hurt too much.

As an immortal, Zeus couldn't die, but if he was careless enough to let his guard down, a powerful blow could destroy his physical body—and that's exactly what happened. Since then, his soul had been pulled to the Underworld, the realm of her infuriating brother-in-law, Hades. Only Hades could restore a god, but reincarnation came with a price. Hera scoffed as Ze-Ze tightened, responding to her mistress's darkening mood.

"He has to wield power somehow," Hera whispered to the snake. "He's no doubt biding his time to bring Zeus back until it benefits him to the fullest." She continued to grumble under her breath and seethed as she remembered the last time she'd tried to find Zeus through her Skyglass. As hard as she'd looked, nothing but inky blackness had greeted her search. She could feel the lord of the Underworld laughing at her, mocking her position as the high goddess of Mount Olympus. What good was her power if she couldn't even break through the wards to the Underworld?

"We'll just have to keep trying," Hera said, stroking the snake between the eyes as she rounded a gentle curve. "Hades has a weakness. We'll find it. Come, darling, Ares is expecting us." Strolling into one of the busiest sectors of the small city, Hera adopted a serene smile as she swayed from side to side. Gods and goddesses greeted her, quick to step out of her path. Hera acknowledged some by name but mostly kept her gaze straight ahead with her chin held high, intent upon her destination.

A few turns later, Hera entered the South End and buried her revulsion. If she lived at the top of the pedestal that made up Olympus, Ares existed in the gutters. Rancid water slithered along hazardous cobblestones, puddling behind sunken stones and drawing flies. Hera gathered her skirts and pressed on.

The bloodred door was visible through the shuffling crowd. It was Hera's small piece of salvation from the undesirable immortals watching her from their lingering posts in crooked doorways and sagging windowpanes. Ze-Ze hissed protectively while her tail whipped back and forth beside Hera's elbow. This part of Olympus was reserved for those who had abused their power or were thought too dangerous or unpredictable to mingle with the higher class.

"Calm, my darling. I know you don't like it, but his kind is exactly what we need." Hera leaned against the chipped door frame and thumped her knuckles on the wood four times. Her confidence was bolstered by the great serpent encircling her neck. Silence greeted her request. Hera clenched her jaw and knocked again, each rap a sharp cry demanding to be answered. Muted cursing could be heard on the other side before the door was ripped back.

"I told you I'd have it next week," Ares seethed but abruptly stopped when he saw Hera. "Oh, Mother. I thought you were someone else."

"Someone come to collect, no doubt," Hera said, raising her eyebrows at her disheveled son. Without waiting for an invitation, she stepped across the threshold into the dank shadows that permeated the small hovel.

Ares shut the door behind her. His bronze eyes shone like an animal's in the darkness. "I was surprised when Hermes delivered your letter. Never thought I'd see you in the South End."

"Desperate times call for desperate measures." Hera fought the shivers that scraped her spine as she regarded her son. His robes were a mess, hair shaved to a stubble, but his eyes . . . His eyes were the worst. They were flickering empty voids, a perfect mask to hide the savagery she knew he was capable of— the savagery she was depending on.

Wrapping the python tighter around her shoulders, Hera meandered farther inside the home. She wrinkled her nose and noted a lazy swarm of fruit flies crawling atop remnants of past meals rotting on the table. A sharp crackle sounded as she ground numerous crumbs on the floor with her sandals. "Are you in trouble?" she asked, fighting to keep the disdain out of her voice.

Ares shrugged as his tongue wet his lower lip. "No more than any of the other gutter snakes that live down here. Let's get to it. What do you want? I know this isn't a social visit." Ares's jaw clicked, his eyes unblinking as he studied her.

"No, it's not. I've set some things in motion, and now it's time to make my threat real," Hera said carefully, afraid to divulge too much. Even though the god was her flesh and blood, she would be a fool to trust him. "I need help. *Your* help."

Ares's jaw clicked again. "Who do you want me to kill?" His fingers twitched at his sides while his eyes slid to the corner of the room. Hera followed his gaze. A great spear stood propped against the wall. The blade was smeared with centuries' worth of rust-colored streaks—constant reminders of all the lives he'd taken, both guilty and innocent.

Hera held up her hand. "No. I need you to make something for me."

Ares furrowed his brow. "Make what? I don't make things. Go see Hephaestus if you want a weapon."

Hera took a step forward, and Ze-Ze hissed and exposed her fangs. "I will not tolerate your insolence, Ares. Listen to my offer, and then you will be allowed to open your mouth." She narrowed her eyes. Ares remained quiet and crossed his arms over his chest. "I need you to create a virus, something vicious and incurable. Something that infects the moment it enters the body. Can you do this?"

"Why me? Why not do it yourself?"

"Are you not the god of war? I thought you'd be excited to inject a little chaos into the realms."

Ares's eyes widened, and his nostrils flared. "And this coming from the same goddess who once threatened to banish me to the mortal world for such violence?"

Hera swallowed and set her lips in a firm line. "It wouldn't be appropriate for me. I do not have the same anonymity that you possess. The other gods, they would know."

"So, you condone my tactics when they're convenient, is that right?" Ares asked, cocking his head. "What do I get?"

"Excuse me?"

"In exchange." Ares left his post on the other side of the table and stalked toward Hera like a lion after a gazelle. He stopped inches away. The python hissed again, but he paid her no mind. "What are you going to reward me with, dear Mother? How much is this virus worth to you?"

Tiny goosebumps prickled over Hera's skin, but she refused to show weakness. She steeled her gaze and stared into Ares's empty eyes. "What do you want?"

"I want what was stolen from me. Give me back Aphrodite," Ares said, his voice deep and gravelly.

"What? That's a ridiculous request. Aphrodite is not mine to give, nor was she taken from you. Your father arranged the marriage between her and Hephaestus long before you two started sleeping together. You want her back? See if your brother will agree to a divorce."

Ares bared his teeth. "Ever since Hephaestus caught us in that damned net, he thinks himself better than me. He knows Aphrodite can't stand him, but he'll keep her for eternity just to spite me."

Hera raised her hands in surrender. "Aphrodite is his wife, Ares. There's nothing I can do."

"Then, find me someone equal to her beauty. I want a woman. I'm tired of taking what I want all the time. I want someone who is mine by right." Ares stepped closer and smiled as she flinched. His hot stale breath clung to Hera's skin. "What's wrong, Mother? Scared I'll get my pleasures elsewhere? With the first woman I see?" Ares chuckled darkly and ran his fingertips along Hera's arms.

A loud snap broke the tension as Ze-Ze pulled back her triangular head and flicked tiny flecks of blood into the air with her forked tongue.

"Ah!" Ares retracted his hand, his index finger now sporting two identical holes that bore down to the bone.

"Don't touch me," Hera warned as she danced out of Ares's reach.

"Cute pet. Good thing she was here." Ares sneered before he sucked the wound. "Who knows what might have happened?" He smiled dangerously again as scarlet blood flowed down his teeth and swelled over his bottom lip.

"Can you make the infection or not, Ares? If this is too difficult for you, I will find someone else."

"Don't worry, Mother. I will craft a toxin so potent it will devour your intended before Apollo can retire his chariot for the day." Ares grinned and spat the gathering blood onto the packed dirt floor. "When do you need it?"

Hera ran her fingers through her hair and looked out the broken shards of glass that functioned as a window. "Tomorrow."

Ares grunted with laughter and wiped the remaining trace of blood off his chin. "Tomorrow? You're joking. It's already midday. I need at least three days."

"Very well. I'll find someone else," Hera said with a shrug and wrapped the bulk of the snake's tail around her waist. "Have a pleasant day, Ares." She moved toward the door, anxious to get out from under her son's hyena-like stare and leave the rest of the filth in the South End behind.

"I can do it, but these tight time constraints are going to cost extra."

"I'm not sleeping with you."

"That's not what I want."

"Then what, Ares? Spit it out."

"Consider the price doubled."

"Oh please, Ares. Isn't one enough?" Hera sighed. "Why do you need two?"

Ares's tongue flickered once more, and his bottom lip shone with saliva. "Mother, please. I don't wish to discuss what I do to my lovers with you . . . Unless you're curious?"

"Goodbye, Ares." Hera wrenched open the door.

"Your infrequent visits are always such a pleasure, Mother. I'll deliver it to you tomorrow."

"Fine, and Ares?" she called over her shoulder. "Do I need to remind you to keep your mouth shut?"

"Depends. What did you have in mind for a punishment?" He arched his eyebrows.

Hera crossed the threshold and slammed the door closed, relieved to have a solid barrier between them.

"He may be a disgusting deviant," Hera spat, "but he's our only chance."

The python hissed in response and nuzzled Hera's palm.

"Thank you. Years entrenched in the military ravaged his mind and robbed him of his empathy. All he knows now is how to kill effectively—a result, I confess, I find most handy to manipulate." Hera shook her head and once again adopted her regal posture. "Come, it's time for us to depart this place and leave the dog to his tricks."

CHAPTER 9

"Bia? Bia? Has anyone seen my sister?" Kait cried into the fields where a large group of anthousais were baling hay. Several earth nymphs looked away from their work and regarded her with curious eyes, but none offered any information.

"You're looking for Bia?"

Kait spun and recognized Miera, the anthousai elder. Her long auburn hair was swept back from her face, and her brows arched with concern.

"Yes, please. It's urgent. Do you know which realm she's in? I was told Madik and Sunti, but I've checked both, and she's not in either."

"Hmm, Sunti would have been my guess as well. She was sent there last week with a team to reestablish the rainforests and inspire growth. Could be that they completed the assignment and returned to Olean. Has no one seen her here?"

"No one. A few anthousais tried to use their sensors, but she's been to so many realms recently . . ."

Miera placed a comforting hand on Kait's arm. "We'll find her. What is this about?"

"Nothing. I just needed to speak with her about a personal matter."

Miera narrowed her eyes. "All right, then. I think we—"

"Kait!" a faraway voice called.

Kait glanced to her right and saw Wei, an anthousai with olive skin and straight onyx hair, walking toward her. "Did you find her?"

The anthousai rubbed her dirty fingers on her equally filthy apron. "I sent my sensors out again and felt a ripple in the earth, much stronger than before. I think she's just returned to Olean."

"Thank you. Thank you!" Kait cried. Her fingers danced, and the wind enveloped her, ushering her to the main square. Landing like a tornado, she touched down and scanned the sea of faces before the wind released her lower body. A few angry grunts echoed in response to her entrance, but she didn't care. If she didn't find Bia fast, she could be a mindless machine in a matter of hours.

Kait sprinted through the gathered nymphs going about their day and caught a glimpse of Bia's red hair a few yards away, but before she could take another step, she collided with a wall that sent her sprawling into the dirt.

"Kait! Thank the g-goddess I found you!" Kait rubbed her shoulder as Bia crouched down next to her. "Sorry about that," she said, gesturing to the large tree trunk that was quickly shrinking. "I d-didn't want to lose you."

"Lose me? I was running *to* you."

Bia blushed and her stutter came out more rapidly. "Oh, I d-didn't know you s-saw me. Well, n-no harm done. I'm so g-glad you're s-safe." Bia threw her arms around Kait's neck and squeezed tightly.

Kait returned her sister's out-of-character embrace before she gently pulled away. "What do you mean?"

Bia's eyes flickered from side to side. "Not h-here," she whispered. She grabbed Kait's wrist. "Come with me." Bia darted down an alley between shops and pressed her back against the wood of one of the structures that shielded them from prying eyes. "Word reached m-me in Sunti about your work with the geyser. A naiad told me you were raving about Dion being bitten. I was worried you had—"

"Cracked?" Kait guessed.

Warm pink color fanned across Bia's face. "Y-Yes. I know you've been struggling since Zeus."

Kait nodded. "You're right; I haven't been myself. But that's not what's going on here. I've been sent omens."

"Omens? Like nightmares? What did y-you see?" Bia asked, her gaze hesitant.

Kait took a steadying breath. "Nymphs. Horribly infected nymphs with a ravenous hunger. First, I saw myself, then one attacked Dion, and just before . . ."

"What?"

"You. You had become one of those terrifying creatures." Kait's eyes welled with tears, and she clutched her sister's hand.

Bia stiffened as the few tears of emotion made her uncomfortable. She took a step back and patted Kait's hand to offer what little comfort she could. "It's okay. It w-was just a bad dream."

"No, they're real—or they will be soon."

"But why? Who would d-do such a thing?"

Kait glanced to her left. Nymphs meandered by, blissfully unaware of the impending danger waiting to be unleashed.

"It's Hera. She's behind all this."

"Hera?" Bia repeated. "What's her p-purpose?"

Kait wrung her hands as she gazed at her younger sister. "You. She's after you. She wants revenge for Zeus."

"I don't understand," Bia said. "Why not just c-come after me?"

Kait shook her head. "She wants to make *me* hurt as revenge for killing Zeus, but her goal is to eradicate the entire nymph race."

"You spoke to her?"

"A short while ago. She bypassed the barriers and visited me in the mortal world. She aims to turn everyone into those mindless things I've been seeing."

Bia's eyes widened. "When?"

"I'm not sure. After she threatened you, she vanished, but I don't think we have much time. She's been working on a way to strike back since the mountain. With my reaction to her nightmares, I think I've given her the perfect opportunity."

Bia's eyes glazed as she fixated on something far away. "We need to warn them. Everyone. All the nymphs, the q-queen. Did Hera say where she'll strike first?"

Kait shook her head again. "No. I don't know how she plans to start, either. The nymphs that attacked me were visions, but there's no way she can plague us all in that manner."

"I'll speak w-with Miera. You find Tahlia. Then, we can address the naiads afterward. We can't incite a massive panic."

"Right. I'll warn Jez, too. Hera made it sound like she was only after us, but she may go after Jezlem."

"Okay." Bia exhaled. "I'll meet you b-back here tonight. We'll come up with a plan to s-stop her."

Kait tilted her head to the side and looked at her sister. "When did you grow up?"

"When our w-world grew teeth."

Kait grimaced as her knuckles rapped the rough bark in a furious tempo. At last, the door opened to reveal a startled Tahlia on the other side.

"Kait, what's going on? I'm in the middle of something," the aurai elder said, angling the door.

"Please, Tahlia. I need to speak with you. It's about the visions." Tahlia pursed her lips and glanced over her shoulder. "Please, I wouldn't bother you if it wasn't important. I only need a few minutes."

Tahlia opened the door a little wider and gestured for Kait to enter. "Fine, come in." She stepped aside and clutched the collar of the sheer robe tight around her shoulders. "Take a seat. I'll be right with you."

Kait watched Tahlia leave the large front room, then took a seat on one of the smooth maple chairs and tried to keep her fingers from casting any accidental magic. Hushed voices carried from the back rooms. Tahlia's abrupt dismissal and scant clothing suddenly made sense, and Kait's cheeks burned. Leaping to her feet, Kait crossed to the door just as Tahlia returned sporting a burnt orange sarong and matching top.

"Going so soon?" Tahlia asked.

"I didn't realize . . . I'm sorry. You're obviously busy."

Tahlia waved her hand, sat down, and crossed her legs gracefully. "Don't worry about it. She doesn't mind giving us a moment. Come, what's happening with your visions? Did you find your sisters?"

Kait resumed her seat and leaned toward her elder. "Yes. I just came from speaking with Bia, and yesterday, I found Jezlem in the mortal world."

"Good, but I assume from your panicked expression that they were unsuccessful in calming your fears?"

"No. In fact, they weren't just visions, but predictions. Hera revealed herself to me in the woods in the human realm and told me she plans to unleash a violent plague to target all nymphs."

"Hera?" Tahlia repeated. "But immortals—"

"I know," Kait cried, holding up her hands. "But she wasn't alone. With her was one of the same diseased creatures I saw before. She crafted it to look like Bia and ordered it to attack me. Please, Tahlia. This threat is real. We must warn the nymphs, tell the queen—"

Tahlia lowered her eyebrows and interlaced her fingers. "Hera, the goddess of protection and purity, built a monster to destroy our entire race? That doesn't make sense."

"I know it's hard to believe, but I swear to Gaia, it's the truth." She slid off her chair and fell to her knees, placing her hands over Tahlia's. "Please, we need to tell the other elders, to prepare for what is coming."

Tahlia shifted her weight and brushed Kait's hands away. "My dear, you need to rest."

"No! Tahlia, I'm not making this up. A terrible plague is coming. Hera said—"

"Enough, Kait," Tahlia warned, raising her voice. "I'm not sure what has happened to you since your encounter with Zeus, but I can assure you, nothing is coming. Hera has no reason to start a war with us."

"Of course, she does!" Kait sprang up from her knees. "Her husband was killed. I *helped* kill him. What could be a stronger motivator?"

"Stop it! I heard this after Hermes. Both he and Apollo were found guilty by the Immortal Council. It's done. Your hatred for the immortals has made you blind. You're grasping at straws and inventing reasons to go after them to ease your own guilt for your involvement in Willow's death."

Kait's mouth fell ajar as if the elder had slapped her. "Invent? Apollo raped and murdered Willow! Zeus raped Jezlem and bewitched naïve nymphs to surrender their halos in a hidden hideout on Earth. What more proof do you need?"

"Did you say Hera is starting a war?" someone asked from the shadows.

The tension immediately dissipated, and the two nymphs' ire cooled with the recognition of a spectator. A beautiful yet severe Amazonian warrior stepped into the light. Her features were pointed, hard, and flawless, and her eyes a mossy green, the color further enhanced by the emerald corset that hugged her muscular curves. Icy white-blond hair swept to the middle of her back, and one of her temples was shaved in the intricate design of her clan.

"Yes," Kait said before Tahlia could deny it. "She plans to orchestrate some sort of infection to wipe out the whole nymph population."

"Are other immortals planning an attack as well?" Akasha asked, alarm coloring her tone.

"Not that I know of."

"Akasha, please. She's mistaken. She's suffering from stress and bad dreams. I ordered her to speak with a healer the other day. There is no threat from Olympus," Tahlia said.

"The fear in her eyes is real, Tahlia. I should go. If a threat is coming, my people must be ready."

"But you just arrived." Tahlia frowned as she gripped the warrior's waist. Reaching up, she tucked a long strand of hair over Akasha's ear to reveal a spiked piercing that resembled a twisting thorn.

Akasha lowered Tahlia's hand. "There's a large nymph presence in Sunti. If she's right,"—she gestured to Kait— "my warriors can help combat whatever Hera is brewing and keep them safe." Tahlia frowned, and Akasha's stern gaze softened. "I'll come back." She pressed her lips to Tahlia's before stepping out of her embrace, then strode past Kait and stopped in front of the door. "I hope you're wrong, for all our sakes." With a lingering look in Tahlia's direction, she slipped outside and was gone.

Tahlia released a heavy exhale once she was out of sight. "Get out."

"But Tahlia, you need to make a statement. Consort with the other elders—"

"When you can provide me with solid evidence of Hera's supposed plague, I will. I can't ask Queen Rajhi to mobilize her soldiers without proof or demand an audience with the Council until you're sure what you've seen is real. Make an appointment with a healer immediately. If she deems you mentally stable, then we'll go to the queen together. All right?" Tahlia sighed and gripped the edge of the door frame as her eyes followed the ghost of Akasha's diminishing figure in the distance.

The last snowflake of the winter storm fell in the human realm as the portal deposited Kait back onto the shores of the frozen lake in Bennington. The moment the shimmering wards of the portal left her skin, she leapt into the sky and disappeared against the gray clouds that still smothered the small town.

The storm may have been over, but the air crackled with electricity. The wind hissed and thrashed nude branches back and forth. Without the sun, it was nearly impossible to gauge the time. Kait assumed it was late afternoon, about an hour or so before dusk. Hopefully, Jezlem wasn't at work yet.

Kait surged ahead in her elemental form. The air tasted wrong, metallic. She spiraled along the angry currents and quickly left the woods behind. Gentle lights glowed as the town crested into view, but the picturesque scene did little to ease her growing fear. All those people could be dead tomorrow if Hera invited her nightmares into the mortal realm.

Kait directed the breeze to the right, past the goods store and pub. Save for the exterior lights, both businesses were empty and dark. She recognized the brick façade of Jezlem's apartment perched near the end of the street and breathed a sigh of relief when she caught her sister's silhouette against the sheer curtain.

Too anxious to change and knock, Kait angled the wind toward the side of the building. She slid through the thin gap beneath the crooked door, and warm air pulsed from the vents and enveloped her, causing her current to rise even faster to the second floor. She hovered for a moment in front of Jezlem's apartment and took in the festive winter wreath that decorated the entrance and the doormat welcoming her arrival. Her sister was thriving in the mortal realm, thriving because she refused to let Zeus's assault destroy her. Kait had escaped the same fate *and* had retained her magic and element, so why was it so much harder for her to move on and find happiness?

Before her thoughts could delve further, Kait funneled through the narrow space underneath the top hinge and entered the tiny studio. Without warning, she separated from the air and materialized in the middle of the living room directly in front of where her sister and Joel snuggled on the couch.

"Christ!" Joel cried, flinging the half-eaten bowl of popcorn they were eating into the air.

Jezlem gasped and clutched her chest. "Kait! You gave us a heart attack."

"It's Hera," Kait said, ignoring the couple's flustered expressions. "Hera sent the visions. She plans to eradicate the entire nymph race."

Jezlem pushed the throw blanket off her lap, letting the flannel material puddle at her feet. "What? Are you sure?"

Kait nodded. "Soon, they'll be real. I don't know when, but I know whatever's coming is coming fast. I came to tell you to be on guard in case she decides to go after the mortal world as well." She turned to go, her magic already casting, but a warm hand pulled her back.

"Hey, you can't rush off," Jezlem ordered, holding her upper arm tightly.

Kait's eyes jumped to Joel, who stared at her with a bewildered expression.

"I have to. I have to warn everyone."

"Slow down. You're upset. Just take a minute. Sit down and tell me what happened. I didn't know what to think when I woke up and you were gone. When we saw Blake, he told us you guys were together, but he lost you in the woods. I was scared." Jezlem hugged her close.

Kait pressed her face into the crook of Jezlem's neck. She wished she could stay there and forget. "It was Hera. She came to me in the woods and threatened Bia. She's safe," she added before Jezlem could ask. "She's back in Olean, trying to convince Meira that Hera's threat is real."

Jezlem wrinkled her nose. "What do you mean 'trying?' Why wouldn't they believe you?"

"Tahlia didn't. She said a goddess had no reason to unleash such slaughter on us, and she wouldn't talk to the queen until I could produce proof."

"What does she want you to do? Bring her a body?"

Kait threw up her hands and pursed her lips. "I don't know what to do. No one will listen to me. Tahlia accused me of making it up, said my past with immortals has made me delusional. She ordered a mental evaluation before taking any further steps. Part of me wants to sit back and let this blow up in their faces, but I can't leave everyone exposed."

"Exposed to what?" Joel asked.

Jezlem ignored him. "I don't care if Tahlia doesn't believe you. Go back to Olean and tell as many nymphs as you can. Send messages on the wind. Scream at them. Make them listen to you."

"It's not that simple, Jez."

Jezlem gripped Kait's chin and stared into her violet eyes. "You can't give up. Don't quit. If you do, they're all dead."

"Okay," Kait agreed. "I'll go back. Don't go out at night, and always have a way to protect yourself. Like I said, I don't think Hera will come after you, but we need to be prepared for anything."

"I'll keep her safe." Joel wrapped his arm around Jezlem's waist. "Er, what exactly am I protecting you from?"

Jezlem released Kait and sank against Joel's slim frame. "I think they're like those yucky people from that movie we watched the other night."

Joel thought for a moment, and his eyes bugged. "Zombies! Zombies are going to come after us? What the hell? Why?"

"Hera is Zeus's wife." Kait sighed. "She wants revenge for his death."

"That's a bit dramatic. Look what he did to you guys!" Joel clenched his teeth. Jezlem stiffened beside him. "But zombies, really?"

Jezlem cleared her throat. "If a man led a mass invasion to avenge his lost lover, you'd call him badassery, right?"

"Badass," Joel corrected with a small chuckle. "But yeah, I see your point. Still, though, I thought Zeus couldn't die?"

"He can't. After his physical body was destroyed, Zeus's soul traveled to the Underworld. Hades either hasn't released him, or Zeus is lying low. Regardless, Hera's hatred for our kind goes back centuries. I think this latest experience pushed her over the edge." Kait glanced at the window, almost expecting to see the goddess's steel eyes.

"Seems backward, though. Why punish you for her husband's affairs?" Joel asked.

"Great question," Jezlem whispered before her voice hardened. "Maybe we can ask her."

"No way. I remember when she tried to burn us up in the hospital. I don't want to get on her bad side again."

Jezlem scoffed. "My hero."

Kait saw the ghosts in her sister's eyes, but also the love she harbored for the goofy mortal. Another face popped into her mind. "Is Blake all right?" Guilt squeezed her stomach.

"Yeah, he's fine. Confused, but fine." Jezlem's words were innocent, but her tone was sharp.

"Good. I wanted to stay and explain, but I was worried she may have hurt Bia."

"I get it, Kait. Just . . ." Jezlem looked uncomfortable.

Kait crossed her arms. "What?" Her question was harsher than she'd intended, but she was tired of her sister treating her like an insolent child.

Jezlem squared her shoulders and made eye contact with Kait as her thumb rubbed little circles on the back of Joel's hand. "Just because Blake's life is no longer in danger, doesn't mean he's not important."

"I know that, Jez."

An awkward moment of silence descended as the sisters stared at one another. Neither one wanted to be the first to look away. At last, Jezlem patted Joel's arm and glanced at the clock on the wall—a silent surrender.

"Okay. Glad to hear it."

The clock ticked loudly, measuring the tension.

"Well, I need to get back and check in with Bia."

"Kait?" Jezlem said and took a step toward her. Kait pursed her lips, ready for another scolding, but Jezlem shook her long blond curls and opened her arms again. "Be careful."

Kait smiled softly and stepped into Jez's embrace. For a moment, they were fifty years old again, just teenagers begrudgingly making up after a stupid fight. She couldn't believe how things had changed. She yearned to leave, but guilt held her in place. "Can you do something for me? Can you tell Blake? I know I should, but—"

It looked like Jezlem might refuse, but Joel saved her. "Yeah, sure," he answered. "I'll let him know at school tomorrow."

Kait's gaze leapt to the sadness in Jezlem's eyes and then flickered to Joel. "Thank you, and tell him I'm sorry."

"For what?"

"Everything." Without another word, she let herself out and slipped into the hallway, leaving behind the warmth and security for the bleak unknown.

CHAPTER 10

A short while later, Kait paced up and down the narrow alleyway, wringing her hands as she awaited Bia's return. She had resisted seeking out Tahlia again. Hopefully, Bia had had more luck. The wind tickled the ends of her hair, bringing with it a sweet earthy scent. She twisted her head toward the alley entrance and exhaled a rationed breath when Bia appeared, her pale skin unscathed.

"So? Did they believe you?"

Bia's shoulders sagged. "No. I'm s-sorry, Kait. I tried. Meira doesn't believe a goddess—one as powerful and prominent as Hera—would do such a thing. What did Tahlia say?"

Kait sighed. "The same. She told me to stop wasting her time. She won't listen to anything I have to say until I have proof."

Alarm shone in Bia's eyes. "What do w-we do?"

"We try to stop this on our own," Kait replied quietly. "We warn everyone, all the realms."

"But without the elders, n-no one will listen."

"It doesn't matter. We'll start slow and spread the story as a rumor. Eventually, fear will catch and the elders will have no choice but to intervene and acknowledge this."

"Once the elders h-hear the stories, they'll know we started it. Won't they discredit us?"

"It won't matter. If we succeed, the unease we create will be too great to strangle."

"But we still don't know w-when Hera is going to unleash this," Bia said. "What if we warn everyone and nothing happens? What if she waits weeks to do anything? What if . . ."

"What if what?"

"What if," Bia continued. "What if all of this *is* only in your head? You went through s-so much. Zeus *tortured* you."

Kait grabbed Bia by her shoulders and squeezed. "Don't think like that. Don't let the elders get in your mind. I saw them. This is real. If you start doubting it, you're going to die. Okay?" She gave Bia a quick jerk, trying to rattle the dangerous thoughts loose. She needed Bia. She was the only one who believed her, the only link between sanity and madness.

Bia nodded and took a deep breath. "Where d-do we start?"

"With the dryads," Kait answered. "None of them have heard about my 'episodes.' They'll make a more reliable source."

"What should we t-tell them?"

"Just drop little hints, small details. Pretend like you heard it from someone else. We'll start first thing in the morning, okay? It's been a long day."

"Okay," Bia agreed, looking relieved. "Try to get some s-sleep." She moved as if to embrace Kait as her hands tapped her thighs, but she spun away instead. Her floor-length skirt swept the patchy grass as she exited the alley into the main square and kept her gaze low.

Kait watched her sister disappear and then peered into the blue sky. As of now, the clouds were wispy, unthreatening, but she knew the horrors that could soon befall them like a thunderous rain.

The sun dipped behind the hills and bathed Hera's gardens in an opulent ruby haze. Fuchsia clouds streaked the sky like glorious wounds, reminding her that beneath all beauty lay a sinister truth. She debated checking the Skyglass again. The last time she had looked, the aurai had returned to the mortal world.

Hera scoffed and ran her hand down the length of her great snake. "Does she truly think me that petty?" she asked aloud. "Can't she see my grand purpose? What would a few dead humans offer me? This is why the nymph race needs to be extinguished. All of them are too consumed with their own pitiful existences."

Uncrossing her ankles, Hera rose from her reclined perch beneath the white dogwood trees and hummed softly while the python uncoiled itself and trailed after her mistress. Hera's thoughts wandered like they always did, back to Zeus.

Do you remember dancing with me beneath the trees, my darling? Do you remember all the love we made while the stars watched with jealous eyes? Why haven't you returned to me, my darling? Don't you miss my kiss, my touch?

A haunting tune filtered through Hera's mind as ghosts swam before her. She had thought they were happy. Yes, Zeus had indulged in numerous affairs, but he always came back, always returned to his queen. Hera threw her arms wide as she welcomed the past. Her eyelids closed while her feet carried her across the soft grass as if Zeus's arms had never left. Her body was poetry, weaving beautiful lyrics in the fading light of another day without him. She danced recklessly, gracefully, and powerfully, pouring all her confusion, frustration, and loneliness into every step. She wasn't sure how long she danced, possessed by the demons singing inside her skull, but eventually, she collapsed atop the cool grass. Dusk had come and gone, scuttling away to make room for the encroaching darkness Nyx wielded, reminiscent of the darkness Hera fought to evade in her heart each day.

"He'll come back," Hera whispered as she stared into the brightening stars. "He promised."

"And you believed him?" a rough voice called from behind her.

Hera jerked into a sitting position, her chest still rapidly rising and falling from her impromptu exertion. "Ares? How long have you been standing there?"

The dark god emerged from the shadows that clung to the outskirts of the orchard where Hera lay. "About an hour. I meant to say something earlier, but you were magic to watch. I've never seen you so vulnerable. So weak." His features hardened to ugly stone as his compliment soured.

Hera's despair evaporated at her son's words. "This is my home. How dare you mock my pain. How did you get in here?" She pushed herself to her feet, staring daggers into the intruder.

Ares tilted his head and raised his eyebrows in mock hurt. "It's not my fault your lock yields under the slightest force, and here I thought you'd be pleased to see me. Especially after tasking me with such an audacious request. Maybe I'll take this back." He slipped a clear glass vial out of the folds of his robes and pretended to study it. "I can think of plenty of other gods who would make short work of it. Or maybe I'll keep it for myself. It would certainly make destroying my enemies interesting."

"You've finished already?" Hera asked, making no attempt to hide her doubt.

"Looks that way, but if it's not good enough for your standards, I can show myself out."

"Wait!" Hera cried. "You caught me in a very private moment. Please, stay."

Ares smiled, and his empty eyes shone like black holes. He didn't reply. Instead, he pocketed the vial and strode forward in the direction of the marble terrace that perched like a giant fist on the opposite side of the lush meadow. Hera followed and called her snake to her side.

"Watch him, Ze-Ze," Hera cautioned. "You know what to do should he erupt."

Hera ascended the ornate staircase and leaned against a pleated pillar, her hawklike gaze never leaving Ares. She looked on in disgust as he helped himself to her wine and emptied the bottle into one of the large glasses that adorned the low table.

Ares spun and took a long gulp, draining half the glass, then sighed and threw his head back. "That's good. This stuff never seems to make its way down to the South End. You're not going to make me drink alone, are you? I thought my success would be cause for celebration."

Hera smiled tightly and left her post at the top of the stairs. Ares eagerly opened a new bottle of wine and filled his glass first before pouring her one as well.

"A toast!" Ares raised his glass in the air. "To heartache and misery. May they chase all the light and happiness from the world." He clinked his glass against Hera's, causing the dark red liquid to slosh over the rim and run as though from a fresh wound down her fingers. Ares ignored her startled gasp and brought his cup to his lips, gulping greedily again until nothing remained.

Hera sipped her wine slowly, her gaze fixed on her volatile offspring. She wanted him gone, back to his despicable hovel. Her nerves bristled. She disliked not feeling safe inside her own home.

"So, let's see it." Hera set her glass on the tabletop. "I still can't believe you finished. How did you complete it so quickly?" She took a seat behind her desk, noting several makeshift weapons within reach.

After filling his glass once more, Ares took another healthy sip and grinned. "As you said yourself, I'm the god of violence and mayhem. I know what toxins incapacitate the mind and steal the soul. The hardest part was procuring them."

"But no one saw you, correct?" Hera worried. "No one respectable?"

Ares laughed, the noise like a raspy cough. "No, dear Mother. None of your great friends noticed the stain you birthed skulking around the apothecaries."

"I just want to ensure you were careful. If anyone were to know I was behind this—"

"Spare me the horror, Mother. My life is ten times worse than whatever punishment they would gift you." Ares threw the remaining contents of his glass into the back of his throat.

Hera took a steadying breath. "You know I have offered to help."

Ares chortled again and drained the last of the new bottle into his glass. "Yeah, I remember. I also remember the price of your assistance. As I told you then, I'm not interested." The tension between them sizzled as Ares swallowed. He dragged the back of his hand across his lips and palmed the vial, bouncing it carelessly.

Hera tensed and gripped the arms of her chair. It'd be just like him to drop it on purpose and smile as it shattered. Ares smirked, no doubt noticing the fear in her eyes.

"Ah, in time, Mother. I think I deserve a reward for delivering before the deadline. It's only fair." His tongue flickered as he stared at her plunging neckline.

Hera shifted and pulled her long curls over her shoulder. "Indeed. You've done well, Ares. I am quite impressed."

Surprise leapt onto Ares's face as he sauntered around her subtle barricade. He positioned his legs on either side of Hera's knees and closed the distance between them. Hera's fingers turned to talons and dug into his chest as she pushed him away.

"Don't be ridiculous. You'll have your women soon enough, and you're also welcome to my wine casks. Take as much as you'd like when you depart," Hera said, fighting to keep her voice even. If she got lucky, maybe he would drink himself to death.

Ares blew a long breath between his teeth and shook his finger at Hera. "That wasn't nice. I don't take kindly to someone raising my hopes and then refusing to give me what I want."

"I didn't raise anything," Hera replied crisply. "You hear whatever you want in that twisted mind of yours." She rose to her feet and angled her body away from her son. "Now, let's see if all your bragging is justified. The vial, please." She held out her palm.

Ares's lips twitched. "Of course, Mother." He placed the vial into Hera's awaiting hand as malice sparked in his eyes.

"Thank you." Hera pivoted away. "Come, Ze-Ze."

The python hissed in response and slithered up the goddess's calf until she rested in the usual spot across her shoulders. Hera's fears ebbed with the weight of the great snake. Ares would be a fool to try anything with Ze-Ze so close. Immortals couldn't be killed, but Ze-Ze's venom caused temporary paralysis that lasted several hours. He was lucky he was able to suck out the small amount she had delivered him yesterday.

Hera tossed her hair behind her, advanced toward the Skyglass, and peered inside the bottomless well. Ares joined her but stood several feet away from the unforgivable column.

"It's potent, as you requested," Ares said, licking his lips. "I suggest using it all. I designed it to target the nymphs specifically, but if other creatures encounter it, I can't promise there won't be any side effects. Within twenty-four hours, all the nymphs should be dead." Excitement danced on his ragged features. This was what Ares lived for: destruction and death.

"That's why you are not in charge. We need to first find a subject to test it on. Then, we release it slowly. I need to stay above suspicion, and if we take our time, it will heighten the confusion. Not only for our prey but for the Council, as well. By the time someone figures out this isn't a bizarre mutation or accident, it will be far too late to stop it."

"That's ruthless," Ares said with a wolflike grin.

"You're my son, after all," Hera replied, her gaze on the small vial. "Where did you think you got it from?"

Ares snickered under his breath and drew closer, carefully placing his palms on the tan stones made smooth from a millennium of spying. "Who are you going to test it on? The nymph you're after?"

"No." Hera pulled the stopper from the mouth, careful not to inhale. The concoction had a sickly sweet scent, like fruit left to spoil in the sun. She peered over the side of the Skyglass and waved her hand. The white clouds hurried out of the way to present her with an unobstructed view of the land below. "Why don't we start in Kairu, the realm farthest from Olean? That way, we can see how fast it spreads." Hera wriggled her fingers, forced the Skyglass to narrow its view, and zoomed in on the lush jungle realm. She was silent for a moment as she considered the few nymphs in sight. "Ah, there. That one is perfect.

Good muscle tone too. She'll be a fast pursuer."

Hera focused the Skyglass on where a pretty naiad relaxed in a shallow pool, oblivious to the gods watching her. The nymph raised her arms and brought a light shower over her head. The droplets absorbed the pale green halo of light that radiated from her skin and dripped down her ice-white hair between her large breasts. Swift drops raced down her skin to her navel as the colors rippled across the water's surface like a moving painting.

"I like her." Ares breathed huskily. "I want that one."

"That's fine, but keep in mind she will be a mindless infectious corpse in a few minutes' time," Hera reminded him. "I'm not sure how much you'll enjoy her then. Don't worry. I'll spare a few for you to keep."

Ares grunted but relented. The naiad closed her eyes and ducked under the calm surface, her nude form still visible.

"Perfect."

Hera reached into the Skyglass and tipped a single drop out of the vial's neck. After a moment of falling, the drop plunged through the thin membrane of the portal and into the pool, a small splash the only evidence of its deliverance.

"What are you doing?" Ares asked. "The water will dilute it. It won't work."

"Doubting yourself?" Hera smirked. "Relax. She's a naiad. They breathe underwater just as easily as above. If the toxin is as good as you say, it should enter her lungs and be absorbed into her bloodstream. It may be even more potent because of her connection to the element."

"But what if—"

"Hush. Watch."

Hera didn't blink, didn't breathe. She stared at the top of the naiad's head, willing her to surface. At last, her calm limbs began to thrash, and she exploded out of the depths of the clear pool. No longer were her features serene. Horrible coughs raked her chest as she fought to clear her lungs. Hera's lips split in a dark eager grin.

"Keep choking," Ares said. "It'll help the infection settle and attach to the tissue." His eyes widened as the naiad's skin flushed and took on a sickly gray hue. Black veins spidered across her naked chest, carrying the infection to her other organs and brain. She continued to hack, unable to draw a breath as her hands fumbled uselessly against her throat. "Just another minute."

The naiad's body twisted, the small uninfected part of her trying to escape its sudden prison. Strangled gargles bubbled in her throat as bile spilled over her lips. "Help!" she tried to cry, but there was no one there. No one save the two gods delighting in her painful last breaths.

The naiad blinked furiously. Sticky yellow pus drooled from the corners of her eyes. With the back of her hand, she wiped it away and smeared it across her cheekbones. As she stumbled up the shore, another violent cough exploded from her lips and sent more bile racing down her chin.

"Here comes my favorite part." Ares leaned closer as his fingernails carved the hard stone. Hera watched him out of the corner of her eye but remained silent as her curiosity won out over distrust.

The naiad's mouth opened once more in a final plea for help, but her voice was gone, replaced with a guttural moaning. Her wild eyes rolled into the back of her head, and for a moment, she stared straight at Hera, as if she knew she was watching—knew she was responsible for her cruel end. The goddess met the nymph's gaze, refusing to show weakness in front of Ares, but the desire to look away from the disgusting scene was so strong it made her heart race.

The naiad collapsed in a heap of putrescent flesh and disjointed limbs. Silence radiated through the jungle. No birds sang, no rodents scurried. Even the leaves had hushed their gentle dance. The earth knew what was coming.

"You weren't supposed to kill them."

"Have faith, Mother. Keep watching."

A sharp crack ricocheted around the clearing. Hera glanced back into the Skyglass just as the naiad threw back her head—so far she must have broken her neck. Her eyes were glassy orbs of white, and her mouth hung askew. Dried bile cemented her features into a permanent snarl. Slowly, she straightened her legs, pushed her deadened corpse off the ground, and climbed to her feet. With blind eyes, she raised her chin in the air and sniffed.

A chorus of faraway laughter echoed, and the nymph's head snapped to the left in response. Another series of cracking bones resounded as her body jerked forward with frightening speed. The nymph crashed through large ferns toward her unsuspecting prey and vanished from view.

Hera leaned back, more than satisfied with the results of the toxin. "Well done, Ares. It's even better than expected."

"Thank you, Mother, but don't you want to watch what happens next? It's going to be thrilling."

Hera waved her hand indifferently. "I've seen enough. Blood and flayed body parts aren't my cup of tea."

Ares frowned, but his eyes sparkled with interest. "That's the best part."

Hera fixed him with a tight smile and crossed her bare arms over her chest. "I am curious about one thing. How did you know the toxin's specifics?"

Ares shrugged. "I created it."

"No," Hera argued. "You knew precisely when it would attack each of the body's systems and the nymph's response. How?"

Ares glanced away. "It's not a big deal."

"You tested it before you brought it to me, didn't you?"

"I had to see if it would work. I know the range of your fury. If it had been a dud—"

"You fool! You could have ruined me! What if someone saw? Who?"

"Who saw?"

"No, you moron! Who did you test it on?"

"A nobody," Ares countered. "Some filthy rat dying in the streets of the South End. She didn't have anyone to miss her while she was alive. No one will care that she's dead."

"Who was it?"

"I don't know. Some forgotten nymph working off her sentence lifting her skirt and spending nights on her knees by the harbor."

"And where is she now? Where did you run this little experiment?"

"At my house. Don't worry. I took care of her the moment she turned."

"How?"

Ares looked into his mother's eyes and raised himself to his full height. "I split her skull in two with a swipe of my spear." A low growl thundered in the back of his throat. "Would you care for a demonstration?"

Hera took a step back and shook her head. She'd forgotten herself, forgotten who she was speaking to. "Good," she said, but her voice was void of its previous malice.

Ares's eyes flared, but he relaxed his rigid posture. "It works. Now what?"

Hera spun away and busied herself with tidying up his empty wine glass and bottles. "Now, we wait and see how long it takes to spread. If they're able to isolate the nymph, then I'll infect another, and another, and another until no realm is safe."

"What about me?"

Hera glanced over her shoulder. "You will go home and never speak of this to anyone or anything you associate with. Is that clear?" Ares started to object, but Hera spoke over him. "Four whores will be waiting for you when you return, aurais in service to Poseidon. They were more than eager to escape the sea. Of course, I didn't enlighten them as to what lay in store with you. Use them as you wish for as long as they last." She left Ares and forced him to follow. She walked briskly as she led him down toward the overgrown wall that towered above them.

"What if you need more toxin? Should I come back or will you come by—"

Hera cut him off and swiped at some hanging ivy to reveal an old iron gate. "Ares, our business is concluded. Do not come back to my residence again unless you receive an explicit invitation from me to do so. Understood?"

"Yes."

"Good," Hera said in a clipped tone as she motioned for him to leave. "Safe travels and . . . have fun tonight."

A feral grin pulled at the corner of Ares's lips as he crossed the threshold. "Until next time, Mother."

Hera didn't reply. With a grand flourish, she pulled the rusted handle shut with a bang so loud that the frame vibrated beneath her hand. She exhaled and stroked the head of her great snake. "First things first, my dear—We get a guard to keep him out."

CHAPTER 11

Kait woke with a jerk. Her eyes snapped open and her fingers curled around the threadbare canvas of the hammock, trying to steady the sudden rocking.

"Up and at 'em, aurai," Anamalla called before she leapt into the crisp morning air.

Biting back a retort, Kait let her head fall against the pillow as the rest of her bunk sisters descended from the thick branches. She glanced up at the pink sky as the sun began its slow climb.

Pink in the morning, creatures take warning.

Kait recited the old rhyme and shivered. Last night had been quiet and peaceful, but she knew Hera watched from above and plotted their destruction with glee. As much as she anticipated the nymphs would dismiss her warnings, she couldn't leave them unprepared.

Kait rolled out of bed and balanced on a smooth branch beneath her. Her lace nightgown fluttered in the gathering breeze as she looked out at the brightening view. Overnight, a fresh layer of snow had sprinkled the forest floor and the temperature had plummeted. Even though the cold didn't affect her extremities, she thought it best to don something thicker in case the beautiful morning turned sickly.

Kait transformed and leapt into the sky. Her flesh evaporated until her elemental form glided along the nearest air current. Directing the wind, she funneled toward the armory. Even though it was early, the armory thrived with activity as most of the aurais exchanged their sleepwear for gowns or trousers, whatever suited their task for the day.

Kait opted for black rather than her preferred gold. Heavy long sleeves gathered around her forearms and snaked up her neck to end in a tight turtleneck. Tough black jeans covered her legs, tucked inside heavy boots. She pulled a black leather jacket from one of the racks farther back and wrapped it snugly around her upper body. Gathering her hair, she tied it back in a high bun atop her head. She had no idea what she looked like, but it felt severe and more importantly, secure. If Hera unleashed her creatures, she wouldn't be caught in a vulnerable dress with her skin exposed to hungry teeth.

Confidence gathered in her chest as she exited the armory, and Kait pointed her boots toward the west where the anthousai clan resided. She launched off the ground, and the icy air swirled in her lungs. She was ready to get started.

"What in all the r-realms are you wearing?" Bia's hands paused mid-cast, her expression one of confusion as Kait entered the modest apothecary hut.

Herbs and crushed powders littered the wooden tabletop in a dizzying pattern only Bia could unravel. Small stone pots each held a different earthy color. The spicy scent calmed her nerves—an involuntary reaction from years of being Bia's guinea pig. Kait assessed her carefully chosen ensemble and shrugged, loving the weight of the jacket.

"I thought it would be easier to fight in compared to that." Kait pointed to the knee-length chiffon dress her sister wore.

Bia shook her head. "I l-love it. Did you have to get special permission to use the leather from the soldiers' stock?"

"No, it's readily available. With the way humans dress today, they keep the armories supplied with whatever we may need to fit in if our assignment brings us in close contact. Come on."

Bia held up her pointer finger. "Give me a moment. I'm just finishing this salve. I thought it might be helpful to have an anti-inflammatory to treat the wounded."

Kait's heart broke at her sister's naïvety. "That's a lovely thought, Bia, but I don't think natural oils can combat this. Hera created the infection from darkness and hatred. She wouldn't risk the Council's punishment if she thought we could stop it." She tried to phrase her words gently, but her throat swelled as she witnessed the way Bia's shoulders slumped.

"There's n-nothing we can do?"

Kait rounded the large table and took the full pot from her sister. "Hey, you know what? I think you should finish. You never know, right? We have no idea what we're about to face. I think it's a great idea to be prepared."

"Really?" Bia asked, her amber eyes wide and guarded.

"Of course." Kait smiled. "Now, how do we finish it?"

Bia stood in silence for several seconds, then rolled her eyes and swiped the pot from Kait's hands. "Oh, give that t-to me. We both know you're hopeless with this stuff."

Kait laughed and placed her hands on her hips. Bia spun away, supporting the pot while she added more herbs. A fresh wave of turmeric wafted through the small space, and Kait sneezed.

"There, that looks perfect." Bia set the newly crafted salve in the center of the table. "Hopefully, if we apply this to anyone who gets infected, it will keep the virus isolated before it can spread through the body."

Kait leaned in, and her waist curled over the wooden edge. The burnt orange salve looked thick. Maybe it *could* function as an antidote.

"This looks wonderful, Bia. Let's get you suited up, and then we can figure out a good method to carry it."

Bia glanced up and looked her in the eye—a rare action for her. "Thanks, Kait."

Together, they navigated the snow. Kait's boots punctured the serene landscape, while Bia seemed to glide atop, leaving only the faintest of footprints behind. They didn't speak as they wandered to another armory. Wary tension blanketed them. Bia managed a swift hello or good morning when they passed other anthousais, but Kait was too consumed with a mixture of anxiety and regret. How many of these faces would be moaning for their blood by week's end?

Half a mile later, they reached the armory and entered beneath the threshold of the large hollow maple tree.

"Take that off and stand over there. I'll find something similar." Kait gestured to her own ensemble as she pointed to a vacant changing stall.

Bia nodded and moved to the eight-foot-high mirror that curved along the left side of the structure. With a thin smile, she greeted several friends also dressing for the day and perched atop a squat wooden stool. Kait noticed her sister's hands fluttering arrhythmically by her sides—a coping mechanism she'd adopted in their early years of life. For all her poise, Bia's anxiety surged beneath her calm façade.

Kait fought to clear her mind and lost herself within the endless racks of material and fabric. She had to focus on one thing at a time. Once Hera's threat became real, they would both have to put aside their fear and fight. It was the only chance they had at surviving, and even that seemed slim.

Kait returned to her sister's side with a pile of folded cloth sandwiched between her palms. Apprehension reflected in Bia's eyes as she rubbed the leather between her fingers.

"I've n-never worn anything like this before."

Kait smiled encouragingly and passed her the bundle. "See how it fits."

Bia discarded her pink dress and swapped the gauzy material for ankle-length black leggings and a simple black tank. A dark brown leather jacket hung off her shoulders, and matching boots encased her feet, the sturdy material stretching almost to her knees. Her long red hair hung down to the small of her back like flames licking the fabric, threatening to set it ablaze.

"Wow. I didn't know you were going to look that good."

Bia offered a wary smile and confronted her reflection. Her amber eyes widened with surprise as she tossed her long hair to the right and cast a small enchantment on the vines dangling from the wooden beams above.

"This feels great," Bia exclaimed. "I was worried the l-leather would be too constricting. I almost look like part of the queen's army!"

"I'm glad you like it," Kait said with a sad grin. "I wish it wasn't necessary, but we can't afford to get tripped up or caught in our gowns. Pull your hair up, too. It'll make it harder for them to hold onto."

Bia shivered in response to Kait's words. Her fingers wove a beautiful pattern along the side of her head and gathered her full tresses in a neat braid before she secured her hair in a tight bun. "How's this?"

"Perfect. Ready?"

Bia nodded and flexed her arms in the foreign jacket. "Our g-garb will certainly make them take notice."

Kait placed her hand on her sister's shoulder. "They will listen. Our plan is going to work." Bia shrugged. "Now, come on. We can't waste any time. I'll take the northern realms; you cover the southern. We'll meet in the main square at dusk."

"What if something happens?"

"Run. Save as many as you can, but protect yourself." Kait stepped forward and placed a kiss on her sister's forehead. "Keep a weapon close and know your way out. I love you."

"Love you t-too," Bia whispered. "Good luck."

CHAPTER 12

The sun hung heavy in the sky, sending waves of searing heat toward the inhabitants of Sunti. Kait sat with a small group of nymphs, indulging in the sweet nectar of the lemon flower.

In the background, a group of satyrs played jovial music from wooden flutes, while others tended the extravagant rows of plump grapes for Dionysus's personal stores. The atmosphere was casual, relaxed, after a hard morning's worth of harvesting. Kait's leather jacket stuck to her skin and prevented her arms from extending. Unable to stand the sensation any longer, she slid her arms free and let the cursed jacket fall to the ground in a crumpled heap.

"Why are you wearing that?" a dryad with dark blue braids asked.

"A precaution," Kait answered before she took another sip of the sweet lemon flavor.

"For what?" a naiad queried.

Kait took a deep breath to steady her excitement. She'd lost count of how many nymphs she'd spoken to. Many of the others were doubtful and had scoffed at the gossip, but a few had listened with true fear in their eyes. Hopefully, the rumors would fester after she left and spread.

"Just something I heard back in Olean," Kait said.

"Are you talking about the monsters?" a dryad asked.

"Monsters?" Kait repeated, giving nothing away.

The dryad nodded as she shoveled a large slice of cucumber bread into her mouth. "Yeah. I heard from a friend that strange beasts were spotted in a few of the realms."

"What kind of beasts?" an anthousai with chestnut eyes asked.

"I'm not sure. She seemed spooked though. Said whatever they were, they had a mouth full of teeth and reeked of dead animal."

"Yeah, I heard something similar," Kait interjected, more than pleased with the uneasy silence that had settled over the peaceful meal. "Except I heard an immortal was behind it. They found some sort of creature and unleashed it into our realms. Apparently, they like the taste of nymph." She nodded to her jacket. "That's why I decided to dress like this. I don't want to find out if that rumor is true."

"An immortal?" a nearby satyr said. "Who would do such a thing?"

Kait put up her hands. "That's just what I heard."

"No way," a skeptical aurai with raven-black hair argued. "If that were true, the Council would never stand by and let it happen."

"True," an anthousai agreed. "But what if they don't know?"

That made everyone pause. Kait glanced up from beneath her lashes and scanned the skeptical faces of those around her.

"What do we do if we see them?" the dryad questioned. "How do we stop them?"

Kait shook her head. "I have no idea. All I know is I've got my magic at the ready, and I'm carrying this with me until whatever is out there is eradicated." She revealed a four-inch dagger from a sheath at her thigh and held it up for all those gathered to see. "Just stay alert. That's all any of us can do, I guess."

"Nonsense." The satyr dismissed Kait's declaration with a snort and wiped his chapped hands on the cedar fur that covered his thighs. "We haven't seen anything of the sort. I wouldn't put any stock in the rumors."

A chorus of voices swelled as the group debated the practicality of Kait's words, but she remained quiet. She had said her piece. Hopefully, it would plant a seed of doubt or fear into their minds. She tucked her blade back into her boot and slipped away from the group, hooking the collar of her discarded jacket with a finger. She slung it over her shoulder and wandered out of the shade toward the nearest portal. Another realm down, one left before she could call it a day.

The translucent film of the portal waved back and forth amidst the long grass a few hundred yards away. Kait sighed and imagined her next destination.

Maybe Kairu won't be as humid.

Kait stepped in front of the shimmering portal, waiting until the wavy image of the favored beach realm appeared. Lush trees and clear water lapped at the frame. She crossed the threshold, but the moment her boots sunk into the sand, she knew something was wrong.

An agitated breeze enveloped her, relaying its unease. Kait's head swiveled. The usually crowded beach was deserted. Without pause, she drew her dagger and gripped it in her palm until her knuckles shone white against her brown skin. Careful to keep the sea at her back, she feverishly scanned the dense trees.

The scene looked peaceful, save for a single trail of crimson blood that soaked the sand. Kait followed it with her eyes, noticing numerous deep grooves on either side as though someone had been dragged away.

Steeling her nerves, Kait knocked the leaves aside and ducked beneath a loop of swaying vines to follow the blood, leaving the sun in exchange for cool shadows. A spot of wetness splashed her cheek. She wiped her face as a piercing scream rent the air.

Kait gasped and jerked back as several more wet drops rained down, splattering her skin. Confused by the lack of rain clouds, she searched the thick foliage above. There, suspended within the tangled vines, were the remains of a nymph. It was clear she was dead. She lay on her stomach, with her neck twisted at such an extreme angle that her face pointed toward the sky. Her rib cage had been shredded, exposing raw pink tissue. Kait's stomach flipped at the gruesome sight and the realization that it was blood that marred her cheek.

Another chorus of screams drew her attention away from the corpse. They sounded close and desperate. Kait sprinted ahead through the large leaves to find the source of the cries. She ran hard and fruitlessly for several minutes. The eerie screams continued, shrill and endless.

Kait closed her eyes and allowed the wind to guide her sight rather than running blindly through the jungle. The wind's vision billowed through the trees until it alighted upon two naiads stuck in the branches of an ipe tree. Below them, an infected nymph with dark blond hair prowled the trunk, leaping and clawing at the impenetrable bark like a vicious piriol. The diseased nymph crouched low and then shot into the air. This time, she managed to hook her arm around a low-hanging branch. Horrified screams crescendoed as the nymph climbed, gnashing her teeth as she went.

One of the naiads opened her palms and unleashed a torrent of water, and the stream hit the nymph directly in the face. The force was too much and sent her reeling back. She lost her grip on the branch and crashed to the dirt floor, landing with a sharp crack, her leg at an unnatural angle. She hissed with rage and launched herself skyward again, heedless of the shattered bone.

Kait's eyes flashed open as she melted into the wind. It had happened faster than she'd thought possible; Hera had created the virus and let it loose to poison the nymphs. To kill Bia. Pushing herself onward through the sticky air, Kait caught sight of bright red streaks painting the leaves and smooth bark of towering kapok trees. Then, she saw the bodies. Dozens of severed arms and legs littered the ground beside motionless corpses. The nymph back in the vines hadn't been the only victim.

"No!" someone screamed and jerked Kait out of her stupor.

Unable to do anything for the dead, Kait raced ahead and reached the naiads a moment later. The sound of clicking teeth reached her from across the small clearing as the infected nymph tightened her grip on the naiad with lavender hair. Tears streamed out of the nymph's eyes as she reached for her friend, but the infected was stronger. With a final tug, she ripped the naiad from the safety of the tree, and together, they collapsed to the ground.

"Sami, get up! Get up!" the other nymph cried, smacking the tree with her hand.

Sami rolled over, nursing a wound to her head. But before she could defend herself, the infected dug her nails into Sami's calf. Kait rushed forward. With her blade clutched in her fist, Kait materialized out of the air and slammed down beside the tangled nymphs. The infected didn't react. Instead, her lips pulled back, and she sunk her teeth into the naiad's thigh, too intent on her prey to notice the newcomer.

"No!" the other naiad screamed as her friend's cry mirrored her despair.

Kait swung her arm and plunged the jagged knife into the infected's back, burying it to the hilt, so far that it punctured a lung. In response, the infected only bit down harder. She seemed mesmerized by the warm blood coating her tongue. Yanking her blade out of the soft flesh, Kait didn't hesitate. She raised the dagger again and thrust it into the base of the infected's skull. The blade slid between muscle and bone, destroying the soft brain tissue within.

Like a puppet whose strings had been cut, the infected's jaw fell slack and her body went limp. Sami whimpered and scrambled away as best as she could with her mangled leg while her friend descended from the branches and hurried to her side.

"Oh, Sami. I'm so sorry. I couldn't hold her off. Let me heal you," the other naiad said. She grimaced at the blood, the gnawed flesh.

"Are there any others?" Kait asked, scanning the trees.

"No, she was the only one. What happened to her?"

"She was poisoned," Kait answered. She bent down and retrieved the dagger, then wiped the infected's black blood on the grass. "We need to get out of here. There will be others."

"What do you mean? How do you know?" the naiad asked as she commanded a steady stream of water to pour from her palms. The cool water washed away the excess blood, but the wound behind was ugly and flayed.

"It doesn't matter. Just trust me. We need to go." Kait scanned the thick foliage and prayed a centaur was nearby. Their knowledge of medicinal herbs was unmatched, and one kick from their hooves would render an infected incapacitated. Unfortunately, the trees were still and empty.

Sami shook her head. "Emya, I can't walk."

Emya focused harder on the raw skin, but no magic she cast mended flesh.

"It can't be healed," Kait explained sadly. "The virus was goddess-born. The magic is too strong for any of us to overcome." Her mind drifted to the salve Bia had prepped only hours ago. There was a very slim chance it would help, but it was with her sister, secured in a cloth pouch at her waist two realms away.

"Goddess-born? That's ridiculous." Emya tried to cast a simple yet effective magic every nymph was taught to cauterize wounds, but the blood continued to flow.

Kait shook her head and glanced away as a shadow danced at the edge of the sun's rays filtering through the canopy. Her body stiffened.

"What is it?" Emya asked.

"We need to move. Hurry. We'll have to carry her back to the portal." She bent down and scooped the injured nymph off the ground. "Get her other side."

"But we have to treat this before infection sets in."

"She's already infected," Kait countered. "I don't know how fast the virus targets the body, but I do know that if we don't leave right now, we're all going to die."

Sami gasped. "What? What do you mean?"

Emya glanced back at the infected's corpse. "But she's dead."

"Yeah, *she* is," Kait answered. The wind shifted, carrying the scent of warm meat toward them. At once, the shadows solidified, and eight disease-ridden corpses swayed on their feet, their blind eyes staring at them.

"B-But . . . that's not possible," Emya stuttered. "I saw the infected one rip out her throat, saw her tear off her arm." She pointed to the dark-skinned nymph in the center, who shuffled lamely toward them. "She was dead."

"Not anymore," Kait said. "I'll hold them back. Take Sami to the portal and get to Olean. Tell Tahlia Kait was right."

"What are you going to do?" Sami asked.

"Whatever works. Go!"

Emya broke into a run, moving as fast as she could while supporting Sami. The army of infected nymphs snarled as their prey ran. They surged forward at once. Kait walked backward and curled her fingers into fists, summoning the wind to her will.

Gargled moans and savage growls exploded as they drew closer. Kait continued her steady pace, ignoring the ravaged bodies and gaping wounds that decorated the creatures who were once her friends. When they were only feet away, she released her shaking fists and roared. A powerful gale exploded from her palms, sending the infected nymphs tumbling head over heels through the air.

Aware she had only minutes, Kait leapt into the sky. She sprinted with the breeze and found Emya and Sami struggling to make it over a fallen log. Kait gathered the wind beneath her and enveloped the naiads to carry them. The weight—combined with her draining energy—was too much, and their toes dragged in the dirt as Kait fought to maintain her hold.

"There it is!" Emya called, pointing at the shimmering currents a few yards away.

"We're going to make it," Sami said breathlessly.

A hoarse cry erupted beside them as an infected nymph sprinted out of the trees to their right and launched herself off the ground. She collided with Sami and wrenched her out of Kait's grasp.

"Help!"

The infected climbed on top of her, pinning her arms down with her knees. She grinned with blind eyes and buried her head in the crook of Sami's neck, her teeth slicing into the vulnerable flesh above her collarbone.

Kait dropped Emya to her feet and severed her connection to the wind. She flipped backward. Before she hit the ground, she unsheathed her dagger, the blade poised for execution. Her boots slammed into the soft earth as she brought her arm down in a graceful swing. Steel slashed the infected's temple in two, instantly halting her feast.

Tears streaked out of Sami's eyes as she struggled to push the body off her chest. Kait bent down and kicked the corpse away with the sole of her boot. "Hurry, the others are right behind us." She hooked her hands beneath Sami's arms. Another chorus of ragged breaths reached them as the wind flavored the air with fresh blood.

"Come on!" Emya yelled. She toed the edge of the portal, ready to leap inside its haven.

Kait stumbled the short distance, doing her best to support Sami's weight, but exhaustion filled her arms with lead and forced her to fight for every inch gained. Behind them, harrowing sounds of biting swelled, and the sickly odor of the dead wafted closer. Emya reached out and pulled Sami and Kait inside the confines of the portal.

"Olean!" Emya cried. Her eyes bulged with fear while the rest of the infected swarmed. They were only feet away, and there was nothing to stop them from entering the portal after them. They were sitting ducks with nowhere to flee.

At last, the portal registered their halos and responded, transporting the trio to their desired destination. Kait watched the descending nightmare. Black drooling mouths, listless eyes, and desperate groans rolled toward them, but their fingers and gnashing teeth collided against an invisible barrier. The portal was a shield, its sensors able to detect an ethereal connection. Without one, the entrants were expelled.

Kairu melted away, replaced with the snow-covered grounds of Olean as the portal deposited them onto the wooden platform. Kait and Emya struggled to keep Sami's paling form upright.

"Help!" Emya shouted as a few dryads arrived from a portal on the far end.

A bald dryad gasped as she raced the short distance to their side. "What happened?"

"We were attacked in Kairu."

"By what?" another dryad asked.

"Infected nymphs," Kait said. "Seal it off. Make sure no one travels there."

"Why?"

"They're still there. I managed to kill two of them, but the others . . ." Kait didn't finish. A flicker of light caught her eye, and she glanced at Sami.

"Your halo," Emya whispered, her eyes full of fear as she regarded her dying friend.

"We don't have much time. We must get her to a healer."

"I can help. Stand still," a dryad with braids said, and interlocked her fingers. The wood beneath their feet rose and pushed them into the air on a sprouting tree. The nymphs clutched one another to keep from falling as the dryad's magic carried them away from the square to a small structure with an intricate symbol carved into the door.

Before they could climb off the smooth bark, the curved door opened to reveal a nymph with a gentle countenance. Customary green velvet covered her skin and marked her as an experienced healer. A small wrinkle formed between the healer's eyes as she took in the unexpected arrivals, but her expression transformed the moment she caught sight of Sami.

"Goddess! What happened? Bring her in!" the healer ordered, her soft voice full of authority. Emya and Kait leapt down and hurried inside with the healer on their heels. She pulled the door shut, and her swift fingers tied on a floor-length apron. "Lay her on the table. How did she sustain these injuries?"

They complied and stepped back to give the healer plenty of space. She applied a sweet-smelling balm to the wounds on Sami's neck and calf. Kait smelled turmeric and wondered if it was the same concoction Bia had created.

Kait took a deep breath and nearly collapsed from heat stroke and exhaustion. "We were attacked in Kairu. We barely made it back."

"Attacked? By what? These bites look humanoid."

"They are. Something has been unleashed. A nymph contracted it and turned savage, bit her sisters. I can't be sure, but I think once bitten, the virus spreads."

"What makes you think that?" the healer questioned, eyes intent on her patient.

"We saw the dead. We saw them . . . come back."

The healer straightened, looking up from Sami's torn flesh for the first time. The broken naiad lay with her eyes closed. Her ragged breaths were the only indication that she was still fighting to stay alive. The healer stepped away from the table and motioned for them to follow.

"Is she going to be, okay?" Emya asked. "You can fix her, right?"

The healer took a deep breath. "I'm afraid not. The wounds aren't deep, but if the dead returned as you said, whatever toxin running through her attacker's bloodstream was transferred to your friend the moment their teeth broke her skin."

"You've seen this before?"

The healer shook her head. "No, but the old texts speak of a terrible plague that afflicted a small population of humans thousands of years ago. The entries describe the dead returning to life, assumed to be controlled by a demonic presence. They were called the *vrykolakas*. Nearly two-thirds of the population was decimated before they discovered a way to neutralize them. It's not quite the same though; her symptoms are different. This is something I've never seen before."

"I killed two," Kait whispered, three if she counted the vision of Bia Hera had created in the mortal world, but she kept that to herself.

"How?" the healer asked.

Kait grimaced. Shame colored her cheeks as she withdrew the dagger from its sheath. The blade was stained black, still bathed in the infected nymphs' blood. "Destroying the head works best."

The healer nodded. "The old texts describe a similar technique. The brain was key. Destroying the brain, be it with a blade, fire, or lack of oxygen, returned the risen to a permanent state of death."

"What was the cause last time? Who created it?"

The healer shrugged. "The source was never identified, though immortal activity was suspected, but Olean has been impenetrable to the gods since the Titan War. We're safe."

Kait's eyes widened at the truth of the healer's words. "Safe . . . unless we breach our own walls."

Emya gasped. "Sami."

All three of their heads snapped up and zeroed in on the empty table.

"Where did she go?" the healer asked, scanning the room.

"Maybe she got better?" Emya guessed, her voice hopeful.

A cacophony of screams shattered the silence as the reality of their mistake erupted.

"I don't think so."

CHAPTER 13

The small group poured out the front door but stopped short at the sheer amount of carnage Sami had accomplished in minutes. Blood splattered the well-worn path that carved through the thin layer of snow. Several nymphs already littered the ground like macabre breadcrumbs. Kait palmed her dagger and cautiously approached the first body.

The healer wrenched Kait's arm back and jostled the knife out of her hold. It fell to the ground with a muted thud. "What are you doing?" the healer asked, aghast.

"She's going to turn, just like Sami. That's how it spreads. We must destroy her brain before she returns and infects others," Kait shot back.

"We don't know if she'll come back."

"Do you want to wait around and find out? Every second we waste standing here, Sami infects another." Kait bent down, grabbed her dagger, and fixed the healer with an unflinching stare. "We have to do this."

The healer flexed her jaw but held her tongue. Kait pivoted on her heels and continued toward the closest nymph. She lay on her side. The skin of her cheek resembled raw meat. Kait peered at the nymph's face and was shocked to see her eyelids flutter open.

"You're alive," Kait said, careful to stay out of the nymph's reach.

The nymph nodded, amber eyes shining with pain. "Something was wrong with that naiad. She bit my face." She sobbed. "Why would she do that?"

"Was that the only place she bit you?"

"Yeah. She bit me and threw me down. I hit my head. I heard my friend scream before I blacked out."

Kait glanced toward a blond aurai a few yards away. She lay on her back in a thick puddle of blood. The crown of her head dug into the ground, and her torn throat was exposed to the sky.

"Check her," Kait said.

The healer's footsteps crunched through the icy snow and halted above the nymph. "She's dead."

"How many bites?"

It was quiet for a minute as the healer inspected the cooling body. "Just one. If the bite hadn't severed her jugular vein, she'd still be alive."

"Oh, goddess," Kait whispered as her hand covered her mouth.

"What is it?" Emya asked, crossing to Kait's side.

"The virus . . . it's changing."

"Changing how?"

"Back in Kairu, the infected that chased us was fueled by hunger. The bodies of her victims were ripped apart, their organs partially eaten, but Sami only delivered one bite before she took off and attacked another."

"What does that mean?"

The healer checked the third body. "This one is alive, too. One bite wound to the neck," she called as she helped the injured nymph sit up.

"She's not hungry. She's building an army."

"But why?"

"Because Sami isn't the one in charge. Hera is the one pulling the strings." An explosion of coughing interrupted Kait's thoughts, and a fountain of stomach bile dribbled over the young nymph's lips at her feet.

"Is she turning?" Emya worried as she vomited up another wave.

"Yes. Find a weapon. Something sharp and sturdy. Go!"

The retching nymph reached for Kait, her fingers feebly trying to grasp the bottom of her pants. Her lips moved as she tried to speak. "Help me," the nymph choked, spraying blood and bile a few inches into the air.

Kait gritted her teeth and curled her hand into a fist around the handle of the dagger.

"No!" the healer cried, but Kait ignored her plea.

With a heavy grunt, Kait plunged the dagger into the nymph's forehead, ending the transformation as she took her life. The soft pink flickering halo surrounding the nymph vanished as her limbs sagged to the cold ground.

The healer stood with her mouth agape. "How could you?"

"She was infected," Kait replied, rising from her crouch. She moved to where the blond nymph lay, but the healer blocked her path.

"She was *alive*," the healer stressed. "You had no right."

Kait stepped toe to toe with the healer. "I didn't kill her. Hera did. I showed her mercy before the virus reduced her to a drooling monster. Now, I need you to get out of my way."

"What if I can save them? What if the ancients found a cure other than dispatching those bitten? Just give me time to search."

"Time is something we don't have. Get out of the way." Kait pushed the healer aside. Screams echoed in the distance, confirming her theory that Sami was out to infect rather than devour, but the healer still refused to move.

"Please, this isn't ethical. Just because someone is bitten doesn't mean they can't be saved."

"We don't know anything about this," Kait yelled. "All I know is what I've seen. Look at how quickly she started to turn. If we don't take care of this, all the realms will be under attack by the end of the day. If you're not going to help me, move."

A flash of dark hair flickered at the edge of Kait's vision as Emya returned, a bronze fire poker clutched in her hands.

"Let me at least prepare their souls for departure to Gaia," the healer begged. "Let them go into death peacefully."

"Kait! Watch out!" Emya cried.

Emya pointed at something behind them with a look of horror. Time slipped into slow motion as Kait scoured to find the source of Emya's fear. Too late she saw the dirt-stained fingers, the salivating mouth as the blond nymph's lips pulled back to reveal eager teeth. The infected's jaws closed around the healer's ankle and bit into the skin like a juicy peach.

"No!"

The healer fell to the ground as the infected knocked her off-balance. Kait pounced and drove her dagger into the top of the infected's skull. The nymph's grip instantly relaxed, but the damage was done. Her dagger grated against bone as she extricated it with a hard yank, and the motion sent the corpse crashing into the bloodstained snow.

Kait cursed and pressed her fists to her temples. Another and another and another she couldn't save. "What can I do?" she cried.

"Nothing. It's too late." The healer grimaced and pulled her foot away from the infected's face. "I should have listened. You're right. The only thing we can do is contain this, keep it from spreading to the other realms. Save as many as you can."

Choked moans climbed out of the third body's throat as she turned as well.

"Go," the healer instructed. "Both of you. Save us."

"What about you?" Emya asked shakily, her eyes glued to the awakening infected.

"I'll take care of her . . . and myself," the healer answered as a tear ran down her cheek.

"Come on, Emya. She's right. We need to go," Kait said. She turned back to the healer and tossed the dagger to the snow in front of her. "I'm sorry."

The healer wrapped her hand around the hilt. "Me too. Now go."

The last infected pushed herself to her feet and threw her head to the side as her eyes rolled back. Kait helped the healer stand and touched her face. Then, she nudged Emya's shoulder, and together, they skirted the infected's twitching hands and sprinted away from the small cottage. They ran in silence until a heavy thud echoed from behind. Kait held her breath as another followed. "Goodbye," she whispered, hoping the healer's kind soul could hear.

Emya cleared her throat after a few heavy seconds. "You need to find a weapon."

Kait glanced down at her empty hands. She debated going back for her dagger, but the thought of having to pull it from the healer's skull was unthinkable. "I'll find something. If you can, use your magic to subdue them, but make sure to destroy the brain."

"Okay." Emya nodded, breathing hard as their legs carried them back to the center of town.

Kait wasn't sure what they'd find, but it wasn't going to be pretty.

The pair ducked beneath the frosted branches of a weeping willow and emerged from the forest, but their hurried pace faltered at the sight before them. There were too many infected to count. Each one hissed like a viper as they hounded the remaining nymphs struggling to hold them off. Kait recognized Anamalla at the center of the frantic group, her eyes steely as she took on three infected at once.

"We can't help them," Emya whispered.

"We have to try." Kait took a determined step forward, but a hand gripped her shoulder and ripped her back. Her heart fluttered in her chest as she waited for the slice of teeth, but instead, a pair of familiar eyes found hers. "Tahlia!" Her gaze swept the elder's stooped frame. Her hair was a mess, and her bare arms and neck were smothered in both scarlet and black blood. "Have you been bitten?" Fear knotted her stomach; Olean couldn't lose her.

Tahlia coughed and shook her head. "No, not yet at least. I'm so sorry I didn't believe you, Kait. I was a fool."

"That doesn't matter now. Are these all the infected?"

"I think so, but I can't be sure. We were able to subdue the first one, a naiad, but she infected numerous others before we figured out how to stop her. She continued to attack no matter what magic or weapons we used."

"Sami," Emya said sadly.

"Destroy the brain. It's the only way to stop them," Kait explained.

"Anamalla figured that out, but not before the naiad bit others. We didn't realize they would . . . come back," Tahlia said.

"The rate at which the bitten are turning is quickening. Soon, it might even be instant."

Tahlia shook her head. "I've never seen a disease spread this quickly."

"That's because whatever this is, it isn't natural. It doesn't follow a typical incubation period."

A series of savage growls erupted from behind. Two infected nymphs crashed through the frozen shrubs. Kait's heart broke as she recognized Dion limping toward her. Yellow bile pooled from the nymphs' mouths and peppered the disturbed snow as they shuffled ahead.

"Get ready!" Tahlia cried, brandishing a long broadsword.

Emya followed suit and raised the heavy poker above her head. Kait glanced down, realizing too late that she had yet to arm herself. She took a step back and spread her fingers, following her own advice and relying on magic to slow them down.

With a groan, Tahlia swung her sword and cleaved one of the infected nymphs' heads from her shoulders. The body continued to charge on for a few steps but then collapsed in a heap of rotting flesh. Dion was swifter and gave Tahlia's sword a wide berth before she cut in, her wild eyes fixed on Emya. The young naiad jabbed at Dion with her poker and was able to knock her off course. Dion ignored the black blood that dripped from her shoulder wound, now intent upon Kait.

Dion threw herself at her, teeth gnashing aggressively as their bodies collided. Before they hit the ground, Kait disappeared into the wind and slipped out from beneath Dion's weight. The infected's head bounced off the cold ground, and her neck snapped from side to side as she searched for her escaped prey. Spying Emya once more, Dion snarled and scuttled across the dirt, moving faster than her broken bones should have allowed. Emya turned, preparing her poker, when a small horde of infected broke through the surrounding trees.

Kait watched in horror as the party of infected closed in on Emya while Dion dove for her legs. The naiad only had seconds to choose which threat was more perilous. Shifting her body away from Dion, she left her back exposed and spun her iron weapon in a wide arc. She caught an approaching infected in the chin and knocked her back as another lunged. Dion crawled closer, her jaws inches away from Emya's swirling skirts. Suddenly, the healer's words wove through Kait's mind.

Destroying the brain, by any means, be it with a blade, fire, or lack of oxygen, returned the risen to a permanent state of death. A lack of oxygen.

With no time to debate the consequences, Kait launched herself at Dion and filled her gaping mouth with a frenzied breeze. Holding her breath, Kait slid down Dion's throat and stopped halfway, expanding until the air filled every available space.

At first, there was no change. Dion pulled herself closer to Emya. But after several seconds, her arms stopped digging into the hard dirt and turned inward, tearing at the skin on her throat. Kait increased the pressure on Dion's esophagus and steeled herself as the nymph's body heaved and rattled. Her hands smacked her chest and neck as if begging for relief.

"What's happening to her?" Tahlia's muffled words reached Kait. She prayed it would only be another minute.

"Goddess, look!" Emya cried. She sounded horrified. Kait assumed there was another outpouring of nymphs, but then she felt it—fresh air.

Dion plunged her fingers into the hollow base of her throat. Her body continued to buck as her brain demanded oxygen. Her fingers dug harder, scraping skin and muscle out of the way to allow an alternative passage for air.

"Kill her!" Emya yelled. A heavy thud rippled along the ground as another infected fell.

Tahlia's strained grunt sounded, followed by the unmistakable whir of a sword slicing the sky. In the next moment, Dion's body went rigid as the blade pierced her skull and her struggling ceased at last. Kait contracted and shimmied back up Dion's throat to emerge between her parted teeth. Inhaling, she drank in the crisp air and sprinted skyward. As she rose, she assessed the scene she'd fled, and her heart ached as she took in Dion.

Half her rib cage lay exposed after her attempt to free the invisible force from inside, and Kait briefly wondered if her friend had been consumed by pain as she tore herself apart.

The surviving nymphs dispatched the last of the infected as Kait directed the wind back to Earth. She spiraled to the ground and alighted out of the wind's hold beside Dion's body. "You two were amazing."

"Where did you go?" Tahlia said. "You left us."

"No. I didn't have a weapon, so I transformed and tried to suffocate Dion from within."

"That was you?" Emya asked. "I didn't know what to think when I saw her mutilating herself like that." She pointed to the obvious carnage at Kait's feet.

Kait didn't need to look. She had felt enough. "It was the only thing I could think of."

"You deprived the brain of oxygen," Tahlia said, nodding with understanding. "That was a risky move, but an effective distraction."

Kait's eyes brightened. "Then, that's how we stop them. An aurai cuts off their air supply and then another nymph finishes them. No one else will have to die." She tried to keep her eyes on Tahlia, but her gaze slid around the small circle of the fallen and rested on every face. So many sweet nymphs dead because of one woman's twisted sense of justice.

"I don't know. We still don't know anything about this virus. What if the aurais become infected from being inside?" Tahlia posed. "We can't sacrifice an entire faction."

Kait shrugged. "I held my breath. If we don't do something soon, we'll have sacrificed the entire nymph race. If the aurais turn . . . then, you know what to do." She stared at Tahlia, her violet eyes as unyielding as her resolve.

Tahlia ground her jaw. "Fine, but we need to act quickly. When we get to the square, find as many aurais as you can and explain the plan. Remember, tell them not to breathe."

Both Kait and Emya nodded as the young naiad gripped her bloodied poker.

"All right. Let's end this."

"Oh, Ze-Ze, isn't it marvelous?" Hera cooed, clapping her hands like an excited child. "The infection is working even better than Ares thought. By midnight, all those despicable tarts will be reduced to drooling piles of flesh." Hera gazed over the rim of the Skyglass and exhaled a delighted squeal as an infected anthousai ripped into a startled dryad. "Perfect, just perfect."

Hera's grin expanded while her silver eyes swept the frantic woods. Ze-Ze hissed softly from her perch.

"Soon, my pet. It's almost time for the grand finale." Shifting the Skyglass's focus, Hera left the turmoil in Olean in exchange for the desert sands in the realm of Taryn. The infection had yet to spread to its borders, but one nymph stood atop the calm dunes screaming nonetheless. Hera chuckled.

The aurai's sister, Bia, was encased in a transparent prison. Tears streamed down her reddened cheeks as her fists beat the walls. It was amusing to watch the anthousai try to cast her way underground, only to realize her cell extended solidly around her. That's when she'd started to dig. Sand covered her hair and sweating skin, the tiny grains embedded deep under her nails. The blood vessels around the anthousai's eyes burst, and crimson stars dotted her skin as her silent wails bombarded her cage.

A strong ripple rocked the walls as Bia's anger and magic surged. The goddess's easy smile fell. The nymph was powerful. Hera spun away from the Skyglass, and her gown swirled with her movements. Soon. Hera would release her when the time was right. She laughed. For all Bia's fighting, only death awaited her. Hades had agreed.

She thought back to her correspondence with the god of the Underworld shortly after Zeus's death. The charming trickster, Hermes, had delivered Hades's proposal with a knowing glint in his eye. It was common knowledge at this point that the messenger was privy to countless secrets. Not only handsome and debonair, Hermes was also wily and clever beyond belief, able to coax the deepest secrets from even the most introverted gods.

Hermes had leaned against one of the stone pillars while Hera broke the emblazoned black wax seal. With hooded eyes, he watched, poised for her reaction. Scanning Hades's elegant script, Hera had attempted to keep her expression neutral, for in her hands, she held her solution to the question she'd lain awake at night trying to decipher.

Hades would willingly help her execute revenge on the nymphs for Zeus's death in exchange for her allegiance when called upon. Hera pursed her lips. She wasn't a fool. Hades already possessed Zeus's power. There was no way he would willingly settle for her mere cooperation when he could have complete control. With her pledged surrender and assistance, when the time came, he would be strong enough to break from his desolate throne and reclaim his position atop Olympus once again.

Hastily, Hera had scribbled her acceptance, putting little stock in the success of Hades's hostile takeover. She might not be able to stop him, but there was nothing which bound her to keep his plans to herself. A quick word with the Immortal Council and Athena could draw up a defensive strategy faster than Cerberus could jump the River Styx.

Let him try. I'll have my vengeance and Zeus.

In the following weeks, the idea for the infection had taken hold. It wouldn't be enough to kill Kaitaini. Death would be far too quick. No, she needed to hurt, to sob until her eyes were too swollen to see. The only way to accomplish that was by killing the one she held most dear.

Back and forth, Hermes had run as she orchestrated the perfect revenge. Hera didn't want to simply kill Kait's sister but to cleanse her soul from the realms forever. When nymphs passed on after their five-hundred-year lifespans, the goddess Gaia sheltered their souls until Olean required more and they began life anew in a different body. It was this perpetual existence that Hera yearned to snuff out. With Hades on board, the possibilities were endless.

"Trust me," Hera purred as her thoughts returned from the past. "It's almost time. The moment I release the anthousai, she'll race right back to Olean. We'll make sure the dear wind nymph sees her sister fall."

Hera ran a triangular nail between the serpent's golden eyes and sat back. "Now, stay here and wait for me. I'm going to get a closer look."

CHAPTER 14

Blood, so much blood, dripped from wooden roof tiles like crimson icicles, transforming the peaceful realm into a surreal nightmare. Scattered about the square were two hundred or so remaining nymphs, each engaged with three or more of their infected sisters. Kait paused on the outskirts of the fight and peered into the cloudy sky.

"Are you happy, Hera? Have you corrupted enough nymph blood yet?" Kait spat under her breath. She knew the goddess was watching. She had spent too much time orchestrating the massacre; she wouldn't miss the violent virus at work.

"Heads up!" Tahlia called.

Kait's gaze snapped back to the scene. Her hands instinctively reached up to block her face as an object hurtled toward her. The sound of clanging metal surprised her as a heavy coil of chain met her palms. "What's this?"

Tahlia swung her sword as she ran into the melee. "We're too far from an armory for a real weapon. It was the best I could find on short notice. Stick to the plan, and be careful."

Kait took a deep breath and gave Emya a quick smile. She spun one of the ends of the chain in a lethal dance. It felt good to have a weapon in her hands. "See you on the other side."

Rushing forward, Kait wielded the heavy chain like a lasso above her head and threw the silver snake in the direction of the nearest infected. The bright links caught the diseased nymph across the face and whirled her around with fierce velocity. The infected swaggered unsteadily, red welts blossoming across her nose and cheek.

Kait readied the chain again and charged closer to deliver a more powerful blow. The infected hissed once she regained her equilibrium, her beautiful face distorted with savagery. Before the nymph could take another step, Kait whipped the cold metal with a flick of her wrist and grimaced as the chain smashed into the infected's temple. The bones caved on impact, and the nymph collapsed to the ground.

Kait stepped over the bleeding corpse, using the chain as fluidly as if it were an extension of her arm. She cut down multiple foes and carved a bloody path through the clashing bodies, but still, her despair heightened. She needed to find an aurai.

She reached Anamalla and ducked as the imposing nymph spun in a tight circle to bring a solid tree limb down on an infected's already bleeding head. Anamalla brushed the clinging hair off her sweating neck and sighed. Defeat shone in her eyes as another tide of infected nymphs surged forward.

"Anamalla." Kait placed her hand on her slick shoulder.

"Kait, you're okay," Anamalla said, relief evident in her voice.

"Yes, but I need your help. I have a way to slow them down, but we're going to need more aurais. Gather as many as you can, then on my mark, transform into the wind and dive into an infected's throat."

"What? We'll reduce what little numbers we have left doing that."

"Trust me, it works. Once they're distracted, our sisters can dispatch them. All of them. This will be over soon."

Anamalla glanced at the advancing mass and gripped her weapon tighter. "All right. You knew this was coming. You tried to warn us, but we—*I* didn't listen. I'm with you now."

Kait touched her cheek. "Thank you, and Anamalla . . . hold your breath."

The nymphs separated and set their sights on nearby aurais. Kait's movements were brutal yet elegant as she wove through the endless maze of growling nymphs. Her chain sliced through matted hair and crazed eyes, guilt weighing heavier with every friend she cut down. They hadn't deserved this end.

She didn't know how much time had elapsed since she broke away from Tahlia and Emya. Realistically, it had only been a few minutes, but surely she couldn't have rendered that amount of carnage so quickly. She followed her friends' stares toward the north of the square. The survivors had all paused to take a collective breath as the newest horde of infected breached the tree line, allowing the sprinting army to advance before launching their counterattack. She steadied her mind and gazed ahead unblinking as she sensed those around her begin to shift uncomfortably. They were exhausted and emotionally drained. Killing went against everything they stood for, but the instinctual need to survive could not be ignored.

The infected nymphs' wild cries polluted the air. Kait let out a long breath and summoned the wind, letting it increase the power of her voice. "Aurais!" she bellowed across the square. Numerous heads swiveled, awaiting her next command, while the disease-ridden nymphs stormed through the thin line of defense. "Together!"

All at once, a dozen silhouettes vanished from sight. Kait joined them and melted into the tornado-like force. She didn't think. Choosing one at random, she drilled into an infected nymph's mouth and expanded the air inside her lungs so it was impossible for her to draw breath. Soon, she felt the familiar tugging sensation of her host fighting to rid herself of her uninvited tormentor, but her struggle was futile. Her movements became sluggish as her brain began to shut down without the necessary oxygen.

Another minute ticked by, and then a wet sucking sound interrupted the infected's self-inflicted war. Her arms flopped to her side as a sharp arrow was yanked from her skull. From within, Kait sensed the moment the nymph passed and hurriedly exited her mouth to attack another.

The plan was working. As aurais infiltrated from within, the other nymphs reacted, killing those infected with clean swipes of their makeshift weapons. A smudge of gray blinked on the horizon. Kait ignored the shadow and jumped into another open throat. She couldn't afford to be distracted.

Again and again, she helped her sisters destroy the infected. She wished their deaths would blur into one, but she personally felt each nymph's surrender and would never forget the sound as their bodies fell to the dirt-strewn snow. After the blade left the eleventh corpse's skull, Kait silenced her guilt and glanced around for a new enemy, but the air tasted different. The flavor had changed.

Still airborne, Kait spun around, surprised to see only six infected nymphs still standing in a perfect semicircle. They seemed frozen. The choir of snarls ceased as the few that remained stared ahead silently with dull eyes. Her friends held their ground and gripped their bloodied weapons, ready for the moment the infected flinched, but their collective confusion was palpable.

What are they waiting for?

Kait spiraled down to the earth and shed her elemental form. She materialized beside a naiad named Iris. "What's going on?"

Iris shrugged. "We're not sure. They just stopped fighting."

"For no reason?" A loud bird's cry erupted overhead as Kait surveyed the square. Up ahead, a shimmer of red hair caught the faint rays of sunlight that climbed through the thinning clouds. "Bia!" Kait cried.

Bia's amber eyes brightened, but the moment their eyes met, hell broke loose.

The six infected nymphs let out furious bellows and sprinted ahead. Kait had never seen them move so fast. In seconds, they were halfway across the square, all charging toward the same target. A flash of dappled gray wings fluttered in the corner of Kait's eye. She recognized the sleek hawk and realization dawned. Hadn't she postulated that the infected were waiting for something? Once Kait had returned to the ground, Hera lifted the brief stalemate and ordered what was left of her army to kill.

Chaos exploded, and time seemed to slow. Kait glanced around for her chain. Her friends swung their weapons, yet none of their well-aimed blows were able to reach the infected. They were suddenly too fast, too agile, and dodged the attacks with ease as they wormed their way forward.

Kait spotted a black object half buried in the disturbed dirt. Crouching, she extricated it and ignored the thick layer of mud that seeped beneath her fingernails. It wasn't the chain she'd wielded, but a shattered chunk of granite. It didn't have the reach she preferred, but at least it was heavy.

Anxious rasps and hungry moans surrounded her. Frantic, Kait looked up to see six drooling mouths closing in. She raised the granite block, calculating the best way to defend herself, yet no matter how fast she moved, she knew her chances were slim. She would be able to take down one or two, but she'd never be able to dodge all those teeth.

Left with no other choice, Kait dropped the stone and called the wind to her once again, but this time, she chose to flee rather than fight. Her fingers spun while her magic crested, but a spark of red made her pause mid-cast. "Bia?" Her sister's face appeared inches from her own. "Get out of here!"

Bia shook her head. "No! This is my fight just as m-much as yours."

The infected stormed closer. Bia slashed the closest one with her sword and caught the nymph across the cheek. Blackish blood oozed from the wound. Kait wielded the wind and blasted the infected in the chest with a powerful strike that sent her hurtling backward.

"Bia, please! I can't lose you, too."

Her sister lowered her scarlet-stained weapon and frowned. "Hera won't stop until one of us is dead, and you're too important to Olean. This will keep you safe. I l-love you."

Before Kait could process her words, the ground fell out beneath her feet, and darkness swallowed her. A rush of cold earth buried her as Bia's magic quickly knitted the dirt and snow back together to seal Kait inside the ground. The last image she saw before dirt showered her face was the tremble of her sister's lower lip as she faced the oncoming mass. Hungry moans crescendoed and created a muted symphony above her earthen prison. Screams joined the cacophony. Kait recognized Bia's shrill yelp and pictured her fluttering hands banging her sides.

"No, no, no! Bia!"

Another scream, raw and broken, ricocheted above, followed by a great thud directly overhead. Panic tore through her chest. She had to get out. She had to help Bia!

Clawing at the frozen ground, Kait grimaced as her nails split while she fought to dig through the cold earth. "Bia!" She tried to pound her fists and flex her elbows, but the dirt slithered into every gap her accelerated descent had created. Cold grains and pebbles bit her exposed neck and pressed into the curves of her ears. Extricating the minimal oxygen from the soil, she held it in her lungs, but she wouldn't be able to remain encased for much longer.

Heavy vibrations shook the earthen ceiling, and loose clods tumbled into Kait's eyes. Muffled screams and cries echoed above. A maternal tug bloomed in her chest. She had to get out! She didn't understand why her sister had leapt in front of her. She remembered the sword in Bia's hand. Bia wasn't the most skilled fighter, but she knew how to wield the blade. She could beat them. Kait's lungs burned as her body consumed the remaining oxygen.

"Bia!" Kait rasped as tears gathered along her lower lashes.

A moment later, hands shot through the soil, hooking into her skin to haul her out. Kait was yanked upward and through the surface. She collapsed on her hands and knees, coughing and spluttering dirt from her sweaty lips. Rather than guttural moans, a flurry of voices enveloped her, their words blurring together to create a monotonous hum like the drone of a bee. Kait's eyes flickered back and forth, searching the cluster of faces for her sister.

"Bia? Where is Bia?" Kait wheezed as she inhaled greedily, expelling more dirt from her throat in her next breath.

The chattering ceased at once, and the entire square fell eerily quiet. Kait frowned and glanced up. All the gathered nymphs were staring at her with sorrow shining in their eyes.

"What? What is it? Where is she?"

Emya helped her to her feet and wiped a trickle of blood off her cheek with the back of her hand. The naiad's eyes welled with tears. "They were too fast. It was already too late."

Kait's stomach clenched, and her throat constricted. Suddenly, the fresh air was her enemy, fleeing from her lungs as she read the grief in Emya's gaze. Following the naiad's stare, Kait turned to look over her shoulder and located the six remaining infected piled high in a crescent shape a few feet from where Kait had climbed out of the ground. In the center of the bodies—splayed and broken—lay Bia.

"No!" Kait dropped to her knees. "Bia, no!"

She crawled over severed limbs and glassy eyes until she reached Bia's side and cupped her sister's sweet face. Her entire chest cavity had been torn open, revealing dark pink organs that had been jostled loose from savage prying. Deep bite marks encircled Bia's arms, calves, and neck. Kait looked at the dead corpses responsible. A few still had large chunks of flesh wedged between their teeth.

"Come back," Kait cried. "Bia, come back!" She willed her sister's eyes to cloud, for her to return as one of the dead, but minutes ticked by, and she didn't move.

"She won't come back," Tahlia explained softly. "One of the infected . . . she grabbed that and crushed your sister's skull while the others . . ."

Tahlia didn't have to finish her sentence. The evidence was before them. Kait saw the granite block she'd held moments before Bia leapt in front of her and recalled the finite thud she'd heard underground. That had been her sister's last moment of this life. Kait had only been inches away, yet she was helpless to protect her.

"She saved me," Kait's voice broke as she touched Bia's shredded hand.

"She loved you," Tahlia said, but Kait hadn't wanted an answer.

Kait shuddered as snot ran from her nose. She wished to bury her face in Bia's hair and hold her close, but the infected had robbed her of that privilege. Bia's body was far too fragile, and the thought of her bones tumbling out of the gaping holes ripped another scream from her throat.

Tahlia placed a comforting hand on Kait's back, but it did nothing to soothe her grief. The elder quietly spoke to the surrounding nymphs. "Spread out. Go in teams of two and sweep the rest of Olean, including the clan's territories."

Vivian—the naiad elder—appeared with a large cut on her forehead. "We'll gather medical supplies and instruct the healers to set up aid stations to treat those with injuries. The other realms need to be searched and any lingering infected executed. I'll ask for volunteers to assist with that."

"Thank you. Inform the queen as well," Tahlia whispered. "Tell her I'll stop by later with a full report."

Kait sobbed heavy ugly cries. Around her, she sensed when the survivors turned away to begin their next task, but Tahlia remained at her side and never let go.

Kait had no idea how long they sat huddled together on the bloodied ground. She held onto her sister's cooling hand as if it were a lifeline while her tears flowed like an endless river. Bia was gone. Her sweet, shy, obsessive sister was now nothing more than blood and bones. She kept squeezing her palm as if Bia had simply fallen asleep as she worked well into the night to finish another tincture. But her sister's stillness was the most unnerving. Bia was never still and hated to be touched. She would have never allowed Kait to hold her as she did. Kait could practically hear Bia's hands as they drummed her legs whenever someone wandered too close.

"Bia, please . . . Please, wake up." Kait stared at her soft features and glassy eyes, praying for a miracle, but none came, and her sister's cool skin grew sallow and waxen. Never again would Kait watch Bia's cheeks flush or her nose wrinkle in concentration. She was truly gone.

Tahlia shifted sometime later and roused Kait from her stupor. In truth, she'd forgotten the elder nymph was there.

"Come, Kait. We need to give Bia's soul space to ascend," Tahlia said, gently sliding her hands around Kait's elbow.

Her soul? Tahlia's words echoed in Kait's empty mind. *No, it couldn't be. It was too soon. They needed to give her a little more time. Maybe her body was trying to heal itself. Just give her a little more time.*

Kait resisted as Tahlia led her away. Inch by inch, Bia's cold fingers slid out of hers and dropped onto the dirt. Tahlia stood her up, carefully supporting her weight to compensate for her wobbling knees.

"Look, her soul is separating," Tahlia whispered.

Kait sucked in a ragged breath and saw what Tahlia described. Gone was death's sickly hue. Instead, a brilliant silver starburst radiated from the center of Bia's shredded chest. The light, faint at first, grew stronger and burned brightly against the gray atmosphere.

Kait watched transfixed as the glowing orb left Bia's body and hovered slightly above her sternum. Kait took an unconscious step forward, but Tahlia held her back. All she wanted to do was cradle her sister's soul. Even though she'd failed to keep her safe in life, maybe she could protect her in death. Another sister lost because of her.

Bia's soul lightly floated toward Kait, seeming just as eager to be near her.

"Careful," Tahlia warned, letting go of Kait's arm. "The mother goddess will be along to collect her shortly."

Kait nodded, not trusting herself to speak. She stepped up, raised her hand to shoulder height, and waited. Bia's soul immediately responded and inched closer until the warm silver mass pressed against Kait's palm.

"I'm so sorry," Kait cried. Her words were barely audible as her voice broke. The soul couldn't reply but enveloped her hand. A shaft of sunlight sliced through the clouds and alighted on the little soul. Kait looked up and felt Mother Goddess Gaia ready to ferry Bia's soul to the heavens until it was time to give her a new life. "I love you," Kait whispered. Time was running out.

Bia's soul hesitated, then drifted away, breaking the seal between them.

"Goodbye." One last heartbroken sob slipped from Kait's lips.

Bia's soul left the earth behind and ascended toward Gaia's soft face. Kait arched her neck, determined to follow Bia until she was gone from sight. A piercing cry, like cackling laughter, ripped the quiet asunder as a dappled gray hawk swooped down and obscured the sunlight, allowing shadows to reign once more.

"It's Hera," Kait hissed.

"Hera?"

Kait stared, unblinking, as the hawk cried again. The bird stopped mid-flight, pumped her wings, and released another screech, and a current of wind coalesced around Bia's soul and forced it to tumble back down to Earth.

"No!"

"What's happening?" Tahlia asked.

"Hera's trying to prevent Bia's soul from reaching Gaia."

Kait's fingers cast, and her feet disappeared into the wind. But before she could complete her transformation, an inky black shadow danced beside Kait and ran its smoky outline along her curves. Then it darted into the sky and cocooned around Bia's soul, smothering her light beneath opaque folds.

"Bia!"

Kait rocketed off the ground, but the shadow was too fast. As she climbed higher, the wispy demon avoided her advance and plummeted back to Earth.

Below, Tahlia spread her arms while her fingers cast a powerful caging spell, but the shadow slipped by and dove into the ground with a thud. The hawk barked and twisted its curved head toward the sky. With one beat of her wings, Hera rocketed into the clouds and fled to the haven of the immortal realm.

"I missed it." Tahlia gasped. "What was that thing? Where did it take her?"

Kait lowered herself back to the ground, clenching her teeth with enough force that the roots ached. Bia's soul had been stolen, destined for a fate worse than death. Now, she'd never return. "She's gone. Gone to the Underworld."

CHAPTER 15

"There must be a mistake," Tahlia said as she hurried to keep up with Kait's long strides. "If we can send a message to Gaia, maybe she can speak with Hades and—"

"And what?" Kait snarled, pivoting on her heels. "Ask him nicely to return my sister's soul? Don't you get it? It's Hera. She's the one responsible for all this! Because of her, all these nymphs are dead. Nothing we can say will help Bia." She spun back around and continued her manic pace.

Tahlia tried again. "Then, we go to Queen Rajhi. She'll know how to fix this."

Kait scoffed low in her throat. "Like she fixed this?" She gestured to the ragged corpses splayed across the ground. "A deadly virus raged within her own walls, yet she did nothing to intervene! Even when hundreds of nymphs were being slaughtered. What makes you think she'd do anything to save one soul?"

Tahlia gripped Kait's arm and wrenched her back. "Lower your voice, aurai. This infection came out of nowhere and took everyone by surprise." Kait opened her mouth to object, but Tahlia held up a hand, silencing her. "It was over before it even began. Our queen would never abandon us, especially in our time of need. There simply wasn't time to mobilize."

Kait narrowed her gaze. She wanted to ignore the elder nymph's wisdom, but even she couldn't find fault in it. "Fine."

Kait yanked her arm free and resumed her brisk walk, heading in the direction of the closest armory. She reached the towering oak tree a few minutes later and shrugged out of her ruined leather jacket as she marched across the threshold. Blood and dirt slathered the fabric. For the most part, the thick material had held up against the onslaught, save for a few rips and slices the infected nymphs' nails had carved. Beneath the sleeves, faint red lines marred her skin. The image of Bia's eviscerated chest flashed behind her eyes. A few scratches meant nothing compared to what her sister had endured.

Tahlia's footsteps tapped the polished wood floor, but Kait paid her no mind. Unraveling from the hollow ceiling were rows upon rows of clothing, from short cocktail dresses adorned with sequins to sturdy cotton frocks. She had no idea what to put on, but she needed something to replace the ripped denim and tattered leather.

Kait shifted aside crimson gowns and white chiffon, but the colors became overwhelming. Blood and teeth. Blood and teeth. Row upon row of horror. Blood and bone. Bia's bones, snapped and exposed, glistening in a darkening pool of red. Faster, her pulse raced as another wave of grief slammed into her. The white dress she held rippled to the floor, and the fabric puddled at her feet, the sleeves bent at unnatural angles.

The room spun. Before Kait could catch herself, the wooden floor rose to meet her. Kait's temple smacked the floorboards with a resounding crack that made her bite her tongue. Blood welled to the surface of the thick muscle and coated her mouth with a sickening copper taste.

Firm hands snaked below her elbows, and the floor rushed away as Tahlia helped her to her feet. Sobs tumbled from Kait's throat, and tears blinded her vision while her elder led her toward the sound of rushing water.

As in every armory, a serene waterfall cascaded from a hidden source and collected in a calm pool lined with large black stones. Kait didn't usually indulge in the warm bath waters, preferring the natural springs, but today she didn't have a choice.

"Raise your arms," Tahlia ordered.

Unable to think beyond her pain, Kait complied. Tears streamed down her face as Tahlia's fingers curled around her shirt's damp hem and rolled it over her head. With a wet slap, it wilted on the floor in a sweaty heap at her feet. Her boots were next. Tahlia gripped the soles and tossed them harder than necessary. One of the muddy heels spiraled to the side and licked a low-hanging gown. A fierce tug, and her jeans and undergarments littered the floor, as well.

"Get in."

Moving mechanically, Kait lifted her legs and collapsed into the black pool, sending a small wave cresting over the lip as water dribbled over the rocks. Kait's eyes flickered around the empty shop, unease growing as the shadows seemed to thicken. Tiny shivers prickled her spine. Someone was watching her. She'd assumed all the infected had been killed, but it would only take one stray to start the nightmare over again, hence the mandatory patrol Tahlia had ordered. A slight breeze rattled the wooden hangers and billowed the colorful fabrics. Kait bit the inside of her cheek, trying to ignore the spike of fear that drilled through her gut. All the dresses were suddenly decapitated bodies swaying across the shining floor.

"Where is Nula?" Tahlia asked under her breath.

"Probably fled," Kait replied as her tears slowed. "Or she's dead."

"Watch your tongue."

Kait pulled her knees to her chest and wrapped her arms around them. "It's not that outlandish. If we look around, I'm sure we'll find blood and—"

"Kaitaini." Tahlia's sharp warning silenced her dark musings, and the sound of pounding water replaced the gurgling moans she'd imagined.

Tahlia yanked out Kait's disheveled bun, and her long chocolate curls fell in stiff waves past her shoulders. A low sigh erupted in the back of her throat once the pressure at her temples released. Her elder turned her attention to the doorless entry.

"Scrub. I'm going to step outside."

Kait complied without comment. The warm water felt good, comforting as it cocooned her naked flesh, but she refused to relax any further. Bia was dead. Nothing could dull the ache, the hollow void ripping her heart in two. Cupping her hands beneath the surface, Kait raised her palms and splashed her face. A necklace of dirt and grime across her skin highlighted where her clothing had left her vulnerable. Again and again, she rinsed, only satisfied when the water no longer ran red down her bruised torso. She turned her attention to her battered arms and hands. Looking at her palms, she noted the heavy layer of blood that still coated them.

How much of this is Bia's?

Kait dragged the soap back and forth over her skin until fresh blood welled to the surface of her wrist. She ignored the sting as the soap bubbled over the wound. The pain felt good, deserved. She intended to rub herself raw, but then she remembered Bia's last words. What good was her sacrifice if Kait went on to hurt herself? Her movements slowed, and her rough passes softened.

"Get a grip. You're no good to her falling to pieces," Kait said aloud.

She lathered her body from her navel to the roots of her hair, washing every trace of the nightmare away. With a deep breath, Kait closed her eyes and slipped beneath the rippling waves, longing to sink to the bottom of the black pool and never surface.

How does it feel, nymph? a cold voice purred, clear over the muted roar of the falls.

Kait's eyes flashed open, scouring the depths for the source, though she was fully aware of who the voice belonged to.

How does it feel to lose the one person you love the most? I only wish you could have seen the pain in her eyes when she screamed as my infected ripped her to pieces. She's dead, and there's nothing you can do to save her.

You're wrong, Kait seethed. *I won't stop until her soul has been restored to the mother goddess.*

Inside Kait's mind, Hera scoffed. *What is your plan, little nymph? Journey to the Underworld and beg Hades to release her?*

Kait was silent for a moment. *Why not?*

A dark chuckle resounded through her mind.

I can't wait to watch you fail.

The goddess's presence melted away but left a heavy pressure on Kait's lungs. It was then she realized she'd been submerged for too long. With a swift bat from her palms, she breached the surface and inhaled a greedy breath.

"By the goddess!" Tahlia cried. "I was about to jump in."

Kait coughed hard, expelling water and saliva in an explosive spray as Tahlia righted her dress back down over her head. Apart from her elder, they were alone. Kait emitted another round of coughs, and her lungs burned as they begged for more air.

Tahlia crossed her arms. "What happened?"

Kait spluttered another pocket of water down her chin, then sighed as she brushed a collection of water droplets off her lashes. "Hera. She was in my head."

"What did she say?"

"She challenged me to go to the Underworld and beg Hades for Bia's soul."

Kait wheezed once more and then exited the pool. She ignored the towel Tahlia offered and stood with her arms out. Her fingers whirred, calling the wind. Instantly, the breeze complied and kissed the water from her skin and wrung her hair dry.

Tahlia wrinkled her nose. "She what?"

Kait turned toward a rack of nearby dresses to search for something appropriate. Her fingers skipped across chiffon straps and gossamer silk to rest on a floor-length gown. It was a deep gold, made of satin with a waterfall of matching sequins and inlaid pearl decorating the bodice. Shimming into the fabric, Kait grinned at the thigh-high slit, impressed with the gown's flexibility. With a dramatic flip, she tossed her hair over her shoulder and strode back to where Tahlia waited. The elder eyed her skeptically.

"Wouldn't black be more suitable?"

"There's not going to be a funeral," Kait stated as she selected a pair of gold flats with hard soles.

"What are you talking about? Bia is—"

"Dead. I haven't forgotten. I'm going." Kait's tone was crisp, resolute. She could feel her grief peeling and shedding like a second skin. She would rescue Bia's soul, no matter what it took.

"Going? Going where?" Tahlia frowned.

"To the Underworld."

Tahlia's eyes bulged. "The Underworld? You can't be serious. Hera was baiting you. Journey to the Underworld is impossible!"

"That's just because no one has ever tried."

"Yes, because it's impossible to get there. The Underworld isn't another realm you can merrily travel to. It's secluded in isolation for a reason. Only the dead can pass through its gates."

"Not necessarily. Theseus paid the ferryman when he helped Pirithous rescue Persephone." Kait left Tahlia's side and marched toward the exit.

"And then Hades trapped them both. You can't succeed! There aren't enough nymphs left to come to your aid when the dark god ensnares you," Tahlia argued. "It could also be a trap. What if Hera is waiting to ambush you the moment you step outside Olean?"

Kait cocked her head. "If she wanted to kill me, she would have laughed as her creations tore me apart. No, she wants to see me suffer. That's why she took Bia." At Tahlia's blank stare, she departed the armory, stepping back out into the wintry air. "Didn't you notice the hawk? The one that circled during the fight? That was Hera's familiar. I first saw her in the mortal world. For an animal, there is no such thing as borders. No realm is off-limits." She stopped speaking, and her mouth formed a small 'O' as her eyes widened. "Of course."

Kait swiveled on her heels, leaving shallow imprints atop the snow.

Flustered, Tahlia mimicked her motions, trying to keep up. "Kait, please think about this. It's too dangerous to leave Olean. Until the teams search the other realms, we don't know how far the infection has spread." Her pace increased to a jog.

Kait returned to the main square, the blood-splattered platform her destination. "I'm not going to the other realms, Tahlia. I'm going to the Underworld."

"But how? No nymph has ever traveled there. It's a hostile nefarious place. Your soul won't last three minutes."

Kait didn't argue. She knew the tales of the Underworld just as well as Tahlia. Her biggest obstacle would be getting past the River Styx, the thin border woven between the land of the living and the cursed souls of the damned. She tried not to think about the flat eyes of the dead said to patrol the river or the touch of their bony hands when they detected an intruder.

Keeping her eyes glued ahead, she did her best to look past the main square-turned-battlefield. She swallowed another hard pill of guilt. Her friends had remained after the fight, toiling with exhausted limbs to remove the bodies and give them a proper burial. Kait knew she should help, but she couldn't delay. Bia needed her. Plus, she hoped with her absence, Hera would refrain from attacking again.

"Please, Kait," Tahlia pleaded as they climbed the stairs. "Hera is one thing, but Hades is a completely different breed of god. He's never going to relinquish her soul."

Kait smiled. "Then, I'll just have to ask nicely."

CHAPTER 16

"Kait? What are you doing here?" Jezlem asked after a shrill yelp. Her keys clattered to the floor as Kait stepped out of the stale air.

"Sorry." Kait eyed her sister's coat and bag in hand as she stood in the dimly lit stairwell. "Are you coming or going?"

Jezlem ran a hand through her tousled curls and sighed. "Going. I'm late for my shift. Is everything okay?"

Kait bit her lip as tears slipped down her cheeks. "No."

Jezlem grabbed her hand and pulled her inside the apartment. Tossing her bag to the floor, she led Kait to the couch and sat down. "What's going on? What happened with Hera?"

Kait took a shaky breath. She had managed to dull the pain since making her decision, but here, staring into her older sister's calm eyes, all she wanted to do was break down.

"Bia's dead."

Jezlem's hands flew to her mouth. "What? What are you talking about? How?" Tears puddled in her eyes.

"Hera attacked, just like she said she would. We fought so hard. There were only a few infected left, but it was a trick. Hera waited until I was vulnerable and directed all of them to hunt me. Bia saved me at the last second. It was almost as if Hera knew she'd sacrifice herself . . . Like that's what she wanted all along." Kait cried softly. "I'm so sorry, Jez."

Jezlem sat in stunned silence, shaking her head back and forth in disbelief. "Not Bia. Not her. Maybe we can ask Gaia to return her soul. If we explain what happened, she might make an exception."

Kait shook her head. "We can't, Jez."

"Why not? We can't just sit here when Bia was murdered!"

"Gaia doesn't have her soul."

Jezlem furrowed her brow. "What do you mean? Who else would?"

Kait licked her lips and swallowed roughly. "Hades."

"That's not funny, Kait." Jezlem withdrew her hand from Kait's clasp.

"It's not a joke, Jez. I swear. Bia's soul was ascending, but a black shadow stole it and plunged underground. It had to be sent by Hades."

Jezlem wrinkled her nose, looking skeptical. "Why would the lord of the Underworld care about a nymph's soul? Nymphs don't belong in the Underworld. They're out of his jurisdiction."

"I don't think it was an accident, Jez. Hades must be working with Hera."

"For what purpose? This doesn't make any sense, Kait."

"I know how this sounds, but Jez, you have to trust me. Bia's soul is in the Underworld, and I plan to get it back," she said strongly, bracing for her sister's reaction.

"Get it back? You can't mean—"

"I'm going down there. If I can talk to Hades, maybe I can persuade him to release her by offering a better deal than whatever bargain he struck with Hera."

"No. No!" Jezlem shook her head. "It's too dangerous, not to mention impossible. Nymphs can't travel to the Underworld. A portal can't deliver you to Hades's doorstep."

"I don't plan on going by portal," Kait said.

Jezlem scoffed. "How, then? You plan on swimming there?"

"I'm going to hitch a ride."

Jezlem pushed off the couch in a huff. "A ride? Kait, just tell me what's going on. I'm feeling too many things to riddle this out right now."

Kait rose to her feet as well. "Animals. They don't have borders."

"What?"

"Listen, I know Hera is behind the kidnapping of Bia's soul. I saw her. I saw her in Olean."

"In Olean? Kait, that's ridiculous," Jezlem said, sounding like Tahlia.

"She wasn't in her physical form. She was in the form of her familiar, a hawk. That means borders to the realms don't apply to animals."

"How do you know it was her? Couldn't it have just been a hawk?"

Kait shook her head. "No, I'm sure of it. The other day when I was out with Blake, I saw her for the first time. And Joel, remember? He recounted the day she attacked them at the hospital. Olean and the human realm are supposed to be forbidden to immortals, but she can come and go as her familiar with no consequences."

Jezlem frowned again and pulled at the roots of her hair. "Fine. Let's say border crossing is possible. You don't have a familiar, and there's no way to travel to the Underworld as your element. Not even the most powerful naiad could make it to the River Styx. So, how do you get there?"

"Haven't you been listening, Jez? I'm going to go by animal."

Jezlem stared at her blankly. "An animal? Which one? You can't just pick an animal. They must be of our world, and then they need certain specifications to get you there and back, assuming Hades even lets you come back. I don't think you understand what you're getting yourself into."

Kait shrugged. "No, I don't, but it's not important what happens to me. All I care about is saving Bia. If Hades relinquishes her soul, I can send her to Gaia. Then, at least she'll have the opportunity to live again. There must be an animal out there who can transport me. All I need to do is find one."

Placing her hands around Kait's upper arms, Jezlem squeezed and stared into her eyes. "I care about what happens to you. You're all I have left. Please, don't do this."

Kait leaned forward and gently kissed her sister's forehead. "Our baby sister sacrificed herself for me, Jez. I can't leave her down there."

Jezlem nodded and sniffled, wiping snot from her nose. "All right, then let me help you."

"But you aren't—"

"I know I can't travel with you, but just because I'm mortal doesn't mean all my knowledge has been lost."

Jezlem crossed to the other side of the room and stopped in front of a large bookshelf, its crammed volumes threatening to explode. She heaved a heavy tome into the air and dropped it onto the rickety coffee table. Kait hesitated, half-expecting the wooden legs to crumble beneath the immense load.

"What is that?"

"An encyclopedia, sort of. It details all the creatures of our world. Joel loves looking through this thing."

Kait sank to her knees, her eyes lit with wonder. She reached out and stroked one of the weathered pages. "Wow, this is ancient."

Jezlem snorted. "It is. I'd guess it's at least a few thousand years old." She settled beside Kait and combed through the first pages. "What are you looking for, exactly?"

Kait shrugged and peered closer at the displayed entry. A two-headed snake called an amphisbaena was depicted. The creature was swallowing a man whole, each head devouring an opposite end. Below, the serpent's magical properties were listed. Apparently, when worn around the neck, the snake granted safe pregnancies to mortals—if it didn't eat them first. She turned the page, uninspired.

"I'm not sure, really. I haven't even heard of half of these creatures. Where did you get this?" Kait asked, skimming another entry that described a vicious empusa that fed on the blood of young men.

"I found it in Olean's library a few decades ago," Jezlem replied. "I thought it was interesting. Sera, the librarian, said I was the only one who had ever borrowed it. Vivian brought it to me after everything happened . . . to remind me of home." A shadow passed over Jezlem's face, but she hastily pushed it away. "Honestly, I've only pulled it out once or twice." The sisters were silent for a moment, each focused on different descriptions. "We should look for something with wings."

Kait frowned. "Wouldn't something with fins work better? I'm not positive of the Underworld's exact location, but I think my biggest hurdle will be crossing the River Styx."

"True, but if things get hairy down there—which I'm sure they will—you'll need an ally, a creature that's not only agile but protective as well. Plus, if it has wings, you can fly over the Styx."

"What about a Pegasus?" Kait flipped numerous pages until she found the desired animal. "A brave creature, loyal to any rider that tames him. The Pegasus is strong, powerful, and quick," she translated roughly from the Greek description.

"Perfect," Jezlem said with a heavy tone of sarcasm. "Only problem is, Pegasus was tamed and stabled one thousand years before you were created."

Kait's heart sank. "By who?"

"Keep reading."

"The wild stallion is now the loyal companion of . . . Zeus, tasked to fetch the god's mighty thunderbolts," Kait finished. "Okay, fine. Maybe not that one."

"What about a Ceryneian hind?" Jezlem asked, perking up.

"A what?"

Jezlem navigated back to the front of the book and flipped through the headings until she found what she was searching for. "There." She pointed to a long-faded drawing.

Kait leaned forward, trying not to get her hopes up. "It looks like a stag."

"Close, it's a doe. A very special doe. I remember reading about it ages ago. It belonged to Artemis, a beautiful doe with antlers of gold and hooves of bronze." She translated the old language. "The Ceryneian hind is aggressive in battle and snorts fire. It is faster than an arrow in flight, its power equal to that of the great Pegasus," she finished. "A skilled swimmer. Huh, it says they like song. Kait, this is perfect."

"Yeah, but if it belongs to Artemis, we're left with the same problem. Plus, I don't see anything in there that mentions the ability to fly, and it may be able to swim, but that's probably in a calm lake, not through a demon-infested river."

Jezlem studied the ancient script. "Its speed might be enough to overcome the flight. Plus, I bet it has a large stride. Look," she began reading again, ignoring the glaring issue of reaching the entrance to the Underworld. "Most Ceryneian hinds avoid ethereal beings and prefer the solitude of swamps or marshlands. All we have to do is check realms that fit that description."

Kait frowned, doubtful. "Jez, you just read that they avoid people. What makes you think that *if* I find one, it's just going to let me hop on its back and travel to the most frightening realm of the ethereal world? This was a stupid plan." She fell back against the couch and held her head in her hands.

"Hey," Jezlem said softly. "We can do this. You can't give up. Like you said, we can't leave her down there. She needs us. She needs *you*."

Lifting her head, Kait nodded, hearing the wisdom of her sister's words. "I don't know if this is going to work, but at least it gives me a starting point. Which realm should I search to find one?"

Jezlem gave her a grateful smile and squeezed her hand. "I'd try Madik. The landscape is relatively uncolonized and full of humid swamplands." She paused and studied her hands. "I wish there was something I could do to help. I hate being useless. You shouldn't have to do this alone."

"Jez, don't say that."

Jezlem shrugged, smiling sadly, and touched Kait's cheek. "Do you need to borrow some clothes?"

Kait glanced down and was met with the smooth skin of her exposed knee. "No, I picked this on purpose." Jezlem's eyebrows arched in surprise and disagreement. "What's wrong with it?"

"Nothing. I think it's an interesting choice, especially for the destination you have in mind."

"It's empowering."

"And revealing. I've never seen you wear something like this. Are you planning to seduce Hades?"

Kait's teasing demeanor fell away, replaced with a stoic countenance. "I'm going to do *whatever* it takes to save our sister."

"Are you serious? Kait, you can't. If you lay with him, you'll surrender your halo and become mortal. Even if Gaia is able to petition the Immortal Council to get your souls back, you'll be stuck in the Underworld." Kait didn't say anything as she picked mindlessly at a loose sequin on her thigh. "Wait, that was your intention this whole time. You don't plan on coming back."

"What choice do I have, Jez?" Kait asked, her voice soft. "We both know Hades isn't going to let her go, not unless he gets another soul in return."

"Have you thought for one second how Bia would feel about this?" Jezlem shot back. Her eyes were cold and unyielding. "She sacrificed herself for you so you could *live*, and you're going to repay her by trapping your soul in the Underworld?"

"It's not like that—"

"Do you want to die? Is that what this is about?"

"What? No, of course not."

"I know you're depressed. I can feel it. Ever since the mountain, you've been different. Lost."

Kait tucked a stray hair behind her ear. "I'm fine."

"Kait," Jezlem said, arching her brows.

"What do you want me to say? You're here, Bia was too busy to see me, and my friends don't get it. They can't understand what I went through, and the worst part is, they don't care. They don't care what he did to me. When I returned, they looked at me like a wounded animal. I could feel their pity but also their indifference. Like I should just get over it. I still had my powers, and my halo was intact. What did I have to be depressed about?" Kait's voice faded to a whisper. "I've had no one to talk to, no one who cares."

"Why didn't you come to see me? It's been months, Kait. Why didn't you tell me?"

"I couldn't. I wasn't strong enough."

"Strong enough? What are you talking about?"

"I didn't want to see you," Kait admitted, fixing her tearful gaze on her sister. She saw the way her words hurt and caught Jezlem off guard. "I'm sorry. You were so happy with Joel, exploring your new life. It was too much for me. It hurt to be around you because I knew I'd never have that joy."

Jezlem was quiet, but Kait could practically hear her thoughts as they flickered across her face.

"You think I was happy?" Jezlem asked at last. "You think adjusting to this life was easy? You don't know anything. You've been too wrapped up in your own problems to consider anyone else's. Yes, your life changed. You experienced something very traumatic, but it happened to me, too. I have the same hurt, only mine went a step further. The difference is, I tried to make the best of my situation. Do you think I like being a waitress? Flirting with dirty men to get a few more tips so I can make my rent? This is a life I never could have imagined. I don't want this. And yes, I am lucky to have Joel, to have someone to lean on and make me smile when the days are particularly dark, but so do you. Blake is a wonderful guy, but you won't give him the time of day because he's not of your world. Well, neither am I anymore. It's your fault you're alone. I'm trying to help you, but it's not enough. No one's help is ever good enough for you. You isolated yourself, so if you came here for a pity party, go somewhere else. I've got better things to do."

Jezlem stood and left the room, slamming the door with enough force to rattle the frame. Kait sat for a moment, too stunned by her reaction and the truth of her words to move. Was she responsible for everything? For the infection, for the wasteful deaths, for Bia? She waited several minutes, but Jezlem's message was clear. She wasn't coming back.

Kait rose to her feet and left the book open to the illustration of the beautiful doe. She glanced around the shabby apartment while her heart ached with regret. She longed to comfort her sister and apologize, but Jezlem was right. Not once had she considered what Jez was dealing with. She'd taken her smiles and laughter for the shallow show they were, too consumed with her own emotions to look deeper.

The tarnished brass doorknob leading to the sinking porch turned too easily in her hands, offering an escape she didn't deserve. "Goodbye," Kait whispered to the walls and stepped out into the night.

CHAPTER 17

Kait's legs stretched over half-buried twigs, punching holes in the snow. She could have flown to the portal, but she wanted to be alone for a time, surrounded by stoic trees and the occasional twitter of a cardinal. If she was honest, part of her hoped Jezlem might follow, but that wish diminished the farther she trekked into the woods with no sign of her sister.

She hadn't bothered to don a coat. If any spectator saw her hiking through the snow in an evening gown, she invited them to think she was out of her mind. She must be for what she had planned next.

Following the magnetic pull of the portal, Kait's feet changed direction and led her to a well-worn path up a familiar hill. She climbed, fitting her feet into the existing footprints that dotted the trail, wondering what it'd be like to step into the owner's life. Would living as a mortal be so terrible? She would have to forsake her element to keep up the guise, but maybe she could attend school and get a job like Jez. She'd have to surrender everything she was.

But you might finally be happy.

Kait exhaled her tumultuous thoughts and glanced over her shoulder to the faraway building she'd departed from. Was Jezlem staring after her? Or was she truly forsaken? Shaking her head, she turned around and collided with a solid object. An unexpected gasp fell from her lips as she flew off her feet and landed on her tailbone.

"Oh, man. I'm so sorry. I was checking my watch and didn't see you." A gloved hand slid around Kait's wrist and hauled her to her feet. "Wait, Kait?"

Kait's eyes popped as the familiar voice triggered her pulse to race. "Blake?" He stared at her in disbelief. His dark hair was covered with the same red hat pulled low over his eyebrows, and his cheeks were chapped a bright red. "What are you doing out here?"

Blake gestured to his wind pants and sneakers. "Out for a run. Your turn. Why are you here?"

Kait shook her head. "It's a long story," she whispered as she stared intently at the gathering snowflakes on her shoulder.

"You disappeared the other day. Is everything okay?" Blake withdrew a small white object from his ear.

"Oh. Yeah. Well, I had to . . ." Kait began, ready to dismiss his concerns, but instead her voice broke and her face crumpled. "No, everything and everyone is gone, and it's all my fault. I thought I could save her. I thought I could warn everyone in time, but it happened anyway, and now they're dead. All of them, because of me." She dropped to her knees and covered her face with her hands.

Blake stood there for a moment, then pocketed the earbud and crouched beside her. Tentatively, he wrapped his arms around her shaking body and pressed his temple against hers when she didn't push him away. "Hey, it's okay. Let it out. I'm here."

Heavy sobs poured from Kait as she leaned into Blake's warmth. It felt so good to be held, to drop the façade of strength. Why had she run away? Why had she never even given him a chance? She buried her face in the crook of his neck and inhaled his scent as another torrent of tears fell. A small flame sparked within her as Blake adjusted his arms to pull her closer, then he kissed her forehead.

The flame grew, licking the inside of Kait's belly, and wove up toward her withered heart, filling her with an undeniable urge to get as close as she possibly could to the boy who held her tight. Before she could throttle the sensation, it spread and directed her mouth forward until her lips found Blake's. She sensed his shock beneath her touch and moved slowly, carefully exploring the brand-new feeling of elation that coursed through her lest she explode. Blake responded. He cupped her face and deepened the kiss.

Kait's body moved on its own. Shifting from her knees, she slid onto Blake's lap and wrapped her arms around his neck. She opened her mouth and kissed him fiercely while her hands spread over his chest and back like vines, eager to encompass every part of him.

Blake pulled away and stared at her with bewilderment. "What's going on?" he asked, his voice rough and raspy. "I mean, I thought you only wanted to be friends?"

Hot color seeped into Kait's cheeks as she rose off Blake's lap and wrapped her arms around her torso. "I know. I'm sorry."

Blake climbed to his feet and hesitantly placed his hands on her shoulders as though trying to keep her close. "It's okay. I want this. I want you, but I know how you feel about me. Has that changed?"

Kait heard the hope in his voice, saw the way his eyes widened with the possibility. She closed her eyes and searched her heart. She couldn't say why she had kissed him, but it felt good to be held, to be vulnerable. For that moment with Blake, nothing had existed outside their lips, their entwined hands. He took away the bad.

Would being mortal be so bad?

The thought drifted through her mind once more, and she pictured a simple life with Blake by her side. Was it so wrong to want someone, to be one half of a whole? Her heart pounded in her chest. She couldn't deny the spark between them, but she wasn't sure if it was out of attraction or desperation for distraction.

"I don't know," Kait whispered. She saw the way his smile faltered and the light in his gaze sputtered. "But . . . I'd like to try."

Blake blinked in surprise. "What? You mean . . . you and me?"

Kait closed the distance between them and unwound her arms, offering what was left of her broken heart. She pressed her lips to his and marveled at the tiny flip her stomach performed when they touched again. "Only if you want to."

Blake smiled and let out a small gasp as he wrapped his arms around her waist and pulled her against him. "Only since you broke my window."

Kait groaned. "I still feel bad about that. Maybe I can make it up to you?" She eyed his lips again.

"I can think of a few ideas," Blake said with a laugh. "Let's get inside, though. My toes are numb." He threaded his fingers through hers and started down the hill.

Kait bit her lip. "Blake, wait. I can't go with you."

"My mom's at work until eight."

"No, it's not that. I have something to do first."

"Okay," Blake said, spinning around to face the opposite direction.

"No. Alone."

Blake frowned. "But I thought . . . I thought you wanted to be together."

Kait sighed. "I do, but where I'm going, it's dangerous. It's no place for a mortal."

"Dangerous how? Why are you going?"

"Bia's in trouble."

"Then, I'm coming with you. I can handle it, Kait."

"Blake, no. You can't. I'll be fine. And I'll come back," Kait whispered, trying to conceal the way her voice wavered.

She knew she was being selfish, inflating Blake's hopes when she might never see him again, but he'd felt so good. Before she resigned herself to the Underworld, she wanted to remember this moment. Remember the way he looked at her, remember the warmth flooding through her as he stared at her like she was perfect. Her breath caught in her throat as she studied his face. Why had she been so foolish? Part of her wished her fate wasn't sealed and that she could come back to this sweet beautiful boy, but love had never been kind to her, and it wasn't about to start.

"At least let me walk you to the portal. That's where you're heading, right?" Blake asked without surrendering her hand.

Kait nodded. "Yeah, I just left Jez's."

"She didn't want to see you off?" Blake glanced over his shoulder as if expecting her to slip out from the trees.

"She, um, had to go to work," Kait answered, keeping her eyes on the snow.

"Oh," Blake said, seeming unconvinced. "So, where are you going?"

Kait inhaled. Her initial instinct was to deflect his inquisitiveness, but this was what she had wanted, to share herself and let go—even if she was only able to experience it one time. They fell into step, and Blake rubbed the back of her hand with his thumb.

"To a realm called Madik. I need to find a creature there."

"Does it have Bia?"

"No. Hopefully, it's going to help me save her—if I can find one, that is. Jez believes I'll be successful, but I have doubts."

"Why?" Blake asked as they trudged up the hill toward the frozen lake.

"The source she referenced is very old. I think I'm just wasting my time, but it's the only lead I have."

"What happens if you don't find anything?"

"I'm not sure. I don't really have a plan B at this point, but I can't leave her. She never gave up trying to rescue me. I can't fail."

"You won't." Blake's words were genuine, and his hand was a pleasant comfort in her own.

They reached the edge of the lake a few minutes later, and the toes of their shoes kissed the encroaching ice. Kait squeezed Blake's hand, then inched her shoe forward, but Blake pulled her back.

"Look, I'm not going to try to talk you out of this when your sister needs you, but just . . . Just remember you don't have to do everything by yourself. Asking for help doesn't make you weak; it makes you smart. I'll always be here. Plus, I don't mean to brag, but my sword-fighting skills have greatly improved since I joined the fencing team."

Kait snorted. "Well, they couldn't have gotten worse."

Blake wrinkled his nose and poked her, eliciting an uncharacteristic giggle as he found the sensitive skin above her ribs. "Thanks," he said before his smile grew serious. "Just promise I'll see you again."

Joy flitted away, leaving behind the ghost of her brief smile. Kait pressed her lips to Blake's but extricated herself from his arms before he could kiss her back. "I'll be careful," she whispered as she stepped onto the frozen surface.

Blake dropped his hand. Kait saw his eyes tighten with concern, but thankfully, he didn't try to stop her. Behind her, the portal shimmered to life, activated by her presence. She whirled to face it and envisioned the marshlike landscape of Madik. She had no idea if Hera's infection had spread to the underdeveloped realm, but the threat of teeth wasn't enough to hinder her, for she would face far worse.

"You didn't promise," Blake called.

Kait glanced over her shoulder, soaking up the wonderful vision of the boy who had risked everything for her and was offering to do it again. The portal read her desired destination and depicted the lush greenery of the swamps beyond. She smiled at Blake as she placed one foot inside the swirling veil, straddling two worlds.

"I know," she answered and vanished inside the swirling winds before Blake could say anything more.

CHAPTER 18

The cold fled, replaced by smothering humidity. Kait lifted the hair off her neck and shivered at the abrupt temperature change. She eased her feet farther into Madik, grimacing as thick mud sludged over the tops of her shoes and filled the narrow spaces between her toes. She grasped the thin fabric of her dress in her fists and tore the elegant train into a jagged skirt before striding into the sucking surface, her heart sinking. The realm was flooded. What little high ground Madik offered now sat submerged beneath a heavy layer of muck.

Kait paused her exaggerated movements as the reality of the potential danger she'd waltzed into registered. She scanned the watery landscape for clawed hands or treading skulls, but nothing stirred. Ready to cast if an infected emerged, she resumed her pace but took care to minimize her motions as much as possible. After twenty agonizing minutes, she had barely waded one hundred yards. Thick mud bubbled farther up her thighs.

"This is pointless." Kait started to turn around when Bia's face flashed in her mind.

I love you.

Her sister's last words made her pause. Bia hadn't thought twice before she'd thrown herself into the enemy's teeth, yet Kait was ready to give up because of a little mud. She touched her fingertips together to call the wind. Her body sank into its warm embrace, and it carried her above the mud instead. She drifted along the current, vigilant for any sign of movement, both from the living and dead. There was little chance Hera's virus had traveled to the desolate realm, but a mistake would grievously cost her. Wandering in haphazard patterns, she grew anxious. There was nothing there. Perhaps, all the creatures had sought shelter from the flood on the outskirts of Madik and were waiting for the muddy waters to recede.

Funneling out of the air, Kait slipped through the voluptuous branches of a bald cypress tree and rested on its raised roots. She exhaled as exhaustion and frustration vied for dominance.

She had yet to rest since the outbreak, but there wasn't time. Any delay on her end allowed Hades more opportunity to manipulate Bia's soul. Her sister's death seemed so long ago, as if the horrific day had bled into endless years. Kait craned her neck and sighed as the hazy sun faltered, losing its grip on the sky as night reared its dark head. She fought her heavy eyelids. Her body pleaded for rest. Without the sun, searching the swamps for the doe would be difficult anyway, and the low visibility left her open to attack from a possible wandering infected. She could regroup and start fresh in the morning.

Kait located a somewhat dry swatch of grass and settled against a smooth trunk to protect herself from an attack from behind. She hummed a quiet lullaby. The gentle notes chased away the heartbreaking vision of her sister's face before the world was pulled out from beneath her feet. Instead, she pictured lazy days spent by the lake while each of the sisters tried to perfect their elemental connections. Bia had always struggled, but she never gave up, even when Jezlem and Kait left her far behind. As more memories swam before her, her humming grew louder, and little words snuck in until a sweet song poured from her lips.

The images morphed, and somewhere amidst her unraveling thoughts, Bia's fiery tresses shortened and darkened to Blake's close-cropped style. A sizzle of pleasure spiked below Kait's stomach when she remembered the feeling of his tongue and the way he'd gripped her thighs as she sat atop him. Their connection was stronger than she'd thought, especially after so many months apart. She traced her curves while she dreamed of Blake's hands touching her, taking time to explore her body. She had delighted in many partners in her youth, but back then, she wasn't interested in taking her time. She preferred making love hard and fast, as it made it easier for both parties to pick up and leave without the awkward conversation afterward. Maybe with Blake, it could be different.

Kait wasn't sure how long she sang, lost between the past and future, but when she opened her eyes, it was to the harsh realization that the sun had fled long ago and the swamp was now cloaked in a midnight blanket. Kait stared in wonder and awe at the sheer number of stars. They were so close she could practically kiss them. Then, alarm flared in her gut when she realized the defined shadows encasing them were also visible. The wind funneled in a terrified rush around her. The lights weren't stars, but eyes, all locked on her.

Kait's first instinct was to run, change into the wind and flee the threat, but she stayed rooted in place, waiting for her eyes to acclimate to the heavy darkness. A sliver of moonlight filtered between the canopy, doing little to illuminate the marsh below.

A soft sound like a wooden horn whistled, and the eyes flickered, several blinking out of sight. In the next moment, the silhouettes shifted, their lumbering gaits more reminiscent of animals rather than the nefarious nightmares she'd assumed. Slowly, she rose to her feet.

"I'm looking for a Ceryneian hind," Kait said.

Muted footfalls fell in response as the once curious animals moved on.

"No, don't go," Kait begged. Desperate, she followed, but the thick mud swallowed her feet. "Wait!" she called, holding the note as if singing a sad song. Hooves paused, and numerous eyes fixated on her again as her melancholy plea reached their ears.

The farthest pair of eyes bobbed up and down. A moment later, golden spots on its back brightened and lifted into the air. The other animals followed suit, and soon the swamp was filled with soft gilded shimmers, imitation fireflies dancing in the air to illuminate their small corner.

Kait gasped in astonishment. The marsh transformed in the quiet candlelight. Standing before her were four does from the book Jezlem had shown her only hours ago. They continued to stare as if anticipating her speech. Her eyes roamed to the doe closest to her. They were giant. Standing regally atop four spindly legs, each one was nearly double the size of a full-grown buck. Elongated antlers adorned slender skulls, and unlike other deer, the antlers appeared to be brushed back, arching in a fluid curve to parallel their graceful necks.

Rich green moss grew from the does' backs, some shaggier than others. The soft fibers hung like spring icicles from their chests and stomachs. Narrow strips of white velvet fur swirled and dotted the animals' hides, each sporting a unique pattern. Kait was in awe. The creatures seemed ancient, their bodies barely distinguishable from the marshy carpet she traversed, yet their eyes were lively and bright, full of wisdom.

"I need your help. I seek a way to the Underworld."

In unison, the does snorted and shook their massive crowns back and forth.

Kait wrung her hands. "Please, you're my only hope. Hades has my sister's soul. One of you must be my guide and ferry me across the River Styx."

"*Must*, my dear?" an old weathered voice asked. "A quest borne of desperation is a folly."

"Bound to fail," another voice said.

"But noble if glory is not what you seek," added a third.

Kait narrowed her gaze, but even in the soft glow of the herd's magic, the speakers remained ambiguous, nothing more than disembodied voices. Briefly, she wondered if the creatures were able to speak, but they were disciplined statues, staring back at her with wide innocence. "Who's there?"

Hushed chuckles like the brush of brittle pages in an old tome surrounded her, just out of reach. Kait tossed tentative glances over her shoulders, and her heart started to race. Something stalked her, something ancient and powerful.

Two of the does broke their trance and departed, swaying on thin legs with a gentle gait that reminded Kait of the giraffes that graced the grasslands of the human realm. They didn't seem bothered by the strange presence, but the voices chilled her. She turned her pleading gaze toward the remaining deer.

"I know it's an impossible request, but I must get there; otherwise, she'll be lost forever." Kait took a step closer and opened her palms as she bowed her head.

"Nothing is impossible."

"Not if you have heart."

"But failure is an interesting spectacle."

Cool breath caressed the back of Kait's neck, polluting the humid air with the scent of wet leaves. She pivoted on her toes and started to cast, eager to take up a more defensive position, but a frigid hand clasped her wrist and froze her movements mid-spell. The agitated breeze dropped with the touch as though her connection had been momentarily suspended.

"None of that, my dear," the first voice said, words raspy and soft. "The Graeae offer aid."

"Unless the Graeae deem you unworthy." The second voice sounded like a snake's, hissing in reply.

The third speaker had a deeper voice, guttural and harsh. "Then, we will deliver you to our sisters, the Gorgons. They're always looking for fresh meat." The same wizened laughter assaulted Kait's ears. She shivered uncomfortably.

"Who are the Graeae?" Kait asked. In her panicked state, she tried to recall her studies of the ethereal realm's history and all its occupants, but her mind was blank. Jez would've known the foreign voices. What she wouldn't give to have her by her side, but of course, that was out of the question. Without a halo, the portal wouldn't activate for her.

A whoosh of air funneled as the chanting voices harmonized. "We are the ones who see all. The past, the present, and the future. We know where you're going and when and how you will die."

"Please, my sister's soul has been claimed by Hades. Do you know a way to the—"

"The Underworld? Of course, we do, but you'll never make it, my dear. Poseidon's minions will claim you before the first wave can swallow that pretty face."

A quiet pop resounded with their eerie chant, and three cloaked hunched figures stood before Kait, bookended by the last two does. The glowing golden embers they released hovered above the small coven. The dim illumination cast light on the three figures' hooded faces. Deep wrinkles carved their grayed saggy flesh, and pert noses pointed skyward, creating the illusion of shrunken cartilage that had been peeled away to reveal the nasal cavities beneath. Kait's breathing hitched when she realized deep black voids occupied the spaces where their eyeballs should have been, save for one, fixed in the left socket of the figure in the middle. The dark brown iris stared at her as a single snaggletooth wormed its way over emaciated lips.

In unspoken unison, the three crones surged forward, and their cloaked silhouettes evaporated in tendrils of smoke against the blackness. Kait spun in a tight circle. The deer didn't move, only continued to stare at her with wide knowing eyes.

A quiet hiss rent the air, and Kait flinched. One of the ancient figures reappeared at her elbow, limbs still somewhat transparent as her shape materialized from the air. Her gnarled fingers clasped the eyeball in her palm. The iris rotated around the glossy sphere as it sought a focal point. With a haggard breath, the crone raised her arm and deposited the eye into her cavernous right socket, using her yellowed nail to spin it around and position it properly. Terror gripped Kait. The women said they offered aid, yet they reeked of death and ruin.

"Settle, aurai," the crone said, her lips droopy and puckered without the support of teeth. "I am Pemphredo. I can taste your fear and feel the alarm flooding your veins. You wish to flee, but that wouldn't be wise, for without our blessing, your task will fail this night."

Kait took a steadying breath. The woman was right; the instinct to melt into the wind caused her fingers to twitch. "Your blessing?"

Another hiss resounded on Kait's right. An identical crone appeared, this one with the snaggletooth. She reached across the small space, hooked her finger into Pemphredo's eye socket, and popped it back into her own. The first sister snarled under her breath but didn't move to take the eye back.

"Yes, a quest as perilous as yours needs a bit of luck. The Gray Sisters can't offer power, but information is just as helpful as a sword, if not more so." Her voice was scratchy, the words barely audible. "Dread weighs heavy in your heart. Deino knows you seek a way to the Underworld, but do you know where its entrance lies? How to escape Poseidon's leviathan? Have a way to traverse the inky black depths to stand in Hades's presence? The way is possible but lost without our insight."

A third exhale brushed the back of Kait's neck, pebbling her exposed flesh. The third sister wound her bony talon around a thick lock of Kait's hair and jerked backward, forcing Kait's body to rest against the frail figure. Reaching out, she ripped the eye from the second sister and pushed it into place on her own face. Kait's knees wobbled at the squishing sound the eyeball made as it pressed against bone and papery skin. "And Enyo sees the horrors that await you. Slithering serpents and nightmares made real. Much blood will be spilled if you continue this path, but it is your own unraveling you should fear the most."

"Please," Kait said, doing her best to angle her face away from the noxious breath pouring from the Graeae's mouths. "I will do anything to save my sister's soul. Did Hades send you to intercept me?"

Coarse laughter echoed, and Deino said, "Dear nymph, Hades does not command us. No immortal can. We simply exist, watching, always watching, for troubled souls seeking guidance, those who have everything to lose."

Kait licked her lips as dread formed a tight ball in the pit of her stomach. "What must I do?"

Pemphredo cackled, her withered lips curling inward over fleshy gray gums. She clapped her hands twice, emitting a muffled sound as her gnarled fingers interlocked. "Journey to Poseidon's kingdom and tell him who you are.

Speak your role in his brother's death aloud."

"He'll kill me."

Deino hissed and fluffed her oversized robes, and her frail body became lost in the charcoal fabric. "Maybe, maybe not. Convince him your actions were just. Poseidon is no fool. He knows his brother and his incorrigible appetite. If the two of you can make peace and he permits you to enter the depths of his realm, bring us the freshest sea foam as a symbol of your union. His naiads only craft it in the first rays of the early morning."

"Be swift and seek him out tonight; otherwise, your quest will be delayed another day," Enyo said. "Prove you're worthy of our knowledge."

Kait's mind raced. She didn't have the slightest clue how to find Poseidon. She wasn't a naiad and had a shaky relationship with water as it was. Yet, the Graeae were demanding she throw herself to the mercy of the ocean and one of the most powerful gods in existence.

"I'm no naiad. I don't know the first thing about navigating currents to find him."

Deino performed an exaggerated shrug and tossed her bald head to the side. "Shame. I suggest you turn back. Seems the prophecy was wrong. Two nymphs dead and the third plagued by cowardice."

Rage flared as Kait's hands curled into fists. "Jezlem's not dead. She is the strongest of us all. She killed an immortal! And I am no coward. Not having the resources is not the same as not having the will. I'll find Poseidon. I'll throw myself off a cliff into the sea's choppy waters if that will prove my resolve to you."

All three sisters smiled, their mouths black slashes across petrified flesh. Enyo fixed the all-seeing eye on Kait and blinked before the dark brown iris clouded to a milky white. "Only time will tell, aurai. Retrieve the sea foam and return to these shores. If you fail, Poseidon will send your corpse to the surface. One way or another, we'll have our answer."

Hoarse cackles bubbled in the backs of their throats as the figures seemed to fold in on themselves. Their skeletal forms disintegrated, large cloaks dissolving against the night sky until only a faint breeze remained. The Graeae vanished as quickly as they had appeared.

Around Kait, the beautiful golden lights that had illuminated the exchange descended to the sodden earth. All of them extinguished in unison the moment they grazed the mud and plunged Kait back into unsettling darkness.

Straining her eyes, Kait searched for any Ceryneian hinds that may have lingered in the Gray Sisters' absence, but they, too, had fled. She was alone. A shaky breath fell from her lips. She could feel the pull of the portal behind her. Madik didn't border any oceans. If she was to attempt this task, she would have to travel to another realm.

Her palms began to sweat as the memory of such a location materialized in her mind. She shuddered; the history of her destination held so much death. But at this point, she'd be hard-pressed to find a realm that didn't offer some sort of horrific memory.

Kait lifted out of the sucking muck into the air while her physical form transformed into the wind. Over the thick mud, she glided back to the human realm, feeling like a mouse lost in an endless labyrinth.

CHAPTER 19

Azure waves crashed against the black cliff base, their white spittle arcing into the air. The cool spray licked Kait's shins. She glanced over the precipice, a solid thirty-foot drop. Her stomach knotted just looking at the rolling surf. Suppose she didn't jump out far enough and was slammed against the rocks or a hungry shark patrolled the sea below . . .

Kait had portaled from Madik into the mortal realm to Hawaii's Big Island. The moment her toes hit the warm earth, terror gripped her. Not too long ago, she'd stood on the same beach, helpless as Zeus's piriol launched its quills into unsuspecting humans enjoying the sun. She could still hear their screams, see the way their crimson blood had splashed across the dry sand. She'd thought the great beast was targeting her. Little did she know she was being herded like a docile sheep straight into the foul god's awaiting arms.

Before the horror unleashed though, Kait had watched a group of local boys cliff jump from this very spot. She remembered thinking they were suicidal to leap from such a height into the unforgiving surf, and the multiple signs labeled *Danger and Off-limits* confirmed her theory. Yet there she was, about to leap into the same frothing mouth.

Three months ago, she'd met the siren Peisinoe on the same beach and recalled she'd had intimate knowledge of Poseidon and his court. She prayed that where she had found one siren, she'd find more. Kait only wished she didn't have to traverse deep waters to locate them. Part of her had considered camping on the sand and waiting to bump into one like before, but patience had never been her strength. Better to get in and get it over with rather than wasting precious hours.

Briefly, she'd contemplated wading into the surf from the shore, but she wasn't a strong swimmer, and after watching the waves' relentless onslaught, she'd decided she'd never be able to break through the rough surf. So, up the hill and over sharp lava rock she'd climbed. She'd already pressed her luck using her powers so often in the mortal world. The last thing she wanted was to alert the Council of her recklessness. The soles of her flats had been shredded by the knife-like stones, and blood trickled down her ankles from where she'd nicked the skin on the rock's hungry teeth.

During her ascent, Kait had yearned to transform into a strong breeze to reach the top and then simply plunge beneath the dark surface, but it was very difficult to phase from one form to another underwater, especially in the high-density salty sea. Plus, once submerged as her element, she'd have no way to direct herself. She'd be no better off than a jellyfish bobbing along with the current. She thought back to the Graeae; nothing about their demeanor had suggested they would appreciate shortcuts.

With a final wince, Kait stepped onto a well-worn rock perched on the very edge of the cliff. Her feet fit into the natural pocket decades' worth of adrenaline-seeking teens had carved as they took turns on the lip. She was bathed in the rosy glow of the sun just beginning to dip below the horizon. The locals were smart enough to avoid the ocean at dusk, but she didn't have the same luxury. If the Graeae were to be believed, she only had a few short hours before Poseidon's nymphs crafted tomorrow's sea foam. She couldn't afford to delay her journey another day. It was bad enough that Bia's soul was trapped with Hades, but Goddess knew what he might be doing to her.

Deciding against a dive for fear she'd foul it up, Kait readied to jump feet first. Her toes slid over the smooth lip and curled reflexively, trying to find purchase where there was none. The sun's honey-colored rays would only remain for a few minutes more. Another thunderous boom shook the cliffside as the waves threw themselves forward, trying to beat back the stone standing in their way.

Kait didn't think. The only thing on her mind was Bia's face. She threw herself forward. A cry stalled in her throat as her body plummeted to the sea. The sensation was so alien to her. As the wind, she had total control, but falling through the sky—and waiting for the ocean to catch her—was terrifying, like an albatross suddenly gone lame. Her dress rippled around her like beautiful useless wings, exposing her thighs and panties beneath. Her hair billowed with her momentum, the tendrils desperate to catch hold of the ledge and pull her back, but it was too late.

The white-capped waves rushed to swallow her in their expansive maw, gurgling with anticipation. Kait squeezed her eyes shut and held her breath when her feet sliced through the surface before the rest of her body followed suit. In a small splash, she was gone, disappearing in the blink of an eye as only a handful of ripples acknowledged her descent.

Salt water rushed up Kait's nostrils, burning the sensitive tissue. Thousands of tiny bubbles cocooned around her exposed skin, the foreign sensation akin to probing fingers. She kicked her legs, and the vast emptiness below her feet startled her. There was nothing to push off of, nothing to ground her. She spiraled through a new sky, frantic and lost.

A flashback of being confined within Jezlem's whirling prison of water one hundred years ago slammed to the forefront of her memory. *Find the oxygen in the water*, Tahlia had ordered as she looked on with disappointment. Kait's frantic limbs stilled. Darting bubbles obscured her vision, but beyond the ascending white orbs, darkness stretched as the last of the sun's rays plunged below the horizon.

Kait's heart pounded, and the muted hum of the ocean toyed with her senses. It was too dark, too open, but she found a small slice of solace in the golden glow her halo radiated, lighting her immediate space like the dim shine of a lanternfish. She wasn't practiced enough in the water to isolate the oxygen molecules, but encased within her lungs, she harbored enough air to manipulate and extend its potency.

Expelling the majority of the pent-up air she held, Kait framed a large bubble with her hands while her fingers glided through the water as she cast. Rather than rising to the surface with the rest of the escaping air, her magic latched onto the oxygen and expanded to form a large air pocket. Propelling her body upward, she broke through the reinforced bubble and sealed the tight space just below her jawline.

Kait inhaled. Now that she'd established some control, she would be able to continuously add to the makeshift chamber from the minuscule molecules around her. However, her solution would only get her so far. Once she started to dive, the oxygen would shrink. Hopefully, Poseidon's kingdom lay somewhat close to the surface or she'd be a bloated corpse come sunrise.

With her first obstacle somewhat tackled, Kait swiveled her body, cupped her palms, and shifted her direction downward to avoid the strong undertow that rolled just below the surface. Several feet down, she no longer felt the lulling pull on her body and was able to swim with ease. Changing direction again, she leveled out and began swimming away from shore.

Kait's arms burned as she performed the breaststroke, her dress ebbing and flowing with her movements. As she swam, she tried not to let her mind wander to the creatures that existed below. Many of them would be hunting. She prayed her silhouette wouldn't invite curiosity.

Farther and farther, Kait swam until at last she paused her stride and floated, aching to rest her sore muscles. She had no way to gauge how far from shore she'd traveled, and she was beginning to have serious doubts about the genius of her plan. The ocean was a massive beast, constantly moving and changing. Seems she'd overestimated her worth. What would Poseidon care if an aurai entered his domain? Not even a single siren had been alerted to her presence.

Disheartened, Kait had begun to kick toward the surface when a large object whistled past her shoulder. Glancing to the right, she noticed a large caudal fin cut through the dim light, its black tip illuminated at the top. Her heart stopped. Blacktip reef sharks didn't usually swim in the open ocean, but there was no mistaking the distinctive tail for a dolphin or whale. Maybe it was migrating, or more likely, she hadn't traveled as far as she'd hoped.

Kait's heart raced as she waited for the shark to return, but blacktips were typically shy and evasive. Again, her memory leapt to the past, back to one of the boring lessons Jez had made her sit through as she studied for her oceanic exams. She recalled Jez memorizing different species of sharks in case she should ever encounter one on an assignment. Thankfully, black tips were part of the more docile group, but if she encountered a bull or a great white, that would be different.

Before Kait could finish her thought, a large shadow emerged on the outskirts of her halo, which highlighted dark stripes painted on a sleek hide. Not a blacktip, but a tiger shark. Powerful muscle swayed with the shark's grace as it navigated the black terrain, its side missing her by inches. She froze, fully aware her magic could do nothing against a full-grown tiger shark. She feared this species the most. Jezlem had told her they were like garbage cans, consuming everything and anything they could sink their teeth into. And right now, Kait was on the menu, her halo a gleaming beacon signaling the dinner bell.

The large shark continued forward, its strong tail just missing her right side. Instinct told her to start swimming, to put as much distance as possible between herself and the circling predator, but frantic movements were the first sign of prey. She couldn't move, yet to stay in place was also suicide.

Without realizing it, Kait had started sucking quick shallow breaths and rapidly depleting her oxygen. She tried to control her fear, but her thoughts raced, too focused on the mouth with teeth hunting her. Her heart thundered, and the sound swamped her ears. She tossed her head back and forth while her terror grew. Ten seconds had dragged on with no sign of the tiger before a harsh hit to her shins sent her sprawling to the left.

The shark then bumped her hard with its nose. A choked gasp fell from Kait's lips as she fought to right herself. Without the sun, it was nearly impossible to gauge which way was up or down. The pressure inside her shrinking chamber grew as she devoured the oxygen, too frantic to replenish it. Again, the shark slunk away, but she was certain it'd be back.

Kait squinted into the darkness as she fanned out her hands, rotating them in a tight circle. Would the predator come at her from the left, right, back, or front? A cold chill gripped her as she glanced down at her feet. She'd lost her shoes upon her violent entrance, leaving her toes pruney and vulnerable. Were great whites the only ones who attacked from below?

A powerful ripple drew Kait's attention to the left, and a silent scream stuck in her throat. The tiger shark charged from only a few feet away. Jagged teeth parted, and its beady black eyes rolled back to eerie white as it prepared to bite. Uselessly, she held her hands in front of her, trying to create a shield to deflect the gaping mouth, but she was helpless. Closing the distance, the shark opened its jaws even wider. There was no escape.

CHAPTER 20

A hard pressure slammed into Kait's right hip as teeth sliced into her midsection, but the sting wasn't as agonizing as she would've expected. Had the shark bitten through nerves? Severed some crucial connection to her pain receptors? Above her, the tiger's enormous bulk rushed by but headed in the opposite direction. Twisting her neck, she saw that talons, not teeth, secured her waist and extended to translucent arms.

A firm nudge to the back of her head caused her to shift her attention over her shoulder. A wide elongated face stared back. Luminous eyes sat above slitted nostrils, and clear skin stretched like a hideous illusion, only heightened by a smile punctuated with hundreds of triangular needle-like teeth. Kait balked in the creature's hold. Something else from the deep had claimed her before the tiger could.

A series of clicks wafted through the water as the frightening monster's mouth twitched. Keeping one clawed hand on Kait's torso, the creature lifted its other arm and pointed a spidery finger. Kait turned her head. The tiger shark raced toward her once again, determination in its eyes. However, before it could penetrate her halo's radiance, a swarm of creatures similar to the one that held her attacked.

The vicious animals used their jaws to tear into the shark's tough hide, and in seconds, the soft golden glow lighting the ocean soured to a dark maroon as the tiger's blood poured from its wounds. Kait watched, relieved and terrified, as the great shark stopped fighting and swam away, choosing life over a quick meal.

Another series of loud clicks chirped in Kait's ear before the creature yanked her downward, towing her body through the heavy sea with ease. She could do nothing to stop her descent. Her captor was too strong, its agile body maneuvering through the blackness with precision and speed.

Kait's lungs constricted. Her small pocket of air was nearly depleted, and she had unknowingly used up the last of her reserve. Her chest balked, spasming as she fought for breath. Her body didn't realize what her mind already knew; she was dying, drowning. Black fireworks exploded behind her eyes as the last of her thin veil of oxygen collapsed, inviting salt water to burn down her throat. It stung her eyes and infiltrated her ears, its onslaught merciless.

She hit her captor's arm as hard as her weakening limbs allowed, and her lungs filled with water. The image of the Graeae appeared, their weathered faces downturned in disappointment. They mentioned they'd seen her death. Had they known it would be a mile under the surface in the clutches of a sea beast? Were they laughing, congratulating one another on their correct prediction? She supposed it didn't matter much now. Kait's head lolled, and the last thing she saw before her vision blurred was the creature's strange smile, its pointed teeth delighting in her final breath.

A harsh thrust slammed into Kait's chest once, twice, three times. Her body jerked upward as she vomited lukewarm seawater over her lips. Bile splashed across the sandy floor, the sound loud and messy. Slowly, she peeled back her eyelids and lay back down, her throat on fire.

"Where am I?" Kait croaked.

She lay on a hard unyielding surface, slightly elevated off the ocean floor she'd just defiled.

"Poseidon's kingdom," a sultry voice answered.

Kait flinched. She hadn't been expecting a reply. After drowning, she assumed her soul would awaken in Gaia's care, but she was far too uncomfortable to be dead. Her wet dress clung to her like seaweed, the once elegant fabric now constricting and sticky. Her eyes and throat throbbed with fire, and she could already feel a deep bruise forming where her assailant had hit her. Dry coughs raked her throat, causing her body to buck atop the hard bed once more.

"Easy, you've been through quite an ordeal." As the woman spoke, Kait's pains dulled, her voice like morphine. A content sigh escaped Kait's lips, and her eyes grew heavy. "Oh, dear. Stop that. He's waiting for you."

Sturdy hands slipped beneath her armpits and hauled her stiff body into a sitting position. "Waiting for me? Who? Where am I?"

The speaker growled, her touch becoming rough as she pulled Kait to her feet. Gripping her jaw, she turned Kait's face to the left. Large blue eyes were the first feature she was met with, along with a small nose and voluminous black hair. She was stunning, but there was an unnerving fierceness that radiated from her. In Kait's semi-delirious state, her mind warred between keeping her distance and the overwhelming urge to press her lips to the beautiful woman's.

"Hush. Don't lose yourself to the illusion." With a quick snap of her neck, the speaker bared her triangular teeth, and her dark skin flushed with the same opalescent sheen Kait recalled from earlier. "Come, you need to walk now."

Realization dawned on Kait as the lovely speaker's beauty settled back over the severe features. The memory of meeting Peisinoe washed over her. She'd been immediately attracted to her as well, hypnotized by her voice, and Peisinoe wasn't even trying to lure her in.

"You're a siren."

The woman nodded, elegant in her stride. Even the way she walked was mesmerizing. She opened her arms in a wide circle and gestured to the space encasing them. Kait blushed. The siren no doubt didn't trust her to not become entranced again if she continued speaking.

Kait marveled at the grand hallway in which they walked. White coral arches created an impressive structure, the dark ocean beyond the sea glass windows indiscernible from within the brightly lit room. Sconces lined every other post. Each was illuminated by a hidden flame as soft teal up-lighting further enhanced the elegance. Beneath their feet was white sand, with discarded shells and pebbles littered throughout.

"How far down are we?"

The siren didn't stop walking but held up her hand and spread three webbed fingers.

"Three miles?"

The siren nodded once more. Silence stretched between them as they wove through the long corridors.

"Did you know a siren named Peisinoe?" Kait asked. "I met her right before her death months ago. She mentioned Poseidon. Was she part of his court? I'm embarrassed to admit I don't know much about your culture."

Her guide sneered, revealing the pointed tips of her teeth. Kait's unease returned, but she understood why the siren chose to answer in her aggressive way.

"She was part of his kingdom, but not his inner court," the siren explained. "One of Poseidon's frequent lovers. He was distraught when he heard of her violent end and enraged when a piriol's quill was identified as the murder weapon." The siren snarled, seemingly making her voice as deep and rough as possible, but Kait still felt the magnetic pull threatening to blanket her agency. She shook her head and focused instead on her bare toes dragging through the sand.

"It was a piriol, raised in secret by an immortal," Kait said. "My sister killed it in the Pyrenees mountains."

The siren paused and touched the tender skin on the inside of Kait's left elbow. "How?"

"She stabbed it with one of its quills, and then Zeus unknowingly crushed its body while trying to kill her."

The siren's brow wrinkled, and she spat a stream of saliva into the sand. "Do not speak that name here."

Kait held up her palms in surrender. "I'm sorry. Trust me, I hold no love for him."

"Why did you come here? What business does a nymph of the sky have with the god of the sea?"

Kait took a steadying breath as a wave of emotion crested behind her eyes. "Hera murdered my sister and orchestrated her soul's descent to the Underworld. The Graeae sent me to see your king to prove my quest is true."

The siren snickered and rolled her eyes. "The Graeae. Meddling old crones trying to play at being the Fates. They do not help. All they cause is misery."

"All the same, they're the only method I have to reach the Underworld unless Poseidon is kind enough to show me the way." Kait bit the inside of her cheek. "I never asked your name."

"Nerissa," the siren replied with a hiss. "And don't get your hopes up on that front. Poseidon is cordial, but you're still an outsider and not even a naiad at that. Did the Graeae say how you will prove your quest to be true?"

Licking her bottom lip, Kait cleared her throat. "If Poseidon will see me, I'll relay that information to him."

The siren chuckled, the sound a melodic chime. Kait felt her eyes growing glassy once again as her thoughts clouded. She was acutely aware of how close Nerissa's body was to hers, her lips . . .

"Snap out of it, aurai," Nerissa warned.

Kait shook her head. "I apologize. I should be stronger than this."

"Don't beat yourself up. You're doing quite well."

"Really? How does your allure work, exactly? Apart from Peisinoe, I've never met a siren."

Nerissa smiled, exposing her double rows of teeth. "Our voices. All it takes is one syllable, and men hurl themselves into the sea, desperate to possess us. Women are not fooled so easily, but it's so much more fun when the prey is a challenge."

The siren cocked her head, her large irises flashing white before she blinked, a silent reminder of how deadly her presence could be. Kait swallowed roughly, unsure if she was joking. Nerissa turned to the left and stopped in front of a towering door with a large golden handle.

"Come. Poseidon is curious to meet you."

CHAPTER 21

The door opened into an intimate chamber. Rather than the ornate splendor Zeus was known to surround himself with, Poseidon's council room was simply furnished. The same bright teal lighting continued into the space, but instead of a grandiose throne or velvet carpet, a cozy sitting area complete with four low-backed chairs was arranged in the center.

Kait's breath caught at the wall of windows beyond the gathered seating. Bioluminescent creatures swam and drifted amidst the thick blackness just past the glass, a scene as incredible and unique as she imagined staring up into the endless kaleidoscope of stars above Olympus would be.

Nerissa gave Kait an encouraging push from behind, and her long talons nicked her flesh by mistake. "Good luck." The siren winked before shutting the door and leaving Kait alone.

The moment it clicked shut, Kait's nerves flew into a flurry. She'd been so transfixed by the natural beauty of the room that she'd forgotten to scan for any hidden predators. With palms raised, she kept her back to the wall as she slid along the perimeter. Stirring the air, she was surprised to find her element responsive.

A strong breeze kicked up to match her anxiety. Was this a trap? Had Nerissa left her on purpose? Poseidon obviously took sirens as lovers, but what of naiads? This deep beneath the waves, would the Council even know if Poseidon engaged in the hunt, forcing nymphs to lay beneath him as he claimed euphoria?

The air rippled with unease. In her periphery, motion flickered. Instantly, Kait was back in the cave, chained to the wall, her magic incapacitated as Zeus touched her, but this time, she wasn't helpless. She sent out a powerful blast of air that billowed around the room. A high-pitched cooing rattled in response as an oblong shape darted to the floor, dragging a collection of tentacles behind a large mass. Her heart raced with panic, and adrenaline surged. She aimed another blast of air, trying to stop the creature as it skirted a chair and dove behind a waist-high bookcase. She needed to see what stalked her. Had Poseidon planted it to attack like Zeus's piriol? Kait sent a shock wave of air along the surface of the floor, causing the furniture to shake unsteadily. A side table toppled, and more cooing erupted, this time louder.

The creature leapt out of its hiding place, and a silent scream tore from Kait's throat. She brandished both palms and created a mini-tornado to incapacitate the monster. The tail end of the twister reached for one of the invertebrate's limbs before a rush of water descended, enveloping the shadow and blocking her attack.

Kait snapped her head to the left and was greeted by a tall silhouette. Water shot from his hands and coalesced around the small creature in a protective embrace before he hugged it to his chest.

"What is the meaning of this?" he boomed like a cannon.

The door shut behind him, and the turquoise lamps burned brighter, bringing the newcomer into sharper focus. His skin was like polished onyx, arms brimming with lean muscle. His chest was bare, a pair of golden hoops pierced through each nipple. A short cerulean sarong wrapped around his waist and exposed toned thighs, calves, and bare feet. Kait took a step back. His head was void of hair, and gold kohl rimmed his dark eyes. The burning halo of the gods radiated from his flesh.

"Poseidon," Kait uttered.

"That's right, and you're the aurai destroying my chamber and terrorizing my pet."

"Pet?" Kait repeated, lowering her hands.

A quiet whooshing sound accompanied the water's retreat, leaving the strange blob-like creature sitting atop Poseidon's hands. He placed a gentle hand on its throbbing skull, as it changed from black to pale red, seeming calmer in its master's hold.

"What exactly is that?"

Poseidon left his post near the door and gave Kait a wide berth. He moved to a table near the windows on the left side of the room and opened a small chest. Reaching in, he withdrew a clicking crab and held it out to the creature. Two arms wrapped around the crab's body and pulled it beneath the folds of flesh pooling in Poseidon's palms. The savage crunch of the animal's beak biting through the shell set Kait's teeth on edge, followed by a wet sucking sound as it slurped up the crab's liquid insides.

The hollow shell fell to the floor a moment later, and the animal turned a rosy shade of red. Kait nearly gagged at the sight of the undulating sack of flesh wriggling happily in the god's arms.

"Pox is a cephalopod, a giant Pacific octopus. One of the most intelligent species on this planet but cursed with an exceptionally short lifespan. Pox is my newest. I rescued her two months ago after she was attacked by a moray eel."

Cradling the octopus, Poseidon took a seat in one of the askew chairs, not bothering to turn it back to face her. Kait followed his lead and moved to the nearest seat, scooting it to face him.

"I'm terribly sorry. I didn't know," Kait said, at a loss to explain the constant fear that haunted her. "I thought, well . . ."

Poseidon cocked his head. "Nerissa told me you were awake, but I don't hold calling hours and run my kingdom less formally than most. I should have been here to receive you, but one of my advisors needed a quick word. Please know you have nothing to fear while in my court, from me or my subjects."

The god's soft voice was a balm on Kait's nerves, easing her fears with the sincerity of his words. His dark eyes were earnest and unblinking.

"Thank you, Your Grace. Your kindness is indeed rare among gods."

"It sounds as if you've had many encounters."

Kait licked her lips. She wasn't up to date on her immortal lineage, but she was willing to wager the sea god was, at the very least, friendly with several of the gods on her list. She prayed that he and his brother weren't close.

"Unfortunately, I have. Apollo, Hera, Zeus, and Hermes." Kait stumbled over the last two. Her nerves spiked the moment Poseidon's brother's name fell from her lips, but she was surprised at how uncomfortable she became uttering Hermes's. It had been over one hundred years since he'd tricked her and tried to take her halo by force. She thought she was past what he had done to her, but just saying his name tore a jagged hole in her crudely patched psyche.

"Whoa, whoa. Easy, aurai."

Poseidon's calm words drew her attention from her cuticles to where he sat. Thrashing about the room, loose papers and miscellaneous objects whipped around as the air kicked up in response to her plummeting mental state.

"Know I have little love for my brother and his offspring, even less for his estranged tigress of a wife," Poseidon said.

Kait glanced at the sea god's face. The agitated breeze settled. "You know Zeus is dead, then?"

Poseidon bowed his head. "Yes, the Council met to discuss the events in the Pyrenees several weeks ago. We sent word to Hades asking when Zeus's soul would be released, but my eldest brother has yet to grace us with a reply. He's either keeping Zeus imprisoned to sate his petty desire for vengeance for his relegation to the Underworld or—the more likely reason—he's too self-absorbed to even realize our brother is at his gates. Zeus's soul could be stranded on the banks of the River Styx, for all I know."

Kait shifted uncomfortably in her chair. "Did you hear that my sisters and I were the nymphs who killed him?" Kait's voice didn't warble as she revealed her secret, and she held the god's gaze without blinking.

Poseidon's brows wrinkled. "I thought a mortal woman was behind the slaying."

"Mortal because Zeus raped her and absorbed her halo. She was a naiad and Zeus's last victim."

"Your sister . . . one of the triad?" Poseidon asked.

"Yes." Kait swallowed the growing lump in her throat. "And now, because of Hera's revenge, my other sister is dead. Her soul is trapped in the Underworld."

"Hera's revenge?" Poseidon's dark eyes clouded. "The seas bordering Kairu were stained with blood. My sirens reported heavy nymph casualties, but they were unable to identify a source, and none of my naiads returned to my kingdom."

"It happened so fast. Olean was overrun with nymphs infected by a virus that caused them to turn on each other. We're still trying to figure out how far it spread. The last I knew, the elders were putting together a squad to comb the other realms while the rest gathered the bodies."

Shame washed over Kait once again. She hadn't meant to abandon the realm after such a devastating loss, but Bia's soul wasn't safe like the others in Gaia's care. Bia couldn't wait.

"But you mentioned Hera. What does she have to do with this?" Poseidon questioned.

Kait exhaled. "She was after me, to hurt me like we hurt her by killing Zeus. Somehow, she crafted a toxin to target my people. She told me her goal was mass extermination, and she almost succeeded."

Poseidon was silent for a few long moments. He stared at Kait and rubbed his palms together. "Are you sure about this? To accuse a high goddess of attempted genocide is no small matter."

Kait's mouth fell open in disbelief. Did he truly think she'd fabricated the story? "Of course. She'd been plaguing me with terrifying omens for days. She even followed me into the human realm—and into Olean—to threaten me."

Poseidon scoffed, doubt in his eyes. "Olean cannot be breached by immortals."

"She found a way."

After setting the cephalopod on the ground, Poseidon sat back and drummed his fingers across the wooden armrest. "If what you say is true, we must go to the Council immediately."

Kait shook her head. "I can't. Hades has my sister's soul. I need to retrieve her before he enacts whatever sinister scheme he cooked up with Hera."

"Retrieve her? As in, journey to Hell? That's ludicrous. Only the dead may enter the Underworld."

Kait leaned forward in her chair and fixed Poseidon with a bright stare. "Which is why I came to you."

"Me? How can I possibly help? You assume that since Hades is my brother, I can willingly flit to the Underworld?"

"Not at all. Before seeking you out, the Graeae found me and offered to relay the knowledge of the Underworld's entrance, but first, I have to prove my quest is true. They tasked me with finding you and confessing my part in Zeus's murder. If I'm able to secure your forgiveness and collect your blessing in the form of fresh sea foam, I will be allowed to continue."

Poseidon pursed his lips and crossed his arms, his expression unreadable. "The Council must be notified. Surely, Gaia has already told them about the attack."

"And does the Council have the power to force Hades to return souls?"

Poseidon's confidence wavered. "No, they have no jurisdiction in the land of the dead."

"Exactly. They'll want proof. Something more concrete than a wispy black shadow." Kait threw up her hands and fell back against the soft cushion.

"But if Gaia saw the attack on your sister's soul, she can testify against Hera."

Kait shook her head. "She didn't. Hera was in the form of her familiar. I doubt Gaia is even aware of the part the goddess played."

Poseidon leaned forward and balanced his elbows on his knees. "Then, we convene the Council. Between your testimony and Queen Rajhi's account, they'll have sufficient evidence to question Hera—"

"And then what? I wait weeks for someone to stumble across a scrap of evidence? Hera's too clever to leave anything that could incriminate her behind. I'll be in the same spot I am now and no closer to saving my sister. I don't have time to navigate the red tape. Please, you're my only chance."

Poseidon exhaled between his teeth, the sound loud and frustrated. Interlocking his long fingers, he stood and paced a short distance away. After a few tense seconds, he pivoted to face her. "If Hades refuses to return your sister's soul, what then? You realize your quest is suicide, right? If you fail, neither you nor your sister's soul will have the opportunity to be made anew. The grand prophecy that spoke of the next triad bringing a seismic shift in the realms will be forsaken, and you will never see the light of day again."

Kait rose to her feet and squared her shoulders. "If I die in the pursuit of rescuing a loved one, that will be enough. And if the realms need reform that badly, I know a dozen qualified nymphs who can easily take my place. Olean will not be forsaken, and at the very least, while our souls may rot in hell for eternity, my sister and I will be together."

A small chuckle transformed Poseidon's grim frown. "You're tenacious, I'll give you that—a trait you'll need to draw on." He nodded and spread his hands in offering. "I accept your confession for murdering my brother. Truth be told, he's deserved far worse for centuries."

Kait grinned, but Poseidon held up a finger.

"Keep in mind that if you do manage to enter his realm, Hades is nothing like Zeus. Our little brother never lost his mindset from childhood. Zeus expects the world to be delivered at his beck and call, a cocky and boisterous asshole. What you see is what you get. But with Hades . . ." Poseidon paused, strode to the large wall of windows, and peered into the inky darkness. "Hades is an entirely different creature, harder to read than smoke. He speaks in dizzying riddles; each sentence is a contradiction of the last. He's slippery and far more intelligent than Zeus or I could ever hope to be. If what you say is true, I have no idea why he chose to align himself with Hera, but you can bet he'll play you just as easily as he's no doubt playing her."

"I understand. I'll do whatever it takes to save my sister."

Poseidon's jaw feathered. "I know, and that is your weakness."

Kait opened her mouth to argue, but there was nothing to say. Hades would hold every ounce of power in their exchange. She was most certainly walking into a trap, but what else could she do?

"Come, with the naiads still in Olean, the sirens need extra time to craft the sea foam. We have time to get you a warm meal and a new dress before it's ready. I don't know if our paths will cross again, but if I can help your cause in any way, you have my allegiance." Poseidon closed the space between them but came to a stop a respectful distance away.

"Thank you, Poseidon. I truly appreciate your kindness," Kait said. For the first time since she'd leapt into the sea, a genuine smile graced her lips.

Poseidon cocked his head and gestured for her to move toward the door. "Don't thank me yet, my dear. You'll be wishing for the tiger shark's teeth once Hades starts with you."

CHAPTER 22

Nerissa pulled the zipper to the top of the dress as Kait swayed on the balls of her feet. "You really should lie down, aurai. Close your eyes for an hour or two."

Kait shook her head, straining to keep her eyelids from fluttering closed. She'd been awake for nearly twenty-four hours, and that included fighting off an infected nymph army and swimming through the rough ocean. She was exhausted, but if she slept, it'd cost her time she couldn't afford to lose.

"No, I'll be fine. Once I get out in the fresh air, I'll perk right up. Being sequestered down here is affecting me more than I would have thought. It's so heavy."

"It's all the pressure. If Poseidon had his way, we wouldn't be in this constrictive bubble, but when other immortals come to call, they don't particularly enjoy our natural habitat." Nerissa rolled her large eyes and looked Kait's new ensemble up and down. "It's nothing much, but at least it covers more than those tattered scraps you had on.

Kait forced her eyes open again and focused on the mirror. Pieces of her old dress lay sprawled about the lavish sitting area in one of the many guest rooms in Poseidon's kingdom. When he'd accompanied her to the room, the sea god had apologized for the ostentatious extravagance. The rooms were built for visiting goddesses.

Kait didn't mind, though she felt like an imposter surrounded by all the finery. It was the opposite of Olean. Instead of natural wood and floral accents, her room shone like a saltwater pearl, every surface glimmering with iridescent elegance. A large sleigh bed stood behind them, and teal curtains the consistency of soapsuds fell in ripples before the glass windows. Several pieces of furniture littered the room, but the one detail she adored was the floor.

Rather than marble or quartz, the coarse sand from the hall extended underfoot. Kait scrunched her toes, loving the way the texture kept her grounded even so far below the surface. Charcoal-gray pants cuffed her ankles and extended upward into a romper. Her favorite feature was the thin gauze strips that trailed off the back like wings.

"I wish we had something sturdier, but down here, we don't have much need for combat gear. The dark color will help camouflage you from sharks, but I don't know how much good it'll do with your halo." Nerissa brushed her long braids off her face and stood with her hands on her hips.

Kait spun atop the sand, appreciating the siren's work from all angles. "It's lovely. Thank you for your hospitality."

The siren shrugged, the light reflecting off her opalescent skin. "Poseidon made the call." Her voice was deep and raspy, a far cry from the beautiful song she'd first spoken with. Kait frowned. Nerissa was speaking like that for her benefit. She hoped it wasn't causing her pain. "I still think you should try to sleep. We can wake you at dawn."

A curt knock rapped on the door. With a defeated sigh, Nerissa left Kait's side and pulled it open.

"Is she rested? It's nearly time." Poseidon's steady voice reached Kait from across the room.

Nerissa grumbled under her breath and swung the door wide so the sea god could enter. "She's out of those rags, but she refused to sleep. I kept telling her." The siren crossed her arms and shot a dark glare in Kait's direction.

Poseidon scanned the large room for Kait, and a small smile tugged his lips when his gaze found hers. "As stubborn as the waves that beat the shore. Is the fabric comfortable? Naiads prefer lightweight material."

Kait ran the transparent sash at her waist through her fingers. "Yes, it's lovely. Thank you, Your Grace."

The sea god nodded and walked closer, clasping his hands in front of him. "Nerissa will escort you to the surface where my sirens are about to craft the morning's foam. Return to the Graeae as quickly as you can. Without the salt to cling to, the foam will only last an hour at most. They'll give you a kelp basket in which to carry it. I fear you'll be limited to your physical form once on land. If you fly, the foam will tear apart."

A small wrinkle formed above Kait's nose as she imagined having to clamber over the sharp lava rocks again, and this time, she wouldn't have shoes to soften the bites. As thin as hers were, at least they'd offered a small amount of protection.

"Thank you. I pray the Anemoi are in an agreeable mood, then. There's nothing worse than when the brothers get in a heated spat. Boreas's cold fronts would certainly make this journey even more challenging." Kait tied her hair in a high ponytail.

Poseidon chuckled. "I remember Boreas in our youth, forever a hothead. I pray your journey back is smooth and your time in the Underworld is brief. I wish I could assist you, but I fear my presence would only cement my brother against your cause. When Zeus burdened him with the task of dominion over the dead, I didn't exactly jump to his defense." Clearing his throat, Poseidon cocked his head toward the door. It was time for her departure.

Kait fell into step with the sea god as he led her through the beautiful hallway. He angled his head to bring his mouth level with her ear and spoke quietly. "In the meantime, I'll travel to Olympus and speak with Gaia and gather her recollection of the events. Word of this infection must have reached the Council by now. I'll also speak with Athena and Artemis. Surely, they'll be able to identify signs of waged warfare over an innocuous outbreak. And as for your descent to the Underworld, I will rescind my wards and cage the Lernaean Hydra for the next twelve hours. I'm afraid I can't leave the gates vulnerable longer than that. My responsibilities aren't just to keep things out."

Kait bowed her head, too stunned to offer her gratitude in any other manner. "Thank you, Poseidon, for everything. I wish this had been my first encounter with a god."

Poseidon's grin faltered, and ghosts swam across his eyes. "I have my faults, just as much as the next immortal," he said quietly, running his hand along his forearm. "Centuries ago, I made a mistake, took what I thought rightfully belonged to me. I'm . . . I'm still trying to atone for my sin."

Kait bit the inside of her lower lip. Even though the sea god had shown her nothing but kindness, she knew all too well the true monsters that resided within the gods, and from the shame in Poseidon's eyes, she realized he was more like his younger brother than he cared to admit.

Kait bowed her head and followed Nerissa away from the sea god's side without another glance. Far above, the stars surrendered their brilliance to the coming dawn. Eos waited for no one.

"Are you ready?" Nerissa asked. She flexed her hands and stretched the translucent webbing between her fingers.

Kait took a steadying breath and glanced at the miles of water suspended overhead. The thin barrier that separated her from the crushing depths rippled with the current and licked her toes. Her thoughts drifted to her sparring session with Jezlem so many months ago, before everything in their world had changed. She hated the sensation of being encased, by water especially— an impenetrable foe that seemed to take pleasure in her misery. She'd barely managed to survive her first dive into the terrifying waves; now, she stood on the precipice of another harrowing plunge. At least she wouldn't have to make this one alone.

"Ready," Kait confirmed as energy swirled across her palms. She'd be able to craft another pocket of air in which to breathe, and with the siren propelling her through the deep, she prayed to Gaia she didn't wind up drowning a second time.

Nerissa flashed her an eerie smile, her serrated teeth too wide in her mouth. "Good. We'll have to do this quickly. Usually, we encourage a much slower ascent. Being submerged at this depth for an extended period allows nitrogen in your blood to expand and form bubbles. Even immortals must be careful, but you don't have that kind of time to waste. Plus, if everything goes well, you'll be dead soon, anyway." She grinned again, a wicked spark lighting in her pale eyes.

"I guess that's a good point." Kait laughed nervously and twisted her fingers, casting her magic to create a halo of air around her head. Nerissa took her hand, and the siren's talon-like nails bit into her soft flesh. "Let's go."

Frigid water swallowed them as the siren broke the seal that kept the crushing depths at bay. With roaring force, the palace flooded, and if Nerissa hadn't gripped her hand, Kait would have been sucked into the frothing whirlpool.

Kait followed the powerful waves as whitecaps slammed into the sandy hall. The dark water grew cloudy as earth and sea collided, but she could have sworn she glimpsed charging stallions amidst the churning spray. A sharp pinch drew her attention forward, and Nerissa's shining eyes floated eerily before her.

"Up," the siren sang, unleashing her full power.

Kait's legs began to kick, overcome with desperation to reach the surface, to complete the command. Maintaining her grip, Nerissa surged through the depths and supported Kait's weight behind her. Faster and faster, they climbed, leaving behind the inky curtains of the unknown. As they passed through the abyss, the sea above slowly began to lighten. Kait's chest swelled with relief, but the desire to continue up, to comply, shrouded her emotions. The siren's power was too strong to allow any other conscious thought.

They passed through the midnight zone and in another dozen strokes, the sunlight zone was visible. Kait's neck ached from the velocity with which the siren dragged her through the deep, and her eardrums pounded from the intense fluctuation in pressure. Her muscles burned with strain, and her ears felt as if they were about to implode. But she kept swimming, kept kicking. Her free hand carved through the water as she tried to reach longer, farther. They were so close.

Black stars bloomed across Kait's vision. Her air pocket was shrinking, her magic dimming. She flitted in and out of consciousness. A school of fish brushed her calves and swept her toes to the side, their current jerking her out of Nerissa's hold. In a handful of swift seconds, her entire world flipped upside down. Gone was the surface or any sense of direction. She was trapped inside Jezlem's liquid prison once more with no strength to break free, tumbling through the expanse as the last of her air diminished. A large shadow loomed as her vision narrowed to thin slits. Another school, a whale, a shark? It didn't matter. Her lungs screamed for air, but she could only reward their plea with salt water before crushing blackness stole the big blue world away.

CHAPTER 23

"Breathe, aurai. Breathe!"

Furious blows drove into Kait's chest, the pain rousing her from a stark sea of unconsciousness. Water burst from her lips in vomiting waves as her lungs expelled the burning liquid.

"Finally. I thought Gaia may have forsaken you."

The strikes ceased, and Kait opened her eyes. Dried salt clung to her lashes and flaked to the warm sand she lay upon as rosy sunshine greeted her. "I'm alive?"

"For now," the siren confirmed, speaking in a harsh tone once more. Kait was grateful. Hopefully, she'd never have to hear the beautiful trill of a siren's song ever again.

"We made it?"

"Yes, and just in time. Look."

Nerissa raised her scaly arm and gestured to an outcropping of dark rocks a few yards offshore. Like surfacing porpoises, five sirens bobbed along the incoming tide. Kait watched, mesmerized, as the calm water rippled and churned, causing delicate sea foam to swell in large plumes. Together, the sirens directed the fresh foam away from the rocks where it rode small curling waves to the beach.

"Here. Fill it to the top." Nerissa handed Kait a woven kelp basket.

Kait dusted the clinging grains from her skin and wrapped her hand around the slippery basin. Wet sand mushed between her toes, and a gentle hiss sounded as the waves slithered up the shore. Her body recoiled from the seawater so soon after her dangerous escapade.

She swallowed her aversion and stepped into the ebbing surf up to her ankles, repressing a shudder. A blanket of foam gathered around her shins, and bubbles seethed and popped as they licked her. She lowered the basket into the airy mass and filled it to the brim with cream-colored lather. Her lips spread in a relieved smile. She'd done it: found Poseidon, confessed her sin, and earned his blessing. Once she presented the Graeae with the offering, she would be one step closer to saving Bia.

Exiting the effervescent sea, Kait cast a slight wind to brush the clinging suds off her flesh before turning to face Nerissa. "Thank you for everything you've done. If there is any way I or the nymphs of Olean can repay the favor, don't hesitate to call."

The siren grinned, and her triangular teeth evoked a twinge of fear. "One day, I might take you up on that. Now, go. As Poseidon said, the foam won't last, and you have a long journey back. Take care not to touch it. The oils will break down the composition."

Kait nodded and slid her palms lower, cradling the basket to ensure nothing but the ribbons of kelp met the precious contents. "I'll head to the portal right away. Thank you."

"I admire your courage and pray you save her."

Without another word, Nerissa strode into the surf and dove beneath an incoming wave. Kait brushed a wet strand of hair out of her face and pivoted atop the sand. As the siren said, she had a long way to go.

Forty minutes later, Kait swiped at the trickling sweat along her brow. She'd thought crossing the lava rock would be the hardest part, but the effort of navigating through the thick humid jungle was beyond comparison. She paused her pace for the sixth time to balance the basket on her hip and slapped the slick skin of her neck where mosquitoes feasted. As an aurai, she rarely had to subject herself to a realm's fauna for long durations and wasn't accustomed to insects. She slapped her shoulder.

The deep pull in her gut guided her feet. Kait could sense the portal was near, but the endless foliage blinded her to its exact location. Glancing down into the basket, her breathing hitched. The sea foam was nearly half-gone, evaporated in the jungle's stifling heat. She had to move quicker and cover more ground if she had any hope of meeting the deadline.

Kait's bare feet sunk into the rich earth as a rose-ringed parakeet sang overhead. She swatted at a waist-high leaf the size of a small table and ducked beneath a moss-covered vine. Her thoughts drifted to Bia. Her kindhearted anthousai sister would have loved to explore the vast tropics and its creatures. She could picture her now, running around with her vials collecting viscous sap, fresh leaves, and nutrient-rich dirt. Maybe one day, she'd be able to bring her back there and enact that exact vision.

A deep rumble pierced the calm. Kait froze and scanned the brush in front of her, sweeping her eyes from side to side. Twigs snapped, and the sharp sound ricocheted. Suddenly, she was back in these same jungles, hunted by Zeus's fierce piriol. Her heart slammed against her rib cage, and her breaths stuttered. He was there. Somehow, impossibly, Zeus was there.

Another guttural grunt sounded, closer this time. Kait itched to cast, to transform into her elemental form and disappear, but the basket in her hands made that impossible. The foam would never survive the wind's velocity. Carefully, she took another step in the direction of the portal. With the basket cradled in the crook of one arm, she raised her other and tapped her fingers. Energy crackled around her hand, ready to launch at the first sign of motion.

Her shaky exhale was the only sound until muted footfalls rang out. Kait pictured the large paws of the creature and swallowed roughly around the knotted scars that still marred the flesh of her throat. She'd never forget the pain of the piriol's four incisors as it held her down while Jezlem screamed for Zeus to stop—the marks were a forever reminder of one of the worst days of her life.

But Zeus's piriol was dead, crushed by rocks in Atlas's cavern. Logic told her whatever she'd heard couldn't have been the great cat, but memories of being hunted through the jungle choked all rational thought. Her instincts screamed to flee. She took another step. Out of the corner of her eye, she caught a flicker of hazy shimmer. The portal was only a dozen yards away.

Kait slunk past a towering plant, hoping to put as much distance between herself and the unidentified creature as possible. A chorus of agitated grunts sounded, and her nerves spiked, kicking up a flurry of wind that stirred the large leaves. To her left, foliage fluttered and exposed a pair of bright amber eyes.

A strangled gasp stalled in Kait's throat as the creature emitted a startled growl, followed by a terrifying shriek as it charged through the underbrush toward her. Before her mind could process the animal she'd uncovered, her feet were racing. All she saw was a powerful black body, beady eyes, and two sharp teeth. Throwing herself into a sprint, she turned and knocked palm leaves and mossy curtains out of the way. Her only thought was of the safety of the portal.

Behind her, the shrieks changed to agitated squeals as her adversary gained on her. Being lower to the ground, with its weight dispersed between four legs rather than two, the animal moved much faster than she could and wove through the dark green labyrinth with ease and familiarity. Kait's fear imploded as teeth grazed the back of her calves, but they didn't bite, not yet. She chanced a glance behind her and was met with furry ears and coarse black hair. The yellowed fangs raised as the animal unleashed another aggressive grunt.

Visions of Kaf slicing her flesh and his poisonous barbs penetrating her back overtook the present, and true terror gripped her. Unable to remain in her vulnerable physical form any longer, Kait dissolved into the air and arched higher off the ground to eliminate the creature's reach. But still, she wasn't safe. The quills of a piriol didn't miss.

Kait wove in a haphazard flight pattern, doing what little she could to confuse the predator. Ahead, the portal rippled in the humidity's haze. She couldn't be sure, but it felt as if she were pulling away from the animal. She peered through the rushing leaves beneath, but there was no sign of the pursuer. She pushed through the last few feet, and the portal's comforting safety embraced her. Kait ordered the air to separate from her body. Her toes brushed the leaf-strewn forest floor. Her vision warbled as the portal awaited her destination.

Madik, she thought hurriedly.

Just then, a creature snuffled into view, sporting the same coarse black fur she'd seen before. But rather than the aggressive pursuit she'd imagined, the animal's movements were slow and deliberate as its snout rooted around in the dirt for grubs and insects. Snout, not jaws. Gone were the fangs, and in their place, two small tusks protruded from the sides of its lips. Gone were the powerful claws, replaced with soft toes. Gone were the fierce growls as the boar shuffled around the path. It was a pig, not a piriol. Kaf was dead, along with his master. She'd endangered the foam for nothing but a frightening fallacy spurred by intense memories. Gripping the kelp basket in her hands, she looked down at the pitiful contents as the portal accepted her destination. The jungles of Hawaii flickered out of focus. Jade green and cerulean sky dissolved and morphed into the dreary gray veil that stretched across the swamplands of Madik.

Kait fell to her knees on the saturated earth as the portal delivered her. A heartbroken sob fell from her lips. In her haste to escape the imagined threat, she'd traveled too fast and sacrificed the sea foam. Only a berry-sized dollop remained tucked beneath one of the folds of kelp. "Bia, I'm so sorry."

The wind shifted, growing anxious. It fluttered the ends of Kait's sodden pant legs. Lifting her head from the pitiful contents, she shivered as the trees' shadows coalesced in a writhing mass, and within a blink, the three Gray Sisters stood before her, hunched like the carrion they claimed to be, feasting on the despair of the hopeless.

"The sun grows high, child, the hour late," Pemphredo said. The goddess of alarm fixed her with a solitary stare while the shared eye alighted on the basket in her hands.

"Though your breaths offer a surprising twist that the sea god didn't drown you," Enyo said in a wizened voice.

The shortest of the sisters, Deino, glided like a specter and tilted her wrinkled neck as she slithered closer. The black scarred pits of her eyes bored into Kait's soul. "Of course, your pulse means little when your hands are empty."

Kait offered the basket with a bow of her head. "I almost drowned in the sea, confessed to Poseidon, and collected the foam. I journeyed on foot back to the portal to ensure its longevity, but I allowed fear to corrupt my mental state. What little remains, I offer you. A small token for a small answer."

"There are no small answers." Enyo sucked her thin lips, obscuring the long tooth for a moment. "For even singular words can become the greatest of keys."

"Or locks," Deino hissed as she pushed her hood back a bit, revealing sparse white hair.

Pemphredo hobbled to Kait's left and snatched the basket from her. The brown iris swiveled, scanning back and forth until it found its prize.

Kait stifled a gasp and kept her gaze trained on the ground, watching the scattering of beetles and millipedes that slipped beneath the Graeae's cloaks. "There's a small drop left," she whispered. "The jungle's climate devoured it in giant licks as I ran."

Deino exhaled. "You say ran as if you are ashamed. Fear is one of the body's most powerful physiological responses. There is no shame in fear, yet you allow it to rule you, defeat you."

Kait glanced at the Gray Sister. "But there was nothing there, just a pig."

Pemphredo spat at the mud, pulled the eyeball from its socket, and deposited it into the basket as she passed it to Deino. "There is never nothing, child. We can taste your nightmares, smell the panic lingering in your veins."

Enyo plucked the eyeball from the salty kelp as Deino's thick nails accepted the basket. Without warning, she stuck out the tip of her shriveled tongue and licked the white sphere. A hum of pleasure thrummed in the back of her throat before she plunged the eye into her own skull's cavity. "The horrors of your past sing to me. So much death, tainted further by guilt. So much burden on your young shoulders, child."

Deino brought the basket to her face and inhaled deeply, her nostrils flaring. She tilted her head and fixed Kait with a hollow stare. "Misery has favored you indeed, yet you did not break. Your success is proof of that."

Kait lifted her head. "Success? No, I failed. The foam is gone. I have brought you nothing but an empty shell."

"It was never about tangible goods, child," Deino said.

Kait furrowed her brow. "I don't understand."

Pemphredo ripped the woven kelp from her sister's grasp and held it before Kait. "What do you see?"

"Seaweed. A basket."

"Wrong again, aurai. This is a gift from the mighty sea god himself. Not only did you fight your way into his kingdom—"

Enyo breezed into view and pushed Pemphredo away to take her place. "You also confessed your sins knowing your admission may very well result in your death. You earned Poseidon's respect and even his blessing." She gestured to the basket.

A cold shiver gripped Kait's frame as Deino clasped her hand. Her skin was paper-thin yet sharp, the brittle bones beneath threatening to puncture the fragile flesh.

"Two of the mighty brothers you have bested. Only the eldest and most cunning awaits."

"Eldest?"

"The lord of death, young one. You've proven your heart is pure and your quest noble. We shall honor our word and reveal the entrance to the Underworld," Deino said, still clasping her hand.

Hope bloomed in Kait's chest. "You will? Thank you, Graeae, for your mercy."

Enyo held up an arthritic hand and looked at her coldly, the brown iris unblinking. "It is not a mercy, child. It is simply balancing the scales. Never allow yourself to be indebted to another, goddess or otherwise, for then they control your fate. We are not granting salvation. The Underworld holds horrors far beyond the gruesome terror you found your own realm plagued with. We're feeding you to the jaws of Tartarus with little hope your soul will survive, but it is not in our nature to be subjective. This is a business transaction, a barter. Poseidon's sanction for the Underworld's entrance."

Pemphredo clutched Kait's wilted hair and ran the strands through her elongated nails. The scent of sulfur and decay clung to Kait's nostrils at the Gray Sisters' proximity, but she forced herself not to flinch to escape the cloying odor.

"Is that what you truly desire, dear aurai? To enter the Underworld and confront the lord of death?"

Kait swallowed, uncomfortable with the Graeae's high-trilling voice. "Yes. I must save my sister."

"It is done. The barter made," Enyo croaked. She plucked the eyeball from its socket with a squelch and presented it to Kait.

Revulsion coiled in Kait's gut as she gazed at the offered organ. The iris faced Enyo's palm, but numerous red veins streaked across the white surface, and the thin pink tissue attached to the back gave a slight wiggle.

Deino wheezed a deep wet cackle. "Every second you delay prolongs the punishment your sister endures. Take the eye."

Kait steeled her nerve and wrapped her fingers around the eyeball, ignoring the way the glossy coating squished beneath her touch. The eye glowed with pale yellow light upon contact, and the iris began to spin, spin, spin until its definition was lost. Vibrating on her palm, the eye thrummed with energy until it paused at last and depicted a scene of incredible beauty.

Jagged white cliffsides stretched for miles, punctuated by thin green saplings clinging to the polished crag. In the center, a shallow river cut through the rocky façade, the aqua water glistening in the sun's rays as if enchanted. It was so clear, Kait could make out the smooth stones underneath until the vision narrowed on a slightly darker depth. The tropical color gave way to muted blues and greens, and a sense of unease gripped her as the current met a sudden end, butting up against gray stones.

"The River Acheron," Pemphredo stated. "In the Epirus region of northwest Greece. Follow the river to this point, where water seems to surrender to earth. Dive down under the mountain. Here, Charon awaits."

Relief warred with terror in Kait's chest. The thought of relinquishing her agency to water once again choked the breath in her lungs. "I had hoped there would be a cave to traverse rather than swim. Is there no other entrance?"

Enyo licked her lips, leaving a trail of saliva in her tongue's wake. "Only if you want to be greeted with teeth." A wizened laugh fell from the Graeae's mouth.

"Never mind. I'll stay with the river."

"Wise choice, dear. Here." Deino pressed a cold hard object into Kait's palm. She glanced down and was surprised to find a silver drachma. Athena's countenance was engraved on one side, while the wise goddess's owl leveled her with a knowing stare from the other.

"What need have I of this?"

Pemphredo waggled her finger before her and smiled, her withered lips giving way to a gummy maw. "Every soul pays the ferryman."

Kait nodded. She'd heard the ancient human legend, but with Gaia as their patron and caretaker in death, nymphs had no need of the coins. She flipped it over once more and closed her fist around it. "Thank you, Graeae."

Deino snatched the eye from Kait's other hand and pushed it into her hollow socket. "One more thing before you go." Deino waved her hand as the other sisters parted to create a small gap between their charcoal cloaks. Out of the low rolling fog, narrow legs more akin to spindles stepped through the cloudy vapor. A doe—or more accurately,—a Ceryneian hind from the earlier herd joined the small coven. It was the smallest of the creatures she'd seen, but as Kait's gaze roamed along the animal's strong stance, she could make out firm muscle beneath the glossy coat.

The doe gave a slight shake of its head. Its bronzed antlers were small, two-pronged, and its mossy mane hung only a few inches, but it stood proud and elegant, awaiting further orders from the Gray Sisters.

"This is Samara," Deino said, gesturing with a curled fist to the creature. "Though young, she is a fearless companion."

Kait slowly extended her hand. Samara sniffed it and nudged her palm with the side of her face. A warm smile felt foreign on Kait's lips as the doe greeted her. "It's lovely to meet you Samara, but I'm afraid I don't understand."

Enyo swished her cloak and brandished the lone tooth in her mouth. "You should know, aurai, that we don't often do this."

"No, we don't often do this at all," Pemphredo repeated.

"It is not the way of the Graeae to interfere with immortal business. We are not the Fates, but your predicament intrigues our curiosities. With a third of the triad dead and another reduced to a mortal existence, what is to become of the prophecy?"

"But Bia's soul isn't dead, and Jezlem already managed to kill Zeus—"

"See? Curious indeed."

Deino's low cackle drew Kait's attention back to her. "You've already proven to be a powerful force, child. One that is not easily dissuaded once her mind is set. We want to see how the events play out when you bring the gods' war to their doorstep. Samara will usher you to the Underworld and fight by your side for as long as she is able. She will by no means give you an advantage over the gods, but it's surprising how much strength you can draw upon when you're not alone."

Kait narrowed her gaze. "The gods' war? Between who? Will this involve all the immortals or only Hades and Hera?"

Enyo shook her head and sucked in her lips to emit a low growl. "It is not our place to reveal events that have not yet come to pass. Fool of a sister, you will do well to remember to hold your tongue, lest I sever it from your mouth."

Deino hunched and pulled her hood over her forehead to shade the eyeball from sight. Samara shook her head and grunted low in her throat. The tension between the three sisters was growing more palpable.

Pemphredo pushed Kait from behind, her bony hands sliding along the thin material across her back. Coldness seeped into the fabric from her touch, prompting Kait forward to escape the uncomfortable weight. Kait plunged her fingers into the leaf-strewn mane of the Ceryneian hind and leapt up, kicking her leg over to sit astride the animal's soft back.

"Be swift and silent in your travels," Pemphredo cautioned. "Find the cave at the end of the Acheron River. Play Hades's game, and let forgiveness into your heart. If you don't, it won't just be your sister's life that will be lost."

"Enough, Pemphredo." Enyo's harsh command sliced through the quiet realm.

Sensing time was running out, Kait bowed her head and gently fisted more of Samara's mane to secure her hold. "Thank you."

The Gray Sisters all turned their weathered faces toward Kait at the same time, five empty orbital sockets staring knowingly while the shared eye rolled. In unison, they spoke. "Horror. Alarm. Dread. Meet them all before you're dead." A cacophony of strained laughter reverberated off the nearby rocks and narrow trees. The wispy fog darkened and absorbed the Graeae's moth-eaten shrouds and gnarled frames. Chills ravaged Kait's exposed flesh as the wind raged. Beneath her, Samara quaked with a similar response and bent her legs into a crouch.

Kait held on, trying to keep her balance without pulling the doe's fur too hard. A moment later, the creature pushed off the wet earth, and the speed with which they lurched ahead was startling. In a single bound, the Graeae and the murky swamplands vanished far behind as the doe raced ahead, dodging trees and haphazard landscapes with ease. Gone was their eerie laughter and the eternal heaviness that seemed to hang over the deep swamplands.

A magnetic energy buzzed half a mile ahead as Samara carried her toward the portal. Kait lowered her upper half closer to the doe's back to help streamline them as much as possible. The familiar effect of the rushing current was so calming, she could hardly keep her eyes open. She settled the side of her face against Samara's velvety neck just below the jut of her antlers. Another leap placed them inches outside of the portal's reach, and the doe stepped inside the swirling pink tendrils without fear.

Kait envisioned the cool shallow waters of the Acheron River, and the portal blazed to life as it read her desired destination. The wind traced her skin and ran through her hair. Her element could tell she needed to sleep, but she couldn't give in, not yet. She didn't know how close the portal would deposit them, and she couldn't leave the doe to navigate blindly on her own.

The portal pulsed with energy, and the drab furnishings of Madik dissolved, replaced with a shimmering kaleidoscope of bold colors against a bright blue sky. The portal emptied onto the top of a rocky mountain where the hillside town of Parga, Greece, was stacked below before the mouth of the sparkling Ionian Sea.

Kait sighed and closed her eyes against the beautiful scenery. "To the river, Samara. Take us to Hades."

CHAPTER 24

Teeth and moans. Dripping blood and choked breaths. The images flickered faster, blurring together in a revolting mass of broken bones and strangled screams. A sob of her own escaped as Kait watched helplessly while the carnage broke out in wave after wave around her, but she couldn't move, couldn't fight. Suddenly, Bia's face materialized, shining with sweat and splattered with extra crimson freckles.

"I love you," Bia whispered just before a horde of infected nymphs reached for her.

"No!" Kait tried to grab her sister and shield her from the crazed bites, but the scene rushed away as she fell into the cold earthen prison. She woke with a start as the sensation of falling triggered her subconscious, and she sucked in a loud lungful of air. The image of a thousand hands tearing apart her sister's soft flesh shattered, replaced by the startling brightness of a jagged cliff rising to meet them.

Instinctively, Kait clutched her thighs and squeezed Samara's midsection harder than necessary as the doe navigated the steep decline of the mountainside. Kait scanned the sparse vegetation as they neared the final drop and was shocked to realize water—translucent as sea glass—sparkled mere feet from her. Without pausing her calculated stride, Samara trotted off and over the edge into the shallow current. A small avalanche of pebbles and loose dirt tumbled in their wake, followed by a deep plunk as both debris and the doe splashed into the slow-flowing current. Lukewarm waves sloshed up Kait's calves and over her thighs before her guide regained her footing atop the smooth submerged rocks that lined the riverbed.

Aquamarine water stretched ahead of them, framed by twin walls of carved stone, dotted with narrow trees. Green vegetation sprouted from crevices formed long ago. The river was warmer than Kait had expected, a rare treat given it was mid-January.

"Samara!" Kait exclaimed in wonder. "You found it, the Acheron River!"

The doe nodded her adorned head once and continued, taking a few sips from the clear fresh water that urged them onward.

"I'm sorry I fell asleep. I suppose it's been a while since I took a break."

The Ceryneian hind only increased her pace, but after supporting Kait's weight for so long, she no doubt needed a rest, as well.

"We can stop if you need to," Kait said, but the doe shook her mossy head and stepped through the stomach-high depths with a powerful stride. "Okay, suit yourself. Thank you for accompanying me. I know it couldn't have been your choice."

Samara gave a brief snort of amusement. Kait didn't have any knowledge of the relationship between the Graeae and the does. Were they able to order any creature to do their bidding, or were these gentle animals simply more sympathetic? Once she returned to Olean, she'd comb the library for more information. A cold shudder rippled through her frame—*if* she returned. Eternal death was a very real possibility, especially when she meant to challenge the lord of the Underworld.

On and on they walked, following the languid current round bend after bend. At last, the riverbed sloped and deepened.

Cool blue water swallowed the pair to their necks, and Kait abandoned her perch atop Samara's back to swim beside her. The doe swam just as gracefully as she ran and showed no signs of distress. That made one of them, at least. The moment the surface surged over her breasts, Kait's anxiety flared. The slow-moving river was a far cry from the middle of the ocean, but panic came nonetheless. Connected with the element of air, water was too heavy, too impenetrable to manipulate, and the memory of being tossed around in its unforgiving grip soured her stomach.

The current sped up like greedy hands pulling them faster. Kait flipped over and angled her head slightly to adopt a natural floating position. They rounded the last curve and came face-to-face with a thick wall of stone. Kait gasped. The dark gradation wove in the shape of a monstrous creature with numerous heads and countless teeth. The Hydra. Her lips whispered a silent prayer that the horrific beast stayed encased in its solid prison. Without Poseidon's blessing, she would've been shredded to ribbons.

"Brace yourself against the stone!" Kait's attention returned to the choppy waters. She'd expected the current to settle, but it was even stronger than before. Alarm flashed in Samara's wide brown eyes as Kait moved to her stomach and readied herself for the impact. They slammed against the white rocks a second later, but Samara floundered, unable to find a foothold with her hooves, and was yanked beneath the frothing surface. "No!"

Using the flat rock face to push herself under, Kait allowed the riptide to sweep her away. She kept her eyes open in the freshwater. A small burst of relief bloomed in her chest when she caught sight of Samara's dark form a few yards ahead. The current increased and dragged her exposed skin along the rough ceiling from the underside of the giant stone. Anxiety spiked again. They were beneath the mountain, rushing to an unknown destination. What if there wasn't an end to the submerged tunnel? The undertow was too strong; there would be no way to swim back the way they'd come.

A stream of air bubbled between Kait's pinched lips. If she died on the outskirts of the Underworld, would she still be able to enter before Gaia claimed her soul? Her limbs thrashed, knuckles scraping the jagged rock. At least she wasn't dead—yet.

The current rushed beneath the mountain and fled from the daylight, plunging into inky darkness and leaving Kait unable to anticipate any turns the river might make. Her gut lurched as she was suddenly shot out of the water. Once her face broke through the plane, she inhaled a large gasp of air, but before she could transform into the wind, her body somersaulted through the dark sky. The ground hastened to meet her. The air she'd just consumed was expelled from her lips as her chest slammed into the packed earth, stalling her momentum at last.

Ragged coughs rained from her mouth as Kait pushed herself onto her forearms. Her lungs burned, her fingers were bleeding, and her head ached with a possible concussion. Wet fur pressed into her bare shoulder, accompanied by the hard prodding of bone as Samara nudged her to her feet with her antlers. Kait stood and winced as a sharp pain pricked her side. She trailed her fingers gingerly down her torso, extracted the silver drachma from her pocket, and massaged the rib the small coin had wedged itself beneath upon her harsh landing.

"Samara, are you all right?" The roar of pounding water drowned out all other sounds as she shouted to be heard. The doe quivered slightly beside her,

her large eyes shining with fear. "I didn't realize the current would shift so quickly."

Kait glanced around at their new surroundings. They stood on a narrow bank to the left of a waterfall. Constant spray peppered the musty air. It was dark, save for a solitary lantern on the other side of the bank that balanced on a ledge of carved earth. The flame within danced, doing little to illuminate the vast space through the ash-stained glass.

Kait walked several feet ahead out of the waterfall's reach and toed the edge of the embankment. It seemed sturdy, but the image of its walls crumbling and dropping her back into the water forced her to step back. Away from the falls, the river was quite narrow, and in the dim glimmer, she could see the bottom of the shallow stream.

Casting a glance over her shoulder, Kait pointed to the lantern. "I'll go across and grab the light. Maybe we can follow this bank and see where it leads."

She moved toward the ledge once more and lifted her foot to enter the now calm current, but Samara bit the back of one of her gauzy straps to halt her progress.

"What's wrong? We can't just stand here," Kait said as the doe shook her mossy head. Samara pawed the ground and flexed her leg toward the darkness. Kait gasped as a sleek black boat appeared in the same shallow water she'd intended to cross, a shrouded figure at the helm.

CHAPTER 25

"Payment." The figure's voice rattled.

Kait squeezed the gifted drachma. Her fingers brushed the beveled edge as she deposited it into the ferryman's outstretched palm. His long bony fingers curled like talons around the silver piece before it vanished in a puff of acrid smoke.

"Board and I shall transport you to Asphodel Meadows," Charon stated.

Kait frowned. "That's not the destination I seek."

Charon cocked his head. The worn gray robe that enveloped his face showed nothing but a hollow black hole. Shivers prickled along Kait's exposed flesh as she wondered if the boatman had any features at all.

"It is not my place to take you to Elysium. That is for Rhadamanthus to decide—"

"I'm not dead, ferryman. I am an aurai, wind nymph of Olean. I have no intention of remaining in your master's realm, but it is with him I must speak. Take me to Hades."

A guttural snarl came from the recess of Charon's hood. "Souls have no power to make demands here."

Another wave of shivers raked her spine, but Kait held her chin higher. She couldn't back down or show weakness, but if she overstepped or insulted the ferryman, he may forsake her and leave them to wander the banks of the Styx for eternity.

"Please, sir. I paid for my passage. Why should the destination matter?"

A low hiss snaked between Charon's lips, but he moved aside, a silent signal for Kait to join him aboard the narrow vessel. With a steadying breath, she stepped off the shore into the gently rocking boat and sat down on a thin plank of wood that acted as a seat.

"Come on, Samara." Kait waved the doe forward, but Charon blocked the step with his oar.

"Passage was only paid for one soul."

Kait's eyes widened. "But the Graeae, they only gave me one drachma. It was meant to convey us both—"

"Only one." Charon pushed off from the bank with enough force to throw Kait from her seat.

Kait's hands shot out to grip the side of the boat to keep herself from plunging into the dark waters. On the shore, Samara tossed her mossy mane and pawed the earth, a forlorn moan echoing from her muzzle.

Kait reached for her, but Charon's icy grip clawed her shoulder and tossed her into the belly of the hull. "Don't touch the water."

"But my friend . . . I can't leave her here."

"Unless you've another drachma, there she stays."

Kait glanced up from her sprawled position on the floor and shuddered. In their scramble, Charon's hood had become askew and revealed a bald skull beneath. What little flesh remained on his bones was the color of curled parchment, and his onyx eyes reflected the rippling river like smooth buttons. His jaw was slightly crooked as if it had broken at one point in time and never properly healed, and the tip of his nose had been severed, creating an eerie orifice in the center of his face. Sagging skin hung off his neck like wrinkled fabric.

Kait couldn't tell for sure if he was dead. He certainly appeared to be more skeletal than human, but an eternity in a sunless tunnel, forced to row every soul from the banks of the Styx to the afterlife, was bound to deplete any healthy body.

With a grimace, Charon pinched the frayed material of the hood and dragged it back over his face. "Take a seat," he ordered.

"All right." Kait begrudgingly settled onto the plank as Charon steadied the rocking vessel. On the shore, Samara continued to watch them, her gaze heavy and pleading, but there was nothing Kait could do. She prayed to Gaia that Hades would extend an invitation for the doe to join her—if she even managed to speak with him. "I'm sorry," she whispered as she watched the Ceryneian hind shrink behind her until the boat rounded a corner and the sweet creature was lost from view altogether.

Charon guided the small ferry down the midnight-black river. With each push, his whole body hunched and coiled, only to then extend with great effort, as if the boat weighed an insurmountable amount and every row cost him all his strength.

"Would you like me to help?" Kait asked hesitantly.

Charon spat. "I told you, the dead have no power here."

"But I'm not dead. I told *you*, I'm a nymph. I came here to find my sister. Hades stole her soul, and I intend to reclaim it for Gaia."

Charon snickered. "Everyone here is dead. The living cannot cross. Styx won't allow it."

Kait furrowed her brow. "I'll show you, then." Twisting in her seat, she flexed her fingers and cast the air behind them to propel the boat forward with a large gust of wind, but the air was unresponsive. Again, she tried to call the element to her fingertips, but it continued to resist. In fact, she felt no connection at all. "I . . . I don't understand."

"You're dead, nymph."

"No, I'm not. We entered the Underworld through the Acheron River—"

"And sacrificed your life. You drowned, nymph. Both you and that horned beast you rode in with. The sooner you accept that, the easier the transition will be for you."

"Dead? No. I don't believe you. I'm not—" Kait lifted her hands to cast again, but this time her breath caught. The boat's warped wooden floorboards were visible through her transparent skin. "This is a trick." She interlocked her fingers and called the wind with more authority, but the air remained stagnant and still, adamant in its refusal. Despair pressed its fingers to her throat.

"There is no other way. You're dead, and unless you can change Lord Hades's mind, you're going to stay that way." The ferryman turned his full attention back to his labors. "Only the dead may enter."

Kait sat in silence for an indeterminable length of time as she struggled to comprehend Charon's statement. Death wasn't part of the plan. How could she barter for Bia's soul now?

The small vessel turned and forked to the right along the River Styx, as another river ran parallel to the left. Kait glanced away from her eerie hands and gazed at the opposite bank. She gasped. Thousands of souls wandered the dark shores. Some were hunched, sobbing into their hands, while others stood stoically at the edge, watching her with mixed emotions. Some stared with vacant expressions, while others spat curses in a dozen different languages.

Kait shrank from their hostility even though a hundred feet separated her from their sneering ghostly faces. "What are they all doing here?" she asked. "Are they waiting to be picked up?"

Charon hissed, never pausing his rowing. "Lost souls. Unfortunate folk who died alone, their bodies left to rot where they fell without a proper burial. As in life, they are doomed, condemned to walk along the river of lamentation. Be grateful for that silver, nymph; otherwise, you'd have been stuck amidst the Cocytus with the likes of them."

Kait swallowed roughly. "And there's nothing they can do to change their fate?"

The opening of Charon's hood rippled as he scoffed in reply. "They should have adopted some morals when they still had breath in their lungs and blood in their veins. Nothing but a hollow eternity awaits them now."

The ferryman pushed the boat along, following the serpentine curves of the Styx. Kait was grateful when the lost specters fell out of sight, but their whimpers and mournful wails still echoed off the jagged rocks. A new guilt gripped her. If she wasn't able to persuade Hades, would the kind doe be forced to wander aimlessly, as well? In her brief scan, she hadn't seen any animalistic souls, but their absence wasn't exactly reassuring. She liked to think they returned to a mother goddess, just as Gaia cared for fallen nymphs, but truthfully, she'd never considered it before, an oversight she deeply regretted now.

Kait turned over her shoulder. "What happens to animals' souls after death? Does Hades reign over them, too?"

Charon's arms stilled, and a tail of ripples fanned away from the wooden craft as he raised his pole from the inky depths. "Hush, nymph. Your silence will be your greatest ally."

Before Kait could ask what the ferryman meant, the boat jostled as it slid across shining opaque rocks at the edge of the Styx. Kait's fingernails dug into the worn wooden bench to steady herself. She tried to remember how long it'd taken to cross the river, but she was at a loss. Time didn't seem to exist in the land of the dead.

"Out you go," Charon said. "Don't let the water touch you."

Gripping the vessel, Kait fought to find her balance. She swung one leg over the side, followed by the other onto the dry stones. The hem of her pant leg dipped into the black waters, and an acrid smell sizzled upon contact. A sharp pain flared in Kait's skull, and a metallic bitterness coated her tongue.

Charon extended a skeletal finger and pointed toward the swirling smoke that coalesced into a quick shape. "A lion," he rasped. "Wrath is the sin that drives you, nymph. Be careful, for the purest intentions result in the darkest deeds."

Kait flicked the damp fabric away from the river's touch and dispelled the prophesized symbol. The moment the contact was severed, the harsh pain in her mind evaporated. She straightened and fixed Charon with a strong glare. "It's not a sin to seek vengeance."

Charon shook his head. The black void that concealed his features sent a wave of unease through her. "No, but the desire to fulfill that vengeance by any means necessary is."

"What do—"

The ferryman bowed his head. "Shhh, he approaches."

Hades.

Kait spun and grimaced as her feet slid on the slippery rocks that glistened like pupils. Gathering her wet curls away from her face, Kait took a deep breath and tried to appear composed. The sound of approaching footsteps, along with a rhythmic metallic clang, thundered off the towering boulders that stretched beyond the shore. Her gaze flickered from side to side, searching for her host, but only stone giants loomed, elongated shadows further darkening the land. A gruff snort erupted on Kait's left as a stream of warm breath blew the hair off her neck. Her eyes widened in fear.

The figure standing before her had a thick muscled hide the color of mud, stretching from narrow hips to wide shoulders. Cords of scar tissue crisscrossed over the creature's neck and cheek. While its head consisted of sharp angles and shadows, its temples curved in a graceful arch into two gleaming black horns. The body of a man and the head of a bull.

Kait held her breath as the powerful Minotaur glared at her with scarlet eyes. Held in its grasp was a menacing silver scythe. The Minotaur dragged it closer across the stones, replicating the same shrill pitch as before. She looked at the lethal blade. It seemed to smile.

"Has death stolen your sense as well as your flesh? What is the meaning of this? Souls with proper payment are to only be taken to Asphodel Meadows. Has an eternity of manual labor taught you nothing? How dare you deliver this to these shores?" the Minotaur spat, its voice low and gravelly. Kait could barely make out the words, but the tone was unmistakable.

"Many apologies," the ferryman replied. "This soul is not like the others. She demanded to speak with Lord Hades."

"And you obliged? Pray Hades doesn't curse you to the banks of the Cocytus with the other wastes of life for this. Back to your post, ferryman!"

Charon bent his head, quickly buried the oar beneath the inky waves, and shoved the small craft away from the shore.

"It was my fault. I didn't want to leave my guide behind—"

"Silence," the Minotaur said. "You do not speak here."

"But I'm looking for Hades."

White smoke exhaled from the Minotaur's nostrils as he leveled the scythe's teeth at Kait's neck. "I said, you do not speak here. You are a soul, nothing more. Open your mouth again, and I will guarantee you never reach Elysium." Kait set her lips in a firm line, unwilling to test the Minotaur's threat. "This way, and keep up."

Unable to do anything else, Kait followed the hulking creature up the mountain. The path they hiked was narrow and steep, and she found herself practically running to keep the Minotaur in sight.

They stopped sometime later, and Kait nearly fainted with exhaustion. She'd grown queasy and light-headed as the strange atmosphere toyed with her vision. Her warden pressed his palm against a well-worn stone to unveil a hidden stairway that curved higher into the blackness.

Kait groaned. Her calves burned with strain. "How much farther?" she asked before she could stop herself.

The Minotaur glared, eyes burning coals, but pointed the silver scythe skyward. "*That* is our goal."

Kait looked straight above. A charcoal dome hung suspended from the cavern ceiling like a crumbling chandelier. She could just make out dull candlelight flickering through the gaps in the stone, transforming the massive stalactite into an eerie skull. Not for the first time, she wished she could gather the wind and ascend the great height, but for now, she'd have to continue to climb.

"Come. We don't stop until we reach the top," the Minotaur barked.

Bright pain jolted Kait awake, slicing through the sudden blackness. She was no longer walking. Instead, she realized with a sick feeling, the Minotaur was dragging her behind him with little regard for the trauma to her body. She tried to pull her hand from his grasp, but her arm had fallen asleep and remained unresponsive. She cocked her head downward and saw the source of her pain. Her pants were ripped, both her knees bloodied and raw as the Minotaur yanked her over the sharp gravel.

"Put me down," Kait demanded, but her voice was only a ragged whisper.

The Minotaur continued forward and jerked her arm so hard it felt as if the bone separated from the socket. She opened her mouth to speak again, but before she could form the words, the Minotaur dropped her weight onto the unforgiving rock path. Her molars bounced off the sides of her tongue, and blood filled her mouth.

"You have a visitor, Your Grace," the Minotaur growled, his deep voice full of reverence.

Kait lifted her head and brushed sweat and blood from her upper lip. Had they finally reached Hades? She knew she should stand to greet the lord of the Underworld, but she was too weak to do much more than hold her head up. Outside her line of vision, she sensed a new figure approach.

"A visitor? Me? That's highly unlikely, but ah, here she is. Is she dead?" The clear voice sounded slightly amused. "I mean, besides the obvious."

"The soul passed out halfway up the mountain, your Grace, but it regained consciousness just as we arrived."

"I see, and why is she so filthy?"

"I dragged it up the mountain, Your Grace."

"Ah, that would do it. Well, bring her in, I suppose. *Gently.* Looks like she's been to hell and back, but she's only just arrived." A smooth chuckle accompanied the sound of retreating footsteps.

Kait shook her head, but the Minotaur ignored her. Scooping her into his arms, he cradled her to his chest, much like how a father would soothe a frightened child. Carefully, he set her down on her feet and didn't remove his hands until she regained her balance.

"Thanks," Kait muttered.

The Minotaur grunted in reply and gripped his scythe, leaving her alone and exposed to face a new threat. From the corner of her eye, she watched as he marched to the side of the room and stood at attention.

"Welcome, welcome. I realize it can be a bit taxing, traveling all the way up here."

Kait's eyes quickly adjusted to the soft candlelight and alighted on a tall figure standing in front of a table carved from white bone. He was clad in dark skinny jeans, polished shoes, and a charcoal gray T-shirt underneath a crisp black jacket. His complexion was pale, appearing even more so beneath a gelled mop of black hair and slender eyebrows.

"Hades?"

"In the flesh." Hades smirked and bowed at the waist. "Pleasure to meet you. It's not often a pure nymph soul washes up on my shores."

"It was not by accident, I assure you," Kait stated. She looked down at her ruined jumpsuit and battered body. "He didn't have to drag me. I was making my way just fine on my own."

Hades shrugged. "You probably were for a bit, but Asterion said you fell unconscious. Don't be embarrassed. Everyone does. It's the air down here. Rather toxic. A feature I designed myself. You see, when I left Mount Olympus to rule the dead, I didn't exactly leave on good terms. So, I designed a few tricks to ensure no one—save for my servants and me—can pass safely through the Underworld. But enough of that. I want to know about you. Why are you here? Or, I suppose a better question is, how?"

Kait raised her chin. "I'm an aurai from Olean. The Graeae gave me the location of the entrance to the Underworld, along with a drachma to pay the ferryman. My guide and I came through the Acheron River to speak with you. My name is Kaitaini."

A small wrinkle of concentration formed in the center of Hades's forehead. "Kaitaini," he repeated. "That's a mouthful, isn't it? You must go by Kait, then?" At her acknowledging nod, his lips curled in a smile. "My, how the plot thickens."

"Sorry?"

Hades waved his hand in front of his face. "Doesn't matter. So, my dear, to what do I owe the pleasure of your company? To find the Graeae in the first place, you must have truly enticed them." His high cheekbones stood out sharply as his jaw tensed. "Especially for them to reveal such a guarded secret."

Kait gritted her teeth at his thinly veiled aggression. "It was earned."

Hades cradled his chin in his hand while his pale gray eyes assessed her, and his pointer finger tapped his flawless complexion. The lord of the Underworld was nothing like Kait had expected. Hades pulsed with manic energy, too wired to sit still, but yet, he was a businessman, calculating as he attempted to anticipate his prey's next move.

Kait cleared her throat and strode forward. "No doubt you're aware of the recent attack on Olean. A deadly infection was conjured and released throughout the ethereal realms. My sister Bia was one of the fallen."

"Oh, sorry to hear that. What a devastating loss." Hades sighed without conviction. "But you must know the departed souls of your kind don't belong to me. Gaia has claim."

"Typically, that is the case, yes. However, during her soul's ascension, a dark shadow captured my sister and plummeted into the earth. I can only assume it was acting on a direct ordinance from you," Kait stated, daring him to look away. Rage bloomed in her gut, and a surge of heat rolled down her frame. For a moment, the powerful response caught her off guard. She flexed her fists, fighting to regain her composure.

Hades put up his hands. "Alas, I know nothing of this. To take the soul of a nymph would pit me against Gaia, and as a result, all of Mount Olympus. I'm not looking to start a war at the moment."

Kait was quiet as she considered the god's response. "So, apart from me, there are no other nymph souls presently in the Underworld?"

Hades arched his eyebrows. "Why? You don't believe me?"

"No, I don't," Kait replied with a crisp snarl. "Has my sister been returned to Gaia, or is she still here?"

Hades's charming smile faltered before the mask slipped back into place. A dangerous chuckle shook his chest. "What do you want, nymph?"

Kait crossed the remaining distance between them and stopped in front of the god. "I want to make a trade. I don't need to know why you took her or the reasons behind your involvement, but I want you to release my sister. Return her to Gaia so her soul can be shepherded to a new life."

"I see." Hades smirked. "And what do I get in exchange?"

"Me."

"You?" Hades chortled. "As what? My personal slave? Darling, look around you. I have hundreds of mindless helots. Why would I need you?"

Revulsion boiled in the back of Kait's throat, but her future was already sealed. If it would save Bia, she would do whatever was necessary. "Persephone is readying to depart for spring," Kait whispered. "You'll be lonely down here until she returns." She took a step closer and pressed her body against the god's relaxed posture. "I know you've heard my name. I know you recognize it. Did Zeus tell you how soft my skin is? Did he tell you how I refused him? I wouldn't refuse you, my lord." The words were bile on her tongue, but she fought to keep her face serene.

Hades brought his hand up and cupped the swell of her breast, running his thumb along the gentle curve. "That is a tempting offer, my dear, but why pay for something I already have?" he whispered, his voice rough in her ear.

Kait jerked out from under the god's touch as confusion contorted her features. "What do you mean?"

Hades shrugged. "Simply that you already belong to me. You're dead. You're already mine." His eyes glistened like cooling coals and hardened to rock. He raised his hand as if to rub her again, but she slapped it away.

"There she is." Hades growled playfully. "The vixen I've heard so much about. Did you really think you could come down here, dangle yourself in front of me, and assume I'd give you whatever you wanted? You're beautiful, but stupid."

"Then what do you want? If my soul isn't enough, what can I give you to release my sister?"

Hades straightened out of his casual stance and fixed his jacket. "*Your* soul may not suffice, but there is one that will." He strolled toward the large balcony that overlooked the expanse of his bleak kingdom.

Careful to keep her distance, Kait joined him. "Who do you want?"

Keeping his eyes on the black river below, Hades's lip curled. "Hera."

"Hera?" Kait coughed in surprise. "But I thought you were working together. I saw her familiar during the attack."

Hades put up a hand to silence her. "When my brother's body perished, I knew Hera would seek revenge. I'd hoped she would be stealthy and singular, but it seems she's made it her mission to eradicate your entire race. As I said before, I don't want to start a war, but war is coming nonetheless."

"War between who?"

Hades took a deep breath. "An attack like the one Hera orchestrated on the lower realms cannot and will not go unnoticed nor, more importantly, unpunished by the Council. Power is about checks and balances, and Hera's rage has made her blind. She's wild and unpredictable, someone I'd rather not take on as an ally."

"I don't understand. You took my sister's soul. You're already helping her."

Hades sighed. "Yes. She came to me weeks ago with a proposition I couldn't refuse. I may have prevented your sister from ascending, but that doesn't matter in the grand scheme of things."

"Of course, it does! She's dead because of Hera. She did this. She's the one who deserves to die. Not Bia!"

"I couldn't agree more."

"Then, why do all this?" Kait asked, exhausted by the revolving conversation.

"Because we must learn to walk before we can run, my dear." Hades fixed her with a wicked grin.

Kait narrowed her eyes. "What must I do?"

Hades's grin turned her stomach. He had her, and he knew it. "I require Hera's soul. Use your imagination, sweetheart." He spun away from the balcony with a flourish.

"Kill her? You want me to kill, Hera? Isn't there another way? You're the master of death. Do it yourself." The words lashed out before she could help herself. All she felt was wrath and fury.

Hades bent over the desk, poring over large pieces of parchment. "My gracious, you really are a stupid creature. Did Gaia gift you *any* intelligence or just that beautiful face?"

Kait left the balcony and slammed her palms on the desk's cool surface. "Look, I came here for my sister. I'm not going to Mount Olympus because you're too scared to leave your rotting dungeon."

A gruff snort echoed from the corner as Asterion charged and brandished his scythe. Keeping his eyes on the papers before him, Hades held up his hand to calm the Minotaur. Slowly, his slate-gray eyes darkened.

The god of death faced Kait. His features subtly shifted. Gone was the charming gentleman. Thick noxious fog emanated from Hades's palms and slithered over the sleek concrete to where she stood. It wrapped around her ankles and bit her calves. The moment the fog brushed her skin, Kait was rendered incapacitated. Her vision turned milky, and her tongue was stitched to the top of her mouth. All she could do was listen as Hades slunk in front of her and gripped her jaw tightly in his fist.

"Scared? You think I'm scared?" Hades hissed. "You forget where you are. Forget who I am. Forget what I will do to you. You think you can come down here and rely on your beauty to keep you safe?" He circled, scoffing at her thin wardrobe and supple skin. "I know what my brother did to you. I know what he desired to do had he the chance. That's not my style. I have no interest in tasting your flesh. My passion lies elsewhere. I get to know my lovers. Such as, how many bones can I break before they plead for mercy? What do their screams sound like? To what length will they go to preserve their life? Yes, I am the master of death, and if you ever challenge me again, you will find out *exactly* what that means. Very, very slowly."

Without another word, Hades released her jaw, and the fog evaporated. Chilling shivers raked Kait's bare skin, sending icy pinpricks deep into her bones. She took a shaky breath and lowered her eyes. The seething rage that had compelled her before evaporated. "I apologize, my lord. I don't know what came over me."

Hades grunted. "Well, that's a start, but your impudence is not forgiven. Don't fall prey to the land of the dead. Remember the air toxins? They seep into the body and pull your greatest sin to the surface. A final test before a soul reaches Elysium. Now . . ." He leaned casually against the desk once more. "Shall we continue where we left off?"

Kait nodded. Never had she behaved with such impudence, especially before an immortal, but she was glad there was an explanation. She thought back to the image of the lion the Styx had conjured upon touching her, along with Charon's warning. Wrath would indeed be her undoing.

"Wonderful." His eyes narrowed to slits as he regarded her meek behavior. "As I said before, I require Hera's soul. Because she's immortal, her soul cannot perish, but as you learned when you murdered my brother, her body can."

"Yes, my lord. I understand. However, there is one foreseeable problem."

"Which is?"

"Hera hates me. You saw yourself what she orchestrated in her quest to hurt me. If I show up at her door, she'll kill me on the spot. There's a chance I can wait until she leaves her residence, but I don't know Mount Olympus, and surely word of my presence will spread."

Hades smiled. "Yes, but you underestimate my sister-in-law's vanity. If you appear before her, begging for forgiveness and praising her intelligence, she may spare you."

"And if she doesn't? If she kills me on the spot? Will you let Bia's soul go free?"

"No." Hades scowled. "If you die, then I will find another way to collect Hera's soul. There's no reward for failure."

Kait knew it was pointless to argue, especially with the volatile god. "Fine. We have a deal. If I succeed in destroying Hera's body, you'll let my sister's soul return to Gaia." She held out her hand and frowned again at the transparency of it.

Hades leaned forward and clasped her hand in his cold ivory skin. "Deal."

CHAPTER 26

"Asterion, bring the lesser soul that accompanied our guest to me, please. They will be leaving shortly," Hades instructed.

The Minotaur nodded in acknowldgement and left the grand room. Kait looked at Hades with questions in her eyes. "Do you have a portal into Olympus?" she asked.

"No. I like my privacy, remember?" Hades said with a smirk.

"Then, how am I to get there? Nymphs are forbidden to enter unless escorted—"

"My dear, I am well aware of the tight restrictions around the ethereal palace. Lucky for you, I happen to know someone who was just about to ascend." Hades's eyes sparked with amusement.

Kait went cold. "Who?"

Hades chuckled and took a seat behind the desk. "I believe you know each other. As I recall, you helped send him to me."

Kait sucked in her breath as a broad figure strode calmly from the shadows. She kept her gaze on Hades but felt the weight of another set of eyes on her back, stroking her bare flesh as if his hands had never left.

"Kaitaini," Hades said. "You remember my brother, Zeus."

Kait set her lips in a firm line and steeled her jaw, forcing herself to swallow the thickening lump that had suddenly taken up residence in the back of her throat. The sound of Zeus's footsteps made her cringe, and the hair on the back of her neck rose like a frightened cat's. All that time waiting in the dark, chained and tethered like an abused animal, flooded through the wall she'd tried to thrust the memories behind. She remembered the feel of his fingers grazing her thighs. The way the skin had split when he cut his knuckles on her teeth. How his wild laughter provided an eerie soundtrack to his psychological butchery.

Zeus had held her hostage for days after chasing her across the ethereal realms. All part of the twisted cat-and-mouse game he'd challenged Blake to play to prove he was a hero. Of course, Zeus had never counted on Kait's sisters joining the fight or being murdered by their rage.

Zeus paused an inch away. Kait noted with revulsion that their arms were a hairsbreadth from touching. She attempted to calm her racing heart, but every fiber of her being screamed to flee. Zeus was a monster, a sadistic savage beneath a golden façade. The memory of his tongue forcing its way between her lips caused her stomach to flip, and vomit burned in the back of her throat. The heavy scent of him permeated their shared space and ignited a dozen more memories. It was too much.

"Please, my lord," Kait said. "There must be another way to reach the heavens. My doe is strong."

"Yes, but going up is much harder than going down, isn't it?" Hades answered. "Besides, this will be a wonderful opportunity for the two of you to kiss and make up, as they say."

"Hades, please." Kait took a few agitated steps away from Zeus. "I can't."

"I was under the impression that you came to me seeking *my* help. I offered you a solution, yet you scorn my aid. Tell me, nymph, do you wish to see your sister again?"

Kait bit her lip. "Of course, but—"

"But her soul isn't worth a few unpleasant hours?"

"Of course, it is, but—"

"Then, it's settled. You will accompany Zeus back to Mount Olympus, posing as whatever tart he's chosen as the flavor of the week. Now, word has gotten around about your death, brother, so you won't be able to return as yourself. Understood?" Hades asked, directing his last question toward Zeus.

Zeus cleared his throat and stepped forward, realigning himself with Kait. "Yes. We can darken my hair and change a few other features. I'll be no different than the lower immortals seeking favor with the greats."

"Excellent, and steer clear of the South End. Rumor has it, one of your sons helped create this vicious disease. Wouldn't want him running off to Mommy and spilling the beans that Daddy's back from the grave early." Hades arched his eyebrows.

Unable to stop herself, Kait glanced at Zeus for the first time. No longer was he a pallid corpse cooling in a pool of blood and ichor. Hades had restored him to his opulent state of grandeur once more. He'd even recreated the muscular arms that had bashed her against rough stones, along with the long fingers that had forced their way inside her.

Kait looked into Zeus's cold blue eyes and pushed away the terror that tickled her spine. "Hera doesn't know you're going back?"

Zeus's eyes wandered appreciatively down the length of her frame. "Not currently," he answered, his voice gruff and husky. "She is aware my soul is here; however, that's where her knowledge ends, and it will remain that way until I say so."

"She killed my sister out of revenge. Revenge for you. Yet here you sit, hiding out until you feel like returning?" Kait spat, bristling with anger. "Hundreds of nymphs died because of you, because of your cowardice."

"Easy, nymph," Hades warned, but his words fell on deaf ears.

Kait stared at Zeus, her fluttering heart beating steadier with every breath as her body burned with fury once more. "You want her dead, too, don't you? You may think you have the freedom to go wherever you want, seduce whoever you desire, but in the end, she's always waiting, calling you back. You're not free, and you never will be as long as she's alive. You're nothing more than a child throwing a tantrum."

Zeus's fist lashed out, attempting to close around Kait's throat, but his hand passed through her.

Hades chortled. "You didn't think I'd be foolish enough to let you within twenty feet of a female with your reputation, did you?"

"Enough magic tricks, brother," Zeus bellowed. "Did you hear what she said to me?"

"I heard," Hades said. "And she's right, too, but that doesn't mean it's appropriate to voice." The god turned to Kait and cocked his head. "Now, for your trip through Tartarus, I suggest returning you both back to your physical forms. You may find it comforting to have something solid to cling to when the nightmares swarm."

Kait balked at the ludicrous suggestion. If Zeus were to touch her again, not even Hades's threats could silence her screams. "No. Absolutely not."

Hades sighed and rubbed his temple. "If I send you in there in your current incorporeal state, you will go mad."

Kait ground her teeth. "I'll be fine."

Zeus crossed his arms. "You seem to be lacking that team spirit you shared with your sisters. I'm not sure I want to travel the bowels of hell with someone who will desert me the first chance they get."

Kait stalked closer to the arrogant immortal and spoke through clenched teeth. "That's where you're wrong. I won't just leave you. I'll break your legs and shatter your arms so you won't be able to even drag yourself after me."

Hades stepped between them and pushed them apart with an amused chuckle. "Now, now. That's enough. Frankly, I don't care what you do to each other, as long as I get Hera's soul in the end. If you want to remain intangible, fine, but if you can't work together and learn to rely on one another, you're never getting out. Do you understand?"

Both Kait and Zeus remained silent.

"Can you handle this? Or should I give your sister's soul to the hellhounds once they're finished with my lumbering brother?"

"Fine. If it will help us get out of here faster, return our physical forms," Kait growled. "But if you touch me, I'll bite your tongue off . . . again." She pointed a finger at Zeus over Hades's shoulder.

Zeus scowled. "Fine."

"Gods, I feel like an overworked parent," Hades complained, rolling his eyes. "Both of you, control your tempers and keep your hands to yourself until you reach Olympus. Agreed?"

Kait nodded once. Zeus exhaled loudly.

Hades leveled them with a look just as the Minotaur returned with Samara. "Perfect timing, Asterion. Friends, it's time to go."

A short while later, Kait sat astride Samara with her eyes trained straight ahead. Behind her, a newly changed Zeus mounted. Hades had altered his piercing blue eyes to a muddy brown, the same shade as his newly dulled locks, and much to Zeus's chagrin, he'd decreased his muscle mass, too, so he wouldn't stand out like the hulking figure he was.

Kait stiffened as Zeus settled into place, and her fingers tensed into claws. Zeus's torso and groin rubbed against her. "Sorry," he muttered, separating himself from her as much as possible in the limited space. Surprise widened Kait's eyes. She'd never known the god to apologize. Maybe he'd taken Hades's threat to heart.

"Now, when you enter the abyss, don't stop, no matter what you see or hear. The tunnel is designed to lead wandering souls astray should they ever get it in their heads that they can leave this place." Hades scoffed. "At the very bottom, there is a portal to the heavens. It is the only way out of the Underworld. So please, try not to get lost, or I'll send Cerberus to find you." His thin lips curled, reflecting how much he'd enjoy watching the great beast bring them back in pieces.

Kait narrowed her eyes. "You said you didn't have a portal."

"I say a lot of things, my dear," Hades replied. He directed his attention to his brother. "Remember, when you get there, lay low. With any luck, our little nymph here will be able to perform her part of the bargain sooner rather than later."

"And then you'll send for me?" Zeus asked.

"Not now, brother." His eyes flashed a warning. The dark god clapped his hands together and took a step closer to the trio. Without a word, he pressed his palm to their chests, one at a time. As his skin met theirs, a silver flame sparked.

"What's this?" Kait asked, unable to touch the dancing spot.

"Your life force," Hades explained. "Only the dead may travel through my realm, but if you clear the abyss, your souls will be restored and the stain of death shall leave you."

Kait nodded, eyeing the silver flame. Would it be that easy for Hades to bring Bia back to life? "Let's go."

Hades stepped back and grinned, offering a small wave. "Have fun. Asterion will show you out." He spun away and called over his shoulder. "Do try *not* to fail."

Threading her fists into Samara's soft fur, Kait squeezed her thighs and urged the doe onward, ignoring Hades's last jest. The doe hesitated, then reluctantly followed the Minotaur down a different path than the one they'd entered on. As they descended the steep mountainside, Zeus slid forward, eliminating the narrow buffer he'd maintained in his brother's presence, but no one was watching now.

"This brings back memories," Zeus whispered, his voice hot in her ear. Kait stared ahead, refusing to bring attention to the way her skin prickled. "You're lucky we're dead. The things I would do to you." He chuckled, amused by the way she jerked her neck out from under his lips. "Funny, isn't it? You helped kill me, yet I don't think I've ever desired you more."

"That's because you're a disgusting vile cockroach."

Zeus laughed, and the deep sound vibrated in his chest. "True, but what luck I have running into you. I have an idea. Rather than going to Olympus and offering yourself to Hera like a sacrificial lamb, why don't we run away? Everyone believes us to be dead. You'd be free from judgment."

"What are you talking about?"

"Come on. I know the only reason you resisted me before was because you were worried what the others would say, what they would call you," Zeus said. "But now, it's just me. We can do what we want." He wrapped his arms around her, but Kait was ready. As his fingers grazed her collarbone, she slammed her elbow back and caught the god in the teeth.

"Gods!" Zeus cried, pressing the back of his hand to his mouth.

Kait glanced back and frowned, disappointed by the lack of blood. "Get this through your thick skull. I don't want anything to do with you, then or now. I came down here to save my sister, not reunite with you. If you touch me again, I'll spear you through the head."

"So, that's a no, then?"

"Our partnership is born of necessity, not choice, you despicable pig. If you try anything, the moment I find Hera, I'll tell her you never had any intention of returning to her and exactly how she can find you."

"Okay." Zeus slid away from her and gingerly probed his front teeth with his tongue.

"Are you finished?" Asterion asked. "Or would you like to find your own way out?"

Kait was silent. She disliked the Minotaur seeing her vulnerable. Her body quivered with disgust, and her breaths were rapid and shallow. It was too much. She'd agreed because Hades warned it was the only way to save Bia, but to force her to work alongside her enemy was beyond cruel.

"This is the entrance to Tartarus." Asterion gestured with his scythe. "An endless prison for truly wicked souls. Listen to what my Lord Hades has told you, and follow it to the end."

Terror sparked in her gut as she gazed into the gaping black hole. "How do we find the exit?" Kait asked.

"I've shared that information with your creature," Asterion answered firmly.

"You don't want to join us? With you as our guide, we'd be out of your hair much faster," Zeus joked, but underneath his casual tone, Kait sensed his anxiety. Tartarus was the epitome of hell. Even the gods were terrified of the monsters that lurked within.

The Minotaur paused and stared at all three in turn. "I don't belong in there." Goosebumps raked Kait's spine. "Pay attention, and don't wander or you'll never get out."

"Thank you," Kait whispered. She broke the Minotaur's stern gaze, unsure what else to say. Asterion inclined his head toward the entrance. She leaned forward and stroked the soft fur of Samara's neck. "Let's go, friend." Behind her, she heard a slight intake of breath as Zeus stiffened. She was terrified but pictured her sister's face. Somewhere down here, Bia was alone and smothered by darkness.

Beside them, Asterion beat his scythe three times and watched with hooded eyes as they edged closer to the entrance of Tartarus. The temperature dropped as inky folds enveloped the trio. A minute later, Kait was blind, her senses held captive by the stifling black.

"What do we do now?" Zeus asked, his question barely audible.

"We trust," Kait answered. "We trust Samara to carry us through."

"Right. We trust my brother didn't just hand us our own rope."

"Quiet."

Kait looked back. Asterion had been completely extinguished. She took a steadying breath and knotted her hands in the doe's warm fur until the animal groaned in distress. "Sorry, Samara." She relaxed her grip. "How long until we reach the end?" She wanted to have faith in their guide, but as they marched farther into the blackness, fear crested like an eager wave. The doe didn't reply, but her hooves kept a reassuring rhythm.

Kait had never experienced true darkness before. An hour or so into the journey, a memory of Madik bloomed in her mind. "Samara, what about the wisps of light I saw your herd release when I met the Gray Sisters?" Kait tried to keep her voice level, but the choking cloud of hysteria was closing in. She knew the journey through Tartarus wasn't going to be easy, but to complete it in total darkness was an unexpected sort of torture.

The doe gave a soft moan that conveyed a negative response. It made sense that if Kait's powers were incapacitated, the Ceryneian hind's abilities would be restricted, as well.

"What's the matter, Kait? Afraid of the dark?" Zeus asked with a snicker.

The sound of her name in his mouth made her cringe, and she arched her body farther from his touch. "Yes, and you'd be a fool if you weren't. We're in the realm of savage monsters, but I suppose that's why you feel right at home."

Zeus said something under his breath.

"What?" she asked, annoyed.

"I said, I'm not the only god to chase euphoria."

Kait's mouth hung agape. "So, rape is okay because you're not the only guilty one?"

"It wasn't like that with the nymphs I attained euphoria from. They succumbed willingly. It was only you and your sister who refused."

Rage boiled in Kait's veins as she recalled the powerful substance Zeus had slipped her sister, the same substance Hermes had mixed into her drink all those years ago. "Just because you bewitched their minds doesn't mean they gave up their halos voluntarily. You drugged them, and when Jez revealed your scheme and refused you, you chained her up with those electrical bonds until you were finished."

"That's not—"

"And Layla? I watched you rape her in the mountains, even though she couldn't give you the high you craved. She begged for you to stop, but the pleas of women mean little to you. You're nothing more than a beast trying to compensate for a small—"

Zeus's large hand fisted around Kait's throat, squeezing hard enough to cut off her words and her breath. He brought his face up close as his words slithered down the shell of her ear. "And you're nothing more than a mound of blood and dirt, created for the sole purpose of pleasuring the gods. Let Gaia brainwash you into believing you're meant to bring balance to nature or whatever bullshit story she spins, but the truth is, you're cattle, and I'm sick of being labeled a monster for taking something that's rightfully mine."

The god snarled and palmed the curve of her backside with his free hand as his wet lips pressed against the side of her neck. Panic flared in Kait's mind, and her body reacted before conscious thought could process the god's attack. Wrenching her weight to the right, she threw both of them off Samara's back as a shrill scream climbed her throat. They landed with a heavy smack against the jagged stone path, but the surprise maneuver succeeded in disengaging Zeus's hands from her person.

Zeus groaned. Kait didn't hesitate. Pushing up from the ground, she pinpointed where the god lay and unleashed a fury of kicks at his face. Her foot connected with a solid object that felt like the side of his skull, and Zeus's responding gasp only cemented her fury. Again and again, she lashed out, kicking and stomping in wild arcs. For the most part, she missed, but the god's pained grunts reassured her she was inflicting some damage, at least. The dark was infuriating, but for the moment, Kait didn't need the light. The blackness had transformed into crimson stars behind her eyes.

Samara pounded the ground beside her, reacting to the sudden surge of activity and rage. Kait felt her broad body brush against her, but she refused to be distracted, to be calmed. She needed to expel this, needed the god to understand how his actions affected her. Kait brought her foot up again and slammed her heel into Zeus's chin as a feral roar exploded from her mouth.

"I hate you! I hate you!" Kait cried. This time, she felt Zeus's palms attempt to bat her advances away, but she stepped back and aimed her assault lower, smashing against his vulnerable ribs. "I can't close my eyes without seeing your face, without feeling your breath on the back of my neck! You're a hideous fiend who deserves to rot in this hole alone for the rest of your miserable eternity!"

Kait spun and clung to Samara's fur, swinging her legs over the doe's back. "Run, Samara, run!" The doe emitted agitated whinnies but quickly obeyed the command.

From behind, Zeus cried. "No! Please don't do this! No!"

Kait squeezed her thighs harder, urging the doe to race as fast as she could through the darkness. She didn't care if abandoning Zeus would make her entrance into Mount Olympus more challenging, she'd find another way. It was worth it to hear the god's pitiful cries. Now, he might understand the helplessness his victims felt beneath him.

The pair raced through the dark. Kait didn't care if they were headed in the right direction; the only thing that mattered was that she put as much distance between herself and the god as possible. Zeus's cries echoed behind her as they fled. She prayed one of the beasts of Tartarus would find him. A surge of vengeance coursed through her as she pictured him being ripped apart. The monster deserved it.

After about fifteen minutes of hard running, Samara began to slow, but with the doe's goddess-blessed speed and long strides, Kait calculated they'd left Zeus miles behind. "Thank you, Samara." Kait sighed as the tightness in her chest relaxed. "Let's see him catch up to us now."

The doe chirped low in response, sounding nervous.

"We'll figure out how to ascend without him. Hades has a portal, after all. It should transport us directly to the gates of Olympus. Besides, you're the only one of the three of us who knows how to navigate to the end of this cursed realm. We don't need him."

Kait's words coursed with power. She'd stood up to her abuser once again and emerged victorious. She hoped he was still lying there too frightened to move, resigned to his fate. He deserved every second.

Samara chortled in agreement and slowed her pace. Kait expelled an anxious breath between her lips in a long stream. She closed her eyes and leaned against the doe's warm back as her lips twitched into a small grin. It was strange that deep in the bowels of Tartarus, she felt the most comfortable she had since entering the Underworld.

Samara grunted to capture Kait's attention, and her eyelids fluttered open. "What is it?" She glanced at the peaks and silent stretch of mountains that lay before them. "Did you hear some—"

Kait's jaw dropped at the sudden change. She could see! Gone was the thick blackness. Instead, the sky had lightened several shades to a thunder gray. It was still dark, but nothing like before.

"What happened?"

Samara only grunted again, seemingly just as surprised by the welcome change. Kait scanned the expansive scenery that stretched endlessly around them. The wide path they traversed was similar to the rocky lane the Minotaur had dragged her up. The pointed rocks made it impossible to see more than a few yards ahead, but at least now they had the small luxury of sight. Kait had no idea why they'd been blessed with this unexpected comfort, but she hoped it paved the way for good fortune for the rest of her journey.

CHAPTER 27

Days, maybe even a week had passed since they left Zeus behind, and the sky grew an infinitesimal shade more hopeful. Kait had yet to become accustomed to the way her body sat quietly. Her stomach didn't groan for nutrition; her bladder didn't demand to be relieved; not even her throat pleaded for water.

It was jarring to be dead, to be a soul able to see, hear, and speak without being plagued by normal needs. Kait supposed it made traveling easier. Being more essence than flesh, her mind didn't crave sleep either, but it was the only reprieve she had. She allowed the doe to set their pace, worried that if she pushed her too hard or too far, she might refuse to go another step.

When they weren't resting, between asking the Ceryneian hind about her family and the intricacies of her daily life, Kait told Samara about Olean and her sisters. Talking helped to stay sane. After so many days surrounded by towers of identical stones, she decided it was no wonder Tartarus had earned the reputation of a hellish abyss. Kait trusted the doe, but there was no way to know for sure if they were getting any closer to their destination.

Kait rubbed her eyes with the heels of her hands and squeezed her thighs, a silent gesture for Samara to pause. "Hang on. My eyes are probably playing tricks on me, but doesn't this place look familiar?"

Samara studied the landscape as the tendrils of her mossy mane swept Kait's legs. The doe chirped but didn't sound as if she shared Kait's suspicions. Rocks were rocks, after all; how much of a variation could there be? Yet, something in the pit of her stomach kept her rooted in place. She didn't know if it was the sweep of the stones' angles or the wide curve of the path, but she knew deep in her bones that they'd passed this way before.

"Was there a fork in the path? Maybe we went the wrong way and somehow circled back?"

Samara shook her head and confirmed what Kait already knew. There had been no fork. There had been nothing but the static lane they'd wandered faithfully the past few days.

"I think . . . I think we're going in circles." The admission felt like a dagger to her chest. There was no way to know how long they'd been stuck following the same loop or how far they'd truly traveled through the realm.

Fear washed over Kait like an icy plunge into a melting lake when winter's reign reluctantly succumbed to spring. Goosebumps pebbled her skin, and her jaw clenched as she hesitantly glanced over her shoulder. The path lay empty behind them, but panic reared and sunk its teeth into her mind. Without the reassuring buffer the last few days of traveling *should* have afforded them, Zeus could be much closer than she'd originally calculated. Visions of him stalking around the bend assailed her and sent her pulse racing into overdrive. She's been a fool to think she was safe. She should've known something like this awaited them. The journey had been too simple, too quiet. Now she was being hunted again.

The instinctual urge for flight caused her palms to tingle, but there was no magic that connected the air to her here in the pits of hell. Kait assessed the path again. No footsteps sounded, but that meant nothing. Scrambling off the doe's back, she raced to the rocky base of a nearby outcropping where a small pile of fallen debris lay. She selected the largest piece of crumbled stone and clenched it in her fist. Then, she climbed onto Samara's back once more.

"Let's go, Samara. Hurry!"

The doe didn't hesitate or question Kait's urgent tone. With her other hand, Kait held the doe's mane and clenched her thighs to remain aloft. Her heart pounded, but her anxiety eased once they began moving. Of course, at this point, he might be in front of them—that's what the rock was for.

The pair raced ahead while Kait kept a sharp eye out for a hidden path or carved steps, anything they may have missed before the sky had brightened to the dull shade above them. She strained her gaze for what felt like an hour but saw nothing but smooth boulders, far too high to climb. Every few minutes, she cast a glance behind them in case Zeus stalked their flight. Thankfully, the road remained empty, but his absence did little to steady the rush of blood in her ears.

Samara's pace wobbled, and the doe's uneven gait drew Kait's attention forward. One hundred yards ahead, an object lay in the middle of the path.

"Whoa, whoa." Kait placed her hand on the doe's damp neck. Samara slowed and came to a stop several feet from the item. From Kait's vantage point, it looked like a piece of farming equipment—a curved steel blade attached to a worn wooden handle. "I'll get a closer look."

Kait slid off the doe's broad frame and winced as she landed on the balls of her feet. It seemed innocuous enough, but they weren't on a farm, and given Tartarus's unforgiving reputation, the blade's presence felt more like a threat than a careless oversight. Slowly, she advanced, alert for movement or sound a concealed enemy might mistakenly emit.

Kait cocked her head and studied the sickle. Apart from a small stain at the base of the blade near the handle, it appeared well-maintained. She extended her pointer finger and traced the smooth side, careful to avoid the steel's bite. The moment her skin made contact, a whoosh of wind threw her hair back, and her eyelids fluttered at the air's sudden onslaught.

A deep voice spoke on her left. "I was hoping I'd be able to meet you. I'm Cronus."

Kait crouched and raised the rock still clenched in her fist. "Stay away from me!"

Cronus shook his head, and his long unkempt gray hair and beard scraped his bare chest. Numerous cuts punctured his arms and torso, angry red gashes that spoke of a savage beating. Some looked quite deep. Pink layers of tissue shone wetly, and a few bled freely.

"I have no wish to harm you, my dear." Cronus spread his arms in a peaceful gesture. "Even if I harbored ill intent, my sons made sure I would never again reach a corporeal state. See?" The Titan plunged his hand into a nearby stone and his flesh disappeared like a ghost.

"Oh." Kait lowered her weapon but didn't relax her hold. Just because the apparition couldn't physically harm her didn't mean he wasn't a threat. Her gaze roamed around the new space. Gone was Samara, along with the endless path and dark gray skies. Instead, golden seams of color wove through the fabricated gray ceiling, imitating a warm sun. Kait's breath caught at the sight. To see something that resembled the afternoon sky after so many days of bleak darkness was overwhelming. Her eyes grew watery, and she ran the back of her hand down her face to hide the escaping emotions. "Where is my Ceryneian hind?"

"She's fine. She hasn't gone anywhere; it is you who has left. The moment you touched my sickle, you were transported to my domain. We haven't left Tartarus," Cronus said, seeing the hopeful light spark in Kait's eyes. "But the small amount of power I still possess allowed me to create a fissure to escape the miserable pit my sons banished me to."

"Your sons?"

"Hades, Poseidon, and Zeus."

"You're their father?" Kait's grip on the rock tightened again.

"Yes. Zeus led the charge against me and cursed every Titan from Olympus at the end of the great war for the heavens. I—along with many others—have been trapped here for millennia."

"Am I supposed to feel bad for you? The Titans abused the nymphs, hunted us down, and raped us like it was sport," Kait spat.

Cronus shook his head. "I'm not here to disagree with you. I've atoned for my sins and the role I played in the destruction of countless lives." He brandished his mutilated body. "My own son, Zeus, chopped me into pieces before Hades locked me in this dungeon. Only after I admitted the truth of my actions did my ravaged flesh begin to mend, though I'm still left with painful sores and cuts to remind me that no matter how much pain I accept, it will never be enough to make amends for those I killed." He ran his fingers along a particularly deep gash, seemingly lost in thought as his mind slipped into the past. He cocked his head a moment later and returned to the present. "I usually resist the urge to meddle with the wicked souls doomed to wander Tartarus, but you intrigue me. Your determination and grit are inspiring. Tell me, what is your purpose? You stalk through this realm with a fire unmatched by any before you."

"I need to kill Hera."

"H-Hera?" Cronus sputtered. "Well, I must admit, that's one I've not heard before."

"She killed my sister and sent her to Hades. The only way your son will surrender her soul is if I send him Hera's in return."

Cronus's eyebrows arched. "That's a tall task with a hefty burden."

Kait nodded once. "Hence why I'm forced to trudge through this cursed realm."

"I see," Cronus said, sounding thoughtful. "And how's your journey been so far?"

She fixed him with a narrowed stare. "You just admitted you've been watching me. How do you think it's been? After I managed to break away from your deplorable son, my doe and I have been stuck in this revolving loop for days, trying to escape the mountains."

Cronus sighed. "Time is a funny thing, isn't it?"

"What do you mean?"

The Titan crossed his arms and smeared a trail of blood along his forearm. "How we perceive its passing."

"I'm not in the mood for riddles or mind games."

"Then, I'm afraid you'll never exit the mountains."

Kait exhaled a defeated breath and put her fists on her hips. "How do I get out?"

Cronus smiled, exposing perfect square teeth. "Well, my dear, you said yourself the path forward is nothing more than an incessant merry-go-round."

Kait wrinkled her brow in concentration. "Right, we've looked for offshoots and places to climb, but there's nothing."

Cronus dropped his arms, and Kait couldn't help but grimace at the flaps of tissue on the inside of his elbows. "That's because Tartarus isn't meant to be scaled. Think about what I've said."

Before Kait could ask for further clarification, Cronus pulled a thin golden thread, and the warm glowing scene that enveloped her unraveled. The beautiful color drained and reverted to the monotone atmosphere once again. Samara chirped at her reappearance and trotted across the few feet that separated them. She cocked her broad antlers so they didn't hit Kait's face as she rubbed her soft forehead against her upper arm.

"Hello, again friend." Kait glanced around for the sickle, but the artifact was gone. Apparently, the great Titan was done giving clues for the day. Her gaze swept the immediate path for any sign of Zeus, but thankfully, they remained alone. "Cronus appeared when I touched the sickle. He gave me a riddle regarding the way out of this endless maze, but I don't understand. What else can we do but continue forward and look for a path that branches off?"

The doe glanced behind them and pawed the ground with her hoof.

"Going back wouldn't work either because we've already come that way? Don't you see?" Kait let her crude weapon roll out of her palm. As it clattered against the stone below, she balled her fingers and pressed them to her temples. "Goddess, help us."

Kait threw back her head and stared into the dark clouds. The image of Cronus's eternally bleeding wounds leapt to the forefront of her mind. They were gruesome to behold, but if the Titan was to be believed and Zeus had severed them completely, they didn't look that bad. She released another loud exhale and rolled her neck. He'd talked of atonement to heal his wounds, but she had nothing to atone for, not yet, anyway.

Had she been wrong to agree to Hades's request? Obviously, she didn't want to kill anyone, but Hades had left her with little choice. How else could she fulfill the god of death's demand?

Kait kicked the nearby pebbles and threw her back against a tall boulder, then slid to the ground. She propped her knees and buried her head in her hands. She knew what Cronus was hinting at, but she refused. She'd rather be stuck in the bowels of Tartarus forever than speak those words. Just the thought caused her stomach to roil, flip, and threaten to expel its nonexistent contents. No. That was out of the question, but there might be something she *could* try that would save them from the ceaseless labyrinth.

Kait tilted the crown of her head up and glanced at Samara. "I think I know what we have to do."

CHAPTER 28

Kait hiked forward—or technically backward—as she led Samara in the direction they'd come. She didn't want to ride. She was anxious enough as it was at the thought of confronting Zeus. Hopefully, she'd be able to work out most of her nervous energy before they found him. She marched with confidence, but on the inside, she writhed in absolute turmoil.

Kait had no idea if her plan would work, but Cronus had alluded to the fact that going forward would only lead to more revolving twists and turns. Her only option was to return, rewind her actions, and meet up with Zeus once more. Hades had stressed the fact that they would need to rely on one another to escape. It seemed the wily god had instituted his own insurance to ensure they both reached the portal. He'd given Zeus a job too, after all.

On and on they wandered, but unlike before, the jagged landscape changed. Instead of sharp precipices, the rocks sloped in a more gradual pattern until the path they trekked started to descend. Kait had no memory of fleeing up a steep incline with Samara, but her memory held little merit after the circles they'd traveled.

"Steady, Samara," Kait warned as the path grew steeper. The large doe bumped against her shoulders, pushing her faster. "Hang on, stop. I'm slipping." She tried to keep her footing, but the slope was nearly vertical, and with the hind's weight sliding against her, Kait's momentum was impossible to control.

Kait's palms grazed the narrowing stone walls, searching for a crevice to hook her fingers into, but the rock had become slick and polished, leaving her with no hope of gleaning any sort of friction to slow her velocity. She bit her lower lip as her breath hitched and the soles of her feet left the ground. Suddenly, there was nothing to brace herself against, no path beneath her. She was falling, somersaulting through the air, unable to even determine which way was up.

Samara gave a startled bellow as she too lost her footing, and seconds later, her bulk slammed into Kait and pitched her to the left. Kait's frantic hands shot out, but only cool air answered her silent plea. She twisted her head and saw a dark slash rising to meet her. She tried to wrench her arms around to cushion the impact, but too soon, the ground reared, and she smacked into the unyielding surface with enough force to rattle her teeth.

Blood welled in her mouth, and her lungs deflated from the painful blow. A loud thud ricocheted beside her as Samara landed several feet away, her beautiful bronze antlers clattering against the ground with a high-pitched screech.

Kait swallowed the bitter taste and groaned as she took stock of her body. Nothing seemed to be broken, but her head throbbed. Inch by inch, she lifted her neck. "Are you okay?" The doe carefully rolled onto her stomach, but her movements were stilted. "I'm sorry. I don't know what happened."

Samara opened her mouth to respond when a huge furred paw with foot-long talons emerged from the opaque ring encasing them and wrapped around the doe's body.

"Samara!"

The doe's brown eyes flared in alarm, and she cried a shrill chirp as the giant claws dragged her backward faster than Kait could lunge.

"No!"

The creature ignored her protest, and both its ghastly limb and Samara's large frame vanished into the inky pools that encapsulated Kait like a dome.

"Samara!"

Kait stumbled forward. Her body had not yet recovered from the hard fall, but she raced to the border of the rippling curtain of black water as quickly as possible. Her chest fell. Another river, this one vertical with no end in sight. Hesitantly, her fingertips combed the cold liquid. Charon had warned her not to touch the water, but that had been the Styx. Were all the rivers in the Underworld hazardous? She was already dead and lost in the darkest abyss; how much worse could her fortune get?

Kait stuck her hand in further, submerging it to her wrist. No scrape of teeth or fiery pain consumed her. With a steadying breath, she withdrew her hand and took a few steps back. The thought of diving into the dark depths terrified her, but she couldn't drown. She flexed her hands and took a running leap, preparing to plunge as far as she could through the barrier, but before she could break the strange membrane, an elongated tail like that of a thresher shark cut through the surface and slapped Kait across the face.

The powerful blow sent her reeling backward. For a moment, she was vaguely aware of her ankles kicking over her head, but she lost consciousness midair and collapsed in a mangled heap, lost to inescapable darkness once more.

Kait knew she was dreaming; the colors were too bright to be of Tartarus as she meandered aimlessly until her unconscious mind conjured the front steps of a shabby little yellow house. Happiness permeated the dream as Kait placed her palm on the faded front door and it gave way beneath her touch. She entered the cheerfully lit hallway, and photographs of Blake and his mother welcomed her. The house was quiet and comforting, a far cry from her reality. A warm presence pressed against her back as Blake wrapped her in his arms. Goddess, she'd missed this gentle boy.

"I wasn't sure I was going to see you again," Blake whispered in her ear.

Kait leaned into the embrace and reached up to trace Blake's scruffy jawline. "You're not," she whispered. "Not really. You're a dream."

Blake chuckled and tenderly brushed his lips along the side of her temple. "So, you're dreaming about me now?"

Kait snuggled closer. "Don't go getting a big head."

"Too late," Blake replied. "The damage is done. My ego has inflated beyond repair. It's huge, massive. Want to see?"

"No." Kait laughed. "I just want to stay here, frozen in this moment with you. I didn't think it was going to be this hard," she admitted. "I'm worried I might lose myself."

Blake hummed. "Then stay. Stay here with me, and stay who you are."

"If only it were that easy." She clutched Blake tighter, rubbing the fabric of his long-sleeved shirt between her thumb and forefinger.

They were quiet for a moment as they swayed back and forth, dancing atop the linoleum kitchen floor. Blake pressed his lips to her hair and spoke, but his words were muted and rushed.

"What did you say?" Kait asked.

"She's watching. They're hungry. Teeth and toes, bones and moons. They're hungry. They're close," Blake chanted and then disappeared, taking his solid presence with him.

Without warning, Kait jolted awake, no longer cradled by the sweet dream as consciousness gripped her like a cold claw.

They're hungry. They're close.

Dream Blake's words cocooned around her and caused her skin to itch. Something was close, skirting the small clearing just outside her line of sight. The strange vertical wall of water was gone, replaced with roiling black smoke that twirled in graceful spirals.

A sudden high-pitched chittering rasped behind her, like that of an insect clicking its mandibles. Kait spun, her breath stalling as she tried to peer through the thick vapor. Heavy slithering accompanied a furious tapping as something large moved through the darkness. Gritting her teeth, she tried to force her mind to remain blank, but images wormed their way in nonetheless and heightened her fear. Visions of a pit full of venomous serpents bloomed, along with ideas of grotesque beetles skittering across the floor, intent on tasting her flesh with their antennae.

Kait released a shaky breath. "It's all in your head."

"I wouldn't be too sure, little one. You never know what lurks in the dark."

Kait flinched, and goosebumps made the hairs on her arms rise. She could barely make out the speaker's words. The voice was a deep baritone, the cadence equivalent to shifting gravel. Terror gripped her as she attempted to pinpoint where the voice originated, but it echoed through her mind like a thought.

"You're a pretty thing," the speaker continued. "Pretty ones don't last long. My children see to that."

A sudden whoosh breezed past her left shoulder and sliced the air with a metallic ring. The same slithering echoed. Kait imagined the muscles of a giant snake, coiling and uncoiling as it tasted the air for her scent.

"Please, I'm trying to find the exit. I need to save my sister," Kait said, hoping to reason with whatever stalked her.

"The exit?" The voice chortled. "There is no exit, stupid pretty thing. This is Tartarus, the domain of monsters and doomed souls. There's no escaping the cruelty that brought you here."

"No, I don't belong here. Hades told us this was the only way to reach Olympus."

The voice cackled, the sound similar to two boulders slamming together. "Hades? That fool knows nothing of Tartarus. Just the thought of me and my children frosts the ichor in his veins."

A cold breeze licked her skin.

"I'm not immortal," Kait explained, wishing her voice were stronger.

"I know that, stupid thing. Your soul is pure. That's why you're still breathing. Though, I sense a darkening. Even the most noble of quests can yield dangerous consequences. Once you get a taste, desire for more sets in like a festering rot, and then you'll only have my realm of horrors to comfort you."

A cold wet sensation wrapped around Kait's neck. She gasped and clutched her throat while numerous prongs explored her skin, tasting her deepest thoughts. The slimy tentacle released, and the voice chuckled.

"Yes, it's already begun to claim you. You have seen death, even delivered it yourself, and you're planning to do it again," the creature stated. "Seems you belong here after all."

"No, please. You don't understand," Kait pleaded, sensing a shift in the creature's demeanor. Before, it had seemed passive, curious even; now the air crackled with tension, a predator on alert. "I'm trying to save my sister."

"Echidna cares not for excuses. Echidna and her children care only for punishment. You claim you are pure of heart? We'll see about that." The monster barked, its laughter so loud and sudden that Kait pressed her palms to her ears to muffle the boom. The ground shook as the massive creature slithered away. As it left, the air whooshed again. This time, three jagged spikes bit into her right thigh, gouging a trio of cuts, each at least half an inch deep.

"Ah!" Kait collapsed as another boom of laughter thundered. Somewhere close by in the darkness, new creatures woke, shifting and stretching as their great mother unleashed them. Heavy footsteps crashed around Kait as vicious snarls rang out. She had to move. If she stayed put, she could not fathom the torture she'd be in for. She hobbled several feet forward but was thrust into blindness when a fresh curtain of opaque silk consumed her.

Another snarl erupted, followed by the snap of gnashing teeth. Dogs or wolves leapt to her mind, and she imagined them ripping her limbs from their sockets and leaving her like a mangled scarecrow. Hot stale breath enveloped her and rolled down her shoulders like a noxious fog. She threw up her hands when a second breath brushed her ankles. Kait twisted her body as the scent of decay washed over her.

"Lovely bones . . ."

"Luscious marrow . . ."

"Crunchy veins . . ."

Voices swelled alongside chittering and clacking as something large licked salivating jaws. A second speaker sang, its tone higher than the first. Claws punctured her skin and dragged languidly down her exposed arms while another set flayed the existing wound on her thigh.

"Give me your thoughts . . ."

"Your terror . . ."

"Your dwindling hope . . ."

"Get away from me!" Kait shouted, scuttling back as the hungry creatures closed in. She threw out her palms and wove her fingers to summon a fierce wind, but her magic was unresponsive. "Goddess, help me!" she cried as a third voice resounded.

"Leave the memories for me . . ."

"The past tastes the sweetest . . ."

"When one's future is lost . . ."

A chilling breeze lifted the hair from her neck as a final pair of claws raked the vulnerable skin of her throat. Ducking out from under the sharp blades' touch, Kait leapt away and ran as fast as her injured leg allowed. Amused roars vibrated the floor, constricting the air around her and filling her ears with their barbaric sounds. One of the creatures reached out a steel claw and hooked it into the gauzy fabric at her waist. With little effort, the stitching gave way. It was a simple demonstration of intimidation, but it worked. Her flesh wouldn't fare any better.

Kait increased her speed, but the pain in her thigh screamed for rest. She glanced over her shoulder and caught a wicked wet gleam blinking at her from the blackness. She didn't know what haunted her or what her next move would be, but she refused to sit around and find out.

The blackness shrank and lightened once again to the same dull gray she'd enjoyed before she decided to attempt this fool's errand to find Zeus. At least now she stood half a chance to defend herself. As she limped a few more feet toward the towering rocks, the stirring of a plan took shape. She brought her toes down atop the rocky path, but rather than solid ground, her foot plunged through the illusion and her momentum catapulted her forward. There was nothing she could do to stop herself, no ledge to grasp. Kait tumbled deeper into oblivion as the hunters' laughter grew.

CHAPTER 29

Falling through the sky was usually easy, natural. There was never any fear, only joy as the air cradled her, ushering her along like a sweet friend. But she was no longer a spirit of the wind, and falling through hell was terrifying.

Like a bird whose wings had been cruelly clipped, Kait careened through the sky, her stomach in her throat as the cold wind forced her eyes wide open. For another few seconds, she fell, with no knowledge of which way was up or down. Leaning to the right, she rolled to her back to look up in the direction she thought she'd fallen from. Only heavy blackness radiated as if she'd been swallowed by a beast and would slide into its stomach with an acidic splash.

Her descent ended more abruptly than that as her spine slammed against a solid structure. Her neck snapped, and her skull crashed into a rock. Stars erupted behind her eyes as her body bounced and flailed like a rag doll thrown carelessly into the corner. She lay there, contemplating the consequences if she remained immobile. Everything hurt, from her knees to her jaw. Exhaustion overwhelmed her like quicksand, pulling her consciousness down, burying her will. Samara was gone. Zeus was gone. Bia was gone. What would it matter if she was gone, too? The world would continue. Hera would be satisfied, and Olean would be safe. Why should she keep fighting?

Don't give up. You're stronger than this. Get up. Get up, put one foot in front of the other, and climb out of this hell, she told herself.

Kait shifted onto her side. She could feel deep bruises forming beneath her skin as her abused muscles pleaded for rest. She ignored her body's resistance, clambered to her feet, and sighed, alone in the unnavigable black again.

A feral scream exploded nearby, bouncing off the rocks like a crazed entity. Kait's palms flexed, poised for attack. Another scream erupted, setting her nerves ablaze. After several seconds, the shrill cries subsided into little more than broken sobs and muffled wails as something scratched furiously at the stone walls. The creature was close and from the sounds of it, injured. Crouching low, she ran the tips of her fingers along the gravel-strewn floor. After a moment of searching, she found a triangular stone with rough sides that would suit her needs. Kait clutched the crude weapon in her fist and straightened, taking a step toward the erratic grating.

"Their eyes, so many eyes, staring, pleading, begging, crying. I didn't mean to. I didn't think, didn't know. I'm sorry. I'm sorry." Fierce whispers filled the space, the speaker's voice ragged and desperate. "Get them out! Take them away. Take her screams. I can't. I can't. I can't!"

Kait stopped short as she recognized the agony in the speaker's voice. She'd heard it a few months ago in the mountains after watching the cavernous ceiling crush the piriol. The tone spoke of true heartbreak, true regret.

Zeus.

"No, no, no! Please, no more!" Zeus cried as the scratching intensified. "Not another one. I said I was sorry. Said it was wrong. Please, no more!"

Kait reached out with her empty hand, and a stone wall kissed her searching fingers. The god's frightened mutterings continued. It sounded as if he was only a few yards away. Three more steps and the coarse stone gave way to a sticky substance like warm honey. She opened and closed her hand. The liquid was tacky, but it didn't prevent her fingers from pulling apart. A metallic scent overwhelmed her, layered with an unmistakable sweetness.

Kait gasped and dropped her weapon to the floor. Ichor—the god's lifeblood—was strewn about the cavern walls like an offering. Zeus screamed again, and Kait couldn't help but smile as he pleaded for whatever attacked him to cease. How long she had waited for this moment. How often she had envisioned subjecting him to the same pain he'd rendered.

"I'm sorry! I'm sorry! I didn't know! No more! Please!"

Zeus's pleas were a symphony, an empowering swell that helped soothe her own trauma. Had he been tormented like this since she left him? Kait's smile widened at the thought. She touched her ichor-covered fingertips together and delighted in the texture as she closed her eyes and rested her head against the wall. How many nights had she lain awake replaying the horrors of his hands, his warm breath on her skin? Did he understand now? Did he know what it felt like to be ravaged? To be forced open, helpless to save himself?

"I was wrong! I was so wrong! Please, take away their screams!" Zeus's shrieks softened to sobs, and Kait heard a steady thudding. She tensed, expecting the god's assailant to brush against her, but then she realized the source of the sound was Zeus slamming his head against the rock.

Good. She hoped he would continue until his skull split like a watermelon, exposing all the wrinkled lobes inside. Part of Kait wished to listen to Zeus slip further into madness and desperation for hours more, but as cathartic as the god's screams were, they did nothing to help her find the exit. She thought back to Cronus's riddle. If she had any hope of escaping, she needed Zeus by her side.

Kait pushed herself off the stone wall and stumbled forward through the dark. Guided by Zeus's incessant cries, she eventually grasped folds of cloth between her fingers and began jerking the fabric out of the way until flesh greeted her touch. Zeus's skin was flush with fever, perspiring from every pore. Roaming farther, she discovered thick gashes that stretched from his neck to his shoulders, bloody ichor oozing from all of them.

"Get up, Zeus. We have to leave," Kait ordered. She hooked her arms beneath his and attempted to haul him to his feet, but Zeus screamed and wrestled out of her grasp, sinking back to the floor.

"No more! I beg of you, no more!" Zeus's shouts crescendoed, and he kicked and flailed like a terrified child. "It hurts. It hurts so badly! I can't take it!"

Soft gray light filtered into the darkness, illuminating the nightmarish scene. The god huddled against the wall, sitting in a pool of golden-red ichor as he clawed manically at his chest and throat. There was no monster attacking him. His wounds were self-inflicted.

Kait wrapped her hand around Zeus's wrist, trying to reach him once more. "Zeus, listen to me. You need to get up."

"I'm so sorry. Can't you hear me? I'm sorry! I'm sorry!" Zeus's words thundered. Oblivious to Kait's existence, he continued to plead with his invisible assailant. Arching back, he slammed his skull against the rocks once, twice, three, four times—each impact harder than the last. A sharp cracking erupted as the bone struggled to remain intact under the immense pressure.

"Zeus, stop," Kait scolded, but her words were in vain. The god was unreachable, trapped within the agony of his own making. This was the true horror of Tartarus. Not the creatures, nor the endless black. The true terror existed in being forced to face your sins and the unbearable atonement.

Kait wasn't strong enough to carry him, let alone free him from his prison. Zeus's screams rattled her teeth. He was in pure misery, locked farther away than she could ever hope to reach. He deserved all this pain and more, but she couldn't leave him. She'd already tried that. Hades's sick sense of humor had tied her success to his. She had to find a way to get the voices to relent.

Kait released her grip on the god's wrist and moved to stand before him. Dropping to her knees, she ignored the way the rocks bit into her skin, the way her thigh burned as the torn flesh separated further. She tasted bile in the back of her throat at her next words.

She spoke softly, so quietly she doubted he would even be able to hear her over his sobs. "Zeus, it's Kaitaini. I am here, ready to work with you to reach the portal. Even after what you've done to me, I am here." As a show of good faith to whatever invisible creature plagued him, she held out her hand, a silent offering of a truce.

Her gentle words wove between the shared space, growing larger and stronger until they seemed to settle in the god's mind. His shoulders relaxed, and his breathing slowed.

"Kaitaini?" Zeus said, his voice withered and raspy.

"Yes," Kait answered.

Zeus reached forward and clasped Kait's hand in his. She jerked back and severed their connection as the memory of his fingers sliding along her bare skin flared. Her heart pounded. This was a mistake. Cronus was wrong. There had to be another way.

The god clenched his eyes shut and whimpered as the mental attack struck once more. "I'm sorry. I'm sorry for what I did to you. I should have never . . . never touched you, forced you to endure that over and over again." His voice broke as heavy sobs racked his chest. "And I'm so sorry that I must ask you to hold my hand now, but your touch . . . it stops the pain." His glassy eyes found hers, and his empty hand shook. "Please, help me."

Kait frowned. She knew her fate if she refused. Ironically, the only way to get away from Zeus was to work in tandem with him now. She bit her lower lip to keep it from quivering as she reached out and placed her hand in his. Her fingers were rigid and stiff, but she held them there even though her instincts pleaded with her to run. "Seems I can't do this without you."

Zeus held her gaze for a moment longer than necessary and sighed. "Thank you."

Kait nodded curtly and rose to her feet, Zeus's hand clutched in hers.

"I know I have no right to ask this, but can we keep holding hands? You have no idea how much it helps."

Kait's nerves frayed at the thought of prolonged contact. How long must she burn to warm him? Why must she be the one to sacrifice? Again, refusal danced on her lips, but he was right. Her touch did seem to help, and as much as it pained her to admit, she needed him to save Bia. "Okay," she agreed after a long pause.

Kait bent down to help Zeus stand and noticed his body seemed to be regulating itself, returning to a normal temperature. Keeping hold of him, she led them away from the ichor-splattered walls and gazed upward. With luck, they'd be able to climb out of the pit, but in her mind, she knew the way out would force them deeper into Tartarus until it had thoroughly tested their fears and laid each of their sins bare.

Swirls of copper and silver illuminated their surroundings, transforming the landscape to an even brighter shade. Zeus had been challenged, and the light was an earned reward for his apology. Following the emerging light, Kait led them through a crumbling archway. Its carved inscription had long faded, save for a few shadowy lines.

"I'm sorry," Zeus whispered, breaking the long silence.

"What?"

Zeus released a breath. "I'm sorry for everything I did. For assaulting you, stalking you, threatening you, forcing my touch upon you."

"You already said that back there." Kait's voice was clipped, and she refused to look at him. Her anxiety spiked as their joined hands grew sweaty.

"I know, but I wanted to say it again when my mind was clear without the pain so you knew it was real." Zeus gave her hand a small tug, enough to force her gaze toward his. He chewed his lower lip and looked unsure of himself for the first time since she'd encountered the arrogant immortal. "I never considered what it felt like, to have someone force themselves inside you. That's what the voices did. They forced me to feel every nymph's pain, and anguish, and guilt, and shame that I caused, all at once. Your sister's pleas were the loudest, and I'm so—" Zeus looked away and squeezed her hand as his voice broke with emotion. "I wish I could take it all back."

Kait narrowed her brows and pursed her lips. "Forgive me if I don't put any stock in this sudden epiphany." She withdrew her hand and wiped the gathering sweat on her hip. She tasted the bitter flavor of wrath once again. To hell if the voices came back for Zeus. She'd done more than enough. "And you should know that I didn't show mercy back there for your benefit. I do not feel sorry for you. I wish those voices could have also subjected you to your victims' physical pain, pressed bruises into your throat, bashed your skull even harder against the rocks, and ripped your ethereal connection away one excruciating fiber at a time. You got off easy, so keep your pathetic apologies for someone who gives a shit."

Zeus's jaw dropped, and his eyes clouded with rage. "I felt everything! They made me feel everything. I bashed my own head. I tried to carve the sin from my skin with my nails!"

"And you think that's enough? A few hours of torture is enough to make up for the countless lives you've destroyed? The innocence you've shattered? The endless nightmares just your voice still conjures for me? Fuck you, Zeus. You have no idea what it means to suffer. Or what it means to wish for death."

Zeus opened his mouth to retort but shut it a moment later. "You're right. I'm sorry."

"Stop saying that. You don't mean it."

"But I do, Kait. I truly do. I don't expect you to forgive me—"

"Forgive you?"

Zeus held up his hands. "I'm not asking for forgiveness, just your patience as I try to correct the mistakes I've made and learn from them. Back there, you said you couldn't do this without me. Well, I need your help, too."

Kait opened her mouth to reply with a snide comment, but the image of the god writhing in blood as he smashed his forehead into the stone lingered behind her eyes. She stood by her statement—he deserved every moment and more—but if it helped lead them out of Tartarus, she supposed she could stand a temporary ceasefire between them.

"Fine, but stay over there, and if you touch me again, I'll find the largest rock I can and impale you so hard with it, you won't be able to sit for the rest of your miserable immortal life. Do I make myself clear?"

Zeus interlocked his fingers and nodded. "Yes, thank you." A tense silence settled over them as they stared uneasily, each waiting for the other to make the next move. He cocked his head and scanned the rocky terrain. "So, what now? Without your doe to guide us, do we even stand a chance?"

Kait grimaced, remembering the fear in Samara's eyes as she was taken by a monster—another friend she couldn't save. Kait took the lead and set a moderate pace as their feet slid over glassy black stones carved into the shape of crawling bodies. She tried to ignore the way the vacant eye sockets watched her. "I believe Tartarus will show us the way out. Tease us when we're close, only to pull back until we've earned it."

"How?"

Kait inclined her head back the way they'd come. "You got a taste of it back there. Whatever evils lurk within your heart, Tartarus will force them to the surface and dare you to confront your sins."

Zeus shivered. "What of the creatures?"

"They're out there, waiting. I met one of them after I lost Samara. She called herself the mother."

"Gods," Zeus swore. "Echidna."

"What?"

"She calls herself the mother because she birthed the great beasts that roam Tartarus, from the sadistic Hydra to the savage Cerberus my brother is so fond of. Echidna is a demon. No one knows whose union she was created from, but the legends say she has a face more beautiful than any nymph, yet her lower half twists and slithers like that of a great serpent. If we meet her again, don't look her in the eye, for they are mesmerizing and lull prey into a stupor before she tears them apart with her venomous fangs," Zeus explained in a hushed whisper.

Kait remembered her fear and the creature's mocking laughter. Zeus made Echidna sound like a mindless hunter, but she knew the mother was much more than that. In addition to her bloodlust, Echidna was clever and patient, a dangerous combination, especially when mice were stumbling around her trap. A cold shiver licked Kait's spine. Together or not, there was a very good chance they would never escape.

CHAPTER 30

It seemed they'd traveled an infinite number of miles through the rocky labyrinth, yet they'd encountered nothing that confirmed they were headed in the right direction. Far off in the distance, a ball of concentrated light burned, their only mecca as they toiled to reach its shores, but it remained a constant distance away. Zeus tried to make conversation, but Kait refused to answer any of the god's inquiries or volunteer any information to help break the silence.

They'd walked for two long segments, pausing to rest in between. Their bodies didn't physically need the respite, but it helped to break up the monotony of endless walking. Thankfully, they hadn't run into any more of Tartarus's demons, but the cuts on Kait's leg had begun to burn with every additional step and leaked a yellow pus. With nothing to clean the wounds, she struggled to keep pace with Zeus as her body fought through alternating waves of fever and chills. Internally, she pleaded to stop, but the only thing more frightening than succumbing to infection was making her enemy aware of her vulnerable state.

"That's it for today," Zeus said. His announcement took her by surprise. His voice rang with authority after so many hours of silence.

Kait's teeth clacked together as she shook her head. "N-N-No, we have to keep g-going. We h-have to find S-Samara."

Zeus shook his head and blocked her path with his body, brandishing his palms, clearly anticipating that she would shrink away from the unwanted contact. Kait tried to push past him, but the path through the tunnel of rock that enveloped them was too narrow. He sat down in the middle of the road, his lips set in a firm line.

"Do you honestly think I can't see how exhausted you are? You can barely stand."

"I can g-go a little l-longer." Kait's teeth chattered, and she grimaced.

"Sit down, Kait. You need to rest. I didn't realize I was pushing you so hard."

Kait's temper flared. "I'm not t-tired, you idiot. I'm sick. I've been b-battling a fever for days."

Zeus's brow furrowed. "Fever? How do you have a fever? We're dead, remember?"

Kait sunk to the stone floor in a disheveled pile, careful to keep out of the god's reach. "Yes, believe it or not, that hasn't escaped my notice. It's probably from my run-in with Echidna before I found you."

"What do you mean?"

Kait couldn't be sure, but the god's tone seemed to hold a note of concern. "She cut me with something. Claws or a blade, I don't know. It was too dark. But whatever it was managed to bypass Hades's reach and poison my blood."

"Where's the cut?" Zeus asked, leaning forward.

Kait angled her body away and hissed between her teeth as the rolling motion sent a wave of nausea through her. "My thigh."

"Let me see," Zeus said gently.

"No! Don't touch me." Kait's eyes flared, and she scrambled farther back on her palms, dragging her body.

Zeus held his hands up in surrender. "I promise I won't touch you, but I need to see the wound. I need to know how badly it's infected."

"Don't t-touch me." Kait's teeth bounced together as her body violently shook with fever and panic.

"I promise. Just angle your leg toward me so I can see."

Kait's eyes fluttered. They were so heavy, but she couldn't rest, not with Zeus so close. With his hands still visible, she stretched her left leg out and pulled the torn fabric away to reveal angry flesh beneath.

Zeus sucked in a harsh breath. "Gods, Kait. Why didn't you say something before? This is nearly gangrene."

"What would it have m-mattered? You c-can't fix it."

Zeus pinched the skin between his eyes. "No, but I could have carried you or tried to clean it had I known. Gods, this is all my fault. What can I do?"

Kait's eyelids closed, longer this time. "Nothing." She shivered, goosebumps pebbling her skin as her bones shook.

"Shit, let me hold you at least. Maybe I can warm you—"

"No! Stay away f-from me."

"I'm not going to touch you like that. I promise."

"No."

Zeus rose to his knees and pounded the stone. "Gods, Kait! Please, let me help you. I know you have no reason to trust me, but I swear on my life, I won't hurt you."

"You're d-dead. It doesn't count. I don't n-need your help."

"So, I'm just supposed to sit here and watch your soul die? What if you can't come back from that?"

"Yes." Kait slid down so that she was lying on the cold ground. She tried to curl into the fetal position to preserve what little body heat she had, but her limbs wouldn't cooperate. She was losing more and more control by the second. Her vision blurred and sloshed sideways. It felt as if she were falling, lost in a whirlwind of color. From far away, she heard a deep rumble like thunder announcing an oncoming storm.

"You're not going to like this, and I'm very sorry, but I can't sit back and watch you suffer."

Two shovellike objects wedged beneath Kait's waist and rib cage and lifted her off the ground. She flinched at the intrusion and kicked her legs, but she was too weak to have any impact. "Let me g-go!" she slurred.

"I'm sorry, but I can't do that. If I can share my body heat with you, maybe we can sweat out this fever."

A rocking sensation overwhelmed Kait as Zeus settled back down onto the floor and propped his back against the rough wall, wrapping his arms around her small frame. A blanket of heat surrounded her as he positioned her on his lap with her temple resting just below his collarbone. The familiar scent of him flooded her nostrils, and the memory of being cuffed to the bed while the god teased and tasted her erupted in her mind, fighting through the fog of infection.

"No, get away from m-me! Get away!" Kait tried to shout, but her teeth were chattering too much for the words to be intelligible. Terrified whimpers fell from her lips. A large hand cupped the back of her head and brushed away her tears. "Stop it! Stop it! Don't t-touch me! Stop!" Guttural screams reverberated deep in her throat as she fought to escape the cage of his arms, but the exertion drained what little energy she'd held on to.

"I'm so sorry. I'm sorry I did this to you. I'm so sorry," Zeus whispered.

Kait pushed off from his chest as hard as she could, but her arms felt like rubber, and her head swam. She couldn't get away, couldn't distinguish which way to even escape. Her heart hammered as her body quaked in his hold, and she grew delirious from the infection. The past and present blended together, the two faces of Zeus colliding into a hodgepodge of monsters. She yearned to twist out of his arms, but her vision narrowed to a thin scope, and then a curtain of darkness doused what little light was left.

I am a song without sound,
    a sun without light,
    a creature of myth,
    but I will kill you tonight.

Crimson images painted Kait's dreams as shifting shadows elongated and shrank, dancing and writhing with increasing power. Yet the moment she tried to focus on one of the shapes, it altered and morphed into another twisted silhouette.

Muscles and blood,
useless when my tricks are done.

Kait forced her mind to pay attention to the swirling dream. If recent weeks had taught her anything, it was that dreams were always far more than fleeting projections. A brush of fine hair tickled her cheek, and she flinched. The unexpected jolt shook the last dregs of sleep away, and the slippery shadows dissolved. She tried to hold on, but it was as pointless as trying to bottle smoke. Another tickle grazed her collarbone, cementing the notion that the voice from her dream had somehow blended with reality. A gentle thud sounded, followed by the quiet hush of feathers.

Fearful of alerting whatever stalked them to her new state of consciousness, Kait peeked through her lashes, careful to keep her breathing deep and even. The same hues of copper and silver greeted her, along with the faraway golden light that acted as their beacon. Peering through the dim lighting, she saw a humped figure, but she couldn't remember if it was another one of the grotesque statues carved into the rocks or if it was a being that pulsed with life. She held her gaze steady for another minute, waiting, daring the large boulder to move.

Beneath her, Zeus mumbled and stretched in his sleep. Suddenly, the uneasy feeling of being watched was the furthest thing from her mind as she realized the god's warm body was draped around her. Her head pounded with pain and terror as she fought to extricate herself from his heavy limbs. What the hell happened? How had she come to be in his lap?

Kait knocked his arms off of her and twisted away, landing sharply on her knees. Off balance, she tipped forward as she fought to reorient herself. Rather than being ravaged by chills, her body now burned as if she'd snuggled a furnace. A weak cough emanated from her throat as memories of the muddled events from the night before slowly formed. She remembered Zeus coming toward her and demanding to help. She'd spurned his hollow attempts, choosing to freeze to death rather than allow him to touch her, but he must have ignored her refusal.

A bitter taste roiled in the back of her throat as she caught the god's scent on her skin. The mountain, the rattling chains, his condescending laughter—it all spiked and made her breaths come in shallow gasps. Arching her arm, she lashed out with her elbow and struck Zeus in the chin with as much strength as she could.

Zeus's head snapped back, and his eyes flashed open as he launched himself off the wall in preparation to meet an assailant. A feral snarl rumbled in his chest, but Kait's elbow smacked him again, this time in the mouth.

"Ow! What the—Kait?"

Kait opened her fist and slapped Zeus across the face. "I told you not to touch me! You waited for me to pass out, even when I told you no!" Zeus put up his hands to defend his face but otherwise took the beating silently. "Keep your vile hands off me! Don't touch me! Don't ever touch me again!" Kait hit him again and again until a deep cough ravaged her chest and forced her to drop her hands.

Zeus held his face in his hands. "I know, and I apologized for going against your orders, but you were getting worse. All I wanted to do was warm you."

"And now I'm burning, and my head feels as if it weighs a thousand pounds!" Kait cried. "I smell like you! You can't understand how horrifying that is! How disgusting and dirty I feel! You've forced yourself onto me again and erased me!"

"No, I'll never be able to truly understand, but I swear it wasn't anything sexual. I was only trying to help."

Something scraped the sole of Kait's foot, deliberate and unhurried. "Don't touch me!" Her shrill scream echoed off the rocks, and Zeus frowned in confusion.

"I didn't. What's going on?"

Pulling her legs in, Kait grimaced as the pain in her thigh drew her attention away from the god. She couldn't bend her right leg. Amidst her fever dreams, the muscles had grown stiff and angry. She ran her fingers along the skin. Dried blood and yellow pus coated the surface, but underneath, numerous maroon streaks drained away from the wound. A rancid smell wafted from the gash. Zeus was right; she had gotten worse.

Movement flickered in the corner of her eye. Kait jerked away, thinking it was Zeus at first, only to realize the shift came from the opposite direction, toward the exit of the tunnel. The rocks along the wall looked different now, more angular rather than the smooth boulders she'd grown accustomed to.

"I didn't touch you, Kait—"

"Shut up." Kait kept her eyes on the rocks as the feeling of being watched returned. If Zeus was to be believed, then whatever stalked them in the dull light was close.

Zeus followed her gaze. "What's wrong?"

"Something's here."

"What do you mean?"

Kait gestured to the pointed statue. As she spoke, the large hump of rock with chiseled edges shifted, its movement more fluid than she would have ever thought possible for a creature carved from the stone. Again, the fluttering of feathers resounded as the rock drew closer, emerging from the dark until the dim lighting illuminated the face of a beautiful woman.

Echidna leapt to Kait's mind, and she recoiled involuntarily—her leg an egregious reminder of her naïvety—but the sounds this creature made were wrong. The movements were too soft, too graceful for the serpent mother.

"Who is that?" Kait gasped, taking in the smooth flesh and golden mane she'd mistaken for rock in the darkness. Surprised by the woman's gentle beauty in the harsh environment, she continued to stare.

Creamy flesh adorned her neck, giving way to supple brown fur, while thick golden hair cascaded down her nude back. The curls nearly masked the joints where two giant wings laced with glossy black feathers erupted. Kait was entranced, hypnotized by the organic fluidity the woman's body possessed as it transitioned to different limbs, colors, and textures. She spied the well-groomed tail of a lion, with powerful legs and claws to match.

"Goddess." Kait gasped. "The Sphinx."

Hearing her name, the Sphinx opened her mouth to emit a soft mewling cry.

Indeed, little one.
You have named me well,
but I fear you lack the knowledge
to escape this hell.

The same voice from Kait's dreams floated through her mind, dominating her thoughts as the Sphinx greeted them.

"Gods no," Zeus whispered, fear coating his words.

Kait hurried away from Zeus to stand before the beautiful creature, favoring her injured leg. "It's an honor to meet you, Sphinx. Perhaps you can help us? We're looking for a Ceryneian hind. She was our guide through Tartarus, but we were separated. Have you seen her?"

"What are you doing?" Zeus hissed in Kait's ear. "It's the Sphinx. Don't you know anything? You don't ask the Sphinx for help. You don't ask the Sphinx for anything. You stay silent and pray your wit can save you."

Kait narrowed her eyes and flushed the god's breath out of her ear with her finger. "I'm asking a simple question."

"And you'll be rewarded with an even simpler death," Zeus mumbled under his breath as he crossed his arms.

Kait focused her attention on the Sphinx again. The hybrid woman stared at her with mild curiosity, her large front paws crossed at the wrists. Kait waited, unsure whether she should restate her question, for the Sphinx only stared. Her almond-shaped eyes gently closed like a lazy cat's. Silence stretched for another minute, and still the Sphinx gave no indication she would reply.

Kait began again. "Uh, I was wondering if you've seen—"

Insolence is dangerous.
Patience a virtue.
To survive my games,
Listening is the first clue.

The Sphinx's voice growled in Kait's mind as the elegant creature flicked her tail in irritation.

Three things you seek,

yet only one I shall bequeath.
If you play,
don't delay,
for time will soon run dry.
"What must we do?" Kait asked.

"Is it a quest? Please, don't let it be a quest," Zeus muttered to himself.
Though part of you travels far,
your feet need not leave.
Answer one riddle,
and then you are free.

The Sphinx tossed her golden curls over her shoulder as a deep purr resonated behind her fangs.

"What's the riddle?" Kait asked, limping closer as her thigh flared with fresh pain.

"Whoa, hold on. We need to be smart about this. We can't just dive in without knowing the consequences," Zeus said. Coming to stand beside Kait, he put his hands on his hips and addressed the Sphinx. "What are the rules?"

The Sphinx cocked her head, her amused carnelian eyes flashing. She crouched on her heels and stretched her front legs, claws flexing threateningly. Her long lashes fluttered while she slid down the rocks with ease. Her sleek black wings ruffled when she landed and straightened to her full height. Kait's eyes widened. The Sphinx towered over her. The creature's wingspan alone must have been at least eight feet.

A rumble like the hooves of a dozen running horses caused tiny rocks at their feet to vibrate. It took Kait a moment to realize the Sphinx was purring. Rubbing up against Kait, the Sphinx wove between them, her body a solid wall of coiled muscle, ready to spring. The foul stench of stale blood radiated off the creature's fur and caused Kait to sputter. Her mind balked, trying to reconcile the strong odor with her stunning beauty. The Sphinx incapacitated her prey with superficial illusions to conceal the true animal beneath until it was too late to run.

Clever little god.
Already, your wits surprise me.
Of course, there is a price
should you fail the riddle given to thee.
One answer you are allowed,

so choose carefully.
If your utterance is wrong,
your blood will turn cold.
Your skin harden to rock,
and you'll join my garden
of those statues you mock.

"Statues?" Kait recalled the strange way the stones had seemed to watch her. Craning her neck, she glanced at the endless peaks. How many souls had played the Sphinx's game, their hopes shriveling to dust along with their breath?

"And if we manage to solve your puzzle?" Zeus said. "You'll show us the way out?"

The Sphinx grinned, her red lips stretching far too wide.
If you succeed where so many others fail,
I shall grant your deepest desire.
The grand feline paused, her gaze intent upon Zeus.
Ensure you know what causes your heart to ail.

Zeus wrinkled his forehead, seeming lost. He returned the Sphinx's stare, unblinking as she sat back on her haunches and her long tail waved languidly back and forth. He let out a long breath and glanced sideways at Kait. "You ready?"

Kait swallowed roughly, her saliva stuck in her throat like glue. "Yes," she answered. "What is your riddle?"

The Sphinx hummed excitedly as her front paws kneaded the rocky dirt.
Very well, my dears.
A riddle it shall be.
But remember, only one word,
or your souls belong to me.

"We understand," Kait agreed. She stood as straight as her injured leg allowed and, for the first time, did not shy away from Zeus's presence, a gesture of solidarity in the face of the Sphinx's intimidation. The god gave her a curt nod in return. If they worked together, they might survive.

The Sphinx's lips parted, and she emitted another soft mewl before reciting the riddle.
You measure my life in hours,
and I serve you by expiring.

I'm quick when I'm thin,
and slow when I'm fat.
The wind is my enemy.
What am I?

The Sphinx arched her brows expectantly, waiting for her prize.

Kait drew in a breath, ready to repeat the puzzle, when Zeus's rough fingers slammed over her lips. She fought to extricate herself from his grip, and his palm muffled her furious curses.

Zeus's other hand wrapped securely around Kait's left shoulder and shook her with one sharp snap. She stopped struggling as he tossed his head back and forth, his eyes screaming for her to listen. He released her shoulder the moment he had her attention and held up his index finger.

One word.

Of course. That was one of the Sphinx's tricks. Kait nodded, her cheeks flushed. She'd almost cost them their lives. Zeus tentatively lowered his hand away from her mouth. This riddle had become much harder than she'd anticipated. The god tapped his temple.

Think.

Kait closed her eyes and tried to remember the clues. Something about serving you. The words leapt into her mind, and she threw up her hands as she mouthed an idea. Zeus cocked his head, his palms at the ready to stifle her wandering thoughts if necessary. Kait waved her hands to signal that wasn't needed and pointed to her wrist, miming a gadget that humans wore. Zeus nodded, following along.

Time.

Kait dragged her fingertip in a clockwise direction several times.

Hours.

The riddle mentioned the object's life was measured in hours and it died by serving. Dropping her head, Kait bowed and held up her palms as if she were worshiping the gods. Zeus nodded, acknowledging the past centuries when humans used to pray to their idols. Straightening, she fixed him with a pointed stare and continued.

So far, they'd recalled hours and servitude. Could it be an imprisoned slave? Kait mouthed her guess in Zeus's direction, but he frowned and wrinkled his nose. Holding his hands close, he separated them widely, only to bring them back together. Thin and fat. Another clue. Kait mimicked Zeus's hands, keeping them narrow, then pumped her arms and pretended to run.

I'm fast when I'm thin.

This sparked the second clue.

I'm slow when I'm fat.

"A human?" Zeus mouthed, but it was too vague. Kait knew the Sphinx was looking for something specific. There was one last clue, something she was very familiar with. Pointing to herself, she pursed her lips and blew a steady stream of air. Zeus pointed to himself.

Wind. Enemy.

Kait nodded. However, this time, Zeus wasn't the enemy, but rather her unfortunate compatriot. Shaking her head, she blew another stream of air and pointed to her chest. The wind was the enemy. Could it be a flower? Broken and forced into submission? She dismissed the idea. None of the other clues made sense for a flower. Quickly, she rattled off natural foes she encountered as the wind.

"A tree?" Kait mouthed. Thin branches swayed fast in the wind, but fat branches moved much slower. The wind was a constant force against a tree, but it wasn't exactly a malicious relationship. Hope surged in her chest as she remembered the second clue. *I serve you by expiring.* Trees were cut down to build homes or other products. A tree must expire to serve.

Zeus tapped his wrist to remind her of the first clue. A tree's life wasn't measured in hours but rings.

A low rumble thundered behind them as the Sphinx smiled.

Only a quarter remains
until your hour dies.
Give me your answer
or your last sighs.

Panic flared in Kait's mind. How had time slipped away so quickly? Her head swam with all the possibilities and the savage fever that tore through her body. She pressed her fingers into her temples and squeezed her eyes shut. She knew she was close. The answer was simple, something small and insignificant that no one would ever guess. Her eyes sprang open and alighted on Zeus. Fear and indecision were written all over his face.

Run? Zeus's expression denoted.

Kait refused. She could barely stand, let alone outrun a winged beast. They had to figure it out. She refused to come all this way only to be defeated by a stupid riddle. With time running low, she looked around, as if the answer might lie in one of the objects surrounding them. Her heart pounded. They only had minutes left. Random objects began firing off in her brain. A river? A book? A memory? A flame? A wound?

Kait froze mid-thought, and her jaw fell slack.

The Sphinx's bright eyes glistened with victory.

One minute left,

and only silence whispers.

Speak now

or my hunger stirs.

Kait spun and stared at the faraway light as the seconds counted down. Kait heard Zeus draw in a breath—ready to guess or beg for more time, she didn't know. But she knew the answer.

"Candle," Kait whispered without shifting her focus from the golden glow in the distance.

What did you say? The Sphinx sounded appalled and insulted.

Kait turned away from the light as a relieved smile split her lips. "A candle. It only burns for a few hours and serves by giving light until it expires. A thin candle burns faster than a fat one, and the wind can extinguish it with the slightest breeze."

Zeus's jaw dropped, and he froze as he waited for the Sphinx to answer. Kait balled her hands into fists, struggling to remain upright as the wound on her thigh surged with renewed pain. At last, the Sphinx spoke.

None have escaped the fate

my riddles have spun.

It seems your quest

is indeed a noble one.

I gave my word

to grant your deepest desire.

Your flesh is healed.

Now, I leave you to reach the end of this mire.

Unless you'd like another test?

If successful, I'll tell you how to navigate the rest.

Kait put up her hands and shook her head. "No, one was enough, but thank you for . . ." Her words trailed away as her mind caught something the clever creature just said.

Your flesh is healed.

Transfixed, Kait looked down and watched as the trio of gashes disappeared. The foul-smelling yellow pus evaporated, and the infected purple tissue lightened back to a healthy pink. The dried blood clinging to her brown skin fell away in a shower of rusty flakes as the sundered muscle stitched itself back into one smooth piece.

"I don't understand," Kait stated. "Why?"

It was the loudest wish.

Buried in your hearts.

My debt paid,

I must now depart.

Before Kait could question her further, the great Sphinx turned and slunk gracefully into the shadows, her padded footfalls quickly lost as she sought another victim.

Kait brushed the backs of her knuckles along the smooth cool skin. No scars or puckered flesh lingered. It was as if the injury had never occurred. "This isn't right. This isn't what I wanted."

"No," Zeus whispered beside her. "It's what I wanted."

"What?"

Zeus closed the short distance between them. He reached out with the tips of his fingers as if to touch where the infection had been cleansed but stopped himself. "I'm sorry. I know we need to get out of here, but you could barely stand, and your fever was getting worse. I can't . . . I can't do this without you, and . . . the thought of leaving you in the dark . . . I'm sorry. I repeated it over and over in my mind to drown out every other thought the Sphinx might hear from you."

Kait blinked, stunned by Zeus's admission. "You did it to save me? But you could have asked for the way out and left me behind. You wouldn't be tied to me any longer. You'd be free to return to Olympus and regain your power. Why do you need me?" Her voice was soft but suspicious.

Zeus took a step closer, careful to keep his hands at his sides. He hung his head. "Don't you see? I'm not strong enough to do this on my own. You've saved me not once, but twice. You made the demons flee from inside my mind, and you bested the Sphinx, a feat no one else can claim. Even before all of this, you never gave in. You did the impossible and killed an immortal to protect yourself and your sisters. I admire you, Kait. You're incredible and resilient. If you'll have me, I'd like to be your friend."

"Don't," Kait spat, throwing out her arm to silence him. "Don't say that."

Zeus frowned but didn't say anything more.

"We need to work together to find Samara and escape Tartarus. That's all. Nothing has changed. I don't want your friendship. When we get out, you're going to aid Hades, and I'm going to save my sister. The dark changes nothing." She clenched her fingers into a fist and stepped away, looking at the faraway light once more. "Come. Tartarus isn't through with us yet."

CHAPTER 31

"I think we're actually getting closer," Zeus said as they clambered over yet another rocky ledge.

Kait sighed. "That joke lost its appeal two days ago."

"Only two? It feels like we've been wandering for a week, and these blasted light swirls only mess me up more." Zeus jumped and swatted the sky where a sparkling bronze swirl hung suspended in the air. His fingers passed through it, doing little to disrupt the transparent light source guiding them on.

Kait scoffed. "That'll teach it. Anyway, it doesn't matter how long it's been. What matters is our progress. Do you really think we're getting closer?"

Zeus paused and stuck his hands on his hips, squinting toward their destination. "We must be. Look. Doesn't it seem bigger to you? Brighter, too? Besides, we can't *not* have gotten closer after walking for days. It defies logic."

"Right, because that's what the realm of chaos boasts . . . logical experiences." Kait rolled her eyes.

"You know what I mean."

Silence settled over the pair as they pressed on, each lost in their own thoughts. Kait tried not to think about escaping the Underworld, tried not to imagine the way the sun would feel or the taste of fresh air. If she let her thoughts wander to such things, they seemed to become tangible—hypnotic hallucinations that tricked her mind with deadly consequences.

Since their last rest, strange things had started happening every time they let their guard down. Earlier, Kait's thoughts had wandered to Samara, and she was plagued with guilt at becoming separated from the gentle creature. Then suddenly, she heard the doe's cry. She'd dashed toward the sound, only to tumble off a precipice over a pit filled with spiked bones. If Zeus hadn't caught her ankle, she would have been skewered.

An hour later, Zeus fell to the ground shrieking about large scorpions biting and stinging his skin after daydreaming aloud of feeling the sun's warmth on his face. Yet when Kait tried to rid him of his attackers, none could be found. It seemed the closer they walked toward the golden light, the more severe their hallucinations became, and it was getting harder and harder to keep them at bay.

Kait skirted a large rock, only to see a deep crevice lying in wait on the other side. "Hey, watch your step up here," she called over her shoulder. "If you fall, I'm not jumping in after you." Silence echoed in reply. "Zeus? Zeus, did you hear me?" She glanced behind her. The messy brown hair and grime-stained robe she'd expected were nowhere to be found. "Zeus? Zeus, is everything all right?"

Kait sucked in her breath as she doubled back, images of the god impaled on another deadly booby trap spurring her on. Climbing over and around the obscure terrain, she caught a quick flash of the silver underlining of Zeus's robe a few hundred feet away.

"Zeus? You're going the wrong way. Stop!" Kait tried to keep the hysteria out of her voice. "Stop!"

She wished she could melt into the wind, fly above the boulders, and reach the god before something lethal befell him first, but her soul remained trapped within her physical form. With her leg healed, her speed was markedly better, but that would do her little good now. They were too far apart. She couldn't reach Zeus in time.

Kait managed to keep the god in her sights as she leapt over small chasms between the stone steps. Ahead of Zeus, a flicker of movement flashed, but it was gone before she could identify it.

"Zeus! Stop!" Kait cried, trying to penetrate whatever spell captivated him. The rocks leveled out, and her stride lengthened. She was closing the gap. "Zeus! It's another trick!"

The god paused, and his steps faltered.

"Zeus, stay where you are! I'm coming, just stay—"

Kait gasped as a collection of shadowy black wisps descended. Willowy tentacles wrapped diagonally across Zeus's torso, slithering around his neck and eyes while he stood motionless, blind to the gathering threat.

"No!" Kait pushed her legs faster. She reached out to knock the god out of the shadow's grasp, but they were too fast. They swept Zeus's legs out from under him, and he fell into their awaiting arms as his robe and features became obscured within the swirling smoke.

"Get off him!" Kait plunged her hands into the dark vapors. Scratching and swatting, she swung her arms to clear them away, but there was no way to tell if her efforts were working. At last, the black vapors cleared, and she was shocked to find she was alone. Zeus was gone.

Black bracelets encircled her wrists before she could step back as the vapors shifted and circled higher up her arms. The force skimmed her shoulders and then dove into her ears. Kait froze as darkness infiltrated her brain and suspended all thought. Unlike the cacophony of rumbles and hisses that had swarmed when the other monsters of Tartarus found her, an oppressive silence radiated this time. She tried to move her arms, but they felt disconnected. There was nothing she could do, no aggressor to fight.

Churning colors danced in her mind. All Kait could do was sit back and watch as they stilled, and images came into focus. Long dark curls and light brown skin appeared, wrapped in a golden halo. Kait stared at her reflection as if looking in a mirror. She watched her lips pull apart in a coy smile as desire flickered in her violet eyes. She was looking at something out of view, but her intentions were clear. Her reflection threw back her head, and a carefree burst of silent laughter ballooned. Kait's curiosity heightened.

A faceless male materialized and gently cupped her chin to guide her lips to his. The real Kait balked, but her reflection relished the stranger's touch and deepened the kiss, pulling him closer. She didn't understand the hallucination. Who was the man? A human? A god? The features kept changing, flickering through colors and shades too quickly to make any identification. The narrow scope panned wider and depicted the entwined pair in a luxurious bed, kissing atop a sea of sheets.

Unable to look away, Kait scrutinized the male, desperate to discover his identity. Green eyes and dark hair. A rush of warmth flooded her as she recognized Blake. He gazed at her reflection with vulnerability, waiting for her to advance the increasing passion. He explored her body with a gentle touch, as if truly interested in giving her pleasure. He closed his eyes when he kissed her and traced her hips as she climbed atop him.

The scene grew more intimate as Kait's reflection shed her sheer covering and began to move in a sensual rhythm while Blake kissed her, his lips trailing from her lips, down her neck, across her breasts, and then back up to claim her mouth. She looked happy and free, in love with a man who loved her as an equal.

The passionate scene blurred to portray a new vision. Kait's reflection reappeared, but this time, she wore a calm demeanor as she stared at a smiling infant swaddled against her breast. The child had her soft brown skin and piercing green eyes, along with a few wisps of dark hair on the crown of its head. Kait almost didn't recognize herself. Never had she gazed at something or someone with such tenderness. Her reflection opened her mouth, silently singing to the happy baby as it giggled with pure delight.

The hallucination was impossible. Nymphs didn't have children, had no need for children. Gaia created each one, and only brought more into the realms when necessary. In fact, Kait had only ever seen children on a few occasions while in the mortal world.

Then, why was her reflection radiating such joy? How did she know what to do? How to hold the infant and make it smile? A sickening feeling twisted her gut. At first, she hadn't noticed anything amiss because her reflection had glowed with such happiness, but upon further scrutiny, her suspicion was confirmed: Her halo was gone.

The Kait depicted in the vision was no longer a nymph, but mortal. She'd given up her ethereal connection and, judging by her content countenance, held the reason why in her arms.

Could that be her life? To surrender her powers and elemental connection for a mortal life with Blake? What if he grew bored of her and fell in love with someone else? What if she ended up hating motherhood and life in the mortal realm? She'd be left alone to wipe snot off their child's face after giving up her whole self for him. How could her reflection even entertain the notion?

Kait looked at the scene again. Her reflection leaned down and placed a soft kiss on the baby's little forehead, and he smiled as his eyes closed, safe and loved. Her reflection glanced up and met Kait's stare with pure adoration shining in every facet of her expression. Her reflection may have been mortal and alone, but there was no denying the incredible amount of love that poured forth from her. Holding the baby, she looked complete and perfect, stronger than Kait had ever seen herself before.

What if the best life is the one you rebel the hardest against? a gentle voice asked, breaking the silence.

The simple question stunned Kait. After Willow's death, a seismic shift had realigned all her priorities, and her only goal in her lifetime was to become a strong and dependable warrior for the realm. Now, her life was full of distractions intent on sidelining her plans. Between Jezlem losing her connection, Blake colliding with her world, Hades's demands, and a second encounter with Zeus, she felt as if she were being ripped in a dozen different directions that all asked her to change and let go of the things *she* wanted.

Kait didn't want to lose herself, didn't want to sacrifice her dreams for someone else's. Yet, the image of her cradling the baby persisted, both taunting and teasing. What if she chose wrong? What if the life she'd envisioned didn't garner half as much happiness as that one moment held?

Make the right choice.

The voice whispered one last time as the bewitching vapors fled her body, leaving her empty and hollow. Kait fell as the momentum of the magic caused her equilibrium to wobble. She landed on her backside with a quiet grunt.

"Kait? Where are you?"

"Zeus?"

Rapid footsteps echoed in response. A moment later, Zeus's greasy hair popped into view.

"Thank the gods," Zeus sighed. "I've been searching for nearly half an hour." He bent down and offered her his hand, but she ignored it and pushed herself to her feet. He retracted his arm and shook his head. "I didn't think I'd find you."

Disoriented from the visions and their sudden departure, Kait crossed her arms in front of her to erect a solid barrier between them. "What happened? Why did you leave?"

Zeus shook his head. "I didn't. I thought I was following you. We were walking, and then I lost sight of you. When I found you a minute later, you waved me on. I thought you'd found a new path, so I followed. It wasn't until I got closer that I realized something was wrong. You weren't you, more like a projection. I tried turning back but was blindsided by all these images. It was as if I fell into a dream."

"What was the dream?"

Zeus pinched the skin between his eyes. "It's fuzzy. The second they stopped, I couldn't recall what had happened."

Suspicion snaked up Kait's spine. The images she saw were branded into her mind. Either Zeus didn't see anything he valued or he was lying.

"I saw Hera," Zeus answered, catching Kait off guard.

"What happened?" Kait asked.

"She was happy. Happy in another god's arms. She'd moved on and finally let me go."

The pair started walking toward the golden light once more, matching strides to ensure neither wandered off again. Kait nodded, hesitant to reply. To Hades, Zeus had claimed that he hated his wife and would do anything to eradicate her from power, yet she noted regret in his tone as he spoke of her now.

"That's good, right?" Kait ventured. "Isn't that what you wanted? To be free of her?"

Zeus didn't answer at first, then nodded in agreement. "Of course. I've been looking to get out from under her hold for a while." He smirked, and a low chuckle fell from his lips, but it didn't sound genuine. Zeus cleared his throat. "What about you? Did those things make you see someone, too?"

"Oh . . . yeah," Kait stuttered. "Just memories of my sisters. Enough to make me homesick for Olean, that's for sure."

"I bet." Zeus sighed. "I'd give my left arm to see the sun again. Hell, even a cloud. Anything that isn't rock."

Their quiet laughter faded as they retreated into their thoughts. Kait didn't know what to think, but the image of the beautiful baby's smile warmed her heart and repulsed her at the same time. Either way, she was terrified of what choices lay in store for her future.

CHAPTER 32

Time meant nothing in Tartarus. Without the sun to gauge the hour, Zeus and Kait simply existed in the now, unable to judge how long they'd trekked over rough stones and crumbling cliffs. Days, weeks, or only mere hours could have passed. There was simply no way to know.

At several points along their journey, Kait questioned if perhaps Cronus had cast his time warp again, for no matter how long they walked, the beacon of light remained a constant distance away. Yet, they'd done everything right, followed all the rules. The only saving grace was that the landscape continued to change and offered new obstacles, which dismissed her theory of being stuck in a loop.

Screams crescendoed both day and night, sometimes far off in the distance and other times in their immediate vicinity, causing them to jump at the unexpected explosions of terror or pain. It became commonplace to catch glimpses of other tortured souls meandering the cursed realm, but Kait was careful to keep her head down and not engage, especially when malignant shadows stalked them.

Kait's leg muscles ached in a dozen different places. After their run-in with the Sphinx, she'd tried to keep her attention fixed on the golden light, but the path was too dangerous and sloped, and it curved at odd angles every few feet. She paused her stride and looked up from the uneven rocks for the first time in several hours and flinched in surprise. The beacon loomed ahead, massive and bright. Shielding her eyes, she peered through the shade of her fingers and was able to make out the silhouette of a stone archway in the center of the blinding rays.

Behind her, Zeus sucked in a sharp breath, taken aback by the sudden closeness of their destination as well. "Is this real?"

Kait started to respond, but Zeus posed a valid question. Maybe the vapors were back, spinning more hallucinations before them. "Only one way to find out," she answered as she slid down a smooth rock on her heels.

Keeping close together, they hurried forward, doing their best to navigate to the archway against the striking glare after so long in the dark. When Kait spied the beacon during the Sphinx's riddle, the light had shone with the gentleness of a candle; up close, it resembled the surface of a brilliant star.

Kait skirted to the side of the formation, eager to discover what lay at the center of the light. Tentatively, her fingers stretched but felt nothing but warm air. She took another step, and her foot plunged into nothingness. A scream caught in her throat, and her stomach flipped as her opposite knee slammed into the rock. Her hands flashed out to stall her momentum. The gritty texture of gravel sliced into her palms and bit her kneecaps, flaying what was left of her thin pants and the first few layers of skin. Hissing in pain, she pushed herself back and collapsed on her backside.

"What happened? Are you okay?" Zeus called.

Kait exhaled through her teeth and scooted farther back for good measure. "Yeah," she replied, her voice strained.

"What happened? I can't see you."

A painful cry fell from her lips as she stood and straightened her injured knee. Kait reached down and felt the damaged skin with her fingertips and gasped when a large wet flap of skin met her touch. "I'm here." Kait breathed through the pain. "I fell, nearly went over the edge." A heavy sob racked her chest as the truth hit her. "It's nothing. There's nothing here."

"What do you mean?" Zeus asked. "There must be. This was the way out!" His voice rose, nearing hysteria as he fumbled against the searing brightness. A moment later, his hands brushed her back and immediately dropped away upon contact, but she could feel him shake with frustration and desperation as if he were trying to hold himself together.

"I really thought this was the exit," Kait whispered. She didn't step away. His presence helped anchor the sinking feeling in the center of her chest. At least she wasn't alone in her heartbreak.

Zeus exhaled a long breath. "It doesn't make sense. Why create a beacon with no salvation?"

Kait shrugged. "Chaos. That's all Tartarus is. Chaos dipped in more chaos."

Zeus hissed under his breath and fumed with anger. "But we came all this way! The Sphinx, didn't the Sphinx point us in this direction? There must be something! What's the purpose of all this, then? To wander for eternity? No, Hades wouldn't do this to me."

Kait was silent as she waited out the god's outburst. "Are you sure? Maybe he has another plan up his sleeve? Maybe he's pledged allegiance to another?"

"No," Zeus barked. "This is the way out. It has to be. It has to be!"

Kait squinted in the direction of the archway. "It does seem strange. Why have such a structure amidst all the other rock?"

"Because it's not just another mess of rock. It's a door."

"A door? A door to what? There's a cliff on the other side."

"Come on. Trust me." Before Kait could protest, Zeus took her hand in his and dragged her the few yards to face the sculpted stones. Kait's breath caught in her throat as blood thundered in her ears. "Ready?"

"Ready for what? Zeus, I just told you, it's a cliff! If we walk through this thing, we'll both go over."

"But what if we don't? Come on, Kait, think about it. You said it yourself: Why is this here? It wasn't by accident but by design. It's here for a purpose. Trust me."

Kait threw off his grip and shuffled back. "Trust you? Why? So you can throw me over the edge?"

Zeus frowned and wrung his hands together. "I know I can't make up for my past deeds, but ever since the vapors forced me to feel the pain I subjected you to . . . I swear, I'm not that guy anymore, and I'd never intentionally hurt you. I want to be your friend, an ally you can count on." His words were soft and gentler than she'd ever heard him speak, but Jezlem had been fooled by this act before, and Kait would never forget the way she'd begged him to stop.

Kait shook her head. Tears threatened as anger pricked the back of her eyes. She'd already felt the brink, felt the loose rock slip out from under her and tumble away. If Zeus was wrong, they would be dead, lost in an endless labyrinth forever. But if he was right . . . The possibility of escape fluttered before her. They'd finally reached the beacon and for the first time, an exit felt so close.

Kait's heart pounded. Never had she followed anyone simply on faith. How did he know? From where did Zeus's confidence stem? What if this was a trap?

"Kait," Zeus said, scattering her thoughts. "Please, trust me."

His voice rang with sincerity, and she recalled the haunting way he'd clung to her hand amidst the vapor's initial attack as he apologized, again and again. Even if the cliff did lead them to another level of Hell, their fate would be the same, still lost with only each other for company. Kait took a deep breath. "Okay."

CHAPTER 33

The archway was just wide enough for them to fit, shoulder to shoulder. Kait gripped Zeus's hand, and her knuckles grew whiter with every step. She knew what lay on the other side: a heart-stopping fall to their demise. Peering through the light with narrowed eyes, she watched as their toes neared the precipice and flirted with fate.

"Nothing's happening." Kait breathed shallowly, beginning to hyperventilate. They were an inch away, the heavy archway directly overhead. She imagined it crumbling and crushing their bodies into a pulpy mess.

Zeus glanced up. "We haven't completely crossed the threshold yet. I think . . . I think we need to step off."

"Off? No!" Kait tried to wrench her hand out of the god's grasp, but he held tight.

"But it makes sense. What better place to hide the way out than in an action self-preservation prevents? Plus, we don't have much choice. If we don't try, then what? Where do we go?"

Kait shook her head while panic built faster in her chest. Her throat constricted, and her body readied to run, to fly as far from the threat as possible. She couldn't fall again, couldn't plunge through the sky without control.

"We go around. We find another way."

"There is no other way. Tartarus isn't like your Hall of Portals. There's only one way in and one convoluted way out. This is our only option."

"But . . . But what if we fall?" Kait whimpered as tears escaped from the corner of her eyes.

"I'll catch you," Zeus said. "You can do this."

Kait's lip quivered, and her body shook. Before she could respond, Zeus leaned in until his lips hovered just above hers. Caught off guard, Kait froze.

She knew what those lips felt like, remembered their touch when the god had crushed them against her hard enough to leave a bruise. Her heart raced, fury battling panic. He was too close, far too close. She needed to move, but one false step and the cliff was waiting to claim her.

Zeus drew back as realization bloomed in his eyes and he read the terror on her face. "I'm sorry. I was trying to get a better look at the edge." He exhaled, and his shoulders slumped. "I apologize, Kait. I didn't even think. Are you ready to try this?"

For a moment, the image of pushing the immortal off the edge flared in her mind with explosive intensity. Part of her would be ecstatic to watch him fall, watch as his body flailed uselessly, powerless to fight off his attacker. But, then she would be alone and—as difficult as it was to admit—having Zeus beside her on this nightmarish journey had somewhat tempered her pessimism about escaping the foul realm. Kait exhaled a shaky breath and nodded her consent at last.

"Okay." Zeus's lips quirked in a brief grin, and together they jumped.

Kait's gut plummeted as empty air encased them, only for their momentum to halt a few feet down. Solid stone rose seconds later. A firm surface collided with the soles of their feet. Zeus and Kait wobbled from the jarring impact but gripped each other and the cliff face behind them for support. A deep rumble groaned, and the intense light dimmed. The harsh brightness drew back, softened by deep shades of burgundy and charcoal. At last, they saw what the golden light had concealed.

Looming rock curved to form a giant basin. The walls were smooth onyx, crackled through with veins of scarlet magma that flowed beneath, which gave off a gentle shimmer. Kait's gaze followed the natural flow of the structure. Situated throughout the large valley was an odd assortment of massive tools, benches, and cauldrons, the latter of which were filled with boiling yellow liquid. The scent of burning iron permeated the air as cooling steel hissed. A steady pounding ricocheted off the rocks. Peering through the rising curls of smoke, she tried to identify the source, but her vision was obscured.

"We need to get down there," Zeus said, as if reading her mind.

Kait scanned the stone ledge that had caught them. "Look. A staircase." Hundreds, if not thousands, of steps descended from where they stood, circling the walls until they reached the base.

"Great," Zeus muttered, noting the exposed right side. "If exhaustion doesn't kill me, vertigo will."

"Come on. Stay close to the wall and take it one step at a time."

Kait nudged past him, pressed her left palm against the stone, and began her descent, eager to put some distance between them. She kept her eyes trained on the path ahead as she fought to calm her racing pulse. Memories of her time spent imprisoned by the god, of his cruel taunts and touches, would only agitate her steps and cloud her mind. If this basin led where she hoped, then she'd be rid of him soon enough.

Their journey was slow going, but it was better to tread carefully than slip and career off the side. After fifty steps or so, the smoke dissipated, but the heat intensified. Beads of sweat collected at Kait's hairline. The temptation to brush her curls back was overwhelming, but she ignored the instinct. It would only take one false move to lose her balance.

A melancholy cry whistled as they continued their descent. Kait paused, straining to identify it. The desperate wail sounded again. The same curiosity was reflected in Zeus's eyes as the clatter of heavy chains rattled several hundred feet below.

"Shut up," a gruff voice commanded. A tinkling of metal echoed as someone jostled a set of chains. "Should eat you raw."

Kait crouched lower to peer deeper into the basin and nearly fainted from shock. Lumbering through an array of tools and instruments was a giant Cyclops. His dark blue skin was covered in soot and sweat. Glistening odorous trails ran down his back and large stomach to a worn burlap kilt that hugged his waist. His hair hung in thick black ropes past his shoulder blades, and a heavy beard covered half his face. Gold jewels were braided into the strands, clinking musically with his movements. Kait's gaze continued down the Cyclops's chest to where twin gold medallions rested atop a mess of wet hair. Cryptic tattoos that blazed with the same intensity as the magma, adorned his stomach, biceps, and neck, depicting symbols from a language long forgotten.

The Cyclops was massive, towering at least thirty feet tall. He flicked a small cage hanging overhead with the back of his hand before grabbing a double-faced hammer and setting himself back to work. A familiar pinging sounded as the monster resumed his pace. Kait looked away from the Cyclops in favor of the cage. It swung dangerously from the monster's touch, but something moved within the thick bars.

Dappled white and brown fur clung to a muscular body in irregular clumps as graceful legs fought to keep upright on the dancing platform. Kait crawled another forty steps as the winding staircase brought her closer. By now, the cage had lost its momentum, offering her a clear view of the single occupant imprisoned within. She released a small gasp, and relief surged in her chest. "It's Samara. She's here," Kait whispered, pointing to the cage.

Zeus followed her gesture, but his features didn't relay the same excitement. "How are we going to get her out? Look at that thing. If we can somehow pry the lock open, we'll still be fifty feet in the air."

Kait frowned, realizing the truth of his words. "We'll figure something out."

The Cyclops's rough baritone radiated throughout the room. "Make this. Forge that. It never ends. Now, Hades demands another thousand breastplates with spaulders? You'd think we were still fighting the Titan War."

"What's he talking about?" Kait asked.

"Don't know," Zeus answered quickly. "Come on. We need to move before he sees us. I vote we turn back."

"What? And leave Samara?"

"Of course not, but we can't reach her from the ground. What good is it to keep going and risk being seen?"

"So, how do we get to her? I still can't shift, and your powers have yet to be restored."

Zeus pointed to the thick metal chain that swayed from an anchor in one of the protruding rocks a few feet above them.

"Is that possible?" Kait asked.

Zeus shrugged. "It's our best option. I'll shimmy down the chain and pick the lock. The cage is level with the stairs, so it shouldn't be too difficult for her to jump the gap."

Kait bit the inside of her cheek. "What if he sees you?"

The god shrugged once more as a small smile pulled at the corners of his mouth. "Let's not worry about that right now."

Their sight became muddled once more as they climbed back into the layer of smoke that rose from the numerous boiling vats, and the vast cavern disappeared.

"Right," Zeus said, stopping their progress. "This is where the cage is anchored."

Kait peered through the haze, barely able to make out the tarnished silver chain. "But it's too smoky. The only way to reach it is to jump. You could sail right past."

Zeus smirked. "Are you worried about me, aurai?"

"No, I'm being logical. You'll fall and break a dozen bones."

"Well, don't fret. You'd never be able to see my body hit from up here." He shrugged out of his soiled robe, tossed the garment to her, and stretched his arms.

The silky material wrapped around Kait's forearm, and the god's scent wafted over her. She dropped the warm cloth to the stairs below and grimaced. Her hatred for him hadn't lessened, yet there was an unnerving pit of unease that formed in her gut as she watched him line up at the edge of the step.

Zeus turned over his shoulder and offered a small smile. "It'll be fine. Samara and I will meet you right back here."

"Okay, just . . . Be careful," Kait whispered, biting the insides of her cheeks until her teeth left an imprint.

"Am I ever?" Zeus's light-hearted mood did little to settle Kait's rising anxiety.

Before she could reply, Zeus reached up and ran his hands along the underside of the rock. Toeing the edge of the stairs, he bent his knees and aligned his body in the direction the chain should be. Kait desperately wished she could blow the clinging fog away or cast a small enchantment to increase his visibility. Without looking back, Zeus pumped his arms and exhaled two quick breaths, then leapt into nothingness.

One minute, the god stood in front of her, solid and tangible; a second later, wispy air took his place, and silence radiated.

One, two, three, four.

Kait counted, attempting to calm her nerves. He should have reached the chain by now. Why hadn't it rattled like before? A vision of Zeus streaming through the sky, hair fluttering across his forehead as his hands reached out, assailed her. She stepped closer to the edge, straining to find the chain.

Let him reach her.

She took another step and brushed her hand through the swirling gray smoke.

Five, six.

Clunk.

A heavy thud echoed, sending shivers up the chain like metallic bones knocking together. Kait exhaled. Had he made it? As promised, she stayed put and rubbed the gauzy material across her stomach like a comfort object. Several minutes had elapsed, and still she waited, gnawing her cheeks with her molars. The chain continued to dance, its links rattling as it mocked her gargoyle-like stance. She remembered the way the Cyclops had gripped the cage, shaking it to torment Samara. What if Zeus had been seen?

Unable to wait any longer, Kait raced down the stairs and out of the opaque smoke, leaving Zeus's crumpled robe behind. She scanned back and forth between the basin and the stairs, anxious to locate Zeus while her feet kept a steady rhythm toward her destination.

Kait stepped down onto the ball of her foot, but the tread crumbled beneath her heel. She slipped, and the world tipped sideways as her heart lurched and her stomach dropped. Crashing hard on her right elbow, she stifled a cry, even as her body continued to slide. The backs of her calves grated against the sharp stones. Her head slammed into a riser, which sliced a sizable gash into the flesh at the base of her skull.

Dazed and disoriented, Kait lay still. Her head and elbow throbbed, and her freshly peeled skin tingled. She had no idea how far she was from the lip, but she couldn't muster the ability to care.

"Kait! Kait, move!" a frantic voice called.

Rolling her head to the right, Kait struggled to find Zeus, but all she could see was brown fur. The pounding of hooves caused her body to shake. A monstrous roar exploded, followed by a sharp whirring sound. Shifting to the left, Kait pulled herself into a sitting position and cradled her head while her focus swam with pain. A flicker of movement flashed as a massive hammer crushed the place where she'd just been lying. She watched in shock while the rock steps fell away and tumbled over the precipice.

"Give me your arm!" Zeus yelled.

Kait didn't know where he was or what was happening; she simply obeyed. She stretched her right arm up out of instinct, and a solid grip wrapped around her wrist, hauling her into the air. The walls blurred as Zeus flipped her back, not letting go until she landed awkwardly behind him astride Samara.

Stars burst behind Kait's eyes as her elbow twisted from the rough force and the shattered bone dug deeper into the surrounding muscle. A painful sob poured from her lips as she wrapped her other arm around Zeus's waist and pressed her face against his sweat-slicked skin. For the first time, she didn't flinch away from the contact. The waves of pain crashing into her were too great.

"Are you okay?" Zeus cried before ducking out of the trajectory of a flying chisel. Its teeth buried into the molten rock above them with a piercing chomp.

"I fell," Kait answered, trying to stifle the tears running down her cheeks. "What's going on?"

An unfinished metal sword clattered behind them and bounced down the steps, eager to taste the doe's hind legs.

"The Cyclops saw me," Zeus yelled over his shoulder. "I overshot the chain. Luckily, I caught the base but had to pull myself up to the top. It was a miracle Samara and I escaped before the Cyclops rammed it. I think he means to kill us." A soft laugh resonated in the back of Zeus's throat. Even facing peril, he somehow managed to remain calm.

"Okay, so why are we heading toward the monster trying to kill us?" Kait asked as the doe charged downward, picking up speed atop the curved staircase.

"I can't stop her," Zeus shouted as the steps in front of them exploded in a blast of rubble and dust. "Hold on!"

Kait squeezed her eyes shut and gripped the doe's slender body with her thighs. She dug her fingernails into Zeus's stomach, remembering she'd left his robe far behind. She pressed the side of her face harder against his back. The sensation of being weightless gripped her as Samara leapt a gap in the stairs with graceful ease.

"You won't escape, immortal," the Cyclops rasped, hair swinging behind him like a dozen nooses. He lurched forward and rushed to a nearby cauldron, knocking the pewter bowl off its stand. The boiling contents slithered across the floor with an angry sizzle.

Golden liquid bubbled and spread, searing table legs and chairs to burning ash. With Zeus and Kait clinging to her back, the doe crouched and extended her powerful legs, launching them clear across the lake of lava. The Cyclops roared as the trio escaped to a safe section of floor, unscathed. Snatching a half-made sword from one of the few remaining tables, he hurled the blazing red metal with furious strength, but the weight of the throw pulled him forward, and he staggered onto one foot to catch himself.

If Kait hadn't been watching him, she would have missed it. Situated directly below the Cyclops, the uneven cobblestones gave way to a narrow wooden panel. She didn't know why or what compelled her thoughts, but deep in her gut, she knew that was the exit out of Tartarus, hidden quite literally beneath the belly of the beast. Zeus groaned and dug his legs into Samara to help guide her out of the sword's path, and it whirled past their heads and clanged to the floor behind them.

"Zeus!" Kait cried as the Cyclops scrambled for another weapon. "There's a door!" She pointed to where the floor dipped and transitioned from stone to wood.

Zeus didn't argue, didn't question her judgment. "Think we're lucky enough that it's unlocked?" Kait scoffed at the absurdity. "We'll find a way to open it, then." With a firm nod, Zeus tightened his grip on the doe's antlers. "That's our target, Samara."

The doe shook her head in response.

"Hold on!" Zeus clasped his hand over Kait's knee for a quick moment before he regained his grip. "Go!"

Samara didn't hesitate. Just as the Cyclops slammed his foot down, the doe sprinted to the left, easily increasing her speed until she was practically invisible. Careful to skirt the cooling lava, she raced around the circular room while the Cyclops's fury raged. He unleashed a wild bellow and chucked anything within reach into the walls and along the staircase. Samara continued her pace, but it was getting harder to navigate the chaotic floor.

Cutting away from the walls, the doe slowed, her sight set on the inlaid door. The Cyclops didn't see them, too intent on destroying the stairs to prevent a possible escape the way they'd entered. Samara jumped over a fallen set of tongs, paused in the middle of the door, and nudged the thick padlock with her hoof.

Zeus rose as tall as he could astride her back. He put his fingers in his mouth and whistled shrilly. The Cyclops spun, murder in his cardinal-red eye. Another guttural cry erupted from the monster as he charged. His left arm drew back, ready to deliver a fatal blow. Samara held her ground as the Cyclops lumbered closer. Kait's panic flared, but she held her tongue, confident her companions had a plan. The Cyclops rushed ahead and punched his arm forward with enough force to split a tree trunk. Still, the doe held her ground.

"Samara!" Kait cried, unable to contain her fear any longer as the Cyclops's blue fist hammered down. At last, the doe sprang out from under their oppressor just before his knuckles reached her. Unable to stop his momentum, the Cyclops's hand crashed through the door and blasted it off its hinges, revealing a swatch of light blue. Fresh air wafted toward them as he hastily withdrew his beefy arm.

"That's it! Jump, Samara!" Zeus yelled.

In one leap, the doe dove through the narrow breadth of cerulean.

"Stop!" the Cyclops roared, stomping on the small doorway with a sandaled foot, but he was too late. The trio sailed across the threshold, claiming victory over Tartarus and its twisted carnival of horrors at last.

They were out.

They were free.

They were safe.

They were alive.

CHAPTER 34

"Eee-owwww!" Zeus yelled, pumping both fists into the air. "We did it! We actually did it!"

Kait glanced back at the door, fearful their freedom was another haunting illusion. However, nothing but endless sky and rolling clouds met her gaze. The portal was gone. She couldn't even detect a faint outline. They were back. They'd bested hell and lived to tell the tale. Kait's grin mirrored Zeus's.

I'm almost there, Bia.

Zeus's laughter boomed like the thunderclaps he wielded. "Can you believe it? We're out! I never thought I'd say that. I thought we'd be stuck wandering down there forever." He lifted his hand to high-five her, and she was surprised she didn't hesitate to return the gesture.

Zeus dropped his head and unleashed another unrestrained whoop of victory. Kait's dizzying thoughts retreated to the back of her mind as she turned to Samara and ran her palm down the doe's velvet skin. "Thank you, Samara. For coming with me, for fighting, and for getting us out."

The doe nodded once in response but remained focused on extending and curling her long legs to glide along the air. Somehow, the incredible doe was flying, leaping from current to current as she carried them high into the clouds.

A quiet hissing drew Kait's attention to her chest. Flickering like a candle battling the wind, the silver spark that signified her life force appeared and blazed bright before, like a dying star, it imploded. Waves of energy rolled down her skin in the aftermath as her soul was revived and restored at last.

Kait's chest jerked forward as she inhaled for the first time since entering the rapids of the Acheron River. Breathing deeply, she laughed as fresh air swirled inside her lungs and the sunshine's glorious warmth kissed her skin.

She was *alive*. Hades had kept his word. She closed her eyes and focused on the soft breeze blowing the light hairs on her arms.

Let me fly.

Kait's flesh immediately dissolved into the wind, and she became one with her element at last. She flipped backward off the doe and soared, no longer plagued by the terrible fear of falling or incessant hopelessness. Her connection to the wind was restored, and with it, her strength. All at once, any remnants of her time in Tartarus evaporated from her person. Her injuries melted away. Gone were the bruises, the fractured bones, the pain.

From a few yards away, she watched Zeus scan the sky for her. He appeared content as he inhaled the same sweet air she danced in. Kait was struck by how different he looked in the light, so disparate from the monster she hated. Surely, his new features helped mask the vicious brute within, yet the change seemed to go even deeper.

Zeus had screamed in agony as the vapors tortured him for his sins and claimed he now understood her pain. It also hadn't escaped Kait's notice how cognizant of his proximity he'd become, always careful not to move too close unless the situation demanded it. She wasn't a fool. To change one's true nature was monumental but perhaps their combined trials had altered his mindset just enough to produce a profound shift from predator to ally. He'd saved her life down there, had even traded a quick solitary exit to heal the wounds Echidna had inflicted upon her.

Kait had no idea what would happen to their relationship now that they'd escaped. In many ways, she realized she'd come to rely on having the god by her side, and that truth scared her more than anything she'd faced in Hades's playground.

"Having fun?" Zeus asked as Kait sent a gust of wind in his direction.

Kait remained in her elemental form, delighting in the strong currents. Part of her wished to prolong the moment, to stay in the sky because it meant a few more minutes of delaying reality. Her next task loomed like a menacing cloud on the horizon. She'd barely escaped one hell, only to plunge headfirst into another without so much as a reprieve. As she swirled through the breeze, her heart yearned to find Jez and see Blake, to kiss them both and assure them she was okay, but Bia was counting on her. Her own desires meant nothing compared to her sister's sacrifice.

Materializing out of the wind, Kait regained her seat behind Zeus and wrapped her arms around his waist to secure her weight. Somewhere along the way, contact with the god had become somewhat manageable.

"Did you enjoy yourself?" Zeus asked.

"Yes. It feels incredible to be alive. I never want to die again."

"Agreed." Zeus laughed.

A quiet moment of silence settled between them as Samara continued to ascend to the tops of the clouds. At the summit, a whole new set of challenges awaited, ready to force them into further uncharted territory. Kait shook the worries from her mind and imagined them falling off her body like rain.

Zeus cleared his throat. "You know we should—"

"Not yet," she whispered as exhaustion overwhelmed her.

At some point, they'd have to talk about how Tartarus had changed their relationship and the new challenges that awaited them in the distance. The moment couldn't be avoided, but for now, Kait stared at the beauty of the sky. After suffocating so long in the dark, she could only focus on taking one breath at a time.

A piercing light flashed behind Kait's closed eyes, jerking her awake. She had no memory of falling asleep, but luckily her arms remained anchored around Zeus as Samara glided beneath them.

"Morning, sleeping beauty."

Kait rubbed her eyes, attempting to shield them from the shine that had woken her. "How long was I out?"

"Not long," Zeus replied. "Though for being a catnap, you slept pretty hard. I think drool is pooling in my waistband."

"Goddess, I'm sorry." Pulling away, Kait gazed at the god's back. Sure enough, a wet trail of saliva covered his tanned skin. "Why didn't you wake me?"

Zeus shrugged. "You needed sleep, and it's not a big deal. I don't mind."

Kait used the ends of her tattered belt to wipe the slime off Zeus and arched backward to reinstate a barrier of space between them. Something grand and gold drew her attention to an object in the distance. Towering gates stood between two massive mountaintops, their summits cloaked in clouds. Delicate gilded vines adorned with curling leaves decorated each picket and extended over the top as if still growing. The ornate structure dazzled in the sun, sparkling like the many facets of a prized diamond.

Zeus spread his arms. "Welcome to Olympus." Kait was speechless. If the exterior was that grand, she couldn't imagine what wonders lay beyond the gates. "Set us down over there, Samara," he ordered, guiding the doe to the left.

Samara switched direction easily, riding a cold air current lower, and carried them to the base of the left mountain. A narrow ledge about ten feet across expanded out from the thick stone, the land solid and strong. As they neared, Kait again marveled at the construction. Olympus seemed to have once been part of the earth until a giant severed it from the land and threw it into the sky. It was magical, and for a moment, she forgot the arduous challenge she'd been tasked with.

The doe's hooves touched down, ending their long flight at last. Zeus slid off first and offered her his arm. Kait gave her hair a quick shake before she vanished into the wind to appear on the other side of Samara. Joy crested through her at the simple act, but too soon, her heart hardened. She knew she couldn't indulge in this freedom for long. Hera awaited.

"Why didn't we enter through the gates?" Kait asked. "Is there a secret way in?"

"No, that is the official entrance to Olympus," Zeus replied. "There are portals on the South End, but those are reserved for merchants. I wanted to stop before we reached the gates because I need to change."

"What do you mean? Hades already altered your appearance."

Zeus gestured to his half-nude form. "Yes, but I don't want to bring about any unwanted attention or questions."

"But we have no other clothes." Kait pointed to her own jumpsuit. Her once lovely ensemble gifted by Poseidon was now covered in grime and ripped to ghastly shreds.

"I have some stashed here," Zeus admitted, sounding sheepish. "You see, Hera was aware of my infidelities, but she thought I left them in the lower realms. I would bring my lovers back to Olympus with me and smuggle them inside to keep them close until I, um . . ."

"Until you tired of them?" Kait finished.

"Yeah." Zeus looked at the ground and traced the rough mountainside until a grin settled on his lips. "Here we are." Wedging his arm into a shallow crevice, he withdrew a plain brown tunic with a hood and frayed black pants, along with a short white shift. Tucking the garments under his arm, he tossed the shift to Kait with a regretful look in his eye. "Sorry. That's all I have. It was easier to smuggle them in if—"

"Everyone thought she was a criminal, sent here to be punished by the Council," Kait said. She held the shift in her palms and ran her fingers along the coarse material. It was common knowledge that nymphs who willingly exposed the secrets of the ethereal realm to humans were dangerous, and if the behavior wasn't rectified after corrective punishment dealt by Queen Rajhi, they were sent to Olympus. The immortals used them for manual labor and the undesirable jobs necessary to keep their great haven functioning. Kait wrinkled her nose. All her life, she'd striven to maintain her reputation, but now, holding the wretched symbol, her jaw clenched. Immortals thought themselves better than all other creatures, and forcing them to wear the degrading shift ensured it was a lesson their "lessers" never forgot.

Zeus frowned. "Look, you don't have to wear it. I'm sorry."

Kait tore apart what little fabric remained intact across her chest and stomach and let the material flutter to the gravel at her feet. She swept the shift over her head, stifling her disgust as it settled across her shoulders. Zeus held her gaze, his eyes never dropping lower than her face. "How do I look?"

Zeus shook his head as he stripped out of his pants and slipped the new tunic on. He crossed the small distance separating them and bit his lower lip. "Awful. I hate seeing that on you. If I had another way inside, we'd take it. You know that, right?"

Kait stared into his muddied irises, searching for the monster who had held her captive just a few months ago. She wished she could erase Tartarus, reset her emotions back to when the only thing she felt when she looked at him was hatred. She missed the wrath that had simmered so close to the surface in the Underworld. It was now clouded with so many other feelings. Kait glanced away and focused on the white shift clinging to her body, then strode forward and placed her palm on Samara's neck. "Come on. We should get going."

"Samara can't accompany you."

"What?"

"Think about it. You're supposed to be a prisoner. You can't roll up with a Ceryneian hind in tow."

Kait froze. She hadn't considered that, but the god was right. She would never be able to get close to Hera with the powerful doe by her side. "Then, act as if she belongs to you. We'll enter and find a place to lie low. That'll give me time to stake out Hera's routine. It's not like Hades told her I was coming. There's no reason I can't accomplish this task from a distance."

Zeus shook his head. "I'm supposed to be a lower god, nothing more than a poor apprentice. What excuse could I give for being responsible for overseeing a nymph's sentence or owning such an exquisite animal? I can only get you inside the gates by claiming I'm your appointed escort. The guard won't ask questions. He'll just assume you've been found guilty after your trial in Olean. Then, the moment we walk in, you'll be delivered to Hera."

Kait swallowed the lump in her throat as the blood rushed into her ears. "Can't we seek another immortal's help? Maybe they could keep Samara, too?"

Zeus shook his head. "There's no one I trust with the truth, and if I take you to someone else, your chances of getting close to Hera will be greatly reduced. You could be stuck here for years."

Kait bit her lip, and her anxiety spiked. Hades would never wait that long. She imagined her sweet sister's soul facing one of Echidna's bloodthirsty children when Kait failed. She hadn't realized escaping Tartarus would be the easier of the two tasks. "But won't *I* stand out?" She gestured to the horrid white shift. "It's not like there's a large population of punished nymphs wandering around. I'll be identified the moment I walk in."

Zeus's frown deepened. "You'd be surprised, actually. Gaia, well . . . Not all the nymphs she creates are sent to Olean. Over the last few centuries, our expanding infrastructure demanded more physical laborers, and she . . ."

Kait took advantage of his trailing thought. "Gaia made you servants."

"Yeah." He didn't look at her. At least the bastard had the decency to appear ashamed.

Fury speared Kait's anxiety. Why hadn't she known about this? How could Gaia agree to that? Creating nymphs so the gods didn't have to shovel their own shit? And what of the nymphs? How could Gaia deprive them of a life enjoying the true potential of their elemental connection? History after the Titan War painted a rosy picture of immortals and nymphs living in harmony to prove the overthrow of the old gods was justified. Yet the whole time, the same practices had endured in secret. What else were they hiding behind those glimmering gates?

Zeus closed the distance between them. "Don't worry. You won't be alone in this. I won't abandon you. I promise."

"Yeah, until *your* task is complete." Kait slammed the heels of her palms against Zeus's chest and pushed him away before she pivoted on her heels. She kissed the soft fur between Samara's gentle eyes. "Thank you for all you've done. Return to your family. I will never forget your kindness and bravery." Her voice wavered as she wiped pooling tears from her eyes. Kait left the doe's side without another word and quickened her pace, grimacing as the white shift rubbed against her thighs.

"Kait, please. Don't act like this. I'm sorry. I'm sorry for what happened to your sister, for what you have to do now—for my past, for who I was. For what a mess all of this is. But please don't shut me out. We have to work together, remember?" Zeus pleaded.

"It doesn't matter, Zeus. None of it matters. This was the plan from the beginning. I offer myself to Hera, and you hide, and plot, and wait for whatever twisted plan you and your brother have cooked up. Either way, you don't have to pretend you need me anymore." Kait didn't slow as she neared the outskirts of the gates.

Behind her, Zeus's footsteps faltered. "But I'm not pretending."

Kait's resolve stuttered. He sounded genuine, but she refused to fall prey to another illusion. For the sake of survival, they'd reached a truce while trapped in Tartarus, but outside those oppressive walls, the fragile trust she'd placed in him had returned to its shattered state once more. Her thoughts shifted to her sister's terrified face as the infected nymphs attacked. No. She refused to jeopardize her only chance to save Bia. Kait rolled her shoulders and hissed, confident in her decision.

"I wish I could believe that." Kait strode away in the direction of the gates.

Zeus jogged alongside her and reached out to grasp her hand. "Kait, please wait."

Kait jerked away as his calloused palms grazed her forearm. The golden gates came into view, along with the guard standing just inside.

"Kait, please."

Kait's strides lengthened. She couldn't do this. Not now. She needed all her focus on Hera. She couldn't risk becoming distracted by whatever lie the god was about to spout. Zeus sighed and his pace slowed as they approached the entrance.

"Halt," a deep voice commanded. "What business have you on Mount Olympus?"

Kait walked forward meekly and bowed her head. As if rehearsed, Zeus strolled forward and planted his hands on his hips. Gone was his vulnerability, his desperation to reassure her. The cold mask she knew all too well was back in place.

"My name is Aristaeus. I've been charged with delivering this convicted nymph to begin her sentence."

The gatekeeper's gaze shifted from Zeus to where Kait stood beside him. She could feel the weight of his stare through her thin shift. Goosebumps prickled her flesh, but before she could turn away, Zeus stepped in front of her and blocked the god's view.

"I would appreciate your cooperation." Zeus's tone was jovial, but his rigid body language hinted at a veiled threat.

The gatekeeper scoffed and consulted a clipboard at his waist. "I don't have any prisoners scheduled for today."

Zeus leaned closer to the rods. "Check again. Or you can summon Hera—the high goddess waiting for her new servant—and explain that *she* forgot to notify *you*."

The gatekeeper's chins wobbled, and his deep-set eyes blinked with fear. "No need for that, sir. No need for that." He hurried to unlock the great gate and stepped back so they could enter.

Zeus gave the guard a curt nod and grabbed Kait roughly by the arm. Her pulse raced, and the wind kicked up, disrupting the wispy white clouds that gathered around their ankles. She was back in the mountains, back beneath the god's harsh touches when he'd thrown her against the hard stone. She inhaled a sharp breath as the wind tugged at the ends of her dress, willing her to transform.

"Stay with me," Zeus whispered in her ear.

He gave her arm a gentle squeeze. His voice was the grounding element she needed, her anchor once again. He was playing a part, just as she was expected to. Kait wrenched her arm out of his hold and shot him a dark look. "I can walk on my own, god."

Zeus smirked. "Not into Olympus. Not on your own."

Kait frowned and turned her attention back to the gates. Even though the entryway had been cleared, she felt a powerful thrumming in her core. She took another step. A wave of energy pulsed and shot her several inches back.

"Whoa." Kait rubbed the tender spot on her chest where the gate's magic had hit when it rejected her. The magic was similar to the portals back home, but this one had quite a kick.

"Believe me now?"

Kait nodded and looked down.

"An immortal must be touching you for you to gain entry. Okay?"

Kait heard the way his voice softened as if he were asking permission to put his hand on her again.

"Come on, then. I haven't got all day to waste on the likes of you," the guard called.

Zeus gently laid his hand on the curve of her shoulder, careful to apply the least amount of pressure needed for the barrier to accept them. "Ready?"

Kait matched his stare. "Yes."

Together, they moved forward, and this time, a warm tingling flooded her skin and combed the strands of her windswept hair. Kait shivered at the familiar greeting as the portal accepted her, and a pang of homesickness pricked her. She'd give anything to return to Olean, but Bia couldn't wait.

The gatekeeper slammed the gates closed once they crossed the threshold. "About bloody time." He relocked the padlock and called over his shoulder, "Riven!"

A gangly immortal with long black hair tied at his nape hustled in front of the gatekeeper. His sheathed sword swung awkwardly from where it hung off his waist, looking far too large for the young soldier to effectively wield.

"Think you can handle this one?" the gatekeeper asked. His tone was challenging as if there'd already been several failures in the young man's past.

"Yes, of course." Riven nodded too many times.

"Good. Then, head out and hurry back. I don't want to find out that you snuck off for a pint at Dionysus's again." The gatekeeper snorted.

Zeus threw up a hand to halt their exchange. "Excuse me, but this nymph is my responsibility. I'll accompany her."

The gatekeeper grinned, exposing the grayed roots of his two front teeth. "Is that so? Well, unfortunately for you, I've no paperwork for this nymph. So, you're not going anywhere 'til that's sorted, all right?"

Zeus's jaw clenched with rage. Kait could only imagine how his injured pride fumed at the lesser god's derision. She grinned and cocked her head. "Rules are rules."

Zeus opened his mouth to reply, but the gatekeeper jabbed the youth in the chest. "Escort this one to Hera's palaces. Be quick, and don't dawdle, lad."

"Yes. I mean, no. I mean, yes," Riven stammered.

The gatekeeper rolled his eyes and gestured toward the lane. "Be off, then."

Riven nodded. "This way, miss."

"Wait," Zeus said. "Just wait. I can take her."

The gatekeeper thrust his clipboard at Zeus's torso, seeing nothing but a dirty beggar bound for the South End once his fifteen minutes of usefulness had expired. "She goes. You stay. Head down to the docks if you need a girl that badly."

"No, but I . . ." Zeus's gaze found hers, and she read the alarm in his dilated pupils, the unspoken words he couldn't say.

"Goodbye."

Kait turned away and focused on putting one foot in front of the other. She swallowed her conflicting emotions and wiped her face of all expression as she marched after the young guard. She didn't have time for doubt or weakness. She was about to face Hera, and she would need every ounce of strength and wile she possessed to stay alive.

CHAPTER 35

The young guard led Kait through the winding streets of Olympus, silent and dutiful, keeping his gaze fixed on the white marble road. Briefly, she considered turning back. Perhaps, she could kill Hera from a distance rather than with the personal assault Hades had envisioned, but she was far too transfixed by the beauty that graced every pillar of the immortal realm to do anything save for gawk.

After leaving the gates behind, they wove along the glistening road and passed a dozen or so vendors dispersed in parallel lines. The loud and raucous atmosphere brought Kait right back to the main square in Olean, and her heart yearned for the soft grass beneath her feet and the smell of Illya's fresh sweet rolls. But she would find none of the comforts of home here. Rather than the warm earth tones and natural shops carved from towering trees, everything about Olympus seemed to float, rooted in nothing but endless sky.

Everywhere Kait looked, the color white dominated. From the stones she traversed, to the ornate pillars that supported the grand temples. It was sophisticated and ethereal, yet cold and rigid in contrast to Olean. Hundreds of gods, goddesses, and indentured nymphs donning the same shift she wore wandered the intricate lanes. The immortals' bright gowns and robes added the only pops of color to the otherwise bleached landscape.

The market bustled with activity as the sun shone, uninterrupted by bothersome clouds. It was easy to blend into the crowd. The immortals gave her as much attention as a piece of furniture, just another servant or laborer carrying out a task. A variety of shops decorated the marketplace, but beyond the single-story structures loomed grand mansions, all emblazoned with the golden seal of the gods. This part of Olympus seemed even more refined, set aside for official business. Kait wondered just how large Olympus was. Over one thousand gods occupied the highest of the realms, but most of it was shrouded in mystery.

Kait turned her gaze upward as shimmering sparkles danced on the languid breeze. Pausing her stride, she lifted her arm, hypnotized by the golden flakes. Several kissed her skin before rolling off to land silently on the marble tile below. She frowned. Even the air illustrated the immense wealth and opulence the immortals basked in every day.

"Exquisite pearls! Gossamer lace! Finest silks!" a chorus of vendors shouted, drawing Kait's attention away from the sky. The guard motioned for her to keep up as she settled back into the bustling market.

Each stall was tucked and elevated a few yards from the main road, designed to force shoppers inside to view the wares and trinkets. Beautiful sheer white curtains billowed gently in the breeze, licking the heels and elbows of nearby patrons as each vendor fought to entice the mingling crowds away from the competition. Kait spied delicate glass figurines, all blown in varying colors. She paused and watched as the young guard continued, oblivious to the fact that his charge was no longer behind him. Patiently, she waited until he rounded an ornate fountain and stepped out of sight. She smiled, celebrating the small victory, and wandered closer to one of the tempting stalls, but her interest was not met with kindness.

"Away with you!" the shopkeeper rasped as he fluttered his hands. "This stall is for paying customers."

"How do you know I don't intend to buy?" Kait shot back, raising her chin.

The shopkeeper scoffed and rolled his broad shoulders beneath a deep orange robe. "What use does a servant have for beauty?" He furrowed his eyebrows and pointed to her attire.

Shame colored Kait's cheeks as she remembered the white shift and realized what he and every other immortal thought—that she was nothing more than trash. Retreating from the stall, Kait collided with something behind her. Her eyes flashed wide as she pictured one of the fragile glass pieces falling to the floor, but instead of a display, dark scarlet robes flashed as a pair of calloused hands steadied her.

"Are you all right?" a kind voice asked.

The speaker towered above Kait. Her head barely grazed the immortal's shoulders.

"Ah, Miss Athena." The shopkeeper beamed, adjusting his sour countenance. "My apologies. I was just cleaning up the shop when some filth wandered in." He glided around the table and reached for the back of Kait's shift.

Athena held up a flat palm to stop him. "That's enough, Strago. Surely, you'd like to help this young nymph, first? If I were you, I'd be grateful for anyone willing to come into my shop."

The shopkeeper, Strago, stretched his lips in a strained grin as the goddess lifted her slender eyebrows, awaiting his reply. He turned his attention to Kait and clasped his hands in front of him. "Were you finished browsing, or can I show you something in particular?" he asked, nearly growling the pleasantries.

Kait shook her head. "No. I'm done."

"Are you sure there isn't anything you need, my dear?" Athena questioned innocently.

"No. Nothing from him."

Athena clucked her tongue. "Ah, you see, Strago? Two lost customers. Careful now," she warned before she steered Kait back into the street.

"Thank you, Your Grace," Kait said, giving a slight bow once they exited the stall.

The goddess waved her hand. "No need for that, dear. I'm Athena, and it would please me very much if you would refer to me as such, as a friend."

Kait nodded, unsure what to say.

"It boils my blood when I see behavior like that." Athena's pale brown eyes roamed back to Strago's shop. "Hopefully, he'll change his attitude. If not"—she paused and brandished her broadsword, retrieving it from where it was strapped across her shoulder blades— "I'm persuasive." She gave Kait a wink before sheathing the weapon again.

"Let's hope the lesson sticks," Kait added. She stood in awe of the fearsome goddess, both grateful and bewildered by her kindness. Athena was known for wisdom but also for her impeccable strategy when it came to warfare. She did everything with a purpose, so what was her intent?

Kait examined the goddess while Athena's attention was diverted. Dark brown legs emerged through the high slits of her leather dress, the fabric pooling in between her knees as the sides brushed the ground. The dress continued up her torso and wrapped around one shoulder, leaving the other side exposed. A heavy brass breastplate stretched across her chest, and a matching belt settled on her hips. Athena's hair was slicked back, and the walnut strands tickled the base of her neck. Even in this seemingly casual scenario, Kait was intimidated.

Athena faced her once more. "How is everyone in Olean and the lower realms? We heard there was an illness?"

"An illness?" Kait repeated. The simple word did little to convey the terror Hera's plague had rendered.

"Yes. The Council met to discuss it last week. We were shocked to learn how many of your kind had perished. Gaia has been so distraught."

A week? Was that how long she'd been trapped in Tartarus? It had seemed so much longer. "No. It wasn't an illness. Not one of an organic nature, anyway," Kait replied through gritted teeth.

Athena's lips quirked. "I was hoping you'd say that."

"What do you mean?"

Athena took a step closer and dropped her voice. Gone was the chipper inflection, replaced by a hushed intensity. "You're Kaitaini, correct?"

Kait nodded. "How did—"

"Poseidon relayed a message several days ago, one that spoke of the true nature of the attack on Olean. He also mentioned that a fierce aurai had journeyed to him before she traveled to the Underworld and urged me to keep a sharp eye out." Athena winked.

Kait licked her bottom lip and swallowed her nerves. It seemed Poseidon was on her side.

"That's no small feat. Demanding an audience with the sea god and the god of the dead on the same day? You must be brave."

Kait's eyes hardened. "Rageful is more appropriate."

"I would expect nothing less if my sisters had been the targets of an envious goddess."

Kait cocked her head. "Your Grace? You know?"

Athena smirked and glanced around to ensure their conversation wasn't discernable to prying ears. "I had my suspicions when my scouts reported multiple meetings between Hera and her son, Ares. Her disdain for beautiful beings has never been a secret, what with her husband's flagrant trysts with other females, my priestesses and other lower goddesses included. Coupled with the reports Queen Rajhi brought to our attention last year of an immortal engaging in euphoria hunts again, it wasn't hard to narrow down the list of suspects."

"Then, why haven't you done anything? Why isn't she behind bars? If you'd acted sooner, my sister wouldn't be dead."

"Patience, aurai. We didn't haul you before the Council after you murdered Zeus because his death seemed a fitting punishment for his crimes. Hera is different. Because of her position and power, we cannot charge her without evidence, and she is adept at covering her tracks. Since Poseidon's letter, I've tried to investigate your claim without arousing Hera's suspicion, but it hasn't been as simple as I'd originally thought. Her private gardens are nearly impossible to penetrate—"

"Miss, there you are," Riven said, his frustration battling relief. "I didn't realize you'd strayed. Come, we must get you to Hera before—"

"Hera?" Athena repeated as her eyes widened.

Kait nodded. "Yes. I'm to serve her as penance for the part I played in her husband's death."

Athena's eyebrows rose further. "Oh, I see."

"Perhaps, we will meet again, and I might be able to offer new insight regarding your inquiry?"

Athena bowed her head, and fire sparked in her smile. "I look forward to it."

Riven grabbed Kait's elbow. His harsh touch suggested he was intent on dragging her if she didn't comply. "Let's go, nymph."

Athena stepped in front of Kait and lifted her arms. "This was my error, soldier. I didn't mean to cause delay."

The guard bowed. His cheeks flushed, and his grip fell away. "No apologies necessary, dear Goddess. I'm sorry to interrupt."

"It's fine. We were concluding our conversation. Enjoy your time on Olympus, dear one. Stay safe." Athena's tone was casual, but her eyes were unflinching chips.

"Thank you," Kait replied. She gave the goddess a final glance and then stepped out from behind her to join the waiting guard. "Sorry."

Riven ignored her and raised his eyes to meet Athena's. "Have a wonderful day, Your Grace." Taking hold of Kait's elbow once more, he guided her toward the edge of the market. Kait pasted a calm smile on her lips, but inside, her heart soared. Poseidon had kept his word, and she now had an unexpected ally in her corner.

The thick crowds fell away as the pair distanced themselves. On the outskirts of Olympus, it was quiet, peaceful even. The small shops gave way to elegant gates and solid fences, each more lavish than the next. A few possessed windows carved of stone, and Kait caught a glimpse of tropical trees adorned with blooming flowers.

"What are these?" Kait asked.

"Private estates for the most powerful immortals," Riven replied. His tone dripped with disdain.

"You don't live here?"

"Not quite, miss." The guard snickered. "This part of Olympus is reserved for the ancient gods. The ones who fought the Titans in the great war."

"Oh," Kait said, sensing the guard's mockery.

"Apparently, the lowly foot soldiers who won them the victory—and who barely survived with the blood of their brothers and sisters splattered across our chests—didn't work hard enough."

"Where do the rest of you live?" Kait asked, amazed at the young soldier's candor. Away from his superiors, his stammer was non-existent.

"We're relegated to the Eastern Annex, miss. Far away from all this. The royals regard us as second-rate citizens."

"That's not fair," Kait said quietly. "No one is lesser than another. No one should be able to force you to do something. No one should be able to control you." Her voice became strong and acidic as memories of Zeus's fists, Jezlem's cries, and Layla's sobs bloomed.

Kait's eyes grew glassy. What had she done? How could she have forgotten her anger, her hatred for Zeus? He was a monster. He'd used nymphs over and over for centuries without a shred of remorse. His actions were unforgivable, yet she'd let her guard down anyway, held his hand, allowed him to warm her feverish body. She pressed a fist to her eyes to stem the flow of tears.

Riven stood awkwardly before her and extended his hand as if to offer comfort, but he let it drop back to his side. "Sorry to go on about my situation, miss. I didn't mean to be insensitive. I can't begin to imagine what life must be like for you. I may not live in a palace, but I have my freedom."

Kait nodded and wiped her eyes again. She knew he meant well, but his words sharpened the sting. She wasn't upset about the clothes she wore, but rather why—why she was there at all. If Zeus and Hera had stayed in their luxurious haven, she'd be back in Olean with all her sisters, together and united. There seemed to be no end to the immortals' greed and vengeance. How had such vain creatures come to rule the whole of the realms?

The guard cleared his throat. "Well, we better get going. Hera's gardens are at the very end of this block," he said gently.

"Okay." Kait sniffled and caged her anger. Crying wouldn't change anything.

CHAPTER 36

They arrived at Hera's gates a short while later. Riven shot her a regretful look as he rang a bell on the smooth wall. A gentle sound like tinkling wind chimes echoed on the other side. Kait took a steadying breath and assessed the residence. Like everything else in Olympus, the walls were impenetrable white marble, at least ten feet high. Her focus shifted to the gate. She couldn't help but scoff when she realized the bars weren't made of the same material, but rather iridescent pearl. Hera had wealth and power, and she'd ensured every object she owned reflected her status.

Kait gripped the bars. There were far too many to slip through. For all of Hera's attention to luxury, the gate reminded Kait of a whale's baleen. She shifted her weight and pushed on the bars, hoping they might have sacrificed rigidity for beauty. Unfortunately, the bars refused to budge. She let out a frustrated groan.

"Shouldn't be too much longer, miss."

"It's fine. Not exactly in a hurry for a life of servitude."

The guard cracked a smile as a figure strode into view on the other side. Hera saw Riven first, and her expression was one of annoyance. Then, her gray eyes slid to Kait. It felt as if an actual weight had dropped onto her shoulders. The malice in the goddess's gaze practically burned her flesh as Kait stood beneath her murderous scrutiny.

"What's this?" Hera asked in a clipped icy tone.

Riven bowed and fell to one knee. "I have delivered the nymph, Your Grace. I apologize for any lateness," he fumbled, his casual diction gone.

Through the slits in the bars, Hera's skeptical features turned steely, revealing the monster she kept buried beneath the flawless surface. The brief glimmer of rage lasted only a moment though before her carefully composed mask resettled.

"Of course." Hera pressed her face against the pearl-laden gate, eyes burning like coals as she regarded Kait. "I expected you an hour ago. Should I express my dissatisfaction with your superiors?" she asked the guard.

"No. I mean, yes. I mean, I am very sorry, Your Grace." Riven rose from his knee but kept his gaze directed at his feet.

Hera sighed dramatically, pulled open the gate, and gestured for Kait to enter. "Off with you now, solider, and don't let it happen again."

"Yes. I mean, no. Never." Riven's eyes slid over Kait one last time as if in pity before he spun on his heel and marched away from Hera as swiftly as possible.

Kait swallowed, both relieved and anxious to see him go. It would be nice to drop the charade, but with the guard's absence, the reality of her situation sank in. She was alone with the most powerful goddess in the heavens, a goddess who lusted for her death. Silently, she waited as Hera sealed the gate. The goddess lifted her arm to her shoulder where a massive serpent perched and stroked it, eyeing Kait with its unblinking golden eyes.

"Well, well, well," Hera hissed. "Isn't this a treat? To what do I owe the pleasure?"

Kait hesitated, unsure how to behave. Should she play meek and humble or stand with strength? Hera narrowed her eyes, as if daring her to respond with aggression. Curtseying gently, Kait raised her hands as a show of peace.

"I come to offer myself to you, Your Grace. The guilt over what my sisters and I took from you has become too heavy to bear. I understand your fury, your need for vengeance. You took my sister, just as I took your husband. I wish to serve you to show how deep my regret runs, and I hope my tribute will satisfy your bloodlust and spare the rest of Olean." Kait prayed her words sounded genuine.

"What a sweet speech. Did Hades teach you the proper way to grovel? Goddess knows he's had centuries of practice."

Kait's jaw dropped.

"Did you think yourself clever? You thought to deceive me with your pretty lies?" Hera growled. "I know why you're here. I know Hades agreed to trade your sister's soul for mine." She fluttered her lashes and cocked her head to the side.

"How?" Kait asked before she could help herself.

Hera toyed with the end of the snake's tail, twisting it around her index finger until her skin disappeared. "Because I have something he wants, and when you want something, the only way to win is to take it." Her hand snapped out and grabbed Kait by the chin. "Well, I'm not playing his pathetic little game. You will be my slave because that's what I want. I want to break you and use you until you beg for death. Hades may be the god of demise, but his wrath is no match for mine."

"I swear, Your Grace—"

"No. No more lies. Ze-Ze will tell me everything I need to know."

Without further instruction, the great snake slithered forward and wrapped Kait in her scaly embrace. Kait held her breath, expecting teeth, but only the snake's forked tongue flickered, her fangs remaining passive. Slowly, she circled her, weaving across her chest, under her arms, and around her neck before returning to her perch atop her mistress's shoulders. Hushed whispers in a language Kait couldn't understand erupted as the snake shared her findings. Hera released Kait's chin as she listened, her gaze far away.

Kait fought to keep her features blank, but her nerves made her hands shake. What had the snake told Hera? What truth could she have gleaned that Hera didn't already know? For a second, Hera's pale eyes widened, her expression impossible to decipher. At last, the snake's whisperings ceased, and the goddess fixed Kait with a cold stare.

"Very well. I accept your pledge but know that you are an intruder in my home, and I will treat you as such." Hera turned to leave but paused as her lip curled devilishly. "But first . . ." Hera reached into the folds of her dress and withdrew a gilded tube.

Kait shifted into a defensive stance and flexed her fingers, ready to cast if necessary. Hera pulled off the top and unsheathed a ruby spike, then coated her pursed lips with the bold color. Kait frowned. What an odd moment to apply lipstick.

The goddess grinned and pocketed the tube with a gentle sigh. Suddenly, she charged and wrapped both arms around Kait's neck, causing her to stumble. The pair collided, and Hera chuckled darkly, caging Kait's body with her own, then captured her lips in a passionate kiss.

Kait was too surprised to do anything more than freeze beneath Hera's onslaught. The goddess's tongue explored her mouth while her fingers ran sensually along Kait's exposed arms. A slight dizziness overcame Kait, and her knees buckled, sending her crashing to the crushed seashell path. Too late she realized and understood the sudden emptiness within her.

The goddess smirked. "What? You didn't really think I'd let you keep your connection, did you?" She threw her head back with a harsh laugh. Manifesting a clear vial with a wave of her hand, Hera spat a stream of golden vapor inside, then, using a manicured nail, perfected her smeared lipstick.

Kait let out a heartbroken sob. She'd just managed to regain her ethereal connection, and within an hour, it'd been torn from her again.

"How?" Kait asked, ignoring the way the sharp shells bit into her knees. "Halos can only be absorbed when an immortal reaches euphoria."

"Is that so, little one?" Hera smirked. "I've lived a thousand lifetimes, traveled to the farthest realms, and do you know what I found? Certain arachnids excrete a fabulous toxin. Once I was able to attain enough, manipulating the properties to achieve my desired effect was simple."

Kait tried to follow. "What are you saying?"

Another dangerous smile split Hera's red lips. Kait wondered if the toxin was what gave them their bloody shine. "One kiss, one touch, and your precious halo sticks to me like glue, transferring from your body to mine. Plus, the best part is the side effect. Whichever halo I absorb, I inherit the power as well. Want to see?"

Hera tilted her head and spread her palms. The air responded automatically to her will. The clear blue sky turned slate gray as the wind in the gardens howled hungrily. Kait gasped.

"You should see your face!" Hera chuckled as her demonstration concluded. "My, that's invigorating, isn't it? Truthfully, I expected a bit more of a fight. And that kiss . . ." She paused. "Imagine Zeus's disappointment when he finally got you into his bed."

Rage boiled within Kait's chest. She pressed her fingers to her upper arm, to the tender skin that was once marred with violet bruises from the beating the god had delivered when she'd fought back in the mountains. Rising to her feet, she fixed Hera with an unwavering stare.

"Your sweet Zeus never took me. I nearly died defending myself from his fists, but I never laid beneath that monster. The truth of that is reflected in the vial you hold," Kait said. "How can you justify his actions? How do you live with yourself, knowing he's forced nymphs to endure his lust? Are you so naïve as to think it was consensual? How does it feel to know your precious husband would rather chase me halfway across the realms than lie with you? And you want him back? You incited a deathly plague upon my sisters to avenge scum like Zeus? You must know how that makes you look, like—"

A resounding slap brought Kait up short as Hera's palm cracked across her cheek. "From now on, I don't want to hear that sweet voice of yours, or I'll cut your tongue from your head," she whispered coldly.

Kait grinned, tasting blood where her teeth had cut her bottom lip. "Why? Did I strike a nerve? You embellish your cheating husband to what, forget the truth?"

Another powerful crack sent Kait's head rolling. Her vision blurred, and her knees buckled, dropping her back down to the crushed shells. Blood welled to the surface of her skin, dotting her visage with tiny red splatters.

"I thought I said I don't want to hear that pretty voice of yours." Hera kicked Kait in the jaw and sent her sprawling onto her back, then swept her long gown behind her as she crouched above Kait's head. A metallic ringing sounded as Hera withdrew a concealed blade. Delicately, she traced it around Kait's lips, kissing the corners of her mouth as the tip dipped inside. "I really should cut out your tongue. You talk a big game, but I wonder if, under all that bravado, you feel pain. Should we test my theory?"

Without waiting for an answer, the goddess shoved the blade inside Kait's mouth and pressed the serrated tip against the back of her tongue. She smiled as a thin river of crimson blood trickled down the length of the knife.

"Perhaps, another time," Hera cooed, withdrawing the weapon with an experienced flick of her wrist. "But I will take this." She dug her pointed nails into the vulnerable skin at the hollow of Kait's throat and whispered an enchantment.

Kait couldn't see what was happening as she stared up at the sky. Only when Hera had finished and released the pressure on her windpipe did she sit up. Silent coughs raked her chest. First her halo and now her speech. Hera wouldn't stop until she'd drained everything from her. After locking Kait's voice in a silver charm around her neck alongside the vial imprisoning her halo, the goddess cocked her head and waved her fingers. "Come. Time to start earning my forgiveness."

CHAPTER 37

When Hades had suggested serving the goddess, Kait had hoped to kill her within the first few days, to slit her throat in her sleep or strangle her pretty neck the earliest chance she got. But Hera was no fool, and she was careful to keep Kait at arm's length. The days bled into one another, and still Kait was no closer to saving Bia's soul from Hades's clutches.

Kait reported to the goddess's pavilion each morning at sunrise, bearing a fresh pot of mint tea. Once Hera arrived and indulged in the warm beverage, she'd return Kait's voice and batter her with questions regarding Olean and the nymphs' culture. From the origin of their elemental connections to the medicinal training they received, Hera devoured every piece of information, but instead of being sated, the goddess's hunger for knowledge only intensified.

After the first week of incessant interrogation, Hera's questions turned personal. She demanded details about Blake and the human realm. The goddess sat stone-faced as she forced Kait to relive every moment from the night Zeus took Jezlem until her sister had driven the piriol's quill through the god's skull. Kait talked and talked each day until Nyx doused the sunlight and the stars danced brightly in the inky black sky. All the while, Hera watched, listened, calculated, and penned every word. Eventually, Hera would set her feathered quill on the large cedar desk and touch Kait's throat, ending their session as she reclaimed her voice. Exhausted, Kait almost welcomed the theft.

Kait responded to every question and silently accepted the coarse jibes Hera hurled at her when she interrupted. She swallowed her rage when the goddess insulted the elder nymphs and labeled the whole of her race harlots who purposefully taunted and teased gods away from their wives' beds. Though Kait's hands would shake and her face would flush, she stifled her fury and put forth a calm façade—anything to perpetuate the illusion that she'd rather suffer for eternity under Hera's wrath if it spared the rest of Olean.

Hera seemed to buy the charade or at least enjoyed witnessing Kait absorb the abuse. After four weeks of being leeched of information, Kait couldn't imagine what else Hera could possibly ask. At first, she'd answered vaguely or lied, but that proved to be even more challenging as Hera's rapid-fire questions tripped her up and the truth was revealed regardless of her attempts at evasion. Besides, Kait didn't see the harm in the goddess's inquiries. The layout and structure of nymph society weren't secrets, and her recollection of being imprisoned by Zeus would only hurt Hera.

The only truth she feared sharing was about her journey to the Underworld and her subsequent wanderings in Tartarus. Every morning, Kait waited and held her breath for the one question that could ruin everything: Is Zeus alive? Yet, somehow, the goddess's musings never veered down that path. Kait was grateful. If Hera figured out Zeus was somewhere in Olympus, she'd surely leave her gardens to seek him out while Kait was left to rot behind the high walls with no chance to kill her. Whatever the reason, Kait was grateful for the delay, for she was no closer to killing the goddess than when she'd arrived.

As Hera dissected Kait, she studied Hera in return. The goddess's gestures, posture, preferences, and direction. Hera was meticulous in her daily routine, a regimen Kait would hopefully be able to manipulate later. Though to be honest, she would have little opportunity to strike. Apart from the long hours spent reciting her history, Kait was separated from Hera, dining and sleeping far removed from her warden's quarters. She'd been there for weeks and still had no idea where the goddess passed her time when she wasn't interrogating Kait.

For the last week and a half, however, Kait had been confined to the orchards until Hera's summons arrived in the late afternoon. From her refined gown and manicured hair, Kait suspected the goddess had left the estate, but to where she couldn't guess. Kait's free hours prior were spent wandering the trees or reading from a small library she'd found carved into one of the hollow trunks. There was even a book about sign language. The collection seemed strange at first, but on the following day, Kait found a name carved into the bark. Canace. The image of the withered aurai in the Thar Desert flashed in her mind again. How many decades had the poor nymph been forced to endure Hera's cruelty? Kait smiled as she traced the scrawled letters, glad the aurai had at least been able to escape to her own tiny haven within this prison.

Kait whiled away the hours poring over the new language, imagining Canace doing the same, while Argus, Hera's guard—a magnificent white peacock—, shadowed her every step. She savored her minuscule independence from Hera and was able to sink into her own thoughts without interruption until the loyal peafowl forced her to the goddess's side.

That was until today. Her new routine was pulled out from under her when Hera's summons arrived shortly after she awoke. Kait assumed the sudden urgency meant today was the day the goddess would quit her vague inquiries and demand to know if Zeus was alive.

With butterflies throwing their velvety bodies against the lining of her stomach, Kait walked to the pavilion as slowly as her custodian would allow in the hope that she might be able to gain control of her nerves before enduring Hera's presence. She paused at the tea cart laden with a steaming kettle beside the stairs and poured the warm tea into a delicate cup. This time, she forewent the saucer, lest the cup clatter and dance upon the ceramic surface as her hands shook.

Kait ascended the few steps, and the narrow handle of the teacup slipped from her grasp when she laid eyes on Hera's languid silhouette draped over the waist-high wall that encircled the goddess's Skyglass. Was she about to fling herself into the bottomless well? The china cup bounced off the marble beneath Kait's feet and shattered into a dozen shards. Acting on instinct, Kait leapt over the pieces, thinking only of pulling Hera back. If her body were lost to the sky, how would Kait ever harness the soul for Hades?

Hera's head raised at the disturbance. "Did you just break that?"

Kait's steps faltered as the goddess regarded her with the slitted eyes of an annoyed feline. The imposing threat of failure evaporated as she realized Hera had no intention of diving into the sky. Kait glanced at the sharp debris scattered behind her and nodded solemnly. It wasn't hard to understand Hera's bewilderment.

Hera lazily unfurled her limbs from their strange position. "Clean it up and then we'll begin."

Kait was surprised to see the loyal python wasn't draped around her mistress's neck but coiled beneath the desk instead. She didn't blame the serpent. The endless void that yawned under the Skyglass was intimidating and unforgiving. She gave a slight nod and crouched to collect the shattered pieces, but from the corner of her eye, she assessed Hera. No longer was her hair meticulously pinned, and her face was void of its usual rouge and eyeshadow. Her long golden waves lay soft against her shoulders, and her gown was far more casual than her typical dress. Clearly, Hera wouldn't be leaving her gardens today.

Hera crossed to her desk. Ze-Ze slithered out of her hiding place and placed herself at the goddess's feet as Kait picked up the last shard. Taking her time, she deposited the pieces back onto the tea cart and returned to her customary position against the pillar. Hera opened the charm that held Kait's voice hostage and crossed her arms, waiting for it to settle in her throat to begin.

The vapor magnetized to Kait's lips and plunged down her windpipe until it reached her voice box. She swiped her tongue over her lip as Hera opened her mouth to speak, but Kait's words escaped before she could overthink her delivery: "Has the Council summoned you? Is that where you've been disappearing to every morning?"

Hera's slender brows arched in surprise before her eyes hardened. "What reason would the Council have to summon me, nymph?"

"A horrendous infection befell Olean and spread throughout the majority of the lower realms. Maybe they're curious as to how such a powerful affliction manifested, or maybe you left some identifier behind."

Hera cocked her head and gave Kait a tight smile. "Of course. The Council has been in touch with Queen Rajhi, but these things happen. Gaia is working hard to replenish what numbers she can, but even your great mother isn't strong enough to create the hordes that were lost in such a short time."

Kait fought to keep her features neutral. Armed with the knowledge Zeus had imparted before she left him behind, she now understood why Gaia was so limited. All her extra efforts went into crafting more servants for the immortals to use and abuse, whom they no doubt discarded the moment they wore out their usefulness. She stifled a growl. If she were to show any sign of aggression, Hera's pets would act or the goddess would rip out her voice before she was able to glean more information.

"So, even Queen Rajhi agrees it was a natural occurrence? Of what? The flu?"

Hera sighed. "No. Your harlot queen seems to think otherwise, but what proof does she have? Her only witness"—Hera gestured to where Kait stood—"wasn't even believed by her own people."

"So, you haven't been accused, then?" The way the goddess's mouth tightened to a thin line answered Kait's question.

"Athena has made several comments."

A thrill rocked Kait's frame. The kind goddess had meant what she said in the market. She was fighting for her.

"I bet she saw right through your lies."

Hera closed the distance between them, seeming to glide atop the floor. Her hand struck out fast and gripped Kait by the jaw. "Whatever you think will happen, whoever you think will save you . . . They won't. No one cares. Athena even tried to call you to testify before the Council, but the other elders wouldn't hear of it, given your reputation."

Kait stiffened as the goddess's cloying breath kissed her cheek. "My reputation?"

"You're erratic and blinded by rage. You've wielded accusations about half the Council—"

"All of which were true! Is immortal prejudice toward nymphs that invasive? Our queen sits on your Council! She's seen firsthand what terrors the gods have forced upon us!"

"Most of those terrors were deemed consensual—"

"Consensual, my ass! You rape nymphs and then invent excuses to save your own skins!"

Hera's grip tightened, and she slammed Kait's head against the thick pillar. "Enough! Enough of your filthy ramblings, or I'll kill you myself and send you right back to Hades."

Kait grinned through the pain that bloomed in the back of her skull. So far, her tactic had rattled Hera, and she was divulging more information than Kait had dreamed. "Do it, then. I already know the way out. I'll come back and cement everyone's foul thoughts of you, an envious murderess."

Hera snarled and dug her fingers into the base of Kait's throat, cutting off her rant. Breathing heavily, she deposited Kait's voice back into the small silver charm of her necklace. Once the lid was sealed, Hera tore her hand away and threw Kait to the floor.

"Get out! Get out of my sight! You're the only one who knows, and I will keep you here until you are nothing more than a rotten corpse to fertilize my flowers. You think this is the first time I've done something like this? The first time I've gotten my hands dirty prying some stupid little tart away from what's mine? I have lived for a millennium. You are nothing more than a fly caught in my web. You're here to serve a purpose. You will never win. Never. Now go!" Hera spat and turned her back on her. "Argus!"

The beautiful white peacock cooed in response and unfolded himself from where he stood sentry at the base of the pavilion steps. His lovely array of eyes sprang to attention, each one turning, watching, staring in endless directions as he collected his prisoner.

"No meals today. Take her straight to her room."

The peacock nodded in salute and circled Kait, brandishing his wings and feathers as wide as possible to herd her off the pavilion. Kait climbed to her feet and stumbled onto the shells. The soles of her feet had protested with blood at first, but after a week or so of enduring the torturous walkway, her skin had scabbed and calloused to a point where the sharp pain had become muted.

Kait glanced over her shoulder, expecting to see Hera's cold gray eyes following her. Instead, the goddess had marched back over to the far side of the ornate Skyglass column. Hera swatted her maroon gown to the side and gripped the edge as she peered down into its depths. Kait craned her neck, anxious to see the contents it contained, but the peacock fluffed his feathers to obstruct her view and urge her onward.

Kait surrendered, faced forward, and continued ahead while her mind whirled. Relief buoyed her. She'd succeeded in keeping Zeus's resurgence a secret and riled the goddess into a furious frenzy instead. It wasn't hard to see how tense Hera had become the past few days, and the explosive exchange confirmed the goddess's paranoid state of mind. Either Athena had persuaded the Council to look harder into Hera's possible involvement or Queen Rajhi had offered other nymphs to make a statement. Kait was the only one Hera had confessed to, but surely Tahlia, Anamalla, and Emya could testify as well.

Locked in the lavish prison, Kait was blind to the events happening back home in Olean and even a few streets over in Olympus. She had to bide her time in carrying out Hades's order to kill Hera. Until then, it was a small comfort to know that the noose around the goddess's pretty neck was inching tighter and tighter.

CHAPTER 38

Dawn broke over rosy clouds the next day as Kait handed Hera a small plate of green grapes and cheese. After their tense argument the day before, she was shocked when the goddess summoned her. Kait's stomach rumbled at the simple breakfast, but Hera ignored the plea and took a slow bite of the crunchy fruit.

"Thank you." Hera grinned as the tip of her tongue slid along her lower lip, ridding it of a stray drop of juice.

Kait resumed her usual position and adopted a passive expression.

"We will be doing something different today. We're going to have a visitor." Hera's tone was indifferent; however, her eyes were alert, shining and sharp.

Kait's eyebrows arched in surprise. From the moment she'd entered Hera's gate, the goddess had made a point to keep her secluded. What had changed? Why invite a visitor now? She ran her fingers along the front of her neck, eyes intent upon the small charm.

Hera clucked her tongue. "No. There will be no need for you to speak. My son Ares will be arriving shortly." She set the plate down on the edge of the desk before she rose to her feet. Hera sauntered toward the pillar where Kait stood as her pale gray eyes bore into her. "You are going to hear things, secrets you already know. Don't do anything stupid, and whatever you do, don't seclude yourself with my son. I need you alive."

Alarm sprang in the back of Kait's mind. She'd never encountered the god but had heard enough stories that his name alone caused her skin to prickle uneasily. Last she knew, Ares had been banned from the lower realms. His aggressive and volatile behavior was a significant public safety risk, enhanced even more when ambrosia or wine corrupted his judgment. In Hera's tone, Kait sensed the goddess's disgust for her offspring, but she needed him as well.

"He will be here soon. Stay out of reach. I'd send you away, but I don't trust you to leave my sight whilst my guard is preoccupied watching my son." Hera scanned the lush grass surrounding the pavilion. Lowering her voice, she fixed Kait with a powerful glare. "Remember what I've said. Don't turn your back on him." A resounding chirp drifted along the breeze like the opening of a lullaby as the peacock announced the god's arrival. Hera didn't break eye contact with Kait. "Do you understand?"

Kait nodded, doing her best to ignore the chorus of shivers that tickled her spine. She didn't know why she was nervous. Unlike her unexpected rendezvous with Zeus, she'd had no prior contact with Ares, nothing to base her wariness on save for stories passed on by a dozen lips. He'd been a powerful Olympian once during the Titan Wars, but that was before his wild antics had provoked the Council. Perhaps, time had calmed him. Maybe he wasn't as terrible as others claimed. But from the way the great snake's body coiled tighter around Hera's shoulders and the goddess's eyes grew grim, she already knew such hope was ill-conceived.

"Stay over there," Hera instructed. She gathered her long peach-colored gown and smoothed the chiffon material behind her as she made her way to the edge of the pavilion. A shaky breath whispered from her lips when she set her gaze on the rising sun and her son's impending entrance.

Kait could practically taste Hera's anxiety as the seconds ticked by. The goddess's private residence was one of the largest estates on Olympus, with the pavilion situated on the westernmost point. However, it would only take the peacock five minutes at most to lead Ares across the gardens.

Following Hera's lead, Kait watched the path. The tension was palpable. She disliked not knowing what to expect. Especially now, without her ethereal connection or voice, she was weak and vulnerable, unable to protect herself. Her fingers itched to summon the wind to her palms, but all her desire was worth nothing as long as Hera held her powers captive.

Argus's eerie call rattled her thoughts and pulled her attention back to the shell path, where the peacock strode forward with his great tail spread. All one thousand eyes swiveled, never looking away from their guest. Kait knew what being the object of all those eyes felt like. Their stare was like a physical weight that laced her arms, neck, and legs all hours of the day. It was a small relief to be free of the intense scrutiny.

Shifting on the balls of her feet, Kait craned her neck to see the god behind the fan of feathers. At first, all she saw was light brown stubble coating his scalp, but a moment later, Argus shifted. Her breath caught in her throat, and her muscles instinctually poised to leap into the wind, forgetting her severed connection. She was taken aback by Ares's appearance as he stalked behind the peacock.

The god was short in stature, exaggerated more so by his hunched shoulders and skittish gait. He paused every few seconds, only to rush forward to cover the ground he'd lost. Kait's eyes widened. He reminded her of a dog that'd been kicked too many times, cowering and edgy, while aggression and anticipation surged in his eyes, ready to explode at any second.

"Good morning, Ares," Hera said, disrupting the silence.

Argus moved to the side of the marble staircase and bowed low, signaling for the god to continue.

"Mother," Ares replied, his voice raspy. He ascended the pavilion and grasped Hera's hand. Kneeling before her, he pressed her fingertips to his thin lips, lingering far too long. Hera cleared her throat, pulled her hand back, and tucked it safely beneath the serpent's body. Ares ignored the slight and rose to his full height, smiling venomously. "I must say, your gardens are divine. I can't believe this is my first time within your polished gates. But no matter, I'm quite used to being the dark stain on our convoluted family tree, though I'm afraid recent chatter surrounding your name is quite scandalous, as well." He laughed, the sound a chilling echo.

Hera narrowed her slate-gray eyes. "Ridiculous gossip, no doubt perpetuated by an envious immortal to usurp my seat of power, nothing more."

Ares cocked his head as he reached the top of the stairs and drifted closer, forcing Hera to walk backward out of his reach. He raised a muscular arm and fixed her with his pointer finger. "Are you sure? Rumor has it one of the nymphs of Olean testified about witnessing a dappled gray hawk after the attack. Let's see . . . Who do we know with that familiar?"

Kait inhaled sharply. Had Tahlia stood before the Council and recounted the moments after Bia's death? Did they believe her?

"Enough," Hera spat. "I asked you here for concrete news from the Council, not deplorable rumors spread by gutter rats."

Ares's dark copper eyes flared with a wild gleam. "Of course, Mother. How could I have forgotten my place? As you know, my seat on the Council was stripped from me long ago, but from what my contacts have gathered, Athena left Olympus for the lower realms the day your house arrest began."

House arrest? The Council had instituted a house arrest on Hera? Was that why her outings had suddenly ceased? Had they found proof to corroborate her involvement with the infection?

Hera's posture stiffened. "For what purpose? She can't possibly hope to find any evidence. We administered the toxin through the Skyglass."

Ares shrugged. "I'm not sure what she's hoping to discover, but Artemis accompanied her, and there can be only one reason."

Hera lifted her chin higher and shook her heavy curls. "The little huntress can track all she likes; there's nothing to find but rotting nymph carcasses."

Kait sucked in a sharp breath, and the air whistled between her teeth. How could Hera be so cruel, so callous? Images of her friends flayed, muscles and innards torn to shreds, hit her with unexpected force, and her exhalation drew Ares's eyes to her corner.

A predatory snarl curled the god's lips. "Speaking of carcasses . . . I didn't realize you'd gotten another one." He took a step toward Kait. His empty gaze reeked of danger. "She's pretty."

"And she's *not* yours." The warning in Hera's tone was clear. "Now, besides a point of origin, what else could Athena's objective be? Did she tell the Council of her plans to travel south?" She waved Ares over to the Skyglass.

Kait released a shaky sigh and held her posture. She'd been the target of many gods' attention before, but none of them frightened her as much as Ares had at that moment. Not even when Apollo melted her lips so Hermes could pin her against the wall outside the speakeasy over a century ago. No. There was something missing from Ares's psyche, some crucial element, and without it, his animalistic mannerisms were left completely unchecked.

The immortals gathered around the waist-high column and peered down into the clear depths. Endless blue sky yawned high above the clouds, but Kait noticed Ares's hesitant shuffles the closer he advanced to the bottomless device, almost as if he were nervous to approach.

Hera perched on the smooth stone rim and brushed her hand through the air above the circular scope. "Tarus."

Kait flinched. It was so strange to hear one of the realm's names spoken by the goddess. It felt like an invasion of privacy as an image of the desert landscape shimmered into view within the Skyglass. She yearned to run over, dive into the image, and get lost in the cool underground tunnels. Did Hera even know about the submerged system? Did her Skyglass function like a portal, or was it simply a detailed telescope? If Kait jumped, would she be able to fall back to Earth and escape the beautiful hell Hera had locked her in?

"Not that I was informed," Ares answered. "She might be down there to collect eyewitness reports. Just because the toxin targeted nymphs doesn't mean other creatures weren't affected. The realms are crawling with lesser beings like centaurs and satyrs. Any of them could have information, too."

Hera hissed, and her great serpent raised its scaly head from where it rested below her collarbone. "Why can't anyone mind their own business?"

"Do you want me to start drafting a new toxin for the beasts?" The excitement in his tone was unmistakable.

Hera fixed him with a hard glare. "Don't be a fool, Ares. With all this heat Athena has thrown my way, it'll only be a matter of time before they question you."

Ares frowned. "Why? Because I'm your son? All of Olympus knows how you despise me. Once my battle tactics helped turn the tide against the Titans and propelled you and Father to power, the pair of you disowned me, turned your backs on me the second you got what you wanted. Kicked me out of the Council and exiled me to the South End with a quarter of my power."

Hera sighed a bone-deep groan that insinuated she'd heard his grievances before. "You got yourself kicked off the Council. You slaughtered an entire human city while celebrating your success. Our hands were tied. You're lucky they didn't inflict a harsher punishment."

She glanced away from the sun-drenched image and slid off the stones to her feet. "You've always been so spoiled, whining about your misfortunes without taking any personal responsibility. You're not a man, just an insolent child. Now, find a way to get down there. Send one of your nasty contacts. I don't care how, but find Athena and dispose of any witness they find who could testify against us."

Ares straightened and cocked his head, facing Hera with an unblinking stare. "Us." His voice was flat, void of all inflection. "Big speech for a bitter old woman. You say I should be a man, yet you continue to order me around like a welp, still wet behind the ears."

Hera scoffed. "Don't be dramatic—"

"You want me to take responsibility for my actions?" Ares shouted. "How about I confess everything to the Council? Show them the methods I used to produce the toxin, as well as your instructions about what it should do."

Hera rolled her eyes. "You have no proof, and your word means nothing compared to mine."

"Do you truly believe that? Seems to me Athena is grasping at anything she can get her hands on. I'm sure if she and Artemis looked hard enough, they'd be able to find some residue from the ingredients used in my kitchen. Plus, there are no doubt bloodstains from the nymph I used to test the venom. My home is filthy, remember?" Ares raised his eyebrow and glared at Hera as a coldness radiated off him. Kait didn't know the god, but even she could tell he wasn't bluffing. "You're on house arrest, Mother. At this point, you're already guilty in their eyes."

Hera dropped her hand and snarled. "You wouldn't dare betray me."

Ares shrugged again and ran his hand along his scruffy jaw. "Of course not, dear Mother, but there's no telling what secrets will pour from my lips once I've had a bit of ambrosia." He smiled, the motion aggressive and cruel.

Gracefully striding away from the Skyglass, Hera closed the distance between herself and her intimidating offspring, her teeth barred. She tucked her chin, and her gray irises rolled upward so only her pearl-white sclera was visible. She looked every bit the terrifying hostile goddess that had confronted Kait in the mortal realm and laughed as she unleashed the decayed illusion of Bia. It wasn't hard to see from where Ares had inherited his vicious demeanor. The two of them stared at one another, neither backing down, like brawling dogs.

"You forget your place, son," Hera hissed. "You think losing your seat on the Council was hard? Or losing Aphrodite to your brother? The despair you felt was nothing compared to what I could do to you."

Ares grinned, his smile seeming too wide for his face to accommodate. "Then, it seems we are at a stalemate, each of us willing to do whatever we must to ensure the other doesn't . . . overstep." He leaned forward and ran his stubbled jaw along the smooth skin of Hera's cheek. Kait watched as Hera barely repressed a shudder. "Until we meet again, Mother."

The serpent's fangs gave an audible snap, and Argus chortled loudly from where he stood below the pavilion. He moved toward the god, but Hera called the peacock off. "That won't be necessary. Ares was just leaving." The peacock expressed a rattling sigh but remained rooted in the lush grass as ordered.

"I guess I'll show myself out." Ares twisted sharply and marched down the steps. His unnerving eyes flashed to Kait for a second before he focused on the path that stretched before him.

Argus beat his wings, the sound a powerful thrum as he displaced the air. A flutter of loose feathers wafted to the ground when his fanned tail shook, and his infinite gaze followed Ares's retreating figure.

Kait didn't stray from the pillar but observed how the goddess maintained her rigid posture until Ares was well out of sight. In appearance, Hera seemed indifferent, untouched by Ares's words and actions, but Kait felt the way the wind pulled and wrapped around Hera's body, holding her tightly. Even though she didn't show it, the great goddess was hurting, falling apart and silently screaming for comfort in a voice only the wind could hear.

A twinge of jealousy squeezed Kait's heart. How could the air abandon her so? It had been stolen from her, severed from the very core of her being. It owed Hera no allegiance. Yet, in the back of her mind, she was proud to call such an empathetic element her own.

"Kaitaini," Hera called, her voice shrill.

Curiosity rather than obedience propelled Kait to the goddess's side. Hera tilted her head slightly as the snake hissed, still riled from the encounter with Ares. "I need you to go to the marketplace and pick up several items," Hera ordered unexpectedly. Reaching into one of the many folds of her gown, she withdrew six drachmas and thrust them into Kait's palm. "Give me a moment to compose the list, and you can be on your way."

Hera sauntered to her desk with her head held high, appearing cool and reserved. Stunned, Kait followed, afraid any delay on her part might result in a change of heart. Standing with her head bowed, she waited anxiously while Hera's feather pen scratched the parchment. At last, a soft tap on the wooden desk signaled the goddess had finished. Kait's hands twitched at her sides, itching to feel the parchment between her fingers. As insignificant as the list appeared, the opportunity to escape the gardens for the afternoon was invaluable. Hera must've either been desperate for these items or desperate to be alone.

Hera folded the parchment neatly down the center, then offered it to Kait. Conflicting emotions crossed her features. With a regal shake of her head, the uncertainty fled from her eyes. "Pick up these items and *these items only.*" She passed over the list. "I expect your return before noon. You may visit the market unsupervised. Is that a regrettable decision on my part?" Hera asked as the great python hissed again.

Kait shook her head and accepted the sheet. An afternoon away from the incessant guard? Suspicion tickled the back of Kait's mind. What was Hera's motive for sending her out? She racked her thoughts for where she could go once free of the garden walls. To be able to speak with Athena would be preferable, but if Ares's report could be trusted, she'd left Olympus. Would it be wise to try to contact another one of the ancient gods who sat on the Council? She tucked the list away in the pocket of her shift, along with the drachma.

"Good. Argus will show you where to exit at the south gate. Knock twice upon your return, and he will escort you in," Hera said. She teased the ends of the feather pen with her fingertips. "And don't get any ideas of running to the Council. Remember, you're nothing, a servant created to wipe the muck off our sandals. Straight to the market and back. If you wander, I shall know and will exhibit no restraint in your punishment." She extended one of her pointed nails toward the smooth Skyglass.

Panic seized Kait's throat. Could Hera truly follow her every move through that? She nodded and raised her hand to her throat.

Hera laughed, the sound hollow and disingenuous. "Not today, nymph. If you have any trouble, show them my signature. That will be an adequate explanation. Now go. I have matters to attend to." With a sharp turn of her head, Hera plucked the feather pen from its rest and set to work writing, abruptly dismissing her.

Disappointment flooded Kait as her voice remained imprisoned, but she maintained a neutral expression. With a swift curtsey, she spun and descended the pavilion, following the peacock to the southern gate. She couldn't be sure, but she thought she heard a quiet sob echo behind her.

CHAPTER 39

The south gate slid open, the hinges protesting as decades of rust flaked to the grass. As soon as a narrow opening appeared, Kait leapt through, still unbelieving that her brief gift of freedom wasn't a trick. Once safely on the other side, she winked at the albino peacock. The perturbed guard clucked low in his throat and shut the gate behind her.

Kait grinned, and muted laughter bubbled over her lips. She was free, at least for a few hours. Setting her feet toward the main hub, she strolled down the lane and pulled Hera's list from her pocket.

Ginger root

Bloodworms

Dill

Datura

Kait was familiar with all the herbs, save for datura. She prayed they would be easy to find. She pocketed the list and continued down the gentle incline. A low cough grunted from somewhere nearby and forced her eyes to widen. She expected to see a meandering immortal or perhaps a Council guard stationed outside Hera's residence to enforce her house arrest, but only an empty lane stretched behind her.

Did Olympus have animals that roamed the opulent city? Kait clapped twice and frowned when the sharp sound didn't elicit any movement from the high grass. Hera's gardens were located at the far end of the street. Unless she was entertaining during Kait's absence, no other immortal would have reason to be there.

Kait pressed on, desperate to leap into the wind. Walking wasn't fast enough. She reached the edge of the manicured lane and turned left, recalling the route to the market with ease. She glanced over her shoulder when another subdued cough echoed. She'd escaped Hera's faithful observation but had given no thought as to what or who she might encounter outside the walls.

Kait quickened her pace and hurried along, her once joyous mood soured by the unmistakable feeling that someone was watching her.

She arrived on the outskirts of the market a few minutes later. A handful of immortals and nymphs in white shifts strolled past, and Kait breathed a sigh of relief at their presence. The heavy feeling of being followed faded as she slipped into the crowd. With one last subtle glance, she checked the road behind her, but nothing stood out.

You're being paranoid.

She withdrew the list once again and scanned the assembled vendors, searching for a table selling herbs and spices. Tucked several booths back, a selection of brightly colored glass vials caught her eye. Kait wove between languid immortals and focused nymphs until she reached the targeted table a moment later. Sparkling like diamonds, dozens of different bottled oils glimmered, displayed on elegant wooden dishes. Beside the oils, gathered herbs and grasses in clear vases dipped up and down in the gentle breeze, and squat pots of various spices sprinkled every available space. Kait inhaled the rich scents, and her heart ached. For a brief second, she was back in the apothecary with Bia.

"May I help you find something?"

Kait flinched in surprise as her hand flew to the base of her throat. There was so much to take in that she had been oblivious to the quiet goddess behind the table. Her hair was pulled back in a tight knot, the dark brown color shining as brightly as a polished chestnut, and she watched Kait like a wide-eyed bird.

"Are you looking for anything in particular?"

Kait nodded and handed over the elegantly scrawled list.

The goddess's eyebrows furrowed at her silence as she accepted the parchment. Anxiety crept into Kait's stomach. She hadn't asked Hera what the ingredients were for, hadn't been able to since her bold accusations were being punished with silence. Besides, she would've been a fool to think Hera would have answered her, anyway.

"I can sell you the dill, datura, and ginger root, but you'll have to go down to the docks for the worms."

Kait nodded again and ran her fingers along the edge of the scalloped tablecloth. She opened her mouth and gestured to the paper with a shrug.

"What are they for?"

Kait gave her a small smile and bit her lower lip.

The goddess smirked and eyed the note in closer detail. "Ah, you're one of Hera's. That explains a lot. The last one was a mute as well." The goddess grumbled under her breath. "Though, I doubt her days of being waited on like the queen she thinks she is will last much longer."

The other one.

A cold wave climbed Kait's spine. Her mind transported her back to the Thar desert and the poor aurai that had served Hera before, the one the goddess had disguised as bait to lure Kait into Zeus's trap. When she'd finally reached her, the nymph was nothing but bones wrapped in petrified flesh. Kait studied the skin on the back of her own hand and imagined all the moisture and blood shriveling away under Hera's magic.

The goddess's movement brought Kait back to the present. She filtered through the numerous boxes displayed on, above, and behind the table, and her deft fingers combed dark green stems and pale yellow blossoms with precision. With a swipe of her blade, the goddess wrapped a generous bouquet of dill with a lavender string and leaned it against the ribs of a small basket. Turning her attention to a row of oddly shaped fungi, she selected a bulbous-looking brown root and placed it beside the dill. Next, the vendor stretched onto her toes, extending her hands into the floral ceiling.

Working her blade skillfully around each flower's base, the goddess clipped a dozen of the beautiful datura blooms. She relaxed her feet and cradled the soft petals like an infant to her chest. Before she placed them atop the other items, she fixed Kait with a somewhat nervous stare.

"Did Hera mention the purpose of this particular request?"

Kait shook her head, her violet eyes wide.

The goddess gently arranged each of the bell-shaped flowers around the ginger root. Kait noted the way she stood each one up as if to shield the centers. Her dark eyes scanned the nearby stalls before she leaned over the occupied basket.

"Be careful with these. Don't eat the seeds." The goddess's voice was low but thrummed with urgency.

Kait wished she could ask why. What did the flowers do? Why would Hera want them? She yearned to speak, but her tongue was nothing more than a useless slab of flesh sewn between her teeth.

The goddess straightened and cleared her throat. All suspicion vanished from her features, replaced by a mask of indifference. "That'll be four drachmas."

Withdrawing the coins from the folds of her white shift, Kait deposited the money into her palm. Her empty fingers then wrapped around the basket's handle, ready to leave, but a stern grip held the basket in place. Kait looked at the goddess and arched her eyebrow in question.

"If you need more, come see me, okay?" Kait nodded curtly, but the goddess didn't relax her hold. "My name is Panacea, by the way. Remember what I said about the seeds."

Panacea allowed the woven basket to slip out from beneath her fingers, signaling she was finished speaking. Kait gave a slight curtsey and slid her arm through the gap until it hung comfortably from her elbow. The urge to ask Panacea about Hera flared strongly in her chest, but she'd already turned away and begun fiddling with one of the arrangements, a subtle message that their exchange had concluded. Would Panacea get in trouble for speaking negatively about Hera? Was it considered treasonous, given Hera's elevated status among the ancient immortals?

Kait left the stall. Maybe she'd be able to catch the kind goddess somewhere less public on her way back. The only thing left to collect was the bloodworms. Hoping to locate a road to the docks, Kait arched onto the balls of her feet, wishing—not for the first time that day—that she could meld with the wind and travel with the breeze.

She swallowed her disappointment and caught a glimmer of rippling cream sails and creaking wooden masts in the distance. A quick stop for the worms and then she could get back. Kait merged into the fluid flow of foot traffic and hastened to the outskirts of the square. The docks looked to be situated about two miles away through a labyrinth of twisting cobblestone streets lined with narrow homes, their bricks so crammed together that the structures' humped shadows threatened to crumble beneath the sun's sweltering stare.

Kait set off on the short trek, eager to be done with Hera's errands. What had Panacea meant about the seeds? Why sell them if they were so dangerous? A waft of unease pebbled the exposed skin on her arms. Was Hera going to kill her?

The Underworld didn't scare Kait; she'd already conquered Tartarus.

The only thing that terrified her was failure. Bia couldn't remain in Hades's clutches. Though maybe that had been the plan all along. Maybe Hades and Hera *were* working together. Soon, he'd possess two nymph souls, rare jewels in his endless collection, and Hera would have the pleasure of killing her husband's supposed lover.

Zeus's face flickered behind Kait's eyes, but she pushed his image away. She'd never been his lover, wasn't even considered a person in his eyes. To Zeus, she was an object to satisfy his lust. Kait cleared her throat and refused to let the memories of Tartarus form. Their journey through Hell had changed nothing. He was a monster, yet she was reluctant to admit that she didn't harbor the same amount of hatred for him as she once had.

Kait adjusted her basket and strolled farther down the street. The sun felt glorious on her bare skin as the breeze tickled her thighs. The afternoon was perfect, but that strange feeling still lingered and made her flesh itch.

Kait recognized the feeling. It was eyes, heavy and lidded, watching as she moved through the streets. Had Hera sent Argus to watch her after all? Or perhaps she'd meant it when she threatened to follow her through the Skyglass. Covertly, Kait searched for an obvious culprit, but the surrounding patrons paid her little mind as they meandered along the alleyways. She frowned. The gaze didn't feel like the steadfast peacock's. Besides, given Hera's current tarnished status, Kait understood why the goddess had sent her off alone. Argus was too recognizable. No doubt, Hera wished to shrink back from the limelight and didn't want anything that could be associated with her strutting about as if flaunting her indifference to the charges levied against her. That would only alienate possible supporters. No. It was far better to send Kait to gather the supplies, for she was just another faceless servant who could belong to anyone.

The uncomfortable shroud intensified, growing heavier with every step. Darkened windows leered as Kait passed, shielding their occupants and intentions. Kait exhaled as she emerged from the alley onto the bright and boisterous docks. Out in the open, the feeling dulled once again, and her breath came easier away from the claustrophobic streets. Vendors barked prices of fresh seafood just caught from the seas of nearby realms, competing with one another for the passing shoppers' attention.

"How 'bout you, darlin'?" one god called. "You have any need for a large salmon in your pantry?"

"Try these, my beauty. Fresh oysters!"

"Your choice of king crab! Only two drachmas!"

Kait shook her head and clutched her list like a guiding torch. She tried to point to get someone's attention, but the vendors were too busy drowning one another out to witness her feeble plea. She wandered over to a vendor at the far end of the pier, away from the shouting and bartering. The god was portly and balding but had kind eyes. He carefully laid his catch out on crushed ice. Wooden crates and derelict barrels lined the edge of the docks, and black nets belched over the sides onto the concrete path under her feet.

The feeling of being watched returned and wrapped around Kait's shoulders like a burlap shawl, itchy and rough. Biting her lower lip, she wove faster toward the vendor, but her ankle twisted in the netting, and she fell. A quiet whoosh of air expelled from her lips as her body tipped sideways. Without the wind, she was helpless, a tower of bones tumbling to Earth with no way of catching herself.

Chapped hands grabbed her and stalled her trajectory before she slipped over the side of the wharf. Kait was confused for a second, suddenly righted when she'd been prepared to crash. Her savior's hands cradled her body, their fingers cupping her shoulder while the other hand grazed her backside. The whole ordeal occurred in a collection of seconds before the stranger planted her on her feet.

"Are you all right?" a deep voice asked.

Kait waited for her equilibrium to reestablish, then her eyes slid to the speaker's face. A familiar sense of dread overwhelmed her. Cold eyes the color of a rusted sword held her like a needle pinning a butterfly to a board.

Ares.

Kait extricated herself from Ares's arms and smoothed her shift, pretending to check for injuries, anything to break eye contact. The weight of his gaze was palpable on her skin, enhanced by his unnecessary proximity. Had he been the one following her?

Picking up several datura flowers that had fallen onto the dirty concrete, Kait forced a smile. She couldn't show him how he intimidated her. Nodding vigorously, she brushed her brown curls out of her face and mouthed a thank-you, then spun on her heels and hurried a few steps away, closing in on the desired vendor.

"Wait, I know you," Ares called. Casually, he grabbed her basket and halted her progress.

For a moment, Kait contemplated dropping the handle and running away, but she was miles from Hera's gardens. He'd easily catch up, and she didn't want to give him any incentive to unleash his temper. As a last-ditch effort, she feigned confusion and tilted her head to look at him blankly. Ares pulled her closer without relinquishing his hold on the basket handle.

"Yes, you're tied to my mother. I thought I recognized you. Sorry I didn't get a chance to introduce myself earlier. My mother never figured out the maternal part." His words were a growl. It seemed frustration and anger still simmered from the spat. "I'm Ares, god of war and destruction. What's your name?"

Kait shook her head and placed her fingertips to her throat.

"Has Hera stolen your voice?"

Kait nodded, disliking the gleam in his empty eyes.

"Interesting. I'm surprised to see you down here. The docks are the common parts of Olympus. Goddesses don't come here unattended, let alone beautiful nymphs. Why are you here? Did Hera send you, or are you trying to run?" Ares's lips curled devilishly. It wasn't hard to see his desire to be the one to drag her back.

Panic leapt into Kait's eyes. Her hands flapped at her sides and uncurled the wrinkled paper from her fist before she thrust it at the god.

Ares wrinkled his nose while he scanned her collected goods. "Bloodworms? Is that all you have left?"

Kait nodded and swallowed roughly.

"Come with me. I'll take you to a place that has them. You'll find nothing but fish and seafood down here. Besides, Hera buys them for Argus. Ever since Hermes slayed him and she restored him into bird form, he will only eat a certain kind. Follow me."

Ares released the basket, but Kait noticed how the simple words resounded like a command. He expected her to obey like one of his soldiers waiting to march to whatever beat he demanded. She wished he would give her more information about Argus. If he'd been forced into serving Hera after his death, perhaps he harbored some ill will and could be persuaded to join her side. But Ares strode off, effectively ending the conversation.

Kait hesitated. Her gut pulled her in any other direction, far from Ares's retreating figure. Surely, someone else could help her, but if none of the vendors were interested before, they definitely weren't going to risk crossing the irritable god of war. Time was running out, and if Ares assumed she was attempting to escape, the thought wouldn't be far from Hera's mind, either.

With one last longing look at the vendor positioning his wares, she left the docks and hurried to catch up with Ares. The god was on the shorter side, but his muscular legs moved fast.

Hearing the patter of footsteps, Ares turned his head and flashed a confident smile. "Good girl. We're nearly there. I can't imagine my mother letting you out of that prison for long. We don't have much time, but it'll have to do."

Kait inclined her head, breathing heavily to keep pace. Her thin sandals slipped into the ruts between the widening cobblestones. This area of Olympus was a far cry from the polished marble and pristine structures that dominated the center. The streets were old and dilapidated, and the crowded shops and apartments were worn with rotten wooden beams that splintered like crooked teeth.

She strode beside him for several minutes, her anxiety increasing with each new abandoned avenue he led her down. Mangy rats regarded them with beady eyes and held their ground as the pair trudged passed. Ares slowed at last, and Kait followed suit. Without her rapid breaths, she realized how quiet it had become. Gone were the sounds of the creaking ships, the competing vendors, and even the comforting staccato of other footsteps pounding the stones. They were alone.

"In here." Ares gestured to a hunched red door beside a large barrel that omitted a ghastly odor.

Kait studied the putrid water within and gagged when numerous drowned insects swirled in the mild breeze. The god held the door open. As she slipped by, she noticed his attention wasn't on her, but rather on the alley behind them.

Across the threshold, Kait stopped short as a musty mildew scent assailed her. She'd expected a dirty bait-and-tackle shop, but the reality was far worse. Rags that may have once been robes were strewn about the dust-covered planks, and crumpled newspapers sporting grease stains drifted lazily across the floor. A solitary chair wobbled on uneven legs, opposite a filthy mattress shoved into the corner. Sweat-stained sheets stretched haphazardly atop the surface, bringing forth a sickly scent in conjunction with the mold. The only light came from the open door behind her and highlighted three vivid facts:

1. This was not a shop.

2. Ares had blocked the only exit.

3. They were utterly alone.

CHAPTER 40

Kait inhaled sharply and backed up. Rather than hitting the doorframe though, her backside collided with hard flesh. Ares's face was poised only inches from her own.

"Whoa, sorry. Didn't mean to scare you. I was just closing the door."

To cement his words, the thick wood clicked snugly into place, banishing the light, the fresh air, and the only means of escape. With steady hands, Ares latched the door and directed her forward.

"Right this way. I always have a stash of bloodworms on hand. I never know when my mother will call on her errand boy." He glanced at Kait out of the corner of his eye. "And I like to be prepared."

Kait's thoughts raced as she shuffled into the center of the repulsive home. It didn't make sense. Ares was one of the most powerful gods; why had he been reduced to living in squalor? Had Hera and Zeus—his own parents—done this to him when they stripped him of his powers? She didn't doubt he deserved the punishment.

The shack was isolated far from any decent immortal, a fact Kait was terrified Ares would exploit. As the god dug through several grimy containers, she slithered to the door. Standing in front of it, she reached behind her body and gripped the handle.

"Here they are," Ares called, holding up a steel box triumphantly. "Took me a second. Sorry it's such a mess in here. I wasn't blessed with the gift of cleanliness." He chuckled casually and sauntered over to present her with the offering.

"I wouldn't look at them if I were you. They're sick revolting little things." Ares smiled. His features were laid-back and aloof. Had Kait imagined his hostility? Was her prejudice against the gods clouding her ability to judge him for who he truly was? A moment passed, and he continued to hold the box out to her. His smile wavered. "Is everything all right?"

Kait nodded. Her cheeks burned with shame. Why had she assumed the worst? He'd saved her from falling and was being nothing but polite now. Returning his kindness with a tight smile, Kait accepted the box and carefully laid it in the belly of the basket beside the ginger root.

Once the worms were tucked away, Kait raised her eyes back to Ares and gasped. In the instant she'd looked down to tuck the worms away, Ares's features had morphed into something rabid and animalistic. Gone was the kind smile, the endearing chuckle. He was a hunter once more, shedding his camouflage.

Before Kait could react, Ares grabbed her by the hair and bashed her skull against the heavy wooden doorframe behind her. Her vision blurred as her knees buckled, but the god didn't let her fall. His arms were there, ready to catch her, all ten fingers burrowing, digging into her shift. Each one tore at the fabric, eager to reach the soft skin beneath.

Flashbacks of Zeus attacking her in much the same manner flooded her mind, and Kait's heart rate exploded. Not again. She pushed through the pain that flared from her bruised head and swung the basket, catching Ares in the eye with the rough wicker.

Ares growled, but it wasn't malicious. He sounded amused. He rolled his shoulders back and sighed, touching the thin slice the basket left across his eyebrow. "Wasn't that fun? I still can't believe you fell for it."

Kait spun and yanked the door handle up, but it stuck firm.

Ares tapped his temple. "An important component of war strategy: Always be two steps ahead of your opponent." From his fingertips, he produced a thin key, a perfect match to the solid lock. Unlike the rest of the hovel, it was the only object that appeared sterile and well-maintained. Fear prickled the back of her neck as he pocketed his prized possession. How many unsuspecting victims had he lured here?

Kait knew there was only one way out. While walking through the filth-ridden streets, she'd noted how the apartments butted up alongside one another. There were no windows, no back doors. Her only escape was the key. Anger simmered behind her teeth as she cursed Hera.

Kait's thoughts drifted back to the last moments when Bia was still breathing, when she'd thrown herself in front of the jaws of the nymphs infected with Hera's poison. The goddess had willingly submerged herself in mud and decay to have a front-row seat to watch Bia die. She wasn't one to shy away from murder, and she liked to enjoy the fruits of her labor. If Ares killed Kait, it would rob Hera of a show. There was no way she'd condoned his plan.

Kait could use that.

Ares sidled up to her, his grin wide and dopey, like a cat hovering above an injured mouse. Kait pointed to the discarded basket, its contents scattered across the wooden floor. She tried to recall the sign for mother and touched her quivering thumb to her chin with her fingers spread. Then, she threw her arm to the left, to the faraway hilltop garden where Hera waited for her return.

The god snickered, batting the edge of her shift where it grazed her thighs with his fingertips. "My mother? My mother won't help you. Even if she knew where you were, she can't leave her luxurious garden. Not that your life is worth her consorting with Olympus's gutter rats, anyway." Ares circled her. "My mother cares only for herself."

Kait pointed to him while her other hand touched her heart, fumbling for a way to stall.

"No. I feel nothing for that woman. Since the moment of my birth, I have been a disappointment, never able to measure up to my siblings. After all these years, do you really think I care what my mother thinks of me? I am one of the most detested gods in the heavens, born to ravage and slaughter. What mother would be proud of a rotten offspring like me?"

He turned his steely gaze on Kait and cocked his head to the side.

"I wanted to take you against the pillar in my mother's garden, right under her nose while she watched me defile you. Maybe then I could ruin a little piece of her perfect paradise. But if I'd stayed and made a pass at you there, she would've forbidden me to touch you. All I needed to do was rile her up a bit, and look." Ares gestured to where Kait stood. "Here you are, alone and unprotected."

The god closed the distance between them and stroked her cheek with the backs of his chapped knuckles.

"Who would have thought Hera would ever do me such a favor? Deliver such a prize practically to my doorstep and steal her voice on top of that so she can't even scream for help."

Kait's mouth gaped at the truth of Ares's words. No matter how hard she cried, no one would come to her aid. Ares's cruel smile widened as he bent his neck toward her collarbone to inhale her scent. Goosebumps pebbled Kait's flesh before her resolve crystalized. She may have been powerless and mute, but she wasn't defenseless.

"As convenient as it is, I admit your silence is disappointing. It ruins some of the fun when I can't hear my prey begging for me to stop. Oh, well. I'm confident you'll make your distaste for me known in other ways."

Ares pulled back his lips to expose canine teeth, eager to taste, but Kait was ready. Years of pankration fighting surged through her limbs as muscle memory overtook conscious thought. Her right hand struck upward, hard and fast, and caught the god in the jaw with the heel of her palm. As his neck snapped to the thatched roof, she dropped to the floor and kicked out in a tight spiral, knocking Ares off his feet.

He crashed to the wooden planks and exhaled a surprised humph. Before he could rise, Kait jumped to her feet and delivered two swift kicks to his face. Ichor trickled from Ares's nose as he groaned and rolled onto his side. A metallic clunk caught Kait's attention as the silver key tumbled onto the floorboards. Her arm shot out, and her fingers closed around the warm metal, but she didn't see Ares's hands.

With immortal speed, Ares propelled his body off the floor and tackled Kait, wrapping one arm around her neck while the other secured her hips. They collapsed, and fresh pain blossomed behind Kait's eyes as her forehead ricocheted off the dusty planks. Ares used his weight to pin her legs down, eliminating any further defensive moves. She threw her elbow back, trying to smack the god in the face, but his amused chuckle illustrated how futile her attempt must have been.

"My turn, darlin', but keep squirming. I love feeling how helpless you are."

Kait threw her elbow again as she thrashed beneath him. She knew it was pointless, but she opened her mouth and screamed as loudly as she possibly could. Despair seized her when her last-ditch cry was nothing more than a puff of air.

"That's it. Scream. Fight back. It makes you taste sweeter," Ares rasped in her ear and tightened his hold on her neck until black spots exploded behind her eyes. His other hand wrenched up her thin shift and exposed her nude backside. She felt him shudder with pleasure as he ran his wide palm across her curves, squeezing and slapping her flesh.

Tears raced down her cheeks. Her breaths came in strangled gasps as her heart pounded. She was back in the alley with Willow, trying to scream through melted lips as Apollo ravaged her friend and Hermes laughed in her ear.

She'd survived Apollo's attack, fought off Hermes, and even bested Zeus, the most powerful of all the gods, but her rage was useless against the brutal desires of Ares. Terrified sobs rattled her chest as she felt a warm pressure graze her thigh. Her toes flexed, and she kicked her feet, trying to roll over, but Ares held her firm. There was no escaping this time.

A ferocious bellow blasted behind them as the door blew off its hinges. Pieces of splintered wood rained down, and heavy footsteps thundered across the floorboards.

"What the hell do you—" Ares yelled, but his words were cut off when a fist smashed into his teeth.

Cold air washed over Kait's naked flesh as Ares's body went sailing into the wall. She pulled her legs into the fetal position, doing her best to adjust the torn shift back to its proper length before rough hands gripped her forearm and yanked her off the ground.

"Come on. Get out of here!"

Kait obeyed without thinking. The god of war recovered from the unexpected blow and staggered to his feet. His robes were twisted around his waist, exposing his lude nakedness, but he didn't shield himself. He licked his teeth and spat a stream of sticky ichor at the stranger's feet.

"That one's mine! Give her back or face the wrath of one thousand armies!"

"Bite your tongue, boy. It's for her sake that I'm not slicing you in half where you stand," the stranger lashed back.

Ares roared and spun toward the corner where a menacing spear waited. The stranger's rough hands touched her lower back, pushing and guiding her toward the exit.

Kait gripped the shattered door frame and clawed her way outside. She risked a glance behind her. Her basket of herbs lay on the floor. The soft petals were crushed, and the ginger root had been pummeled to slime. Even if the contents were in usable condition, nothing could prompt her back inside the shack. The bloodstained blade of the spear hurtled through the air.

"Go!" the stranger shouted as they both ducked.

Ares readied for another attack, trashing his home as he scoured the mess for another weapon. The dark-haired stranger faced the god. From his stance,

Kait could tell he wasn't going to let Ares off easy. "You've always preyed on the weak and vulnerable, exacting your savagery on innocents to prove your strength. You're not strong. You're a coward."

The sunshine in the alleyway dimmed as thick clouds billowed across the darkening slate-gray sky. Kait frowned as a familiar scent accompanied the shifting weather. Charcoal and petrichor. Realization sizzled through her mind at the same moment a lightning bolt careened through the house and struck Ares in the chest. The blast sent him reeling backward, and he collapsed in an immobile heap. Smoke curled from his body and snaked upward, collecting in a tangible fog across the low ceiling.

Zeus turned and clasped Kait's hand, joining her in the narrow alley. Kait flipped her empty hand over to expose her palm to the sky.

"No, he's not dead, but his memory of this affair will be foggy. Come, we need to get you away from here."

Kait allowed the god to lead her down the street, fighting the panic that constricted her chest with every step. Her breaths were shallow gulps as they ran. The phantom touch of Ares's hands gripped her legs. He had been so close to taking her. To killing her. They rounded a corner and followed a flight of stairs back up to the central marketplace, but once the scent of cooked flesh was well behind them, Kait ripped her arm out of the god's hold and refused to go any farther. She collapsed against a cold wall away from the prying eyes of passing immortals, and tears blurred Zeus's silhouette.

It'd been weeks since she left the god behind at the entrance to Olympus. His darkened hair had grown long and shaggy, and his skin looked weathered and rough. The same brown tunic concealed his body. Even though his eyes resembled tepid mud rather than blue sky, she recognized the immortal who'd helped her survive Tartarus.

Zeus tried to take her hand once more, but she knocked it away and crossed her arms. After Ares's assault, the last thing she wanted was another pair of hands touching her. "I'm so sorry—"

"How?" Kait mouthed as tears carved thin trails down her cheeks.

Zeus cleared his throat. "I followed you. I should have announced myself the moment you left Hera's, but I was worried you would order me away. It felt good just to be next to you."

Kait ignored the small tremor of relief that enveloped her in his presence. She furrowed her brow as she fixed Zeus with a quizzical stare.

"Why?" Zeus guessed. "You know the answer to that." His voice softened. "When we parted, I didn't expect to . . . miss your company, but I felt it like a hole in my chest. I couldn't stop worrying about how Hera might have been treating you. I had to see for myself that you were all right. I camped outside Hera's when I heard she'd been placed under house arrest in the hope that she'd send you out. I didn't plan on revealing myself, but then I saw Ares . . ." Zeus's jaw hardened, and the muscles ticked with rage.

Kait hugged her arms around her torso. Zeus had been the one following her. The tears flowed faster as the adrenaline from her escape calmed. A tornado of emotions surged within her at Zeus's return. Part of her wished he would throw his arms around her as she sobbed into his chest, but her fury was too great. Ares's attack had dredged up terrifying memories that still haunted her nights. Both gods had humiliated her, made her feel weak and powerless. She shouldn't have needed to be rescued because she never should've been assaulted in the first place.

Zeus's shoulders fell when he saw the way her eyes burned with the accusation that he was no better. Like father, like son. He took a step closer, shook his head, and dropped his eyes to the tiles below. "I'm sorry. I told you how sorry I am. I'm not that guy anymore. Tartarus changed me . . . *You* changed me."

Kait's stare softened at the genuine regret in his voice.

"I'm sorry I let him get that far. At first, I thought Ares really was taking you to a shop, but as he wove deeper into the slums, I recognized his destination. He moved so fast that I lost you for a moment. Thank the gods I found you when I did." Zeus took a step closer and raised his hand as if to trace the curve of her cheekbone but dropped it to his side when Kait flinched back. "Has Hera been treating you all right? Are you eating?" Zeus asked to disrupt the silence.

Zeus had committed monstrous acts—nothing would erase the past—but things were different now. Since Tartarus, he acted like a new person. Still, she hesitated to trust him. After Hermes's lies and tricks so long ago, coupled with the nightmares and pain Zeus's cruelty had rendered, she wasn't sure if she would ever be able to place her faith in anyone other than herself. She nodded curtly to answer the god's question but held her arms even tighter, sticking her elbows out like spikes.

"Good. I've been so worried about you. Do you have a plan yet?"

Kait shook her head. Her gaze wandered from Zeus for the first time and peered at Panacea's stall over his shoulder. She didn't know the time, but from the sun's position, it was late.

"What is it?" Zeus asked, glancing behind him.

Kait gestured toward the stall and her missing basket. She'd even lost the list. No doubt it was balled up on the floor along with all the other rubbish rotting in Ares's shack. What had she needed? Worms, ginger root, sweetgrass, and some type of flower? She groaned into her hands, imagining the punishment Hera would gladly enact when she returned late and empty-handed. She'd whip her for wasting so many hours, ignorant to the horror Kait had endured.

"The vendors are beginning to pack up for lunch. I can grab what you need. I'll take care of it." Zeus turned to leave, but Kait grabbed his hand before he could take a step. The idea of losing sight of him and being left alone was too much.

Zeus frowned when he saw the panic in her gaze as if he were solely responsible. He clasped his hand over hers. "Do you want to come with me?"

Kait nodded and wiped her face with her shift. Together, they jogged hand in hand across the square toward the table covered in greenery. Panacea's eyebrows arched in surprise as they rushed into her stall.

"May I help you?" Panacea asked, setting down a half-filled wooden crate. Her gaze drifted across Zeus's tall form to rest on Kait. "Oh, you're back." Wrinkles formed over her nose. "Did you lose your items?"

Kait nodded, trying to keep her composure. She could still feel Ares's hands grabbing her, his stale breath licking her ear. The urge to cry gripped her again. She couldn't pretend everything was okay. She'd take whatever punishment Hera threw at her for not bringing the items if only she could break down behind the confines of the garden's high walls. Kait waved her hand, turned on her heels, and started to walk away.

"Wait, hold on," Panacea called. "Dill, ginger root, and datura?"

"Yes, that's right," Zeus said.

Retracing her steps, Kait returned to the table and tilted her head in question.

"I followed you, remember? I watched you buy them the first time," Zeus whispered under his breath.

"Here, it's no problem. I can gather them for you again," Panacea said.

Working swiftly, the dark-haired goddess soon had a new basket arranged, an identical match to the one she'd left with earlier. Kait dug in her pocket, but her fingers clasped only a single drachma. Goddess knows where the other one had ended up, but it wasn't enough. Slowly opening her closed fist, she revealed the solitary coin with a pained look on her face. The items cost four drachmas; to barter for less was an insult.

"Here," Zeus said, his own pockets clinking. "Put yours away. Hera will want to see change, especially if you didn't find bloodworms."

He tipped the coins into the goddess's palm, the small pile too large for her grasp.

"Oh, no, it's only four. That's far too much," Panacea protested, catching a few falling coins with her other hand.

"Keep it. We appreciate your recollection and the accommodation. Is that all you needed?" Zeus asked, inclining his head to Kait.

With a slight nod, Kait answered yes and smiled at Panacea.

"Have a nice afternoon, then." Panacea returned to covering her wares as an unreadable expression pinched her features.

Zeus handed Kait the new basket. "I think I should say goodbye here. If Hera or her devil peacock see anyone accompanying you back, it'll arouse questions we don't want to answer."

Kait nodded and rubbed her fingers along the basket's handle while she stared at the polished stones beneath their feet. She didn't know how to say goodbye to Zeus, didn't realize she had missed him, too. She wished she could vocalize her gratitude. Without his interference today, she would be a bloody mess on Ares's dingy floor.

Zeus stood there quietly for a moment. "I'm so sorry for what my vile son attempted and even more sorry for the unpleasant memories it stirred. Before you get lost behind your wall of thoughts, know that I'm never far away. I will always be here if you need me. You're not alone, okay?"

Zeus cupped her chin, and Kait allowed him to guide her face upward until their eyes met. Muddy brown irises gazed at her, but she could still see him, see the god who both terrified and protected her. She didn't believe people could truly change, but it seemed as if Zeus had begun to listen, after all.

"Bye, Kait."

He didn't embrace her, simply dropped his hand and headed back toward the slums without another glance in her direction.

Kait exhaled as his simple brown tunic blended into the mass of gods peddling their way home. Was he going back to Ares's? Rage overwhelmed fear as she pictured the god of war. She hoped the filthy beast was too broken to move.

She tossed her dark curls over her shoulder and took a steadying breath. It was harder than she would have thought to watch Zeus go, and already her anxiety fluttered with vulnerability as her shield departed. All she wanted to do was crumble in the wake of the assault, but she couldn't afford to give in. Bia was counting on her, and Kait had an even bigger adversary still waiting.

CHAPTER 41

The warm peach sky of afternoon arrived. The once dark clouds that had roiled above Ares's house were gone, and instead, gold ribbons curled elegantly above the arcing sun. Kait raced up the hill to the lofty private gardens as the basket swung haphazardly in the crook of her elbow.

Hera's walls loomed. Veering off the path, Kait headed toward the back gate tucked within a wall of ivy. Her breaths fell in shallow gulps as she tried to remember the next step. The goddess told her Argus would be awaiting her arrival, but the method to signal her return had fled her mind.

Kait raised her arm, and her knuckles scraped the grainy wood. Before she could properly knock, however, the door was wrenched open from the other side. Rather than the stern peacock, Hera's beautiful cold face greeted her.

"Where have you been?" Hera seethed. She snatched Kait by the thin strip of fat on the back of her arm and yanked her inside.

Hera didn't release her grip, only pinched Kait's skin between her fingers harder. The goddess towed her through the tall grass. Once they reached the polished plateau, she pushed Kait down and smirked with satisfaction as she fell to her knees, unable to catch herself in time.

"Get up. Give me the basket."

Kait pulled herself to her feet and righted the ginger root that squashed several of the datura petals. Hera ripped the basket out of her grasp and rifled through the items. Her eyes narrowed as her lips pulled back in a snarl.

"Gone all day and you have the audacity to return without everything I asked for?"

Hera whipped back her hand and slapped Kait across the face. A flash of white exploded behind Kait's eyes as her neck recoiled from the assault.

"Who were you with? I saw you! I followed you with my Skyglass. Who is he? Who's the beggar I saw you with?"

Kait fought to keep her features neutral as she raised her eyes back to the furious goddess. It was no surprise Hera had kept tabs on her. Hadn't she felt she'd been watched all day? Zeus, Hera, Ares. So many eyes all waiting for her to trip.

"Answer me, whore!"

An amused smile caused Kait's stinging cheek to twitch. She touched her muted throat, a lock without a key. Realization bloomed in Hera's expression. Hastily, she opened the charm around her neck and unleashed Kait's captured words. Pale vapor lifted out of the tiny box, stretching and swirling through the air as it drifted to Kait like a magnet.

Kait inhaled and guided her voice back to where it settled comfortably in her larynx. She sighed, appreciating the beautiful sound.

"Spit it out, aurai. Who did you meet with?"

Kait cleared her throat, coaxing her voice back after its long absence. "No one. A beggar, as you saw. I needed help gathering the items you required. The first vendor didn't sell bloodworms. She pointed me in the direction of the docks and told me to try my luck down there."

"You've been gone for hours. What else were you doing, and where are the worms?"

"I was looking for a stall that offered them when I bumped into your charming son."

"Ares?" The color drained from Hera's face, briefly punctuating her rage.

"Yes. He told me I was wasting my time at the docks and ordered me to follow him instead."

"You didn't."

"What choice did I have? He was insistent and grabbed me before I could protest, whatever good that would have done. Then, he tricked me into going inside his disgusting home, where he tried to rape me. He laughed and said he would've taken me right in front of you if he thought he could've gotten away with it."

Kait took several deliberate steps toward the goddess, empowered by her own voice.

"How could you have raised such a monster? Do you know how many women he's assaulted? Do you bury all the atrocities your filthy offspring has committed as long as he leaves you alone? Does the Council know how sick and disturbed he is? Why is he free, running around Olympus?"

"Enough, nymph. You speak of matters that don't concern you."

Kait's jaw fell slack. "Don't concern me? Your son tried to rape *me*! If not for the beggar who happened along, he would've succeeded. Why haven't you done anything to contain him?" Hera glanced away and twisted her hands. Kait's eyes widened with realization. "Because you're terrified of him. You're terrified of what he could do to you if he had the will. You're terrified he'll tell the Council everything."

"Shut your mouth, aurai."

"Take back my voice and make me."

Kait's fingers spasmed, desperate to call the wind to her palms. She felt a gentle stirring—as if her element were waking from a deep sleep—but her connection wasn't strong enough for any substantial magic. She watched the way the goddess's lips pursed. She'd hit a nerve and loved the feeling of power it gave her to witness the mighty immortal's discomfort.

"Tell me, was working with your vile son worth killing my kin? Was it worth having all of Olympus hate you and celebrate your fall from grace? Zeus is a bastard, motivated only by his own selfish desires, yet you waged a full-scale war against my kind for killing him—doing what should have been done centuries ago—and then sit here and pine for his return!"

The moment of weakness displayed by the goddess earlier evaporated, replaced once more by her steel façade. "Don't preach to me. You're not the epitome of virtue, either. Nymphs may avoid being intimate with immortals, but only because of the risk. When your lot isn't concerned with losing your ethereal connection, you spread your legs for anything and everyone, filthy half-breeds and humanoid beings that are hardly more evolved than animals." Hera's gray eyes bristled with ice. "It started as revenge, but the wider I looked, the more I realized the need for your entire race to be eliminated."

Hera slunk toward Kait and cocked her head to the side. "Nymphs are nothing but weaker copies of goddesses, flawed renditions that beg to be dominated. I can see why my husband fell for you, why my son tried to take you. Gaia molded you to be perfect, irresistible, and fragile. That's the most appealing part. Watching you break."

Securing Kait's wrists in her fist, Hera pressed her body against her and palmed Kait's breasts with her other hand. Her fingertips danced across Kait's thin shift and pinched her nipple.

"Get off me!" Kait rasped as she broke out of Hera's hold.

Hera chuckled and released her without resistance. Kait's cheeks flushed. It'd been for show, a simple demonstration of the goddess's power, but fury ripped through Kait's psyche. She was sick of immortals taking whatever they wanted without repercussions. Without pause, she drew back her arm and rammed her fist into Hera's nose. The thin cartilage gave a satisfying crunch. Hera gasped and cradled her face.

"Don't ever touch me again," Kait warned, flexing her right hand.

A single drop of ichor trickled out of Hera's nostril, but she didn't wipe it away. Instead, she smiled as it ran over her lip and graced her tongue.

"How long has Zeus been back?" Hera asked, her eyes bright.

Kait frowned. "What? What are you talking about? Zeus is dead."

"Is he?"

"Yes. Wasn't that the whole point of your game? The reason you killed my sister?"

Hera paused, and the silence was tangible. Kait's flesh prickled as the goddess regarded her with hooded eyes. How could she know? Hera headed toward the marble column that held the Skyglass. She perched delicately on the edge and brushed her hand across to disturb the navy clouds within.

"Show me the Underworld."

Hera's request was a gentle whisper but rang as clear as a scream across the pavilion. Kait flinched, determined to remain where she stood in case the goddess saw through her flimsy front.

"For quite some time—since your human sister rammed that quill into Zeus's skull—I've scoured the Underworld for a glimpse of my beloved." Hera kept her gaze on the Skyglass and peered into the swirling tendrils. "I couldn't see anything at first, and then I specified my search, able to trick the wards Hades instituted against me." The tendrils stilled and revealed an image Kait recognized of the jagged mountains that bordered the River Styx. As if the blood in her veins were magnetized, Kait's legs moved involuntarily and carried her to Hera's side. "I thought I saw him, a brief glimmer of his soul, but nothing concrete. Do you know why that is?"

Kait swallowed. "Because he's not there."

A slow smile spread across Hera's honey-rose lips. "Because he's not there," the goddess repeated. "How smart you are, Kaitaini. So, if my husband is no longer imprisoned in the Underworld, where is he now?"

"I don't know."

Kait licked her lip, trying to keep her focus steady. She didn't know how Zeus's disguise worked. Could it fool the Skyglass?

Hera clucked her tongue and set her icy gaze on Kait once more. "Oh, I think you do, my dear. Do you often let dirty beggars touch you?" Hera picked up her gown between the tips of her fingers. The movement caused the soft taffeta to rustle, like secrets spilling.

Kait opened her mouth to argue, but what could she say? Especially if Hera had watched as Kait clung to him in the market and witnessed their intimate parting.

Hera narrowed her eyes. "I don't know what plans you've concocted in that pretty head of yours, but I have no intention of being destroyed, especially by the likes of you. Hades will never possess my soul or my power. He'll have to find another way to wage his pathetic war."

The god of death's words filled Kait's mind. "He said you went to him with a proposition he couldn't refuse. He upheld his end of the bargain. He stole Bia's soul for you. If he's planning a coup, then I can only assume you vowed to help. Do you really think Hades will allow you to simply back out?"

Hera tossed her head, and her honey-colored curls grazed her shoulders. "As ruler of hell, he has dominion over every soul that crosses the River Styx. Presumably, he's already taken Zeus's power or, at the very least, drained enough to ensure Zeus would be far too weak to stop him. He doesn't need me. He wants me, broken and pliant. I never had any intention of actually fulfilling his demands. I bow to no one."

Kait exhaled, shivering in response to the raw power that emanated in waves off the hostile goddess. "That's why he sent me. He never trusted you."

A cold laugh boomed from Hera's lips. "Of course not. You can't trust any immortal. We're all out for ourselves. Hades was a fool to send you. To think *you* could destroy *me*."

Kait straightened, empowered by the goddess's dismissal. "Maybe he saw the breadth of my rage and realized that will not rest until my sister's soul receives justice for what you've done."

"Justice? You offered yourself to me, claiming your servitude as penance for what you and your filthy kin did to Zeus. Do you want to know another secret? Do you want to know why I let you stay here?" Hera moved closer, her painted lips snarling. "Do you remember when my python touched you that first day? She has a very sophisticated sense of smell. Can you guess what she gleaned from your skin, nymph?"

Kait swallowed. She recalled the short flight from the portal to Olympus. Remembered wrapping her arms around Zeus's bare torso, the flavor of his scent on her lips when she'd woken against him.

Hera leaned closer. "That's right. No amount of fire and brimstone could disguise Zeus's scent radiating off you, as if he'd laid claim to you. I allowed you to stay, knowing you would lead me right to him." Her teeth flashed menacingly, and the Skyglass revealed Zeus in his beggar's disguise. "So, I ask again, nymph, where is my husband?"

Kait took a steadying breath. "That doesn't look like Zeus to me. If Hades released his soul, then he should've returned to you. Unless he doesn't love you like you thought. Maybe he finally realized how intolerable you are? Maybe all of this was designed by Hades? He knew you'd jump at the slightest hint that Zeus might have returned. Maybe you played right into his trap? Or perhaps, you'll allow me to kill you. Then, you can search the Underworld yourself."

Hera raised her eyebrow as Kait finished speaking and set her lips in a thin line. "Perhaps, another time. Argus?"

An eerie cry echoed as the white peacock unfolded himself from his subtle perch atop one of the surrounding columns. In a plume of white feathers, the bird fluttered into the sky to land beside his mistress.

"Double your sentry. She is not to sleep, eat, or bathe alone. Understood?"

The stoic guard chortled in reply, turning his beady eyes to Kait. She hadn't expected anything less, but the extra supervision was hard to swallow, especially after her brief taste of freedom this afternoon.

"That is all, nymph. Go to bed. You have a big day tomorrow."

Kait was more than happy to leave Hera's presence, but she recalled the forgotten basket and spilled items. It would be a fitting punishment if the goddess waited for her to fall asleep, then commanded her to fetch them in the middle of the night.

"Would you like me to retrieve the goods you requested?"

Hera waved her hand, her attention already focused back on the changing depths of the Skyglass.

"Dispose of them. They're wilted and ruined by this point. Obviously, the task was too challenging for someone of your stature."

Kait bit her tongue. She jumped the few steps leading away from the pavilion, back to the spot where the goddess had grabbed her. As she walked, she fought to keep her breathing under control. She needed a plan. She was running out of time. Hera was so close to the truth.

"Wait, nymph," Hera called. "Aren't you forgetting something?"

Kait closed her eyes, deflating. For once, she'd let herself hope that Hera may have forgotten or maybe, now that her true intentions were aired out in the open, no longer cared.

Argus squawked and directed Kait back to the Skyglass. Hera withdrew her hand, her fingers spread to claws. Kait hesitated before the goddess and stared defiantly through her. A coy smile tugged at Hera's lips as she plunged her curved nails into the hollow space at the base of Kait's throat.

Without meaning to, Kait gasped. "No." But the word was stolen from her, nothing more than a hoarse sigh.

Hera smirked and guided the glowing voice into the prison that hung from her neck. "Try not to be so pathetic. I might like you more. Now, go."

Argus chirped again, the sound sharp and shrill. With what little grace and dignity she had left, Kait departed the pavilion with the peacock nipping at her heels.

It didn't take long to reach the scene in front of the gate. A breeze had separated the bouquet of dill and scattered it across the shell path. Kait kicked the misshapen ginger root as hard as she could. The lumpy brown plant arched high into the air and bounced into the towering shrubbery that lined the walls, disappearing in the tangled foliage. The peacock sounded a warning, but Kait rolled her eyes. After the day she'd had, it felt great to hit something.

Kait scooped up the discarded dill, crushing the brittle stems in her fists. Her toe nudged the basket, but instead of sending that flying too, she picked it up and shoved the broken herbs inside. All that remained were the datura flowers. The colorful petals cartwheeled atop the seashells, and a few wandered into the lush grass. Kait plucked them up with her thumb and forefinger, admiring the vibrant purple color drizzled amidst the cream. She noted numerous spiky green orbs extending from the stems. They looked like teeth eager to taste her finger. Were these the seed pods Panacea had warned her about? Aware of Argus's fervent attention, she collected the rest of the datura and deposited them into the basket with the same indifference as the rest of the contents.

Kait gestured to the immaculate path and fixed her warden with a raised brow. The peacock chortled and gestured with his long neck back to the tiny overhang where her sleeping mat awaited. Usually, the long walk to her quarters depressed her and reminded her of how little she had, but not tonight. Tonight, energy hummed in her veins from the little secret tucked securely in the basket.

After all these weeks, Kait had a plan.

Night crested, black and silent. The stars were tucked away as Nyx unrolled a thick blanket of clouds over their ancient eyes. Kait strolled into her semi-private room. Only three walls enclosed the space, the front open to the elements and her guard's ever-watchful eyes. She huffed and swung the basket, playing as if she'd forgotten to throw it away. The peacock followed her movements as she placed it beside her cot, his docile feathers gently quivering.

Settling into a roosting position, the peacock lowered his elegant body to the ground a few yards away from the entrance of her makeshift shelter. With a loud hush, he fanned his feathers wide and erect, brandishing eyes that never blinked. Only then did her guard relax for a short respite.

Kait shrugged out of her torn shift. The thought of sleeping in the present one disgusted her. The memory of Ares's hot breath and the way the material had bunched in his fists as he pawed her flesh caused the hairs on the back of her neck to rise. With little choice, Kait lay atop her straw mattress, ignoring the bites as numerous sharp ends irritated her naked back. She tried to force her thoughts to something, anything else, but Ares's wild gaze awaited her every time she closed her eyes. Even now, secured behind Hera's high walls, she felt exposed and vulnerable.

After her imprisonment under Zeus, she vowed she'd never let another god touch her, yet Ares had managed to put his hands all over her body. Kait's defenses had been nothing more than the buzz of an irritating gnat. Her eyes burned and released the pent-up tears and fear that had gripped her since she'd met the god down at the docks. She blamed Hera. If the goddess hadn't hijacked her powers and stifled her voice, Ares would no doubt be missing one, if not more, of his appendages tonight.

Hot tears raced down Kait's cheeks and puddled in the ends of her dark hair as she unleashed a silent scream and pounded the mat with her fist again and again. It wasn't fair. She wasn't okay. She felt like a failure. She knew the defensive art of pankration, knew the body's vulnerabilities and how to hit hard. She knew how to inflict fatal injuries without the help of magic, but Ares was the god of war and a crazed one at that. Her downfall had been fear, and her hesitation had allowed him to gain the advantage over her. No more. It was time to shift her strategy. Without bothering to wipe her tears away, Kait reached into the basket and withdrew a datura flower. Again, the spiky green pod entranced her.

Don't eat the seeds, Panacea had warned.

If Hera was after the seeds, she would've taken the flowers, but once she saw the wilted petals, she'd told Kait to discard them. Perhaps, the petals held a medicinal purpose. Maybe Hera didn't know about the seed's potency. Kait's heart ached as she pictured her sweet sister grinding herbs and flowers with her mortar and pestle. Bia would know the uses for datura and would no doubt scold Kait for her lack of knowledge.

Soon, Bia.

Argus made a low warning sound in the back of his throat as he observed her twirling the beautiful flower in her hand while tears continued to soak her hair. She covered her chest with the threadbare blanket and offered the flower to the noisy peacock.

The fowl shook his head. Kait supposed her guard had deemed the flower innocuous enough to allow her to indulge in its wilting petals without sounding the alarm, and maybe, just maybe, he felt sorry for her. She sighed and rolled the flora's narrow stem between her fingers. She wouldn't be able to taint any of Hera's food or drink with the seeds; the peacock watched too closely. The only way to get the goddess to ingest them would be through smoke and mirrors.

Kait carefully ripped the soft petals into strips and let them flutter to the grass as her tears slowed. Argus's feathered eyes stared, but there was no threat to his mistress from the flower's destruction. Using her thumbnail, Kait sliced into the soft flesh of the pod. A watery substance trickled down her finger and omitted a bitter odor. She peeled the thick skin back, and a dozen black oblong seeds deposited into the bowl of her palm, shiny and wet. Could it be this easy? Would these inconspicuous seeds kill Hera?

The desire to slip one onto her tongue was strong, but what was their potency? Was one sufficient? One tiny pill of death? Kait's violet gaze slid to the left, eyeing her semi-sleeping guard. She imagined slipping one of the seeds into the fowl's morning grains. Would he spasm and choke or simply drop dead? Guilt made her stomach sour, and she pushed the thought away. No matter the peacock's allegiance, he didn't deserve to die.

Kait leaned over and deposited the remaining ruined petals and seeds in the belly of the basket, then exhaled and closed her reddened eyes. She couldn't deny her frustration. After weeks of fruitless searching, at last, she'd found a method to destroy the goddess. But, without proper knowledge of administration and their effectiveness, what good were they? The titles encased in Canace's secret library flickered through her mind, but there were none pertaining to botany. Shifting on the thin mat, Kait tried to relax and prayed her dreams would deliver the answer instead.

CHAPTER 42

"Wake up, you lazy thing," Hera's crisp voice demanded, heralding the dawn.

Kait blinked the sleep from her eyes and rubbed the crust from the corners. Blearily, she gazed at the stern goddess. The dusty morning highlighted the scowl on her face. Kait propped herself on her elbow and adjusted the thin blanket that lay bunched over her nude body.

Hera crossed her arms at the wrists. "You will go back to the market this morning. I need fresh fruit from Dionysus and scones from Hestia for my breakfast."

Kait cocked her head, a refusal on the tip of her tongue. After yesterday, the thought of venturing out beyond the high walls frightened her. Ares knew where she resided. No doubt he was waiting to exact his revenge the moment she stepped outside. Plus, why would Hera want her to go back out? Was she hoping she might lead her to Zeus?

"I realize you may be hesitant. Argus can accompany you."

Kait shook her head to refuse the guard, then touched her chest and gestured to the wall.

"Good. Go now. You will be back in half an hour." Hera tossed two drachmas at Kait's feet, then pivoted atop the grass, and her long pink skirts billowed with the movement.

Kait rose and stretched the kinks from her limbs as her guard chortled under his breath, encouraging her to move faster. She rolled her eyes and wandered over to the little wash area. She sighed as the cool droplets tickled her hairline and ran down her neck. After drying herself on a thin towel, she ran her fingers through her tangled curls. She wished for a mirror, but there would be no helping her disheveled appearance, anyway. To the right of the shallow bowl hung a new shift, one clean and void of holes. Her eyebrows arched in surprise at the unexpected gesture. Then again, if she ventured out of Hera's walls in a torn shift, it would reflect quite poorly on her guardian and encourage questions Hera would probably rather not answer. Kait slipped the shift over her head. Hera was only protecting herself.

Returning to her sleeping mat, Kait scooped up the coins and bounced them in her palm. As she turned, her eye caught the black seeds in the basket, now dry and dulled from their exposure to the cool night air. On a whim, she pocketed them along with the coins, just in case Hera decided to clean up while she was out.

Argus clucked his tongue and narrowed his eyes. Kait withdrew them from her pocket and offered them to the bird in the shallow bowl of her palm. She held her breath, awaiting the fowl's reaction, but managed to keep her face expressionless. After a minute of scrutiny, the bird pumped his wings and inclined his slender neck toward the south gate. Clearly, he had no knowledge of the dangers of datura seeds, but she also sensed he sympathized with her a small fraction. He observed her day and night. Of course, he saw the bruises, the fingerprints that dotted her naked flesh as she dressed. Argus wasn't an ally, but she detected a softness growing in his stare.

Kait pulled her greasy hair into a tight bun. Would it be too much for Hera to allow her to bathe with more than a cold cloth and a rough bar of soap? She yearned for a hot bath, to sink below the perfumed surface as the oils of rose and lavender soothed her dry skin. Alas, water was another luxury the goddess held hostage.

Argus called, his wailful song clipped to convey her expiring window. Kait slipped on her flats and followed the peacock downhill to the gate. Her heart thumped as her fingertips brushed the smooth wood several minutes later. Would Ares be so bold as to wait right outside? Shivers sent a rush of cold air down her body. His savage eyes leapt to the front of her mind. Or maybe he'd stalk from the shadows. Kait couldn't decide what was worse.

Zeus will keep you safe.

The thought escaped before she could reel it in. No. It was dangerous to think of him that way. She didn't want to count on him, didn't want to place her trust in him. He was a tool, nothing more, the quickest way to enter Olympus. If she allowed herself to think otherwise—to think he might have honestly changed—she would only set herself up for more heartache. Zeus was a god, her enemy. Why was it getting harder and harder to remember that?

Dawn crested over Olympus and bathed the gardens in rich light. Argus was right; Kait was running out of time. Swallowing her trepidation, she pushed open the gate and took note of the empty lane, feigning confidence as she heard the door shut behind her. Unlike yesterday, there was an emptiness to the air. Kait frowned. She was relieved Ares wasn't nearby, but that emptiness meant Zeus's absence, as well.

Kait left the residential neighborhood at a brisk pace and came upon the market a few minutes later, but this early, the once bustling square was quiet and sleepy. Only a handful of vendors were present, setting out their wares and decorating their stalls with fresh products. One of the early risers was a pretty goddess with a thick braid down her back. White flour was splashed across both of her cheeks. She furiously kneaded a large blob of sticky dough.

Kait assumed the goddess was Hestia, already working harder than everyone else because it was her rolls and pastries that would be in high demand when the rest of Olympus awoke. Kait wandered over to her stall, hesitant to interrupt as the goddess continued to beat the dough, seeming lost in the rhythm. Kait knocked on one of the wooden posts that supported the peaked white roof, a friendly smile on her lips. Hestia glanced up, but her hands never ceased their movement.

"No bird today?"

Kait cocked her head in question.

"Usually, Hera sends her peacock to collect the scones. My first customer every single day. She likes to eat them while they're hot. Go on over to Dionysus's stall while I finish with these. He's not here this early. Just leave a drachma in his coffer and take a handful of fruit. I recommend the grapes."

Kait nodded and headed off in the direction Hestia had indicated. In the northeastern-most corner of the square, a small but lush copse of trees grew. Ripe oranges, pears, and apples hung suspended from narrow branches, while plump grapes, blueberries, kiwi, raspberries, and dragon fruit occupied long curling vines. She sighed in frustration. She'd forgotten the basket, but maybe the seeds' toxicity would rub off onto the fruit while in her pockets and she could test their potency this morning.

Kait withdrew the drachmas from her shift and tossed one into the coffer. It made a shallow plink. Obviously, Dionysus didn't empty it regularly. In her haste, several datura seeds rolled out of her pocket and scattered to the gravel stones below. Kait's gut clenched as the dark kernels seemed to disappear. She dropped to a crouch and used her nail to sift through the pebbles. One, two, three, four, five, six, seven. Her gaze swept the ground for more but only gravel met her search. She pinched the small cluster that still remained in her pocket and sighed. She had to be more careful. Kait straightened and exhaled. The recovered seeds huddled in the shallow bowl of her palm, and her pulse slowed. They were her only hope. Kait cleared her throat, then selected an orange and a bushel of grapes and stuffed everything into the deep folds of her shift.

With the fruit gathered, Kait turned to head back to Hestia's stall. A flurry of wings erupted at the edge of her vision. Clutching her chest, she stumbled and bumped the table with her backside. At her feet, a tiny hazel owl pecked at the ground around a long-fallen apple, then tilted his head and stared at her with wide yellow eyes. Slowly, Kait raised her hand to wave at the creature.

"Glaukopis, come," a sweet yet stern voice called.

The owl flew upward in a graceful arc and landed on a muscular forearm. His goddess wore her hair in the same slicked-back manner as the first time Kait had seen her, but she was void of the breastplate this morning. A chic yet simple scarlet dress that ended just above the knee hugged her athletic frame.

"Kaitaini," Athena said. "It's been weeks since I last saw you."

A genuine smile lit up Kait's face as she closed the distance between herself and the goddess. Athena stroked the little owl's breast feathers with the back of her pointer finger. "How are you? Is Hera treating you all right?"

Kait grinned and held her arm out, then pulled it back into her stomach before moving it up to the side of her mouth to sign *Welcome home.*

Athena frowned. "What's happened to you, dear?"

Kait shook her head and pressed two fingertips to the hollow of her throat.

Athena's gaze hardened. "The witch took it, did she? Not surprising in the least."

Kait pressed her fingertips to her forehead to ask the goddess if she had learned anything while in the lower realms, eager for information.

Athena sighed and stroked the tiny owl once more. "I spoke with many creatures regarding the outbreak, particularly the speed in which it was able to spread. It must have been horrific to witness." Kait bit her lip but refused to let the bloody images form. She couldn't afford to be plagued by guilt; she needed to focus. "In Kairu, a clan of satyrs believed their water source had been contaminated after a witness reported seeing a naiad become infected while bathing. Bouts of cholera broke out not long after the area was cleaned and bodies were disposed of. At first, they were frightened they would turn as the nymphs did, but their symptoms were curable. Artemis"—Athena gestured toward another stall where a heavily freckled goddess with glossy chestnut hair gathered in a thick braid down her back alongside a quiver of arrows, stood inspecting a display of arrowheads— "followed the stream and located a small pool that fed it deeper in the jungle. The witness confirmed it was the same pool that made the naiad sick. The water was clear, yet all the flora surrounding it had withered and died. Artemis took samples of the water, and they are being analyzed now. With luck, it will give us the insight we need."

Kait exhaled, relieved the wise goddess hadn't given up and believed there was more to find. She touched her chin and lowered her palm in thanks.

Athena offered her a tight smile, but her eyes were tired. It seemed she wanted to find evidence against Hera even more than Kait did. "So, what has she sent you out for this early?"

Kait tapped her bulbous pockets and gestured to Hestia's stall a few yards away. Smoke curled from the top of the woodstove and carried the scent of warm bread on the wind. Her mouth watered as she imagined biting into the fresh loaf, but she knew better than to get her hopes up. Only a hard pear awaited her for breakfast if Hera decided to end her imposed fast at all.

"Ah, we can't have the queen eating cooled, bread now can we?" Athena snorted under her breath. "I'm glad to see that other than making you dumb, it seems she's kept you in good health, otherwise. Though—" Athena's cheerful mood clouded as she tilted her head and ran her gaze down Kait's frame. "Did she give you those bruises?"

Fear and disgust roiled in Kait's gut as the memory of Ares's savage grunts and stale breath assaulted her. She pointed to the few marks that marred her face but then pulled the collar of her shift to the side to reveal a necklace of purple fingerprints. Touching her thumbnail to her forehead with her fingers spread, she then brought it to her chest to sign *Man*. Following that, she raised both of her hands in front of her and moved them from side to side: *War*.

"Ares," Athena growled. "I meant to speak with him before I left." Her face darkened with fury, then changed to one of horror. "I just realized . . . Your halo."

Kait nodded and pointed in the direction of Hera's gardens.

"Thank the goddess," Athena whispered. "You were able to escape?"

Kait nodded again as she recalled the way Zeus had charged in and struck his own son in her defense. Without him, the outcome would've been horrific.

"I'm sorry, my dear. Believe me, this will not go unpunished. I'll head there right after I bring my findings to the Council this morning." Athena reached into the pouch tied at her side and handed Kait another drachma. "Here, make sure you get something warm for breakfast, too." She delivered a swift wink and a kind smile.

Before Kait could ask her more about the lower realms, the wise goddess spun away and strode back toward the center of the market. Kait watched her go, admiring the regal manner with which she carried herself. Perched elegantly atop Athena's shoulder, the little owl turned his head in Kait's direction.

Kait smiled as she watched them go and clutched the gifted coin. The bread would be a treasured gift, but her joy stemmed from Athena's promise and the possibilities her findings might yield. It could be the evidence the Immortal Council needed to formally charge Hera. A flash of dark brown pulled her thoughts back to the retreating pair, and she gasped as Athena's owl fell backward onto the marble floor with an audible thud.

"Glaukopis!" Athena cried, falling to her knees. Using one hand, she cradled the tiny creature's head but didn't move to pick him up. "Artemis!"

Kait rushed over, quickly joined by the huntress.

"I don't know what happened. He was fine a moment ago." Athena didn't cry, but her voice wavered.

Artemis crouched beside Athena and gently rested her fingertips on the bird's frail chest. "His heart is racing. Does he have any ailments or allergies?"

Athena shook her head. "No, nothing."

"Any recent change in diet?"

"No, I prepare all his meals."

"Did he ingest any sort of foreign substance, maybe by accident?"

"Not that I'm aware of. Oh, Artemis, what could have done this?"

The creature gasped, wheezing for breath, his once alert stare now cloudy and unfocused.

"He appears to have been poisoned."

"Poisoned?" Athena repeated. "By whom?"

Kait rubbed her sweating palms on her shift, careful not to squish the grapes. Her fingers brushed the collection of hard bumps in the deep recess of her pocket. The datura seeds. She fished them all out. She'd had twelve but her breath caught as she realized two were missing. She presented them in her palm and thrust them toward the goddesses.

"What's that?" Athena asked, her amber eyes full of distrust.

Artemis inhaled sharply. "Are those from the datura flower?"

Kait nodded and patted her pocket. She pointed to the owl as she recalled him pecking the ground at her feet. She hadn't realized all of them had fallen from her pocket before.

Without pause, Athena leapt up and transformed. Gone was her flesh, her hair, her gown, all replaced with sleek feathers. A tawny owl, much larger than the little one that clung to life at her feet, shot into the sky. Following Athena's flight, Kait winced when she flew off into the rising sun's rays, but before her vision had even recovered, Athena was back with sooty pebbles clutched in her talons. She emitted a high-pitched screech, then dropped them beside Artemis, her large eyes staring intently at Glaukopis.

The huntress scooped them up, opened the little owl's beak, and thrust the black rocks down his throat. Kait looked on helplessly as the creature lay far too still. Athena spread her wings, about to soar away for more, when Glaukopis wheezed, coughing and spluttering with great effort. Artemis pressed the bird's diaphragm, forcing him to vomit up what little was in his stomach. Black bile, complete with half-digested mouse legs and three oblong seeds, splashed atop the white marble.

Athena's feathers lengthened and shimmered as she transformed back to her physical form. "Thank the gods." She stroked the bird's head. They waited with bated breath and exhaled a collective sigh of relief as Glaukopis hopped up, shook his tail, and ascended back to his perch on his mistress's shoulder.

Kait wiped a tear from her eye and pointed to the black liquid that stained the polished stones.

"Activated charcoal," Athena said, answering her muted question. "It's one of the rare antidotes for datura poisoning."

"Where did you find that?" Artemis asked.

"Hephaestus's workshop."

"And where did you get those seeds?" Artemis's tone was clipped as her gaze slid to Kait.

Kait gestured to a nearby stall. She didn't see Panacea's table yet, but surely she'd set up later. An uneasy feeling settled in the pit of her stomach. Would the kind goddess get in trouble for selling her the flowers?

"Panacea has a booth that offers medicinal herbs . . . Did you get them from a vendor in the market?" Athena asked, turning her attention back to Kait.

Kait nodded and was relieved at the absence of any tension in their faces when they spoke Panacea's name.

"She's serving Hera," Athena added under her breath as she and Artemis rose to their feet.

Kait watched the huntress's amber eyes narrow.

"Did Hera tell you to buy datura?" Artemis asked.

Again, she nodded. Panacea could vouch for that. Doing her best to sign her way through the lack of language, Kait pointed to the seeds and shook her head back and forth. Extending her pinky and thumb on one hand, she placed her thumb in front of her mouth and twisted her wrist, so the back of her hand was now shown: *Accident.*

"Datura possesses medicinal properties. If the petals are ground, they *are* a natural anti-inflammatory." Athena glanced at Artemis. "Maybe Hera wasn't aware of their toxicity."

The huntress didn't look convinced but sat back on her heels in silent surrender. Kait sighed, glad to no longer be held captive by Artemis's calculating stare. Athena took a steadying breath and pointed to the remaining seeds displayed in Kait's palm. "Make sure you dispose of those promptly. They're highly potent. That little handful you have would kill Hera in minutes."

Artemis cleared her throat. "If only we'd be so lucky."

Athena didn't agree, but her lips quirked with amusement. Kait returned the seeds to her pocket, unsure what to do next. She was a few minutes late with Hera's breakfast, but she couldn't exactly excuse herself from the goddess's scrutiny.

Athena must have sensed Kait's anxiety. "Go on. Grab your goods from Hestia before Hera sends out a search party for you. Remember to use the drachma to buy a loaf for yourself, as well." Kait nodded, smiling graciously, and gave a curt wave goodbye. "Oh, and Kaitaini?" Athena called. "Stay strong and be careful."

CHAPTER 43

As predicted, Hera was furious when Kait returned a few minutes late. Again, she indulged in a long rant about Kait's incompetence, one that resembled last night's scolding. She'd taken an extra five minutes to savor the warm bread that now filled her belly, and she stood silent as the goddess's harsh words rained down. Along with Athena's reassurance, the comfort of enough toxic seeds in her pocket to destroy her enemy gave her much-needed hope. Soon, she'd be free of Hera's tirades, and Bia would be safe in Gaia's care.

This time, Hera didn't bother restoring Kait's voice for an explanation. Instead, Hera snatched the fruit and cool scones out of Kait's hands once she reached the end of her speech. "Just go, and do not return until I summon you."

Kait's eyebrows arched as Hera turned her back on her and carried her breakfast to the Skyglass column. Did she suspect Kait? Had the Skyglass revealed the secret seeds buried in her pocket? Hera didn't act as if she'd seen the exchange between Athena and Kait. She was, no doubt, busy combing the whole of the South End for Zeus's beggar countenance. Kait had simply been bait.

Kait departed Hera's side and strolled through the lush grass with Argus following dutifully behind her. Out of the corner of her eye, she observed Hera and took stock of the way the goddess sat. She was hunched and tense, her vertebrae raised like sharp discs that jutted out beneath pale skin. Had she lost weight? Already, it seemed as if Hera had forgotten her, too absorbed in the shifting visions the Skyglass depicted.

Kait eyed the albino peacock as he preened his feathers, every bright eye unblinking as they followed her. Maybe the goddess hadn't forgotten about her completely. Kait felt the seeds bump against her thigh and prayed that Hera saw something in her search for answers that would beckon Kait to her side once more.

Five days dragged by without so much as a glimpse from Hera. There were no errands, no visitors, not even any interrogations to help pass the time. Instead, the goddess sat, clinging to the rim of the Skyglass from the moment the sun rose until it was too dark to see the images displayed within.

Kait tried to keep calm, aloof, but she was terrified. What if the seeds' toxicity expired? What if they shriveled to dust? She held the one opportunity to save Bia in the palm of her hand yet remained powerless to alter her situation.

On the sixth day, as Kait began to go mad from curdling anxiety, her poor luck shifted. Just before noon, Hera summoned her to the grand terrace. Kait climbed the marble stairs, barely able to control her nerves, and gasped when she caught sight of the goddess for the first time since returning from the market.

Hera's appearance had become a horrifying caricature of the effervescent beauty every immortal radiated. Her once elegant posture was now crooked and emaciated, and her bony shoulder blades stuck out of her dress like fossilized plates. Greasy curls hung from her skull like damp seaweed, and her cheekbones were hollow and gaunt, covered by stretched graying flesh. Her eyes burned brightly, but gone was her confidence, her power. All Kait saw was desperation.

Her eyes roamed over Hera's empty back. The great snake wasn't in her usual place atop her mistress's shoulders but rather coiled in a heap at her feet. No doubt, the python's weight had become too much for Hera's frail bones. Kait couldn't understand how the goddess had lost so much weight so quickly. Kait sharply and repeatedly, tapped her foot to draw Hera's attention away from the Skyglass. Slowly, the goddess glanced up, her features unchanging as her eyes came to rest on Kait.

"How long have you been in love with him?"

Kait frowned at the accusation. Before she could shake her head, Hera unclasped the silver charm, and Kait's voice slammed into her windpipe, nearly knocking her off her feet.

"Tell me, nymph."

Kait cleared her throat, startled by the sound after so long without it. "With whom?"

"Zeus, you imbecile."

Kait's frown deepened to a scowl. "I'm not in love with anyone."

"Not even that pathetic mortal from the mountains? I thought he saved you," Hera said in a mocking tone.

Kait swallowed roughly. Unease squeezed her gut. Until Hera mentioned him, she hadn't thought of Blake once since entering Olympus. There wasn't room in her thoughts for distractions. The only thing that mattered was Bia, but guilt still weighed in her stomach like a heavy stone. How long had she been gone? Eight weeks? Nine? She thought back to their goodbye, the sweet kiss they'd shared, but it was hard to recall that brief moment of happiness with him now.

"I'm not in love with anyone."

Hera pursed her lips, unblinking. "Is that so? Tell me then, why do you dream of Zeus almost every night? I've been watching you, watching your dreams, over-exerting my powers to steal them away before you even realize you've crafted them. Shifting faces, blond hair, dark hair, but always the same smile, the same ending."

"What ending is that?" Kait had no recollection of dreams regarding the god. Even her nightmares had ceased. She furrowed her brow. Hera could be bluffing, trying to force her to admit some obscure truth. Her gaze slid to the Skyglass. As far as she knew, it couldn't show specific dreams or thoughts, only an objective view of people as they were in the present moment.

Hera's eyes hardened. "A baby. A beautiful blond-haired child in your arms."

Kait sucked in a breath as the image from the vapors in Tartarus leapt to the forefront of her mind. In her vision, the child had been dark-haired, but she remembered his rosy cheeks, how soft he'd felt.

How right he felt, Kait's subconscious added.

Kait frowned and opened her mouth at the same time the great snake hissed and slithered toward her mistress's calf. Hera yelled, her voice shrill and fragile, recapturing Kait's attention. "Look at me, nymph! How long? Where is he? Where is he?"

Something wasn't right, and it was then that Kait saw it. Hera twisted her thinning frame and exposed the contents of the Skyglass. A beautiful baby boy cooed in a set of delicate arms as chubby fingers toyed with a brilliant golden curl. The vision wasn't of Kait, but another goddess Kait didn't recognize.

"You know that's not me," Kait explained. "And I've never heard of such an ability to steal dreams. It seems to me you've poured all your power into scouring the heavens until you've found someone to support your wild claim in the hope I'll admit to a deranged affair with your husband, but I don't know where Zeus is. If you're all done with your tricks, I'll return to the orchard."

Leaping off the short wall bordering the Skyglass, Hera crossed the distance between them as her bony fingers extended into claws. She latched onto Kait's arms and dug her nails into her skin, snarling inches from her face.

"I know you're keeping him from me. Where is he? Give him back! Give him back to me!"

"Get off me!" Kait cried, arching her body as far away from the crazed goddess as possible.

Argus chirped from his perch, startled by their raised voices. He took several steps forward, but Hera turned on the white peacock.

"Get out of here! Go watch the front gates!"

The fowl tripped over his own feet, seemingly taken aback by Hera's ferocity. He flapped his large wings and soared over the enraged goddess before she could strike him, as well. She and Kait wrestled, each gripping the other's arms, attempting to remain upright, but Kait underestimated Hera's strength and more importantly, her rage.

Wrenching her arms upward, Hera upset Kait's balance and chucked her to the marble floor. A pained grunt fell from Kait's lips as her cheek slammed against the unyielding stone. Then, Hera's foot connected with her jaw and sent her sprawling onto her back. Hera breathed like a hungry lion, preparing to clamp her jaws around Kait's throat and deliver her back to Hades. Never had Kait seen Hera so unraveled, so animalistic. Not even her excitement on the brink of the infection could have rivaled the savagery now reflected in her eyes.

Kait rolled onto her stomach and crawled as her bare feet scrambled for purchase on the slippery marble. A swift kick to her side brought forth another groan from her lips. This time, though, Hera's foot caught in the fabric of Kait's shift and forced the dress to ride up over her hips. Four round seeds tumbled out of her upturned pocket and skittered into sight.

"No!" Kait cried involuntarily.

Hera's head snapped to the left at Kait's outburst. The goddess leapt over her and crouched down to gather the black seeds, flicking them into her palms with elongated nails. "What are these?"

"Please, give them back. They're all I have," Kait said.

Hera stiffened. "All you have of what? Of Zeus? Did he give you these sweets? Feed them to you while you lounged in his bed?"

Kait shook her long hair. "No, please. Don't eat them!"

The great snake squeezed its mistress's leg. Ze-Ze's amber eyes were locked on the seeds, and she hissed long and low as if in warning. Could she sense the toxicity? The danger her mistress clutched?

"In what realm do I obey you, nymph?" Hera spat. Before Kait could utter another word, Hera opened her mouth and tossed the seeds into the back of her throat.

"No! Hera, please! Spit them out!"

Ze-Ze's jaws snapped wide, her four large fangs white and gleaming. Kait was sure the serpent was about to strike, but rather than attack her, the snake buried her teeth into the thick muscle of Hera's thigh instead.

"Ze-Ze!" Hera jerked the snake's triangular head away, dislodging her pet's fangs from her flesh. She hurled the giant python to the ground, seething. Hera staggered toward Kait as a deformed smile dominated her mouth. "Too late, nymph. You want your precious berries? You'll have to cut them out of me."

Kait pushed herself onto her hands and groaned as she settled into a seated position. She exhaled the pain that flared in her ribs and brushed the hem of her shift back down over her thighs. "Those weren't berries." Her voice was clear and strong, suddenly void of the previous heartbreak.

"I don't care what they were, as you are no longer in possession of them."

Slowly, Kait climbed to her feet, exaggerating the movement. The poison had affected Glaukopis only a few minutes after he'd ingested the seeds. He was much smaller than Hera, but then again, Hera took three times the amount the little owl had.

"I've been holding on to them for a few days now, trying to figure out what to do. It's no secret I came here to kill you. Hades has my sister's soul, and the only way he'll release her is if I give him yours instead."

"We've been over this, nymph. I have no intention of going to the Underworld or letting you outside these walls again. I am untouchable and will continue with my goal to wipe out every nymph in all the realms!" The two women skirted each other, the snake's unconscious body the only divider separating them.

"The seeds weren't a gift, but I wasn't lying when I said they were all I had. After so many weeks, I finally figured out a way to kill you." Kait spoke quietly.

Hera scoffed. "With seeds? The acids in the stomach are too strong for anything to take root."

Kait stopped pacing, fixed Hera with a cold stare, and cocked her head to the side. "What about poison? Are the acids enough to stifle that?"

Hera paled to a ghostly tone as worry shone in her eyes for the first time. She looked down and walked her fingertips across her stomach. Kait caught the way they trembled.

"Datura seeds, in case you're wondering. Panacea warned me when I bought the flowers the other day. She was concerned you might use them on me, so I beat you to the punch. Did it taste good? Eating death?"

Hera's gray eyes shifted from side to side. Kait scanned the patio as well. Save for a few porcelain teacups and a vase, there was nothing Kait could use as a weapon. She longed for her element.

"Athena was the one who gave me the idea. She and Artemis practically insisted on your destruction. Seems you don't have many friends here."

Hera raised her chin and held herself at her full height. "Friends are a form of weakness. I am a goddess, the most powerful on Olympus. You think you've won? Think you can kill me? You're going to have to try harder than that, little nymph."

Hera smiled a wicked ugly grin, and terror gripped Kait. Why wasn't the toxin affecting her? She couldn't delay any longer. Hera would die today.

Kait lunged toward the flower vase. She wrenched it off the marble pedestal and spun, preparing to smash it over Hera's skull. Blunt force trauma was her only option now that the seeds hadn't worked. The painted ceramic flew from her fingers, but Hera cackled and spread her palms wide.

Fierce winds poured from Hera's hands and forced the vase backward as a choked breath stalled in Kait's throat. How could she have forgotten the goddess still wielded her magic? Kait threw her body to the ground and fell flat on her stomach as she dodged the vase seconds before it smacked into her head. Hera spat in frustration and commanded the wind to spiral back, the vase still enclosed in its grasp. Before Kait could move, the wind funneled toward her and smashed against the back of her skull.

Ceramic shards exploded, cutting Kait's flesh. Blood welled to the surface and trickled down her ears and neck. Without pause, Hera raised her hands. The wind slipped beneath Kait's body and levitated her into the air. Blood dripped onto the marble-like macabre raindrops. Hera pushed her hands to the left, and the wind mimicked the motion and slammed Kait into a solid pillar. Her body collapsed to the ground in a broken heap.

"Whoa! That felt good!" Hera laughed giddily. "I should enslave more of you. Imagine if I had the power of earth and water, too. I'd truly be unstoppable!"

Pain seized every part of Kait, shaking, gripping, and burning her limbs and insides. Her breath rattled in her chest. Her head pounded. Nausea struck as her vision swayed and the world tipped sideways, sloshing from side to side.

"What did I tell you, nymph? You're no match for me! Nothing! You will never save your sister, and Hades will never control my power. You've lost, thrown away your one opportunity."

Ze-Ze lifted her head, waking from her stupor. The goddess crouched down and stretched out her arm to allow the snake to slither into place across her shoulders. Hissing low in the back of her throat, she gave Hera a warning.

Kait's head beat a steady rhythm, but at least she could see straight. Rising onto quivering elbows, she balanced on her knees. The goddess righted herself and Kait watched as the snake's tongue tasted Hera's breath. Ze-Ze shook her head and settled into place on the goddess's shoulders, but Hera wobbled and fell forward. She landed hard on her knees as the additional weight of the snake forced her to collapse. The great python opened her jaws and hissed as she was thrown down once again.

Hera's eyes widened with understanding and fear. Kait was right. The python had been trying to save her mistress. "Ze-Ze, I'm s-sorry," Hera stuttered as her body began to spasm.

Kait clambered to her feet as the goddess's limbs went rigid, her fingers twitching and curling at unnatural angles. Hera's eyes rolled into the back of her head, the whites gleaming as her facial muscles seized. A choked gasp issued forth from between her crooked lips, and her complexion soured, turning yellow and sickly as the poison attacked her lungs and prevented her from drawing breath.

"You can't kill me," Hera wheezed, the words garbled noise. She twisted onto her back, and her spine bowed outward, pushing her stomach and breasts into the air while her neck curved to the right. The glass vial encasing Kait's halo clattered atop the marble but didn't break. Hera tried to reach for the snake, but her elbow refused to bend, her arm stiff and skeletal. "Ze-Z—"

Hera's last word fizzled into a strangled gurgle as the light in her eyes faded to a glassy sheen. She resembled a broken mannequin, one whose limbs had been contorted. Kait stared for a minute, too stunned to move. She'd done it. She'd killed Hera.

A wave of relief crashed over Kait, and her body shook as tears coursed down her cheeks. Hera was dead. Dead! She didn't have words. She'd waited so long for this since the goddess had appeared to her in the woods outside Blake's house. All those weeks spent wandering in the dark of Tartarus, followed by the weeks of imprisonment in Hera's walls. Hades would have his prize, and Gaia could make Bia's soul anew. At last, her sweet sister would be safe.

The heavy vibration of the snake's movement staunched Kait's relief, and she sucked in a startled squeal as Ze-Ze slithered between her feet. Kait waited for the serpent to turn on her, but her muscular frame was drawn to her unmoving mistress instead.

Ze-Ze coiled beside Hera's collarbone and laid her diamond-shaped head atop her sallow skin. Minutes had passed since Hera exhaled her last breath. Kait's mind whirled back to the present. She had no idea what to do next. Was she supposed to trap Hera's soul, or would it find its way to the Underworld by itself? Before another thought could form, silver vapor poured from Hera's mouth and coalesced into a shifting sphere. Kait froze, afraid any movement would influence the soul's direction and waft it out of reach. The snake's calm demeanor changed as she narrowed her gaze on something behind Kait and snapped her fangs. On the edge of the raised patio, in a sea of rolling fog, stood Hades.

The god of the Underworld looked strange surrounded by sunlight and Hera's elegant furnishings. His skin was bone white, his chiseled cheekbones the most prominent feature beneath his translucent eyes. His black hair was once again gelled to perfection, and his thin lips blended in with the rest of his face. Kait shuddered. He resembled a grinning skull.

"Well done, Kait," Hades said. "I must admit, I had my doubts." The fog billowed as he glided forward, cloaking his feet so he appeared to fly. He approached Hera's corpse and eyed the soul that hovered above her blanched lips.

The snake hissed again, but Hades wasn't fazed. He extended his arms just as Ze-Ze uncoiled. Launching her muscular body into the air, the serpent struck, fangs bared. Without diverting his eyes from the glowing soul, Hades caught the snake by the throat with ease. The moment Hades's fingertips brushed Ze-Ze's scales, the great python went limp and succumbed to death at once. Kait couldn't tell if the god had broken her neck or if his mere touch was enough to kill.

Hades tossed Ze-Ze's long body over his shoulder, and Kait cringed as the loyal animal landed on the rim of the Skyglass. For a moment, nothing happened, but then the snake's thick middle slid into the center of the small tower. A twinge of pity fluttered in Kait's stomach as the snake's tail and head disappeared and spiraled down to Earth. She knew how frightened Ze-Ze had been of the bottomless glass, always tightening her grip every time Hera wandered too close.

"Yet, here you stand, while the great Hera lies at my feet." Using both hands, Hades cradled the soul and gazed at it like a mother would a child. "Don't be angry, my dear," Hades cooed to the silver burst in his palms. "I've got big plans for you." He lifted his chin. Kait stared silently as the god brought the soul to his lips and pushed it onto his tongue, swallowing before she could protest.

"Wait!" Kait cried, but Hades's throat illuminated from the inside as Hera's soul plunged into the dark cavern of his stomach and was lost from view.

Hades turned to her with an amused expression. "Don't fret, darling. Simply a method of storage until my projection returns to my domain. The wards bar me from entering Olympus, but I wrote in a small clause that allows me to penetrate the barrier as long as death is present. The arrogant Council signed it, confident that death would never breach their walls. For immortals, death is a faraway notion, a mortal fear; yet, here I am." He smiled, and Kait shivered as the small gaps between his teeth shone with a remnant of the soul's sparkling color.

"What about my sister? Is she in there, too?" Kait asked. Her voice quivered with nerves, and her finger shook as she gestured to the god's stomach. If Hades went back on their deal, she'd have nothing and no way to hold him accountable.

"No."

Kait crumpled, unable to remain standing. "You promised me Bia's soul."

She gritted her teeth to keep the tears at bay.

Hades put up his hand. "Relax, nymph. I am a god of my word." He untied a black pouch from his waist. With deft fingers, he manipulated the thin strings and pulled it open. Kait held her breath. The contents glowed with the same silver light of Hera's soul. "You can take her out if you like, but I assure you, it's her."

Gently, Hades passed over the cloth pouch, and Kait released a relieved sob as her pent-up tears flowed. Happiness overwhelmed her as she pressed the pouch to her chest. "Oh, Bia. It's finally over."

Hades cleared his throat. "Not quite, my dear. You still need to return to Olean and restore your sister's soul to her body."

"But . . . her body is nothing but bones and rotting flesh. I thought to give her soul back to Gaia."

"I took the liberty of crafting a new body for her, unless you'd rather I use the blood and matter for someone more deserving?"

"No, please! I'm sorry. I didn't know such an act was possible." Kait brushed tears off her cheeks.

"The body won't be exactly the same, mind you, but it should be fairly equal. I'll watch for your arrival. Once you portal back to Olean, it'll appear to you."

"Thank you, Hades."

Hades waved his hand dismissively. "You delivered Hera's soul to me. We're square, my dear. Oh, but before you leave Olympus, I suggest taking that." He pointed to Hera's corpse. At first, Kait was confused. Then, she saw the shimmering golden liquid encased in the clear vial about the goddess's neck. Her elemental connection. Hades arched his manicured eyebrows. "Might come in handy."

After cinching the drawstring tight, Kait tucked the pouch deep into the folds of her shift, comforted by the light weight where it rested against her hip.

Hades pivoted sharply above the smoke and paused, his finger to his lip. "One more thing. Your Ceryneian hind has been in my possession since you entered the front gates. I think she's sick of the Underworld. I know I am." A column of smoke plumed in the grass several yards away. Bronze antlers cut through the film, and the beautiful deer emerged a moment later.

"Samara!" Kait exclaimed. They ran toward one another. Samara stopped just shy of the grand pavilion, and Kait leapt off the platform, landing beside her friend. She wrapped her arms around her velvety neck.

"I'm so glad you're safe!"

Kait pressed her face into the soft fur and inhaled the scent of damp earth and charred wood, then pulled back as the aroma of death and decay infiltrated her nostrils. Guilt swirled within her as she imagined the gentle doe trapped in hell all that time.

Hades raised his hand, and his fingers fell in a graceful sequence. "I must be off. I'm afraid I've got work to do, and you've got visitors."

"Visitors?" Kait repeated. She followed his gesture toward the back gate but saw only the high bushes that enclosed the wooden entrance. "Who—" she began, but when she looked back over her shoulder, Hades was gone, vanishing as silently as he had materialized. "Do you see anyone?" Kait asked Samara as she ran her hand down the deer's neck. Samara didn't respond. Instead, her large brown eyes dilated with fear, trained on something in the distance. "What is it?"

Kait followed the doe's gaze, and her breathing hitched. Sprinting toward them in the tall grass was Hera's albino peacock with Ares directly in the fowl's shadow, a terrible gleam in his eyes.

CHAPTER 44

"Oh, Goddess," Kait whispered.

A horrifying scream pierced the tranquil garden, like a woman being strangled. The peacock's feathers flared, all one thousand eyes snapping awake. Argus let out another tingling shriek. Even from afar, he knew something wicked had befallen his mistress. Ares charged through the grass beside the bird. Kait couldn't hear him from where she stood, but she remembered the feeling of his breath on her neck, the way it had clung to her like a rippling film. She broke out of her trance and pushed Samara forward. "Hold them off. I need to restore my connection!"

With a curt nod, the doe lowered her head, bronze antlers glimmering lethally. Sprinting like an arrow let loose, Samara accelerated to her maximum speed, lost in a blur of color and movement, streaking from side to side. Kait watched, unable to look away. Only feet separated the doe from the others.

Samara skirted the peacock and aligned herself with Ares, not slowing down. With a resounding crack like that of the earth splitting, the doe collided with the god, finding her mark. The next scene unfolded as if in slow motion. One moment, Ares was an unwavering bullet bearing down on her, but once Samara clashed against his chest, his direction reversed. Kait's jaw dropped. The god hurtled backward through the air, his muscular arms useless as they pinwheeled over his head.

A ravaged cry shifted her focus. Argus was closing in on the pavilion, and Kait was still powerless. She raced to Hera's side, dropped to her knees, and yanked at the silver chain that held her magic hostage. There was no clasp to free, and the shiny cord was too strong to break in half. Grunting, she clasped one hand around the vial. With the other, she tried to tug the chain over Hera's head, but the goddess's stiff frame proved too heavy, and her neck was too contorted to lift the necklace off.

The sound of crunching shells echoed as Argus's claws clattered atop the path. Only a set of stairs and a few yards of stone remained between them. Out of time, Kait grimaced and snuggled as close to Hera's corpse as possible. The goddess's blank eyes stared at her, mocking her struggle even in death. Kait looked away from the dull pupils, brought the vial to her lips, and poured the golden contents onto her tongue. She tilted her head to get all the liquid, but then her chin brushed Hera's cooling skin. Reflexively, she flinched, and the vial slipped from her fingertips. What little contents remained splashed out of the tube and spilled across the marble floor.

"No!"

Was it imperative that she drink the whole thing? Would her magic fail to return to its full strength? For a second, Kait considered slurping it off the floor, but a dark shadow blanketed the sun, followed by a terrible screech that split the air. Argus stood over Kait, his sharp beak poised above her forehead.

Kait brandished her palms and poured all her energy into igniting her magic, but the wind refused to obey her call. Either she hadn't consumed enough of her halo or it hadn't absorbed into her bloodstream yet. Either way, she was defenseless.

The peacock cried and drilled his pointed beak toward her face as Kait dodged his thrust. Hovering in the air, Argus extended his scaly legs and flexed two long claws. This time, he didn't miss. His talons raked down Kait's arm and torso, and the force of the attack rolled her out from under Hera's corpse.

Kait tried to cover her face with her uninjured arm, but the peacock leapt atop her, ripping and scratching at her flesh. The thin shift she wore offered little protection against the onslaught, but her focus wasn't on herself; it was on the small pouch in her pocket. She couldn't let Argus destroy it or risk Bia's soul disappearing.

Kait cried out in pain as the peacock's claws carved a deep gash just under her collarbone. Blood spilled in a hot torrent down her chest. She had to get away, had to get up. Argus struck again, but this time, Kait managed to catch hold of the fowl's ankle. She wrenched his leg back with all her might. The peacock stumbled, sacrificing his position atop her to save himself from careening to the hard stone.

Kait pushed herself up with great effort; her wounds burned from the exertion. Again, she called the wind to her, but the breeze remained uninfluenced. Panic seized her heart.

Argus charged and dispelled Kait's frightened thoughts. With no magic, she planted her legs in a fighting stance, fists raised as the muscle memory of pankration took over. She let out a deep exhale, thrust the heel of her palm up, and caught the peacock in the jaw. Thrown off-balance, Argus wheeled and staggered to the right. Kait took advantage of his momentary stumble and delivered three swift kicks to the bird's middle, then brought her leg upward and kicked him in the soft spot of his throat. A choked gargle sounded in response, but she didn't stop. She flanked the peacock and punched her hands through the shield of feathers to grip his slender neck.

Rough veins ran along the backside of the feathers and cut Kait's cheek. She wrenched her head back as far as her neck allowed and dug her fingers into the animal's windpipe. She rasped with the effort it took to hold the bird in place and applied even more concentrated pressure with her thumbs, pinching the narrow airway shut. Argus flapped his giant wings, whipping his body to loosen Kait's hold, but she held tight.

Tears poured from her eyes as she squeezed the peacock's neck harder. She'd never killed an animal—an innocent—before, but she knew if she didn't, the guard would never let her leave in one piece. Another minute passed, and Argus's struggles weakened. Still, Kait clung on as a heartbroken moan fell from her lips as she remembered the gentleness with which he'd interacted with her. "I'm sorry."

The peacock's feathers went limp, and his beautiful eyes draped over her body. Shivers combed Kait's arms, causing the hairs to stand on end. It felt as if his many lashes blinked against her bare skin. At last, the bird's head fell to the side. He was dead.

Kait released her hold and dropped the magnificent peacock. He landed with a hushed thud at her feet. Overwhelming guilt and regret washed over her as she emerged from beneath the veil of feathers. Her breath fell in choked sobs, and her bottom lip quivered as she stepped away from the pile of mounting corpses.

Kait expected her palms to be stained bloodred, but the light brown hue was even worse. Apart from Hades, no one would know her sins, and she wasn't finished yet. Kait craned her neck and scanned the lush grasses for Samara or Ares, but the gardens radiated an eerie stillness.

Bright pain erupted as Kait raised her hands above her head—a sharp reminder of the deep gouge Argus had cut through her muscle. The front of her shift clung to her breasts, soaked with blood. She needed to find a healer. Her eyes went wide at the thought of an anthousai, and she hurriedly patted her side. Bia's soul was still safely tucked inside.

With one loved one secured, Kait's gaze wandered to the faraway gardens. Where was Samara? A cluster of fruit trees drew her eye. The expansive orchard was the only place within Hera's walls where one could hide compared to the open vulnerability of the meadows. She knew Ares wouldn't exercise restraint against the doe and would use the tight shaded forest to his benefit.

Kait ran, the soles of her feet slapping the marble stones and carrying her down the stairs and over the path to land on the soft earth. The wind stung the wound across her chest, along with all the other gashes she'd sustained under Argus's attack.

Kait was so focused on entering the orchard that she didn't notice the way the wind had shifted. Rather than pushing against her, the current turned warm and malleable, welcoming her body instead. A delighted smile stretched across her lips as the element tunneled into her hair and massaged the strands like a familiar lover. Kait marveled at the power that surged in her palms. Her connection had been restored at last.

"Hello, wind. Let's do this."

Without slowing, Kait leapt into the azure sky and closed her eyes as the current cradled her, inviting her home. Midair, she folded her fingers, and her flesh disappeared as tiny gas molecules replaced her hair, toes, and arms until she was indistinguishable from the breeze. Renewed hope and strength coursed through her and pushed her faster over the gradual hills.

"I'm coming for you, Ares."

CHAPTER 45

Kait crested the hill and soared above the treetops. Even from this vantage point, she was blind. The thick foliage presented an impenetrable barrier. She would have to enter the labyrinth of branches and leaves to find her Ceryneian hind and whatever assault awaited her. The wind raged in response to her anxiety about seeing Ares again. Kait took a steadying breath and descended in a graceful arc. Memories of the god's calloused hands pinning her arms in place overwhelmed her as she left the sunlight behind and exchanged the bright rays for damp shadows.

The trees were quiet, as if they all held a collective breath. Kait remained in her elemental form as she slithered around gnarled trunks and raised roots. A sparrow called cheerfully in the distance, either unaware of the danger or unconcerned. Sparse sunlight filtered through rustling leaves and dappled the mossy path like enchanted sprites leading the way.

Kait directed the wind forward and spiraled in a tight corkscrew. Lethargic bumblebees droned from blossom to blossom, their steady hum normally relaxing but now unsettling. Between their monotonous drone and the air rushing past her ears, she was deaf to the delicate sounds of her enemy. Lowering the breeze to the grassy carpet, Kait alighted from the air and materialized. Her hearing improved, but she disliked how vulnerable her physical form left her.

The trees sighed and whispered to one another as she ran past. She wished she could tell if they were on her side. She switched direction and veered to the right, leaving behind the elegant orange blossoms for squatter hunched apple-bearing saplings. In this part of the orchard, the atmosphere shifted. Rather than the fresh innocence that had first welcomed her, the apples' sweet scent turned her stomach. Kait picked up her pace and averted her eyes from the fallen fruit at the base of each trunk. The skins were peeled back, flayed by numerous hungry ants and beetles. She swallowed roughly and prayed the rotting fruit wasn't an omen. A set of pale legs stretched onto the path ahead.

"Samara!"

Kait staggered to a halt. The doe lay on her side, her head lolled onto her front legs. One of her beautiful bronze tines had been snapped off, and a scarlet gash slashed across her side that extended from the front of her chest to her stomach. It looked deep, the work of a large hunting knife. The soft white fur covering her belly was stained pink and darkening by the second. Samara was losing too much blood too fast. Kait fell to her knees on the maroon-soaked grass and stroked the doe's damp head. At her touch, Samara wheezed, flinching with life, but then her eyes squeezed shut as if breathing were too painful.

"I should have been by your side. I'm so sorry, Samara."

Another breath rattled in the doe's throat and her pupil rolled until she found her. Tears pooled in Kait's eyes and ran down her cheeks. She brushed her hand down the doe's neck and sawed her lip with her teeth as she felt the gentle animal shudder with death.

"You never gave up on me," Kait whispered, thinking back to when the Graeae gifted her the beautiful doe in Madik. "I'm sorry I couldn't get you home."

Samara twitched one last time and exhaled a laborious sigh as she surrendered at last. Kait leaned forward and kissed her, closing her eyelid so the wretched flies wouldn't find it. Her heart ached. So much death in such a short span. Was Bia's life worth so many others? For the first time, doubt crept into Kait's mind. In Olean, she'd been enraged by the fact that Hera and Hades had so easily stolen Bia's life, yet here she was doing the same exact thing to quench her own sense of vengeance. Charon and Echidna's warnings flooded back to her as she considered the mounting bodies. It seemed her wrath had indeed darkened her soul and she belonged with the monsters of Tartarus, after all.

Wiping the dripping snot from her nose, Kait stood and shook her head. She couldn't afford to think like that. She'd come this far to save her sister. If she gave up now, Samara's, and Argus's, and even Hera's lives would have been sacrificed in vain.

Clearing the last few tears from her eyes, Kait exhaled, and the wind turned frantic. Hot steel licked the back of her calf and peeled the first few layers of skin off the muscle.

"Ah!" Kait collapsed to the earth as a dark chuckle resounded through the trees.

"Hello again, sweetheart." Ares twirled a curved kukri blade in his fist. The tip glistened with fresh blood, while the spine boasted a darker color. "How nice you got to say goodbye—or apologize, I mean. Must be an incredible feeling, to have someone die for you. I personally don't think your life is worth it."

Kait pressed her palm to the back of her leg and winced with pain.

"Does it hurt? I hoped it would. Took you a bit longer to find us than I anticipated, but I entertained myself just fine." He gestured to Samara's lifeless body. "I assume Hera's dead?"

Ares phrased the question indifferently, but the touch of fear in his voice was unmistakable. Blood pulsed down Kait's leg as anxiety flared. How could she hope to defeat the god of war if she could barely stand? Remaining in her crouched pose, she nodded. Ares's relief was palpable.

"Excellent news. Why then, I daresay it's just you and I. Alone again, though this time I won't stop until I've had my fill of you. I might let you enjoy your own pleasure before I slice your throat, but I haven't quite decided."

Kait growled. "You're not going to touch me."

Ares threw back his shaved head and guffawed. "I've got the knife, honey. Now, down on all fours and arch your back before I cut off your head. I won't be needing that part."

Faster than Ares could blink, Kait shot four concentrated orbs of swirling wind at the immortal. One sailed over his shoulder, but the rest slammed into his chest, throat, and wrist. The last hit forced the knife from his hand, but he managed to catch it before the wind could carry it away.

"Oh, got our power back, have we?" Ares leered, his gaze bright and wild. "Two can play at that game."

Withdrawing a heavy spear from his back armor plate, Ares stormed toward her. Kait rose into the air and called the wind. She was out of reach of the knife, but the spear could strike easily. Good thing she didn't plan on letting Ares—or his weapons—get that close. Kait flexed her hands, and a fierce vortex erupted from her palms, forcing the god backward.

Ares groaned with frustration as his sandaled feet slid over the grass and dirt. For all his strength, he was helpless to combat the wind. Kait continued the onslaught, her fingers shaking with the effort. She couldn't keep it up much longer.

Ares's back rammed into a tree. He plunged his kukri into the rough bark behind him and smiled while the wind stretched and distorted his lips. Kait knew he could feel it, feel the power weakening. He lifted the spear in his other hand and aimed, ready to let it fly the moment her magic faltered.

Kait's whole body trembled as her power drained. After so many weeks of disuse, she was weak, only able to exert energy in short bursts. The tips of her toes grazed the long grass as her magic petered out. Ares's grin widened, and he heaved the spear.

Kait watched it leave his fingers and cut through the still air with ease and precision. Her heels bounced on the firm ground while the air around her sizzled, blowing the nearby leaves every which way. Sunlight glowed between the gaps, and the golden rays highlighted the razor-sharp head of the advancing missile. Another three seconds and it would be buried in her chest.

Rather than duck, Kait leapt into the air. Extending her limbs, she twisted her torso and rolled over the spear tip, avoiding it by millimeters. The rush of air from the spear blew the ends of her hair, then it catapulted forward and buried into the base of an apple tree. Bark exploded on impact, and splinters of wood rained down.

Kait's neck snapped after she landed in a split on the grass just as Ares's fist collided with her cheek. Her teeth sliced into the inside of her lip, and blood sprayed onto her arm as her vision wobbled, but she remained upright. Ares peppered her face with two more quick jabs, causing a torrent of crimson to spout from her nose. She fell face down on the ground while fireworks of pain burst behind her eyes. A hideous chortle slithered into her ears. She'd thought Ares a savage beast before. Turns out, he'd been going easy on her.

"Seeing stars yet, nymph?" Ares asked as he circled her like the vultures he favored. "This is such a turn-on, seeing you splayed out like this, your blood coating my knuckles." He raised his fist to his lips and licked the crimson drops with his tongue. "You taste good, but I know you can offer me something sweeter."

Ares kicked her feet apart and knelt between her legs, tracing the curves of her calves. Kait's head spun, and her face felt raw and swollen. She heard the god grunt behind her, felt him shift from side to side as he moved his tunic aside, felt the heat coming off him. Garnering her strength, she closed her eyes as Ares's hands squeezed her thighs and forced her shift over her backside.

"Now, I get to see why my father hunted you so avidly. Let's hope you live up to the hype."

Her energy restored, Kait melted into the wind and slipped out of Ares's grasp. He cried out in frustration as he tried to catch her in his palms, but she wove straight through his fingers to rematerialize at his back. He was armed to the teeth. Ares's armor boasted numerous slits, each one occupied by a different blade. She removed a push dagger from its sheath, her movements fluid and precise, as if they'd been practiced. She flicked the blade into the air, caught it around the T-handle, and plunged the steel into the tender flesh an inch below the god's hairline. The blade sunk to the hilt and cut easily through muscle and sinew until it scraped the top of his spinal cord. A sharp inhale was the only evidence he'd registered the pain at all.

"How's that? Do I compare to all the other nymphs you forced beneath you?" Kait spat and spread her hands, aligning them with his back. A great blast of wind pulsated from her palms and propelled the god end over end. Ares landed on the churned earth, and his face ground against the fresh dirt.

Kait dropped her arms and tossed her limp curls out of her face. The back of her hand was caked in blood and sweat, but she exhaled with victory and relief. It was over. She blew a long breath between her pursed lips and let her head fall back. Too late, she realized a dark figure was watching her. Panicked, she looked to Ares, stunned that the immortal had recovered so quickly, but her enemy still lay on the ground where she'd thrown him. The stranger threw back his hood to reveal dark brown hair, muddy eyes, and a mouth creased with worry.

"Zeus?" Kait asked. "What are you doing here?"

"I thought you might need help, but it appears you have things well under control." He closed the distance between them, and his concerned expression deepened. "I was in the market keeping an eye on Ares when I saw him rush away. I tried to follow, but he cornered me at the bottom of the hill just outside the gate."

Zeus pulled his brown cloak aside and revealed his tunic. A brilliant red starburst soaked the fabric directly over his heart. Kait gasped. Without thinking, she pressed her hand to the wound to stem the bleeding. The futility of what she was attempting hit several seconds later. Was she really trying to heal an immortal? Kait pulled away and looked down as her cheeks burned.

"That was silly of me," Kait whispered.

"It wasn't." Zeus paused and touched the edges where her fingers had just rested. "You can't imagine just how much that meant," Zeus said. His voice was soft, shy even.

Kait furrowed her brow. "What do you mean?"

Zeus hugged his torso. "That despite everything between us, your first instinct was to help and not hurt me. It gives me hope that maybe I truly am becoming a better person, and you can see it."

Kait cleared her throat and shook her head. "I didn't even think. I just saw more blood and reacted, but . . . I guess I was worried you might've been in pain. I mean, if you even feel it."

"Even though I can heal myself, it still hurts. If that little fool had practiced his weaponry skills, he wouldn't have missed my heart, and I'd be back where I started."

"The Underworld wasn't that bad," Kait joked.

"This time, it would be." Zeus's voice softened. "I'd be away from you."

Kait's gut clenched, but this time, it wasn't solely out of hatred and disgust for the immortal before her. Back in the Pyrenees, she'd wanted nothing more than to spill as much of his ichor as possible. Yet now, the moment she'd caught sight of his wound, her only thought had been to save him, to keep his heart beating. The shift was cosmic. Was it possible someone's character could change that drastically? Could she truly forgive him?

Zeus was careful to keep his distance. Her thoughts tumbled over one another as her heart and brain battled. They'd reached the precipice, the moment that had been building since Hades revealed Zeus in the Underworld. It would be so simple to dismiss Zeus and return to Olean. She'd never have to see him again. So, why was she hesitating?

Memories of their journey through Tartarus unfurled behind her eyes. There was no doubt Zeus had started off as the same brutish fiend she'd helped kill, but as the past flashed before her, she recalled pivotal moments that illustrated the change the vapors had influenced: the night Zeus held her close as her fever raged, offering what little comfort he could; how he'd wished for the Sphinx to heal her wounds rather than to escape; and when he'd volunteered to save Samara from the Cyclops's keep, even though it put his own life at stake. His reformation hadn't ended once they escaped Tartarus, either. The whole time she was imprisoned behind Hera's walls, Zeus had waited to ensure she was okay, and when Ares tricked her, the god had chosen her over his own son. He'd also remained cognizant of her boundaries and only touched her out of necessity when peril threatened her safety. For all appearances, it seemed as if Zeus had truly changed, or, at the very least, was putting in a solid effort to try.

Kait chewed her bottom lip. It was easier to believe Zeus had changed for the better when she was looking at a different person. "Show me the real you. Can you undo Hades's spell?"

Zeus frowned, his mouth tight. Was he as nervous as Kait was? "I can try. I don't have much of my power back. What little Hades allowed me to keep, I used on Ares that day he took you to his home. Give me a minute."

Zeus furrowed his brow in concentration. At first, nothing happened, then slowly his brown eyes lightened to bright blue. A ring of amber lingered around the pupil. His crooked facial features shifted to symmetrical perfection, and his dull hair bleached to dirty blond. Gone were the rags he'd worn all those weeks, replaced with navy blue trousers and a matching waist-long vest, embellished with dull gold thread. Zeus exhaled a heavy breath as if the seemingly simple transformation had cost a great deal. He stood before her, a tarnished rendition of his once former glory, but instead of confidence, he regarded her with a wary expression.

"I'm sorry if this makes you uncomfortable," Zeus said, but he didn't look away or shield his original form.

Kait took in his handsome visage. An involuntary shudder raced through her, but as she stared into his eyes, it became clear that the feelings of hatred and aggression that had been branded so strongly on her psyche had weakened enough to allow her to view him in a new light. She'd seen him at his most vulnerable during the ultimate test in Tartarus. It wasn't going to be possible to forgive everything Zeus had done, but she was surprised to realize she was willing to accept him as he stood now—an ally she'd come to rely on.

"It does." Kait inhaled a ragged breath and released it with a quiet sob. "But looking at you, I . . . I forgive you for what you did to me."

Zeus stood there, appearing stunned as tears welled in his eyes. "You . . . forgive me?"

A choked gasp stuttered between her lips as a tear of her own trickled down her cheek. Kait nodded and wiped it away. "Yes. I forgive you." She extended her hand and offered Zeus a small smile.

The moment she spoke those three words, it felt as if a leaden weight in the center of her chest burst into thousands of fragments. Suddenly, her breaths came easier, and the tight smile she wore widened as a wave of warmth flooded her body. Forgiving Zeus was the hardest thing she'd ever done, but until the moment she finally believed she was ready, she'd been blind to how destructive harboring all that hatred had been to her own well-being. Her entire frame felt lighter, and the wind kicked up in a cheerful funnel around them.

Zeus clasped Kait's offered hand in his and placed his other hand on top as he let his tears run freely down his face. "Thank you. I promise I'll never be that guy again."

Kait had never put much stock in promises. Actions spoke far louder, but Zeus's behavior had already proven his words to be true. She had no idea if she would ever fully trust the god, but for now, she was content with this small truce.

Zeus squeezed her hand once more. A gust of wind kicked up and stung their eyes. "Whoa." Zeus shielded his face from the sudden surge and released her hand. "I'm sorry—"

"No, it wasn't me." Kait blinked against the onslaught. "The wind is anxious." She glanced down as dread pierced her gut. "Oh, no." Upon seeing Zeus, Kait had forgotten about Ares and the small dagger she'd plunged between his vertebrae. The grass surrounding them was empty, save for a slightly discolored depression where his body had lain. Kait's jaw dropped in horror.

"What's wrong?" Zeus asked.

"He's gone."

CHAPTER 46

In the next breath, twin cinquedeas sliced through Zeus's chest. He pushed Kait away seconds before the tips of the blades carved her too. She stared at Zeus, at a loss for words. Surely, he could heal himself again, but the amount of ichor running down his torso spoke otherwise.

"K-Kait," Zeus stammered. His arms twitched in front of him as if he were caught between reaching for her and wanting to keep her out of danger.

Ares leered from behind his father and grinned wolfishly. "Hello, Father. I thought that was you. When you beat me the other day, it reminded me of the lashings I used to receive as a boy. Such fond memories. You and Mother were wonderful parents to all your offspring—except me. I don't know what I did to make you think I was unworthy of love, but job well done; my heart is a black pit, rotten to the core."

Kait sidestepped Zeus and brought herself closer to Ares.

"Ah, ah, ah, nymph. None of your tricks or I'll pull out these daggers, and he'll be dead in seconds. I won't even let you say goodbye."

"Don't do this, Ares." Kait held her hands out in surrender. "He's your father. You don't want him dead."

"Why is that? Do you think my spear missed his heart by accident earlier? Has he been saying I'm a lousy fighter again?" Ares snaked his neck over Zeus's collarbone and spat in his ear. "If I wanted to kill you quickly, I would have, old man. No, I want to watch the light leave your eyes and your jaw fall slack as you fight to draw your last breath."

"Ares—"

Ares threw his head back to face Kait. "Think you know me? Think you can get inside my head? What do you know about love? Abandonment? You're nothing more than a drop of blood and a handful of dirt." Ares twisted the cinquedeas clockwise, and the movement elicited a strained cry from Zeus.

"You're right. I don't know what it was like for you growing up." She had one play to distract Ares, but just the thought of the suggestion churned her stomach, and if she wasn't quick enough . . . "If I can't appeal to your better nature, then how about your greed?" Slowly, Kait brought her hands in and slid her sleeve down to expose her shoulder. "Let him live, and I'll give you euphoria."

"No," Zeus wheezed, but Kait ignored him.

Ares scoffed. "Sorry, nymph, but euphoria is nothing compared to the pleasure I'll reap killing this bastard." Ares shoved the blades farther, and Zeus gasped. His eyes glazed; his breaths grew shallow and futile.

Kait lowered her head. She knew what she had to do, knew it was too late to save Zeus. Her heart clenched as a single tear trailed down her cheek. At last, she'd granted him forgiveness, but the Fates were cruel. She righted her shift and beheld the god. Even as his heart fought to beat around the daggers slicing it in two, he never looked away from her.

"Going to cry, nymph?" Ares mocked.

Kait lifted her head. "Yes, but first . . . I'm going to kill you."

Kait threw out her right hand and closed her fingers in a tight fist. Her nails sliced into her palm, but she squeezed harder and let the energy build. Her power thrummed, eager to be released. She delayed another ten seconds and then uncurled her fingers. The effect was immediate. Her magic rippled, and fierce wind projected from her body, enveloping her target. Ares choked as Kait manipulated the air around his throat and constricted the oxygen while increasing pressure on his windpipe. Her lips stretched into a fierce smile as she strangled him from afar.

Ares's eyes bulged, and he clawed at his neck with one hand, but his desperate fingers batted empty air. Zeus moaned as Ares twisted one of the daggers. Kait relaxed her attack, but Zeus shook his head.

"Keep going," Zeus urged.

In her moment's hesitation, Ares sucked in a sharp breath, and his reddening face cooled. He withdrew the blades from his father's back and shoved Zeus's body away before he charged Kait with both bloody cinquedeas drawn.

Kait didn't watch Zeus fall. Her gaze zeroed in on Ares, on the brutality scrawled across his features. She recognized the confident gleam in his eyes.

He knew she would die by his hand. Kait stacked her fingers and planted her feet. In response, the wind swallowed her, replacing her physical form with clear vapor.

Ares stumbled, unable to stop his velocity. Kait materialized and yanked him backward with the wind. Slamming her palms together, she thrust them up and tossed Ares into the sky. She caught his weight a dozen feet off the ground and suspended his fall. Rotating her pointer finger, she spun his body so that he faced her and hung him upside down.

Kait didn't smile, didn't speak, just stared with a blank expression. She remembered Ares's hands, his breath, his possession as he touched her. With deliberate patience, she cocked her head. She'd always been the deer in the scope, but this time, she wasn't prey. She was the hunter, and she wouldn't stop until she'd eviscerated her quarry.

Kait separated her palms by inches. Instead of focusing on Ares's throat, she commanded the wind to tunnel into his mouth, nostrils, and ears until she felt a sizable force collect in his gut. Then, little by little, Kait squeezed again, so forcefully that her hands shook and her clawed fingers trembled with exertion. This time, there was nothing to distract her. Her only thought was watching Ares's face purple as he hung like a discarded marionette.

Ares pinwheeled his arms and let knives fly in her direction, but Kait didn't flinch. One of the blades buried into the ground between her feet; the other sailed directly toward her chest. A look of triumph created a strange frown on the god's upside-down face, but Kait was ready. Without acknowledging the approaching weapon, her torso evaporated into colored mist and reformed the moment after the dagger sailed through.

Despite his failure, Ares chuckled, throaty and loud. "Can I tell you a secret? Gods don't need to breathe."

Shivers tickled her spine as she recalled the way his father had revealed the same thing against her ear in the mountains. "I know," Kait explained flatly. "I'm putting pressure on your other organs instead, pushing their weight onto your heart and lungs. Now, your heart is working twice as hard to pump blood to the rest of your body, and all that blood is pooling in your brain—far more than is supposed to be there. You'll either die of heart failure, or your blood vessels will rupture, triggering a brain hemorrhage. Personally, I hope it's the latter. I want to see you bleed."

Panic crossed Ares's features as he tried to sit up, but his heavy muscles pulled him down like an iron anchor. Kait squeezed harder and increased the pressure from within his abdomen. Her violet eyes sparkled as his stomach swelled and the organs crushed one another. She wasn't a healer, but she could tell Ares's body was beginning to shut down.

Kait held the god steady and dragged the wind down his body, lashing his thighs and the vulnerable pieces between like the crack of a whip. The god fought to keep his features neutral, but Kait caught the way his jaw clenched.

"How does it feel, Ares? To be touched without consent?" The wind grew rougher. "Does it feel good to be helpless? To know your pleas for mercy won't stop me from hurting you?"

Kait lashed the wind again. This time, the god's eyes flared wide with pain. Wrath fluttered in her chest, begging her to hit him harder. He deserved it. He deserved to have his limbs ripped off one by one for what he did to her.

"There's so many things I want to do to you, Ares." Kait's voice wavered as her fury crested, and a snarl ripped from behind her teeth. She tightened the wind's hold. She could picture all the ways she could delight in torturing the god, and the visions inflated the wrath swelling within her. Out of the corner of her eye, she spied Zeus, deathly white amidst the dark green grass. His screams in Tartarus flooded her mind, and the memory pricked her surge of vengeance. He'd faced his sins, greed, pride, lust; and apologized for them. Charon's words gripped her again.

The desire to fulfill that vengeance by any means.

As much as Ares deserved to be punished, was it worth sacrificing her own humanity? No doubt he deserved to die, but if she prolonged the act and took pleasure in his pain, then she was no better than him. Kait exhaled a long slow breath and calmed the wind's assault. It was time to put an end to this nightmare.

The purple coloring of Ares's face spread up his chest and arms like a tree taking root.

Just a few more minutes.

Ares continued to squirm, fighting to break free of her hold, but at last, his movements grew languid and his arms flopped, his fingertips dangling limply above the grass. Then, Ares's eyes rolled into the back of his head, the whites gleaming as his brain fought to stem the onslaught of blood pouring into his skull. The leaves rustled with a quiet hush as if an invisible audience waited with bated breath for the finale. Kait located the rhythm of Ares's heart and heard the way it banged desperately, growing weaker with every echo.

Kait flexed her fingers and increased the pressure one last time. In the next four seconds, she knew it was over. Blood and ichor gushed from Ares's eyes and nostrils as his brain imploded. Gasping with exhaustion, Kait let her arms collapse to her sides. The moment her focus dissipated, Ares dropped from the sky and crumpled into a mangled heap of ichor and limbs.

It's almost over. One more act.

Kait seized one of the cinquedeas at her feet, gripped the bone-like handle, and closed the short distance between herself and where Ares lay. With a flick of her head, she tossed a strand of hair out of her eyes, crouched down, and drove the dagger into the god's skull. She refused to make the same mistake. This time, she would ensure he was good and dead.

Steel slid through flesh and bone and buried into Ares's swollen forehead. Golden-red ichor burst upon impact and peppered Kait's face with hot spray. She sucked in her bottom lip, and the flavor of copper, plus the sweet tang of ichor, filled her mouth. An exhausted sigh climbed from her throat as she wiped the slippery fluids off her brow and lay back in the cool grass. Long green tendrils tickled her sweating skin and reminded her of Bia's gentle touch. She patted her hip and the small pouch secured there.

"Soon, Bia. I'm almost there," Kait whispered and closed her eyes.

She'd done it. Hera was dead. Ares was dead. Bia was safely in her possession, but the greatest triumph was within Kait herself. She was proud that she had been able to control her wrath and harness its potency before it had poisoned all of her. With great effort, she peeled back her eyelids and stared at the blue sky through the sun-dappled leaves. How she wished to simply lay there and rest, but she was so close to completing her journey. She had to finish.

Kait let her head fall to the side, and Zeus's motionless form met her gaze. Memories fell like rain as she remembered staring at Zeus's corpse once before. The first time, she'd laughed, but now, her heart pinched in uneven shards, and her chest felt hollow and sore.

Kait rolled onto her stomach and pressed her forehead to the damp earth as tears pooled beneath her chin. Everything was wrong. Last time, she was surrounded by friends and family. They'd celebrated their victory, alive with the hope of starting a new chapter. How had it all changed in just a few short months? Everyone had grown while she stayed rooted in place. Even her feelings for the boy who'd risked his life to save hers seemed non-existent in her heart now. A slow clap woke her from her thoughts. Hades appeared beside her, his image smoky and translucent. Kait propped herself up on her elbows, too weak to stand.

"It's not often I'm surprised, but killing three immortals in one day? I'm impressed, my dear."

"I didn't kill Zeus. That was your nephew."

Hades waved his hand. "Tosh. It doesn't matter. My halls are going to be quite full, not to mention loud, when this family reunites."

"You're not going to resurrect Ares, are you?"

Hades lowered his chin. "I must, darling." Kait's face fell. All her efforts to kill the bastard had been for nothing. "However, he has been rather naughty. Maybe a few hundred years wandering Tartarus will improve his attitude?" He pivoted in his polished shoes and gathered the small silver soul-burst that slipped from between Ares's lips. Once the soul was safely ingested, Hades turned and sauntered toward his brother's corpse and swallowed Zeus's soul, as well.

Kait sighed when the dark god straightened and smoothed a faint line in his suit jacket. "Well, I'm off. Lots to plan."

"Wait!" Kait called, pushing herself off the ground. She bit the inside of her cheek. "Are you going to bring Zeus back? You know, like you did before?"

Hades tilted his head. A condescending gleam shimmered in his pale eyes. "He will need to play a part, but can I be frank, my dear?" Kait nodded and wrung her hands together. "Forget everything that transpired between you. You may think he's changed, but I know my brother. It's not in his nature to put others before himself. He will grow bored and revert to his old ways. I've watched him rescind promises for a millennium. Though his vows sound good at the moment, he doesn't have the capacity or willpower to follow through. But I will say . . . There at the end, it really did seem like he cared for you."

Without another word, Hades vanished. Coils of smoke lingered in his wake. A weak cough raked her chest as Kait inhaled the slightly sulfuric plume of decay and brimstone. Alone for the first time in weeks, she surveyed the carnage that marred the idyllic orchard.

Exhaustion clung to her frame. Now that there was no one to feign strength for, Kait's shoulders slumped forward, and her feet shuffled one after the other until she reached the spot where Zeus's body lay. Déjà vu assailed her as she took in his shredded chest and graying face beneath a trail of ichor that stained his lower lip and chin. Last time, she'd grinned as she watched Jezlem spear his skull with the piriol's quill and laughed as his corpse paled. Now, as she stared at his pierced chest and diced heart, an overwhelming sense of loss settled across her shoulders like a weighted blanket.

Zeus had pushed Kait out of Ares's daggers' reach and encouraged her to finish her assault on his own son, even though it meant enduring more pain himself. Zeus gave his own life to ensure Kait killed Ares, not because he wanted his son to die, but because it was the only way to protect her.

Kait sank to her knees beside Zeus's shoulder and placed her hands in her lap. Hades's words wove through her mind. She knew it was foolish to believe Zeus had changed, but maybe going forward, he would be an ally for nymphs and could help bring about equality between the different races. She meant what she'd said when she forgave him, and the only way to hope for a better future between immortals and nymphs was to trust.

Kait leaned over and breathed against Zeus's cold cheek. "Prove him wrong."

EPILOGUE

Kait didn't look back as she exited the orchard. Her future didn't reside with the broken immortals in the grove but in the velvet pouch at her hip. Samara was gone. Zeus was gone. Hera was gone. She was alone again, but this time, hope rather than despair buoyed her.

Without a clear destination in mind, she strolled through the lush meadows, and habit carried her to the pavilion. Emptiness radiated from the marble terrace without Hera's manic presence and the imposing python. Kait half expected to see the peacock in her shadow.

You killed him, remember?

Kait's throat closed as she swallowed her guilt. Despite Argus's allegiance, the innocent creature should not have died. She abandoned her darkening thoughts while she climbed the steps and traced her hand along the back of Hera's lounge chair. The old Kait would have bottled her regret, allowed it to eat at her happiness and fester like an untreated wound. But after everything she'd faced, what was the point of holding on to something she couldn't change?

The glossy marble was warm under her feet as she rounded Hera's desk. Once, the drawers had been tidy, their contents filed and organized. Now, however, the chaotic jumble was the perfect parallel to Hera's crumbling state of mind. Curious, Kait picked up a wrinkled letter but let it slip from her fingertips without absorbing any of the words.

Like everything else, what did it matter? At last, her task was over. She'd won, emerged victorious over two immortals, and held her sister's soul to prove it. The urge to return to Olean was stifling, a physical force pulling her home.

Kait's chest ached as she yearned for simple days spent lounging along the river and creating beautiful little eddies of leaves and curling petals. She wished she could go back to a time before everything had imploded, to when all three of the sisters were still ignorant to the cruelties of the world. But Jezlem was mortal, and Kait didn't know if the sister she now carried would be the same gentle soul who'd leapt in front of a mouth full of teeth to save her.

Kait meandered farther across the pavilion toward the Skyglass. A mixture of terror and excitement caused her heart to accelerate. If she looked inside and asked it to reveal her next destination, what future did she hope it might depict? Olean, in its wondrous simplicity? The human realm, where she might find happiness with Blake? Or the start of a new era between nymphs and gods with Zeus standing behind her, the one person whose dizzying and convoluted past left more questions than answers?

Kait peered inside, careful to keep her tumultuous thoughts behind her teeth. As she beheld the endless cerulean sky below, she realized she didn't want to know what tomorrow would bring. Her mind quieted while she observed the scattered white clouds, some no more than gathering wisps, as if they couldn't make up their minds what to become, either. Part of her wished to throw herself into the ocean-like sky and let the Fates steer her body wherever they deemed. But she was an aurai; it wasn't in her nature to subject herself to the whims of others. She commanded the wind and piloted the current toward her own destiny.

Still, what sort of life was she destined for? She'd dealt with more than any nymph her age or older had endured. Had she and her sisters already fulfilled the prophecy of the triad, or did more hardship lay in store for her family? Kait grimaced, unable to stop her next thought before it manifested.

With Jezlem being mortal, are we still considered a triad?

Kait shook her head as another layer of guilt settled in her chest. No future felt right. If she returned to Olean and never set foot outside its borders again, she would forfeit any relationship with Jezlem. If she chose to explore a future with Blake, what would their entwined lives be like? How would he explain her differences to his friends? How would he feel when they all started having families? Would he leave her for a mortal who could bear his children, a real woman as opposed to the drop of "blood and dirt" Ares had labeled her? Or would she maybe one day love him enough to give up her elemental tie and fulfill the vapors' image, the one of her holding a beautiful baby in her arms? And what of Zeus? No matter how many times she tried to convince herself that he remained the same monster who'd hunted her across the realms, his words and actions had proven otherwise and inspired hope that one day nymphs and immortals would truly be equals. No more borders or subservient classes, just harmonious existence.

The possibilities swirled in a kaleidoscope of colors and faces behind her eyes. Then, putrid black smoke cloaked the shifting visions as Hades's polished smile stretched. It was futile to imagine her future when the dark god plotted to overthrow the realms. Why hadn't she paid more attention? Hades desired Hera's soul to eliminate any threat against his uprising, but when did he plan to invade? How? What was his plan?

At a loss, Kait sighed and rubbed her temples. She was tired, so tired. The only thing compelling her to continue through the mad chaos had been Bia, and now that her sister's soul was safe, she could barely keep her eyes open.

Kait slid her backside onto the smooth stones encircling the Skyglass and swung her legs over the brim. A serene smile graced her lips as her feet dangled above the empty sky. There was no straight answer, no magical cure for what ailed her torn heart. She rubbed the velvet pouch between her fingers. The first step was to reunite Bia's soul with her body. If she could trust Hades—and strangely, Kait found that she did—her sister's new body would be waiting for her.

The expansive blue void called, a familiar lullaby. If nothing else made sense, her connection and place amongst the sky did. With the pouch knotted tightly, Kait pushed off the stones and left her jumbled thoughts hovering above. Soon, she would have to face them, decide what her true purpose was and who to spend the rest of her life with, but not today.

Her stomach gave an involuntary lurch as her body plummeted through the Skyglass. Cold vapor kissed her skin as clouds rose to meet her and her hair twisted in a tornado. Kait acknowledged its anxiety as the air willed her to change, but she loved the pressure as she barreled toward the ground. Loved the feeling of its rough fingers cradling her body as the wind fought to keep her airborne.

Seconds after falling, the Skyglass became invisible. White clouds and blinding sunlight blocked her prison. Kait was more than happy to see it disappear after so many weeks spent locked away in Hera's gardens. Diving forward, she lay on her stomach, arching her spine so her toes and one arm pointed back at Olympus. Her other hand clutched the pouch. At peace, she watched the mountains and trees below loom larger, growing closer as her velocity increased. Kait's breath caught in her throat, but there was no need to scream.

The sky around her rippled as she entered one of the lower realms. The ground was only a few thousand feet away, but still she did not shift to her element. Thick humid air escaped out of the leafy canopies as the tropical realm of Sunti welcomed her.

At last, when Kait's stomach brushed the tops of the jade canopy, she melted into the wind. Now, instead of falling, she drifted, spinning until she couldn't tell which way was up. Rich dark brown earth rose to meet her. Kait settled atop the rainforest floor as a warm breeze and then relented her connection with the wind to allow the heavy shadows that stretched across the forest to cradle her physical form. Far above, a strong gust blew and parted the thick green ceiling. Past the varying shades of blue stratosphere and wispy clouds loomed Olympus and the watchful Skyglass, only now there was no one left to peer into its knowing depths.

AMONG THE BURNING

NOTE FROM THE AUTHOR

This book has endured a rollercoaster of a ride to publication, and I am so grateful to all my readers who patiently waited for this sequel. In 2022, my publisher canceled this series because they claimed, "Sexual assault survivors are no longer trending," and therefore stories that included their voices were dismissed until a time when, "People might care again."

As a survivor of multiple sexual assaults, their attitude, which is echoed by so many others, made me sick to my stomach. From a young age I was taught to be polite and to put others' needs before my own. I learned that sentiment also extended to the people who abused me.

If survivors speak out, name names, or try to file a report, we are either told it would be a waste of time, are labeled liars, or told it could ruin the abuser's life. No one ever asks us, "Are you all right?" because we are expected to get over it and move on. They don't understand the trauma assault yields, how it haunts and infects until we are a ghost of our former selves, constantly watching and calculating the intentions of those around us. Our joy has been stolen, and replaced with a cold intelligence because someone is always there to take advantage.

In America, someone is sexually assaulted every sixty-eight seconds, and that statistic is only regarding reported cases. By speaking about my own assault and writing this series, I hope to raise awareness and compassion for survivors and help create a better world that listens and supports rather than silences. Our stories deserve to be told whenever we decide *we* are ready.

ACKNOWLEDGMENTS

Among the Burning would not have been possible without an incredible community of people. To my editor, Chelsea Cambeis, thank you for diving back into the ethereal realm and making this novel as strong as it can be. To Neil J Hart, thank you for another stunning cover and your flexibility. To my beta reader Christyn West, thank you for taking the time to read this manuscript twice and provide the critiques needed to elevate it. Thank you to Sam Moran for proofreading on such short notice. To all my ARC readers, thank you so much for your time and enthusiasm for this project. To my sister Mercedes, thank you for making me laugh and pulling me out of my head when the stress becomes too heavy. Our van cries are the best therapy! To my husband, Daniel and my wonderful kids Jack and Joanna, thank you for being bright lights and loving me every day. And lastly, thank you to all the survivors who took the time to talk with me about your own stories of abuse. Whether online or at a book show, I am honored that you were comfortable sharing your experiences with me, and I will always carry them. I am so proud of each of you for finding your voice.

ABOUT THE AUTHOR

Caytlyn Brooke is an award-winning author known for writing gritty stories with endings that are rarely happy. She attended UAlbany where she studied psychology and developed a habit of staying up far too late reading. She is married with two children and a fat orange cat. She lives in the Soaring Capitol of America and can be found playing in the sunshine or watching old movies. This is her seventh novel.

AMONG THE BURNING